PEAK CROSSER

ADAM J. MANGUM

Empire of the Peaks

BOOK 1

Rocket Crossing, LLC • adamjmangum.com

Cover design, interior design and map by Megan Hemmert

Published by Rocket Crossing, LLC

2nd Edition, December 2016

To Mitch for showing me how to dream, to Marc for showing me what's possible, and to Kathleen for making it possible.

ACKNOWLEDGMENTS

A thank you to all of my readers, including Brad Hemmert, Karalyn Hill, Michelle Kopp, Dan Lee, Lindsey Lobner, Kayla MacNielle, Beth Maki, Todd Maki, Kristi Perkins, Jenny Reinsel, Chris Sorensen, and Aaron Taylor.

Also, a big thanks goes to the entire crew of Writing Excuses, the best podcast in the writing biz. Thanks to Brandon Sanderson for being an inspiration (and for critiquing my first few chapters), to Mary Robinette Kowal for helping to hone my craft, to Dan Wells for his courage, and to Howard Taylor for his wit. And to all of the Writing Excuses 2014 Retreat alumni, thank you for spending the best week of my writing career with me.

Peak Crosser was also made possible by a host of crowdfunders who took a chance on an unproven author. These include my parents Don and Diane, my in-laws Darryl and Bonnie Lee, my younger sister Rachel, Ross and Nikole McBride, and my older sister Jenn.

I also got to work with two talented editors, Julie M. Rodriguez and Kristine Kerr. The book was made better by their efforts. Megan Hemmert provided the beautiful cover and a gorgeous interior.

Big thanks to my brother Marc who passed away in October 2015. Marc made a movie and showed me what's possible when you commit to a dream. We miss you Marc, but you live on in all of us who knew you.

I also had some help from my daughter Lena who created names like mrakaro and cosow. All four of my daughters (Lena, Clare, Jane, and Hannah) provide all the imaginative fuel a writer could ask for.

The biggest thanks goes to my wife, Kathleen. Five years ago she told me to stop talking about writing a novel and do it. And so I did. Thank you, love. You've enabled me to find myself and live my dreams; I can think of no greater gift.

THE EMPIRE OF THE PEAKS

1 | STRANGE ENCOUNTER

Heavy rain pushed against them, and it restricted their vision in the diffused twilight. If Zornan had been traveling on the ground, the mud and reduced visibility would be frustrating, not life-threatening. But he wasn't on the ground. He rode a giant, hawk-like mrakaro toward the sheer face of a dark mountain.

He slowed Silver, his mrakaro, as they approached Shisnath, the sprawling city hidden mostly in shadow at this late hour, especially with these black rain clouds blocking any remaining sunlight. Slowing reduced the pelting of the rain against Zornan's skin, and he reached up to clear water from his face. But it did no good; any water he cleared was replaced immediately by the rain.

Why would Shisnath's ancient inhabitants build a city on the side of a cliff facing a shade-forsaken desert? It rarely rained in this part of the southern Empire, but when it did, it was as if the skies were trying to make up for a hundred days without.

Zornan guided Silver closer, but the wind and the rain fought their approach. Silver struggled to maintain their altitude at the city's third level. But she'd done this before, in even worse weather than this. So though the entire rain-drenched affair annoyed Zornan, he knew she'd get them safely inside the Peak Crosser keep.

Silver angled her wings, catching a gust which corrected the altitude and pushed them across the cliff and over the walls of the keep. She landed on the damp ground, the walls providing refuge from the wind. But nothing provided relief from the deluge.

Zornan dismounted, his already soaked feet splashing into a puddle. He reached up and tried to wick the water off Silver's feathers, but it was useless; they were both completely soaked, and since the rain continued, getting her dry would be impossible.

A young lad approached, an apprentice to the keeper, his face mostly invisible under a large-brimmed hat.

"Greeting, Peak Crosser," the boy said through the rain's dense noise.

"Welcome greeting, young apprentice." Zornan slipped the boy a copper and headed for the dry confines of the keep.

Silver screeched as Zornan walked away, her complaint ringing through the yard. The Shisnath keep was small and provided little shelter for the mrakaros and cosows kept there.

"Sorry, girl!" Zornan yelled through the rain, grimacing at his partner's unfortunate circumstances. Silver would spend the rest of the storm soaked and miserable, but there was nothing Zornan could do about that. Zoran closed his eyes and felt the weather around him. The rain would stop in a few hours, so she'd have a chance to get dry and sleep before they left in the morning.

The keep was empty, which suited Zornan. His fellow Peak Crossers could be as chatty as women on a festival day, and Zornan tired quickly of their constant gossip. He chose a seat at a table next to the roaring fire, hoping the added heat would dry him some before he retired to his room. He ordered tuber stew and a glass of emperor berry juice, refusing the keeper's offer of cuije; the local liquor was too strong for his taste. He'd be miserable enough in the morning without a hangover.

As if the infuriating rain had not been enough, two other Crossers entered the small common room, mugs of cuije already in hand as they chose the table next to his.

"What are we celebrating, again?" one of the men asked, his speech slurred to match his glassy eyes. He wore a short beard, speckled with gray.

"Jurg, you're as drunk as you are ugly. We celebrate nothing today." The second man was more sober, his face curved into a scowl. "The Empire and all its minions can rot below the Infinite Mountains for all I care."

"Shhhhh!" Jurg, the drunk one, hissed like a snake. "Language like that is treason."

"But that's how I feel. How could they do this?"

Curiosity tickled Zornan, but he ignored it. Whatever bothered the man was likely a long tale, and Zornan needed to sleep so he could wake early in the morning and get home.

"The Empire can do what is likes," Jurg replied. "That's why they call it the Empire."

"Shut your mouth, you stupid drunk. You don't even make sense." The angry one buried his mouth in his mug.

Zornan's stew arrived just as a third man entered the common room. The man was tall, his hair long and dark. He was dressed in bland gray clothing, not the tight-fitting brown of a Peak Crosser. His face was smooth and his walk fluid. Crossers didn't shave for days, and they all walked with a gait caused by hours aflight on giant flyers. The man was not a Peak Crosser.

"This common room is for Peak Crossers." The angry Crosser glared at the newcomer, echoing Zornan's thoughts.

"Technically, the common room is open to all High Tradesmen," the newcomer replied, his voice deep and formal.

"What trade do you belong to?" Jurg asked before taking another drink.

"A Magistrate," the man replied.

A Magistrate? Zornan looked back at his stew. No man wanted to tangle with a Magistrate, certainly not a lowly Peak Crosser. Zornan did not know the law, but he assumed a Magistrate did. Maybe any of the High Trades could come into the common room of a keep, but in his thirteen years traveling the Empire, he'd never seen any but fellow Crossers.

The stranger walked across the room, standing next to Zornan's table.

"Greeting, Peak Crosser."

Zornan looked up at the man. He didn't wear the stately purple robes of his trade, but he wore its grace and formality in his eyes.

"Welcome greeting, Magistrate."

"May I sit?"

Zornan nodded. Yes, the mountains frowned on him now; a wind-blasted Magistrate joining him for supper.

"Come on Jurg." The angry man stood, spitting the words. "It smells too much like the Empire in here."

The two other Crossers walked out, leaving Zornan alone with the Magistrate.

"What brings you to Shisnath?" the stranger asked.

"I'm a Peak Crosser." Zornan hoped his curt reply would give the man reason to leave.

The man smiled. "Not a talkative one?"

"Not really."

"Any idea what had your friend there all crossed up?"

"Not my friend," Zornan said through his stew. "And no."

"So you haven't heard?"

Zornan exhaled deeply. There was no way he was getting away from this, at least not until he finished his meal and got reasonably dry by the heat of the nearby hearth.

"Heard what?"

"About Master Lascrill?"

Lascrill, his master at the Peak Crosser Academy, would be an old man now.

"No."

"Not one for words, heh?"

The man smiled again, but Zornan did not return it.

"Well, Crosser," the man continued, "I can tell you all about it."

Zornan exhaled again.

"Lascrill has been accused of treason."

Zornan set his spoon in his stew and looked at the man. Lascrill? Treason? Lascrill had been Master of the Peak Crosser Academy for nearly thirty years. What treason could he possibly accomplish while living among initiates and hatchlings?

"I hadn't heard that." Zornan reached back for his spoon.

"I've spoken with many Crossers over the past week since the news came from Bristrinia. Your kind are angry, think the Investigators of the High Trades framed him."

Zornan's initial reaction matched the one the Magistrate described. He'd liked Lascrill, despite the man's mocking Zornan at the time for his quiet nature. Lascrill had mixed his lessons on navigation, weather, and giant flyers with lessons of honor and loyalty to the Empire. This hardly fit a man accused of treason against the Empire.

"I'm sorry to hear that," Zornan replied, his voice flat.

"You're not angry?"

Zornan shook his head. "No. I hope the Investigators are wrong, but I know nothing about it. Maybe they're right."

"Remarkable." The stranger looked Zornan up and down, assessing him like the aviary masters would a young hatchling. "You're just as he described."

"Just as who described?"

"Lascrill."

Zornan almost spit out his drink.

"What? You know Lascrill?"

"Yes, quite well, actually. We were initiates together long ago."

Zornan scooped up the last of his tuber stew and took a final drink.

He stood to leave. He wanted nothing to do with this conversation, wherever it was headed. He didn't really believe Lascrill could be a traitor, but he didn't fancy flying into this storm.

"Sit down, Zornan."

Zornan slowly sat. Did he have to obey the command of a Magistrate? He wasn't sure it was required, but he thought it wise to do so. The man's tone sounded more like a command than a request.

"I need your help," the stranger continued. "Lascrill said you could be trusted, that you could be counted on."

Zornan looked around, but the room was still empty. "An accused traitor vouched for me? I'm not sure that's a great endorsement."

The stranger laughed, but the sound was forced, like an apprentice laughing at his master's ill-timed humor. "Maybe not, but it's all I have. I need you to carry something of great value for me—to a place only a Peak Crosser can go."

Zornan shook his head. "Then make your request of the keeper here, and an assignment will be made. I'm under a contract, and I only carry for my employer."

"No." The Magistrate shook his head. "This is not the type of request you make through official channels. I know the law, Zornan. This must be done outside its bounds."

By the peaks, this was getting worse. "I'm sorry. I cannot help you."

Zornan stood to leave again, but the man grabbed his arm. His grip was strong. Zornan looked back at the Magistrate; his eyes were eager, and concern creased his forehead.

"Please, Zornan. My fate hangs in the balance. It's possible that the entire Empire hangs in the balance."

"You'll have to find another way."

The man released his arm. "There is no other way. You are one of the only people in the Empire I can trust."

"Good parting," Zornan said, heading for the stairs.

Before climbing the stairs, Zornan looked back to the Magistrate. The man sat there, his hands over his face, slumped against the table, his earlier posture of grace and authority gone.

Zornan turned and climbed the stairs. He wanted no part of that which sank a Magistrate into so much grief.

2 | HOMECOMING

The morning light overtook the darkness, peeking out above the mountain spires. Billowing clouds, which just moments before had been invisible, whitened against the harsh, dark colors of the Infinite Mountains. Some of the clouds reverently hugged the peaks, while others glided above the majestic range. Zornan gripped Silver's harness and steered her toward the valley. They were almost home. They were almost home. The storm had delayed their arrival a full day, but they were almost home.

His conversation with the Magistrate in Shisnath still bothered him. What made a Magistrate, one of the most powerful men in the Empire, fret like a nervous hatchling? And why would Lascrill, a man he'd known long ago, recommend Zornan for anything?

As Silver banked to their left, Fallindra came into view. With sharp eyes honed by his Peak Crosser training, Zornan could see the city in detail: people milling about in the dim light, animals grazing in the pastures outside of the city, and the Peak Crosser keep on the city's northeast edge. His well-trained ears could hear the beginning of the day even at this distance: the baying of animals looking for breakfast and the farmer chopping wood on the edge of town.

Zornan focused on his destination and saw Mistar, the Peak Crosser keeper, out in the yard, ready as always. He urged Silver into a steeper descent toward the keeper.

Mistar's young apprentice and cousin, Giltar, ran up just as Zornan and Silver completed their landing circle. Giltar was his older cousin's opposite, as vivacious as his master was stoic.

Zornan pushed Silver to circle one more time. The mrakaro's giant wings flapped as she slowed and prepared to land several feet from the master keeper and his apprentice. Silver gently landed on the dew-wet grass, planting her feet. She tucked her wings close to her body and nodded to the keepers to let them know it was safe to approach.

Zornan unhooked his legs from the leather harness and slid off the bird, landing deftly on the ground.

Giltar nodded to him but stopped halfway through the nod and squinted his bloodshot eyes in pain, undoubtedly the remnant of a long night. After shaking off the discomfort, the apprentice approached Silver and began dismantling the harness.

Mistar walked toward Zornan, his peg leg sinking into the dew-covered ground with every other step. He greeted Zornan with a hand on his shoulder. "Welcome landing, Crosser."

"Welcome greeting," Zornan responded.

"How long will Silver be with us?"

"Two weeks." Zornan stretched his legs and arms, shaking out the stiffness.

Mistar's lips curved upward, his subtle version of a smile; he loved Silver almost as much as Zornan did. "Very good, Crosser. As always, Silver will be treated like she was my own."

Zornan returned the smile and walked away from the keep and into the city.

It was early morning, and the streets were slowly coming to life. A local shopkeeper—Zornan could not remember his name—nodded deferentially, properly accounting for his lower station.

Down on the ground for less than ten minutes and Zornan already ached for the sky: for the clear views where he could make out the terrain, feel the currents of the wind, and chart the best path. On the ground everything was too close, and everything was on top of you before you could properly see it. And navigating people was worse than navigating the Infinite Mountains.

He walked through the city, returning nods to a few residents. Their returned greetings were stiff and formal, not like the ones they shared among themselves. He was High Trade, after all, and an outsider. His marriage to Calla had made him part of the town, but it did not make him one of them.

As he passed The Water's Edge, one of the city's common houses, he noticed two strangers standing just outside. Fallindra was small enough that any stranger stood out, but these two were more conspicuous than a yellow-feathered mrakaro.

The first man's dark skin marked him as someone from the east or the north, not a native of the central Empire. He was several inches taller than Zornan, and Zornan was considered tall by Fallindran standards. But what made him stand out most was his dress. His pants were dark and loose-fitting. His shirt was white silk, not the rough fabric Zornan wore. The stranger wore a blue vest decorated with intricate black patterns. A sudden chill shot up Zornan's back. That pattern marked the man as an Investigator of the High Trades. Other than Zornan, there were only two High Tradesmen in the valley. It was possible the rat—as other High Tradesmen commonly called the Investigators—was here to see him.

Standing next to the Investigator was a large man in the maroon clothing of an Enforcer. They both stood casually, as if they belonged at the entrance of The Water's Edge. But they didn't belong there any more than a wolf did among sheep.

As if called by Zornan's thoughts, the Investigator broke from his conversation with the Enforcer and made his way straight toward him.

"Greeting, Peak Crosser," the Investigator said, his voice pleasant and his smile bright.

"Welcome greeting, Investigator."

"I don't mean to bother you so soon after landing, as I'm sure you'd like to return home to rest. But I do need to speak with you. Could you spare a few moments?"

He'd asked nicely, but Zornan had little choice. You did not deny the request of an Investigator of the High Trades. "Yes, of course, Investigator."

Zornan followed the man into The Water's Edge, the hulking Enforcer following closely behind. The common room was empty this early in the morning except for two women washing the floor. The Investigator dismissed the women, and he and Zornan sat alone at a table. The Enforcer stood off to the side, his eyes on Zornan, and his arms resting across his massive chest.

"My name is Crisdan, Investigator of the High Trades," the stranger said. "I assume you know why I'm here?"

"I don't have any idea."

The Investigator smiled. Zornan didn't think Investigators were allowed to smile, and this man smiled like an undertaker after a plague. "I'm sure you've heard the rumors about Lascrill."

"Only recently. A few other Crossers mentioned something about him in Shisnath. I don't pay much mind to idle gossip, but they said he was a traitor." Zornan left out the fact that the strange Magistrate had actually told him about Lascrill's troubles. That seemed like the sort of thing you didn't tell an Investigator.

"In this case, it was more than idle gossip." Crisdan leaned forward onto the table. "Lascrill has been accused of treason against the Empire and of conspiring to kill the Emperor himself."

Zornan's eyes widened. Treason? Assassination? It seemed so strange when played against the man Zornan had known.

"I am investigating Lascrill," Crisdan continued, "and as part of that, I'm reaching out to some of his former pupils."

Zornan nodded. "But Lascrill trained almost every Peak Crosser in the Empire. Are you talking with all of us?"

Crisdan shook his head. "No, just those he mentioned in his writings and notes. Though he escaped, we obtained years of correspondence between him and his co-conspirators."

"I was mentioned?" Zornan shook his head. "I hardly know the man. I've only spoken to him once since I left the Academy."

Crisdan smiled again. "Regardless, you are mentioned prominently and frequently. Any idea why Lascrill would single you out?"

"None." Zornan could feel the tension rising between them as Crisdan turned from pleasant conversationalist to interrogator.

"When was your last meeting?"

"Four or five years ago, when we happened upon each other in Bastanda. I was there delivering a message from my employers. We shared a drink and swapped stories of my Academy days."

"Nothing since then?" The mirth was gone from the Investigator's face. His look intensified, as if he were peering into Zornan's soul.

"None at all. Honestly, I wouldn't even know of these charges if I hadn't overheard the Crossers in Shisnath. I don't talk to many others, and I keep in touch with no one in my High Trade."

The pleasantness returned to Crisdan's face. "Of course. I apologize for the intrusion. Just tying up all loose ends." Crisdan stood. "Please, be on your way."

Zornan stood as well. "Sad parting, Investigator."

"Sad parting, Peak Crosser."

Zornan quickly walked from The Water's Edge and into the street. There was nothing sad about this parting.

Crisdan slid back into his chair, placing his hands on his chin. He continued to read Zornan's emotions as the man left The Water's Edge and headed for home. All of the Peak Crosser's emotions were easily explained: worry, frustration, and deep concern for his family. The man would have been easy to read even without Crisdan's Investigator abilities.

"He's as guilty as can be." Stargarn sat opposite Crisdan, his enormous frame barely fitting the chair.

"Why do you say that?" For an Enforcer, Stargarn was intelligent, but that was like saying he was the biggest guppy in the tide pool.

"He was nervous. And he lied."

"Everyone's nervous when they talk with me, Stargarn. That's hardly evidence."

"What about the fact that no one in town really knows him besides his wife's parents? Why would he be so private if he had nothing to hide?"

Crisdan had trouble remembering before he had his abilities, before he could sense emotions like they were scents floating in the air before him. Was everyone without Crisdan's blessing as thick as Stargarn when it came to understanding the emotions of others? How could you live like that, guessing all the time?

Crisdan shook his head. "Maybe he's just a private person. That's also evidence of nothing."

Stargarn huffed and looked away. He was an Enforcer who loved to play Investigator. Crisdan did not need to worry about job security.

"Fine," the Enforcer said, "but he's mentioned all over Lascrill's communications. Isn't that evidence?"

This was Stargarn's first valid point. Zornan's name appeared in Lascrill's private notes and in letters written to Lascrill. The foolish traitor had kept all of his correspondence, a treasure trove of knowledge about the rebel Kuthraz. Much of it was in code, but much was plain. Lascrill and his confederates had not called each other by name, but it was clear that the other two leaders were High Tradesmen as well. That narrowed the search somewhat.

One passage in a letter to Lascrill stood out: *I hope you are right about Zornan. I need someone honest, someone who can take what I most value to safety. Please confirm that Zornan is that man; we cannot delay.*

Unless Zornan's name was used as code, Lascrill had enormous respect and trust in Zornan. But it was possible they were taking this too literally, that the use of Zornan's name was no more than a false trail laid by conniving rebels.

"Zornan is not a rebel, not yet," Crisdan responded finally. "He's not lying about his relationship with Lascrill. Though he lied about one thing…"

Stargarn leaned forward, eagerness filling the space between them. "What?"

Crisdan scrunched his face. "It was a strange thing to lie about. Someone else told him about Lascrill."

"Maybe it was someone from the Kuthraz," Stargarn said, his face triumphant, his pride flowing.

Crisdan shook his head. "No, he wasn't really aware of the rebels. I'm not sure that's it." It was curious though.

"Is it possible he fooled you?"

It was Crisdan's turn to huff. It was possible, but few in the Empire learned to deflect their emotions from an Investigator. Crisdan felt the disbelief and frustration leaking from Stargarn, confirming that his abilities were sharp.

"So we leave, then?" Stargarn asked.

Crisdan shook his head again. "No, there's something here. Though unlikely, it's possible Zornan fooled me. And the Peak Crosser keeper and his apprentice both lied, and…" Crisdan didn't know how to say it without confirming Stargarn's fears, but the apprentice had been hard to read. Whenever Crisdan had asked about Zornan, the young man had gone blank. Not someone hiding emotion, but a blank slate, like among aged people who'd lost their minds. But when Crisdan asked about another topic, the apprentice snapped back to normal.

"No," Crisdan continued. "We'll stay in Fallindra a little longer. Zornan is the best lead we have. No harm can come from being thorough."

Stargarn nodded, his satisfaction and pride filling Crisdan's senses. An Enforcer who thought he was an Investigator, like a man who wished to be a fish. Crisdan knew he was right about Zornan, and he certainly wasn't going to put his trust in the intelligence or intuition of a man who'd been blessed with increased strength and endurance throughout most of his body, except for the lump sitting atop his large shoulders.

Calla stood in the kitchen, sprinkling powdered sugar on a hot breakfast cake, Zornan's favorite. Unlike her mother Caladria, who knew her farmer husband would be arriving at dusk or a shopkeeper's wife who knew the approximate hour the shop would be closed, Calla never had more than a few minutes to prepare. She had started the cake early that morning in the hope that Zornan would arrive today. It was the third straight morning she'd made a cake.

Calla had a secret arrangement with Giltar to have a stable boy run across town and give her the news as soon as they had sight of her husband and his giant bird. Zornan was taking a little longer than usual today. If it had been any other man in Fallindra, she'd have thought he stopped to talk about the weather or whatever men talked about. But Zornan never stopped to chat. Whatever had delayed him had given her time to finish the cake and the girls time to decorate. Windsa and Caldry were running around the house's main floor, carefully placing flowers and ribbons throughout. They treated each of their father's returns like a festival day. So did Calla. She thanked the moons each time for his safe return.

This time brought added anxiety. With that Investigator in town asking questions about her husband, Calla's heart held a little more worry. But she wouldn't let dark thoughts dampen this moment.

She pushed those thoughts aside as she sprinkled the last of the powdered sugar. She heard the front door open and Windsa shriek. "Dadda! You're home, you're home!"

"Hello, little buttercup." Zornan's quiet, deep voice still thrilled Calla.

"Dadda, Dadda, Dadda!" If it were even possible, little Caldry shrieked louder than her older sister. Calla came around the corner to see her husband with both of his little girls in his strong arms. Smiles lit their faces, their eyes wide and their joy escaping in little squeaks. Zornan's smile was nearly as large, and his eyes darted between the girls like he did not want to miss a moment of either of them.

Zornan's tight-fitting brown uniform was covered in dust and sweat, but the girls did not care that their father smelled as bad as his mrakaro. After a few moments, Zornan's eyes met Calla's, and he smiled softly. His smile created the same intense feeling it had when he'd first courted her. His hair was short, the same dusty brown it had been since the day they had met. His eyes were a gray-blue, and his wind-worn face was like leather pulled over stone. He was beautiful.

"Dadda," Windsa said as her father put her down, "you're always too fast. We aren't done getting ready."

"No ready," Caldry added, her voice as sad as she could make it.

"Yes, what are we going to do?" Calla smiled brightly. "You always ruin everything."

Zornan moved toward her, and she met him halfway across the room. The embrace sent a jolt through her as their bodies pressed together. He kissed her lightly on the ear, the closest thing to his lips. They parted slightly, enough to bring their faces together.

"It is so good to see you, Calla." His eyes held worry.

"The Investigator?" Calla guessed at the cause of his mood.

He nodded. "But let's not ruin the festival." He turned to the girls. "Show me what you've done."

They spent the morning eating and laughing. Zornan chased the girls around the house, even though he was exhausted and craved rest. After a few hours, the girls went outside to play near the garden, and Zornan and Calla were left alone in the kitchen cleaning up.

"You should go rest, love," she said.

"I doubt rest would come." He stopped what he was doing and stared out the window at the girls.

"What did the Investigator want?"

"Something I don't have."

Communicating with Zornan could be frustrating. He was not a verbal man, and many in town thought him unfeeling. But he felt deeply—deeper than most—and hid those emotions below the surface. She'd learned the cues written in his actions and on his face. He was worried for Calla and the girls, even if she didn't understand why.

"What is it?"

"They think me part of a rebellion. My old teacher Lascrill is accused of treason, and I think they're looking carefully at Peak Crossers whom he may have recruited to whatever deeds he was planning. He mentioned my name in many of his correspondences."

"Lascrill? You've hardly ever mentioned the man."

Zornan turned and smiled. "I hardly ever mention anyone."

She laughed as she cuddled into his chest. "True."

"I wasn't close to him. He was a boisterous, clever-spoken fellow, and he used to mock me for being silent. I endured it because he was an excellent teacher, the best at the academy." Those words were high praise from Zornan, as he rarely extolled anyone.

"And they think you've been recruited?"

"Maybe. How long has he been in town?"

She pulled away. "Several days. He talked with Mother and Father, and he's been asking about you all over town."

"Did he come here to the house?" Zornan's eyes narrowed, and he took a deep breath.

"No. I think it would be improper to question the wife of a High Tradesman when he's not there."

"I don't know High Trade law very well, but you might be right." Zornan stared out the window at the girls.

"I am right. I went to the library, and Doothban helped me look it up."

"You are amazing, Calla." He kissed her, and the thrill from their earlier embrace raced through her again. He led her by the hand away from the kitchen.

3 | DARK THINGS

Zornan stood facing the unnamed Magistrate, both standing in the empty common room of The Howling Dog. The Magistrate pleaded with Zornan to take his cargo to some unknown place. His countenance was different from their encounter in Shisnath. He looked sad, broken. He was desperate, as if whatever task he hoped Zornan would take held the fate of his life and the Empire in its execution.

Zornan continually denied his pleas, and the stranger became more and more agitated with each of Zornan's rejections.

Then the Magistrate pulled a knife and rushed him.

Zornan shot up in bed, his heart racing, his hand reaching for the short hatari that lay on the floor nearby. A dream. It had been a cursed dream. It was so real, so vivid. Zornan did not dream like that often, and in that moment, he thanked the three moons for his lack of imagination. How could a man sleep with frequent visions like these?

As he began to ease back into his bed, his sharp ears heard a sound, a faint noise from the first floor. Having the hearing of a Peak Crosser could be annoying at times like these, with inconsequential sounds echoing in the near silence of night: a mouse beginning to make his home in the walls, the floor and foundation of the house settling, one of the girls turning over in her bed. Usually he could ignore it, but the frightful dream had driven him to a startled wakefulness. He rose to have a look. Maybe he could expel a pest before it became a bigger nuisance. He thought of leaving his hatari by his bed but decided better of it; he could use the staff to strike a pest if need be.

As Zornan stepped out of their room and into the hallway, he heard another noise, this one louder. It wasn't a mouse. Had Windsa gotten out of bed and wandered downstairs? He peeked in the girls' room as he passed, stepping softly as not to wake them. No, they were both asleep in their small beds. What in the name of the emperor was making that sound?

He gripped the hatari tighter. With only a thought, the small, milky brown stick grew into a full-length staff. Each end of the hatari sharpened until it became a point that could pierce most armor. Zornan stood at the top of the stairs, waiting for another sound, but nothing came. The stairs were noisy, at least to him, but he knew where to step to be quiet. Before reaching the last step, he heard a third sound, like one of the girls brushing past a curtain. It was close, near the bottom of the stairs. As his right foot softly stepped on the final stair, the wood creaked ever so slightly. He paused and then stepped out into the parlor.

A dark form streaked across the parlor and into the kitchen. Zornan barely caught a glimpse as it zipped by. Even with his sharp eyes, he saw no detail of the phantom, only the outline of something large and dark, maybe as large as a person. He wasn't even sure if it moved on two legs or more.

Zornan sprinted into the kitchen, stopping just inside the doorway, the hatari pointed toward any potential threat. But it was empty, the open door the only evidence that anything had been there. Zornan crossed the kitchen slowly, scanning the room for hidden surprises.

When he reached the door, he could see out into the dark night, the moons and the stars providing just enough light to make out some details. He saw the stalks of vegetables in the garden. He saw the outline of the wooden wagon Calla's father had crafted for Windsa as a gift for her second birthday.

And he saw the creature. It stood at the edge of the tree line, and Zornan had nearly missed it in his scan of the yard. It looked like a man, on two legs, crouched almost to a sitting position. Before Zornan could make out any more detail, it moved, vanishing into the complete cover of the woods. He took a few more steps into the yard, but the closer proximity did nothing. Whatever that unnatural thing was, it was out of his range of sight.

Zornan's rapid breaths and fast-beating heart raced against each other, and he inhaled deeply to try and slow both. Part of him wanted to pursue whatever that thing was, but his growing fear froze him in place. This beast, man, creature—whatever it was—might be impossible to catch, even in the light of day. What other powers besides inhuman quickness did it possess? And while he hunted it, what would prevent it from circling back to his house to finish whatever it had started? He couldn't leave Calla and the girls to face that nightmare alone.

He slowly backed into the house and closed the kitchen door. He knew he was unlikely to sleep, not with his heart still racing and his mind churning. Fallindra held few dangers, except for tonight.

4 | A DIVERSION

Days had passed, and Calla worried for Zornan. Exhaustion filled his face and slowed his limbs. He did not always sleep well when he was home, being more comfortable under the stars and in the company of a mrakaro than in a bed. But this was different, and Calla worried about the toll. He was not enjoying his time with the girls as much as he usually did, and he hadn't touched her since that first day. Was it the Investigator? She wanted to ask, but Zornan usually shared when he was ready, so she urged herself to be patient.

Early that morning, Calla's parents arrived from their farm outside of the city. It was a good diversion, something to take their minds off their worries. Her mother, Caladria, was a calming presence, and her mothering of the household appealed to Zornan. And despite his reticent nature, Zornan enjoyed conversing with Calla's vociferous father, Thandar. The man never met a topic upon which he did not have a dogged opinion.

"But Zornan, the High Trades are a form of slavery," Father repeated one of his favorite arguments. "Most of you are forbidden to marry or to have children. And you cannot live and work as you see fit. That is slavery, Zornan, or at best, indentured servitude."

"But I am free," Zornan replied calmly, though his face betrayed his amusement at Father's resolute tone. "I come and go as I please. I'm no more a slave than a shopkeeper or a tailor." Zornan smiled. "No more a slave than a farmer, who cannot work when it rains but must when it doesn't."

"Lunacy." Father sat up in his chair in the parlor, his hands flying away from his body as if to flip Zornan's argument aside. "I am my own master. Maybe the gods exert their will over me, but no one else does. I owe no money, I answer to no one."

"Again I must disagree. I believe your master sits in this very room."

For a moment, Father's animated face looked puzzled, and then he laughed. "Oh yes, well, marriage is a topic all its own."

They sat in silence for a time. She could tell Zornan was enjoying it, and that her father was searching for a new topic.

"I hate to intrude, Zornan, but…"

"It's no intrusion, Father, I'm sure." Zornan had taken to calling her parents "father" and "mother" shortly after they were married. He rarely spoke of his own parents, and when he did, it was with a deep-seated anger. Her parents were his now.

"What about the Investigator? Any idea why he's here?"

For a split second fear flashed on Zornan's face, but it disappeared just as quickly. "He is investigating a Peak Crosser-turned-rebel named Lascrill. He asked me a few questions about the old man, but I'm sure he's left Fallindra by now."

"He has not," Thandar retorted. "I ran into Thistid yesterday, and he saw the Investigator leaving The Howling Dog earlier in the day. The man had a room there, and still does, as well as two bruising fellows who must be Enforcers."

"It's no worry, Father," Calla said. "Zor was not close to Lascrill. I'm sure the Investigator will leave soon."

"He is all the talk of the town," Caladria interjected, not looking up from her crochet. "Many of the young ladies pass by the Howling Dog more frequently, hoping for a glimpse of the mysterious man and his escorts."

"Mysterious?" Father's face lit again. "He's not just mysterious, he's a demon."

"Demon?" Zornan poked at Father. "The Investigator looked quite human to me."

"Of course he did," the older man replied, leaning closer to Zornan and lowering his voice. "Demons can change forms. Even little lads know that." Thandar leaned back and smiled. Though Father believed in the supernatural and Zornan did not, he could still have fun with what he knew Zornan thought nonsense.

"Come, Father, how is he a demon?" Calla asked.

"Investigators can read your mind, and they feed off fear like we feed on food."

Zornan shook his head, but Father wasn't joking any longer, and Calla had heard the stories of Investigators learning secrets by prying thoughts out of a person's mind.

"I know you think it's all training, Zornan, but Investigators and Enforcers are not like Peak Crossers or Magistrates. They are given power. Maybe your blessing was a formality, but their blessings are supernatural."

Zornan laughed. "Oh, Thandar, I wish I could convince you that the Empire is not filled with dark assassins, fearsome giants, and constant intrigue. The truth is much more boring than that."

"Maybe so, maybe so." Father sat back, his mind churning over these dark thoughts. But as quickly as his apprehension came, his face returned to a smile. "Thistid did not just mention the Investigator—he also suggested I join the boys in a game of brithdal tonight at The Water's Edge. Hopefully it's not too much of an imposition if we stay here tonight. The game will end rather late."

"And you'll be much too drunk to make it back to the farm."

Thandar smiled at Zornan's rebuke, and ignored the judging looks of his wife and daughter.

"Well, a game of brithdal is not complete without drink and food. You should come, Zor. The boys would get a kick out of gaming with a High Tradesman."

"You know I don't gamble." Zornan's expression was flat. Gambling had been a vice of Zornan's father.

"I would never suggest such a thing, lad. Just come and be around us. Drink, tell some stories of your travels. We'll play brithdal, and you can try and keep your mind off of Investigators and rebels. Nothing helps rid a man of demons like a good drink."

"Or conjures them," Caladria shot back.

"My dear woman," the old man smiled, "don't you think the lad needs something to ease his mind?" Father's pleading eyes turned toward Calla, and she couldn't even keep a false stern look for more than a second.

"Of course, he should go," Calla said, and then turned to Zornan. "Who else would guide Father's unsteady feet?"

5 | A DARK NIGHT

Once Thandar's friends had finished their gambling (meaning Thandar had lost most of his coin), Zornan joined the game of brithdal and had a few drinks. One of the only things Zornan brought willingly from his childhood was a love of games of luck and strategy. He won seven hands in a row before Thandar and his friends begged for mercy and called it a night.

Zornan guided Thandar through Fallindra's deserted main street. He felt dizzy and a little disoriented himself thanks to a few drinks. Thandar had as much to drink as Zornan, and the older man was stumbling like a child after spin-and-run. The man was leaning heavily on Zornan's shoulder, his grip tightening each time he stumbled. Thandar did not drink often enough to handle it well (Caladria forbade liquor in their home), and he was not as fit as Zornan. This much pine beer meant a slow, wobbling ramble from The Water's Edge across almost the entire city to their home.

"Great game, lad, great game. So close to winning the pot." The man's words were slurred, and his eyes seemed intent on closing as he fought heavy blinks.

"Of course, Father. So close." Thandar had not been close at all. Brithdal was nearly as fickle as Luck herself, and Thandar's luck had been poor all evening.

Out of the corner of Zornan's eye, three men walked out of the darkness between two small wooden homes and into the street. Fallindra was a safe city, with little danger day or night, but their sudden appearance brought Zornan quickly out of his mild drunkenness.

"Stay still, Father." Zornan reluctantly let go of the man, but Thandar did not fall. Zornan eased the hatari from its holder on his back, and took two steps forward to create a little distance between himself and Calla's father.

The two men in front were short and fat. Both had swords strapped to their waists. The man in back was taller, with long hair pulled back behind his head. The light of the moons and a lone street torch danced on their obscured faces.

"Greeting, Peak Crosser," the tall man spoke as the three of them stopped a dozen paces in front of Zornan and Thandar.

He could see the men better now. The two shorter men had dark beards and greasy black hair. They looked identical, save that one of them wore his sword on his left hip while the other wore it on his right. They wore the same scowl on their faces. The third man stood behind, taller by a head. He had a mocking grin and confident air. The man carried no visible weapon, and his leather clothes looked like what High Trade apprentices wore at the academy. His face was clean-shaven, its only blemish a large scar from his lower lip down his chin.

With the way these men appeared, Zornan thought a formal greeting seemed out of place.

"What do you want?"

"Oh, Peak Crosser," the tall man said, "nothing really. Just a few questions about an old friend of yours. And we'll need to take your hatari as well."

"No. If you want my hatari, you will have to claim it." He turned his head to the side and whispered to Thandar, "Step back a few paces." Zornan extended his arm, his hatari parallel with the ground. The rod extended to its full length, and spearpoints grew on each end. This display was the traditional fight challenge of hatari wielders, and Zornan hoped it would intimidate his attackers.

The two shorter men grinned the same feral grin and drew their swords, one in his left hand, the other in his right. They looked back at the taller man, who nodded, and they rushed Zornan in a dual attack.

Zornan blocked one blow and stepped back to dodge the second man's slash. He twirled his hatari around, blocking each man's second attempt. They were skilled and fought well, their feet balanced. And they coordinated their blows, though Zornan used the long hatari to parry each attempt. They were fast, but Zornan could be faster. He gave up some ground blocking their attacks, using the first few moments to judge their abilities. His long-forgotten training sprang into his mind, breaking through the drunken fog.

He spared a small glance toward Father. The older man stood behind him, stepping slowly back. Zornan wanted to tell Thandar to run, but he wasn't sure the man was able to in his inebriated state, and Zornan couldn't spare the focus.

The left-handed brother came with a downward blow, which Zornan blocked easily. As the right-handed brother attacked a split second later, Zornan jabbed with the end opposite at the butt of the right-handed man's sword, dislodging it from his grasp and taking a chunk of his hand. The right-handed man cupped his hands together and screamed.

The other brother stepped back and looked at his wounded companion. He growled, his knuckles going white against his pommel. His stepped forward, raising his sword in a strong, downward thrust.

His anger made him too aggressive, and Zornan easily countered three ferocious blows. Zornan blocked the fourth with a swing of his hatari, which knocked the man off balance. Quickly stopping the motion, Zornan planted his feet and jabbed the spear end into the center of the man's chest. The hatari went right through him, the sharp end reaching out his back. Zornan withdrew his weapon and stepped back as the left-handed attacker slumped to the ground, dying.

Zornan turned to see the other attacker pick up his sword with his off hand and turn to face Thandar. The older man was watching the left-handed attacker die and did not see the other man approach.

Zornan moved quickly toward the wounded bandit, who turned to face him. Zornan's heart raced like it had a few nights before, but he felt nothing of that terror. Rage melted any fear, and the first brother's threat toward Thandar untethered any restraint.

Zornan swung the hatari down hard at the man's left arm, crushing it between his elbow and his hand. The thief howled in pain and dropped his sword, falling to his knees. Zornan spread out his two-handed grip and thrust the hatari in a blunt attack at the man's face. The weapon slammed against his nose with a sickening thump and crack. The second brother slumped to the ground, motionless.

With the two brothers out of the way, Zornan turned to the taller man. "Walk away now, villain, or you will join your friends in the final sleep."

The last attacker smiled broadly, his eyes lighting up like a man looking at a pretty woman. "Oh no, Peak Crosser, I think you underestimate me. I am not leaving without the answers I came for."

The tall man pulled his own hatari from a holding place behind his back. With his right hand, he extended his weapon in front of him, and the hatari grew to full length.

This man was not a common rogue, and that realization drained any poise Zornan had gained in fighting the brothers. If this attacker could manipulate a brastilia weapon, then Zornan was facing a trained High Tradesman. Yes, Zornan was faster and stronger than most men, but those advantages were gone against another High Tradesman, especially against one who was likely more practiced and less drunk.

The man's grin turned into a grim scowl as he lowered his hatari into a two-handed fighting grip, twirling it once. It was his turn to try and intimidate Zornan.

Suddenly, the attacker wheezed like a sick dog and slumped to his knees, dropping his hatari as he braced himself. A dark arrow stuck through the man's neck, blood flowing down to his chest.

Zornan stifled a scream.

The tall villain gasped again and fell lifelessly onto his face.

Zornan scanned the buildings where he thought the arrow might have come from, but he could see nothing. No figure in a window. No shadow in an alley. No movement. It was as if the arrow had been shot from one of the moons by a hero of old. What under the light of those three blessed moons was happening? For several moments Zornan stood there, the bizarre circumstances freezing him.

Shaking himself free of his fright, Zornan stepped forward and retrieved the man's hatari, slipping it into the holster on his back. He kept his own hatari at the ready, though it wasn't likely to help him; blocking an arrow in this light would be complete luck.

Zornan turned around. In the fear of the moment, he'd almost forgotten about Thandar. The old farmer was standing in almost the exact place where Zornan had steadied him. He was shaking, his hands gripped tightly together just below his chin. His eyes were still fixed on the corpse of the brother who had tried to attack him.

"Come, Thandar, come." Zornan placed a hand on the man's shoulder and guided him into a nearby alley. Thandar sat as soon as they were around the corner, burying his face in his hands. Zornan wasn't sure if he was weeping or just frightened. Zornan could feel his own arms shaking and sweat covering his entire body despite the chill of the evening.

Zornan took a deep breath and tried to shine some reason on the events and clear the fear gripping him. But what could reason make of all this?

Zornan peered around the corner to see if the archer had revealed himself. He blinked several times, trying to understand what he saw. All three assailants were gone, as if they, too, had risen to their feet to escape the archer. In the darkness, Zornan couldn't even see any sign of blood.

This is impossible! Zornan's mind shouted. But as Thandar often said, "Not believing in something doesn't change its reality." If Zornan trusted his mind at all, then all of this was indeed happening. Just like the other night with the dark figure he'd chased from his house, his mind had no rational explanation for what he'd seen.

He turned to Thandar. Calla's father was more composed, no longer seated but crouching at the ready. He was looking to Zornan for direction—or maybe an explanation. Zornan had no answers, but he knew they needed to get off the streets.

"We need to move now," he whispered to Thandar. Zornan grabbed the man's arm and guided him through the dark alleys toward home as quickly as the two men could move.

6 | THE NEXT MORNING

Zornan lay in a cave, a familiar spot where he frequently rested during his journeys. He was close to sleep, and Silver was flying around an adjacent valley stretching her wings and looking for prey. The cave, high in the mountains, was the perfect spot to camp: isolated, private and comfortable.

As his mind drifted toward sleep, a sound like rocks being displaced by a small animal brought him back to full consciousness. At first he thought it was Silver returning, but it was too soon, and Silver could not be that quiet. Zornan eased out of his blanket and grabbed his hatari.

A man burst into the cave, brandishing a sword. He rushed directly at Zornan, screaming wildly.

As the man's first blow came down, Zornan blocked it with his elongated weapon. He easily parried each strike and then became aggressive, forcing the man backward. Behind his attacker appeared the long-haired bandit and the brothers, each holding a sword. Standing behind them, with his hands behind his back, was the Magistrate from Shisnath. All four men rushed Zornan as well. The attacks were too much, especially in the confines of the narrow cave. He fell back against the cave wall, desperately trying to block each blow. The first attacker cut his arm, and then the long-haired bandit thrust the sharp tip of his hatari at Zornan's throat.

Zornan shot out of bed, sweat dripping down his face, his hatari gripped to his chest.

He looked around in panic, trying to find his attackers. He tried to calm his breathing as he scanned the spare room. He was home on the second floor of his house in Fallindra, not in a cave full of villains.

He cleared his mind of the dream and the confusion of startled wakefulness. Yes, he could remember now. After the attack in the city streets, he and Thandar had returned home. After helping Calla's father into the room downstairs, he'd slipped into this room. At first he'd wanted to stay awake, but exhaustion must have conquered him. Dim morning light floated through the window, and he could hear someone stirring downstairs, probably Calla preparing for the day.

Before the attack last night, Zornan had only killed one man. It was the man in his dream who had attacked him in the cave. The man had been waiting outside Zornan's remote camping spot, likely for some time, watching for a Peak Crosser to make camp there. Whether he was there as a thief, to test his fighting skills against a High Tradesman, or simply a madman looking for blood, Zornan would never know.

The Peak Crosser had tried wounding him, had tried not to kill him, but the wild and strange man attacked ferociously even after several serious wounds, as if pain and reason were foreign to him. Finally, Zornan stuck his hatari through the man's chest (much like he had done to one of the brothers hours before), and moments later the man had stopped breathing. Silver had returned a few minutes later and carried the man's body off the ridge. Zornan never knew what she did with it.

Until last night, that had been the only mortal fight of his life. And now he had killed two more and watched a third catch an arrow in his neck. At that moment, he was glad to be the kind of Peak Crosser who delivered items between valleys and not the kind that fought in the Emperor's army. These tense moments were proving too much for him, with nightmares plaguing his sleep and constant worry likely to plague his daytime hours.

A knock at the front door made him jump. While some merchants and farmers would likely be up and about, it was still very early to call on someone. Zornan started to stand but sat again quickly. His head ached and the room seemed to spin. *Calla can deal with whomever has come.*

Calla stood in the kitchen, working beside her mother on a meal to help their husbands recover from an evening of drinking and gaming. Zornan was passed out in the extra room on the second floor and Father in the guestroom on the first floor. Both men were still dressed in their clothes from the night before. Calla smiled, hoping the diversion had been good for Zornan.

A knock at the door interrupted her thoughts.

"A little early for visitors," Caladria remarked.

Calla nodded but set down the dough she was kneading and removed her apron. It was improper to answer the door dressed like a servant, especially for the wife of a High Tradesman.

She glided into the parlor and almost tripped on Caldry.

"Sorry, Mamma."

Calla smiled. "Go play with Windsa outside. We want to let Papa and Father sleep." The small girl disappeared into the kitchen and out the back door.

Calla smiled again and reached for the door, but her smile disappeared as she opened it. The tall, dark Investigator stood there, flanked by an even taller man dressed in the maroon uniform of an Enforcer. Ninel, the town constable, stood a step behind.

"Greeting, Lady Calla." The Investigator was as striking as all the women in town had said he was. His skin was the color of richly stained wood, and his hair was curly and hung to his shoulders. He was not as large as the hulking man behind him, but he was fit and strong.

"Welcome greeting, Investigator." She tried to flash a smile but was sure she failed. She turned to the Enforcer and Ninel. "Welcome greeting, Enforcer, Constable."

"Welcome greeting, Calla," Ninel replied, his eyes betraying his discomfort. The Enforcer made no pleasantries.

"Is your husband available?" the Investigator asked.

"I'm afraid he's not feeling well. He was out late last night with my father."

"May we come in?"

She flinched at the question, which was likely not a request. "Of course. Forgive my bad manners." She motioned for them to enter.

The three men walked into the parlor. The Enforcer folded his arms behind him, rigid and formal. His hair was blond, and his eyes were as blue as lake water. His face was square and plain. Ninel, who was built strongly himself, looked like a pesky younger brother standing next to the Enforcer.

"We need to see your husband." The Investigator's voice was calm, but insistent.

"Of course." She turned toward the stairs. "Zornan. Please come down here now." She made her voice as calm as she could but infused it with urgency. She hoped he would come quickly.

Zornan did not disappoint. He moved deliberately, the effects of the drinks painted on his worn face. He reached the bottom of the stairs and squeezed her hand. His expression was empty.

"Greeting, Investigator, Enforcer. Good morning, Ninel." His voice was cracked and rough. He did not seem himself; his face and posture seemed to carry more than a late night.

"Welcome greeting, Peak Crosser." Crisdan motioned to the chairs in the parlor. "Shall we sit?"

"Of course," Zornan offered. "Please sit."

Zornan and Calla sat opposite the three men. The Investigator's piercing eyes did not leave Zornan's face, as if he were trying to pry into her husband's soul. Even though she was sure Zornan had nothing to hide, the Investigator made her very nervous.

"I would like you to tell me about last night." Crisdan's words were a command, not a question. He sat on the edge of his chair, hands resting on his thighs.

Zornan took a moment to respond, his eyes fixed on the Investigator's intimidating gaze.

"Last night? I went to The Water's Edge to watch Calla's father and his friends play brithdal."

"I'm more interested in what happened on your walk home."

Zornan's face finally broke, and he looked scared, even terrified. Calla had never seen him look like that. What could possibly have happened on their way home? Zornan looked over at her and smiled weakly before he spoke.

"As Thandar and I were walking home, we were attacked by three thieves. They wanted my hatari, and I think they wanted to ask me about Lascrill, but our conversation never got very far. I believe I killed two of them, a slimy pair that looked like twin brothers. The third and I never fought because he was killed by an arrow to the neck."

Calla stared in disbelief. An attack on the streets of Fallindra? That was unthinkable. But she knew Zornan was an honest man and didn't drink enough for this story to be fantasy.

"An arrow? In the dark?" Crisdan's doubtful tone mocked Zornan. "And you never saw who shot it?"

Zornan shook his head. "I know it sounds like an impossible shot, but that is what I saw."

"And what happened to the bodies? Why didn't you rush to me or the constable?"

"I was afraid that the attacker who killed the third thief was going to attack us. I was with an unarmed, untrained, older man. I needed to get him back to safety."

"Is that all?" Crisdan's glance was intense, and it shifted between Zornan and Calla. Actually, his eyes spent a long time locked with hers. What was the man looking for?

"No, after Thandar and I got to cover, I looked back into the street. The bodies were gone."

Ninel and Crisdan looked at each other.

"Gone?" Ninel said incredulously. "How could three dead men walk away, Zornan?"

"Hold your tongue, Constable." Crisdan glared at Ninel. "You cannot question a High Tradesman."

"Apologies, Investigator." Ninel humbly looked at the Investigator's feet.

"I know it sounds impossible," Zornan continued, "but that is what happened. The men disappeared from the street. At that moment, honestly, I was frightened, especially for Thandar. He was quite drunk, and as I said before, unarmed. I needed to get him home."

"It happened as he said." Father stood near the doorway, and all eyes shifted to him. "Everything he told you was true. Zornan saved my life, and I don't know how those men disappeared, but they did."

The Investigator turned his piercing eyes on Father. Calla was proud of him; he did not shrink at all under the Investigator's glare.

"Very well." Crisdan turned back to Zornan. "Do you have any evidence of this encounter, besides your word?"

Zornan looked to the floor, his forehead creased in thought. He quickly looked up. "Yes. The taller thief, he brandished a hatari before being killed by the arrow. It rolled out of his hands, and I picked it up."

"May I see it, please?"

Zornan paused before responding. "Of course." He stood and walked out of the sitting room, returning a moment later with a hatari that, to Calla's eye, looked exactly like his own. He handed it to the Investigator.

"I need you to come with me, Zornan. I would prefer to have the rest of our conversation out of your home. Even this conversation has been a disrespect to your wife, to your children, and to your wife's parents." The Investigator switched his glance back to Calla, smiling warmly. Calla returned the gesture with a smile of her own, the best she could create under the circumstances.

"Certainly, Investigator. May I come see you in an hour or so?"

The Investigator's smile vanished more quickly than it appeared. "No, Peak Crosser, I would ask that you come now. No delays."

Zornan nodded gravely and turned to Calla, taking both her hands in his. "I will be back soon, love. Let the girls know Father is coming back...soon." The last few words pulled deeply at Calla's emotions. How quickly would he return? What was this all about? Calla wanted to reach out and embrace him, beg him not to go.

"I will tell them," she said as calmly as she could muster. "Come back as soon as you can."

7 | INTERROGATION

The constable's building was a simple structure with five rooms. There was a front room where the constable greeted others. The second room was one Zornan had never seen. It supposedly contained written files from the constable's investigations, a history of all that happened in Fallindra when the constable or an Investigator was involved. The only door to this room was from the constable's office, which was the third room, connected to the front. The fourth was a holding area, usually used for letting drunken commoners sleep off a bad night. The final room was the largest, filled with six chairs, two tables, and three small cots. The room had two doors: one from the constable's office and one leading to the alley behind the building.

It was in this room that Zornan sat in a chair as Crisdan Investigator paced across from him. A table lay between them. One small, opaque window hung in the ceiling, letting in some light while obscuring the view of curious passersby. Additional light came from two small oil lamps. The dancing shadows and feelings of fear reminded Zornan of the night before.

The same Enforcer who'd been with them at The Water's Edge stood there, his face carved into a scowl, his eyes locked on Zornan. His constant glare increased Zornan's apprehension.

Crisdan paced the room. He had not spoken since they'd entered, except to ask Zornan to sit. If this was meant to make Zornan more nervous, it was working. The Investigator held the thief's hatari, absently fingering its inscription. All brastilia weapons were engraved with the name of the owner and the name of its maker.

As if reading Zornan's thoughts, Crisdan stopped pacing and turned to face the Peak Crosser.

"Do you know whom this hatari belongs to?"

"I assume to the man I encountered last night."

"No." Crisdan sat down in a chair across from Zornan, placing the hatari between them on the table. "This belongs to an Enforcer by the name of Hasmalle. Do you know Hasmalle?"

Zornan shook his head.

"He was killed almost a year ago, assassinated on the streets of Nandria in front of dozens of witnesses. He was stabbed in the neck from behind by a cowled attacker with a hatari. When the local constable recovered his body, his hatari had been taken. Everyone assumed a passerby had stolen it because all the witnesses said the assassin struck and then ran, leaving no time to take Hasmalle's weapon. And now it shows up in Fallindra." Crisdan leaned forward, locking his eyes with Zornan. "Have you ever been to Nandria?"

"Yes, several times as part of my contract with the Priests of Cazdanth. I usually get there two or three times a year."

"Yes, and you were there the day Hasmalle was killed."

Zornan's eyes widened. How could Crisdan know that? Zornan had been there about a year ago, but he wasn't sure exactly which days or for how long. When you visited many of the same places year after year, the visits blended together into blocks of memories.

"How do you know that?"

Crisdan examined Zornan, not with suspicion but more with curiosity. "The Peak Crosser keep records in Nandria will confirm you left later that day."

"Are you accusing me of killing this Enforcer?"

"No, no." Crisdan laughed, which Zornan thought odd. What about this situation could possibly be funny? "You have his hatari, but that is not proof. I'm accusing you of killing a different Enforcer by the name of Doorsal. The tall man from last night."

"I killed? I told you, I killed two men, twin brothers I believe, after they attacked me. I watched the other man get shot by an arrow."

"But we have a witness who says he saw you kill Doorsal in the street last night, from behind, sticking your hatari through his neck. The other Enforcer, Hasmalle, was killed the same way. And we found Doorsal's dead body last night in an alley, with a hole through his neck."

"But that's not what happened!" Zornan shouted his response and stood with his hands on the table, his face drawing closer to Crisdan's. Despite the aggressive rebuttal, the Investigator did not flinch.

"So you say, but our witness says you killed Doorsal in cold blood, no provocation."

"Who is this witness? I demand to see him."

"Sit down, Zornan." Crisdan's tone was not critical or harsh, but soft, almost like a father gently chastising a child.

Zornan sat but still fumed. He considered himself good at controlling his emotions; Calla often tried to playfully goad him into getting angry, usually with little success. But the events of the last few days had ignited his rage into an intense pitch, and he was having trouble controlling its path.

"You must understand, Zornan, I am on your side. Investigators of the High Trade exist to protect High Tradesmen. I'm not looking for a way to trap you. I am looking for a way to help you, but I'm finding it difficult. If you want to help me, please keep a calm mind."

Zornan breathed deeply and nodded. "Yes, Investigator. I want to help. But I don't understand why my word is being overridden by some commoner or Low Tradesman."

"It is not. Our witness is not even from Fallindra. The man who claims you killed Doorsal is a Magistrate."

A Magistrate? A wave of despair struck Zornan harder than if Crisdan had punched him in the face. The word of a Magistrate was like the mountainous peaks dotting the empire: set and unmovable. Magistrates were trained to uncover the truth, were bound to only speak truth, and were, in many ways, the highest of the High Trades. And a Magistrate claimed that Zornan had murdered this Doorsal. Trillia was the only Magistrate in the area. Had she seen last night? Who else could it have been?

"Trillia?"

Crisdan shook his head. "The name of the Magistrate is High Magistrate Stethdel."

Zornan shook his head. A High Magistrate in Fallindra? He wasn't sure how many High Magistrates there were, but they ruled their High Trade and were the final arbiters in the Empire's most important disputes. If a regular Magistrate's word was as strong as a mountain, a High Magistrate's word was as constant as the light of the sun and the moons.

The Investigator rose and walked around the table, placing his hand on Zornan's shoulder. "I will try and think of a way to help you, Zornan, but I will not lie to you. Unless Stethdel changes his story, which would be a very odd and almost singular occurrence, there is little I can do. If you did, indeed kill Doorsal..." Crisdan squeezed Zornan's shoulder as he tensed and started to protest. "I know you say you didn't, but you may need to come up with a reason why you did, one that doesn't involve the existence of two men we can't find or an almost impossible shot of an arrow. You need a story that Stethdel cannot dispute, one in which what he saw makes sense and doesn't condemn you. Do you understand?"

Zornan nodded, but he didn't understand. Was Crisdan telling him to lie? What reason could Zornan give to kill another High Tradesman from behind without provocation? Crisdan was hinting that there was some possible justification that could potentially save him from punishment, but Zornan knew little of the law and its intricacies.

"As you say, Investigator." The full weight of Zornan's exhaustion pulled on him. Restless nights, dark visitors, and now a life-crushing accusation. Zornan wasn't sure he could even stand.

"Please give me your hatari. A High Tradesman under an accusation like this must surrender his weapon. Go home, Zornan. Try to rest. I wish I could console you otherwise, but the next few days are likely to be as long and as difficult as this one has been."

Zornan stood, removed his hatari, and gravely handed it to the Investigator. He hadn't even thought about the possibility of having to relinquish his weapon, but he was falling into numbness, and giving this up seemed small compared to what he might face in the future if a Magistrate found him guilty of killing one, or maybe two, fellow High Tradesmen. He walked from the constable's office and into Fallindra's streets.

Crisdan sat back in his chair as the door closed behind Zornan. He fingered the Peak Crosser's hatari now, feeling Zornan's name and the name of the weapon's maker intricately carved in the ancient tongue. Coincidentally, it was made by the same priest who'd made Hasmalle's hatari.

Crisdan knew Zornan was innocent, something he had suspected even after Stethdel's accusation early that morning. Everything besides the High Magistrate's words screamed innocence. Zornan was naive and honest to a fault. If Crisdan was sure of anything, it was that the events, as inconceivable as they might seem, happened just as Zornan described them.

But Zornan's innocence was irrelevant; the word of a High Magistrate superseded the truth.

Why would the High Magistrate build this elaborate plan to trap Zornan? Discovering Stethdel's motives would be impossible. Crisdan was forbidden to read the mind or emotions of a High Magistrate unless commanded to do so by one of the High Investigators. But turning off his abilities was like someone asking him to stop breathing, and while he didn't dive into Stethdel's emotions, Crisdan knew a lie when he felt one.

Crisdan pushed these thoughts aside and returned to Zornan. Before the accusation, Crisdan had envied the man. He was clearly and completely unaware of the world around him, despite his extensive travels as a Peak Crosser. He did not know the origins of his own abilities, which was not unheard of among Peak Crossers. But this Peak Crosser was also unaware of High Trade law and didn't even have enough guile to catch Crisdan's meaning on concocting a good motive to combat his accusation.

Was Stethdel trying to discredit Zornan? Was Zornan really a confederate of Lascrill and involved in the Empire's political intrigues? The answers eluded him.

Crisdan's High Trade blessing made him acutely aware of everything around him, even when he did not want to be. As he walked into any room, he was aware of the fears and secrets of each person. He could feel them. And it tainted his entire view of the world and humanity. Zornan carried none of that burden.

But what Crisdan envied most was the Peak Crosser's wife Calla. As an Investigator, marriage or any committed relationship was strictly forbidden. Crisdan had relationships with women, but they were fleeting. Crisdan wanted something more substantial, the support that only a good woman could provide.

Calla was that kind of woman. His brief interaction with her that morning let him know that. She was pure, true and faithful. And she was beautiful. Because of the High Counselor to the Emperor, it had become the fashion among the Empire's elite women to mirror the High Counselor's extreme thinness. In addition, it was the fashion for women to wear tight clothing that accentuated their skeletal features. Crisdan did not find that style attractive. He preferred women like Calla, women with substance.

Crisdan cursed himself for letting his thoughts wander back to Calla. It had been bad enough that he had stared at her during the questioning at their home and that he had let his thoughts wander to being alone with her. She was faithful and true, and he was the man who was likely recommending her husband appear before a Magistrate faced with a charge of murder. Those circumstances did not portend romance.

Romance, he thought, cursing himself again. *She's married, and I'm forbidden. What is wrong with me?*

Stargarn walked close to the table, his satisfaction potent.

"Do you still think he's innocent?"

Crisdan had to be careful now. Though Stargarn was under Crisdan's command, his true allegiance sat with his High Trade, and doubting the word of a High Magistrate was something the Enforcer may feel compelled to share with his superiors.

"I think this is more complicated than it seems," was Crisdan's measured response.

"That's not an answer, Investigator. Maybe your view is clouded."

Crisdan looked up at Stargarn. Did the man suspect his feelings for Calla? No, Crisdan would be able to feel his distrust or suspicion, but the Enforcer felt of pride and self-righteousness. And he wasn't observant enough to have picked up on anything not laid out clearly before him.

"And you gave him advice." Stargarn's words were an accusation.

"Do not question my methods, Stargarn. I am the Investigator here, not you, no matter how much you want to be." The other man stiffened at that, anger spiking. "I serve all High Tradesmen, and my advice was nothing out of the ordinary." But he knew it was a lie as soon as he said it. Most of his kind would not have encouraged Zornan to lie.

But it didn't really matter. Zornan seemed intent on speaking the truth, which would do nothing but drown him.

8 | THE HIGH MAGISTRATE

Zornan had intended to go straight home, but he didn't want to face Calla yet, or Thandar or Caladria. They would have so many questions, and he didn't want to give the answers, not until he had time to digest it himself and wrestle with the likely outcome of all this: banishment from the High Trade or his execution. What he wanted most was to hug his two girls and hold them tight.

Intent on avoiding those conversations, he made his way to The Water's Edge, his hunger pulling at him, distracting him. He needed his mind to be clear to reason all of this out.

The Water's Edge was nearly empty, and the innkeeper quickly served him emperor berry wine and morning stew. Every sound echoed in the small common room, not like the night before during the game of brithdal—before Zornan's life had been ruined.

His mind kept wandering back to his dilemma, searching for a way out. But there was nothing to find. It was the word of a High Magistrate against a lowly Peak Crosser. Only having the Emperor himself as the witness would have been worse. Zornan could no longer fight the dread seeping through his entire body, paralyzing rational thought and dousing any hope still flickering inside him.

Intent on trying to guide his mind to anything but the dark paths ahead of him, Zornan looked up. The tavern keep was gone, and the room was nearly empty. It was a slow time of day, but The Water's Edge typically had more men than this at any given time. As he took another drink, he became aware that he wasn't entirely alone. He could feel someone behind him and could see one side of the outline of a tall man at the edge of his vision.

Before he turned to look, the man spoke.

"Greeting, Peak Crosser."

He turned to see the Magistrate he'd encountered in Shisnath. Zornan began to dismiss the man but decided to hold his tongue.

The tall Magistrate walked around the table and sat opposite Zornan. "I hear you've come across a bit of trouble. I might be able to help with that."

Zornan's anger boiled, but he pushed it back. "How would you know that?"

"Because I am the witness to your murderous act."

Zornan gasped, stunned. "You're a High Magistrate? You're Stethdel?"

"Why yes, I am. I'm sorry for not introducing myself properly in Shisnath, but the situation required some discretion, and to be fair, you never asked my name."

"Why do you haunt me so? Leave me alone. You've won. You promised a storm, and now I'm caught in the middle of it. Did you come here to gloat?"

"My goal is not to ruin your life, Zornan."

"Well, it should be. Because you've accomplished that in a most spectacular way."

"My goal is to transport something, off the regular record. It's something of immense worth to me personally, and I need it carried by someone who is not involved in any way in the political traps of the Empire. You were that man. You still are that man."

"Ha." Zornan took a long drink, draining his glass, wishing for more. "I thought you'd be more aware, as a Magistrate, that I can't do that now even if I wanted to. Crisdan took my hatari, and I'm sure he has men watching the Peak Crosser keep. I cannot leave Fallindra, and I cannot take your precious item. I am stuck, and you're the one who placed me in these binds. All because I wouldn't help you and take your vague quest!"

Each word fueled his anger, and he could feel it overflowing like the North River after a storm. He had only felt this angry once in his life: when his father sold him into the High Trades. He wanted to hit Stethdel, hurt him. But what little rational thought remained constrained him. Assaulting a High Magistrate would only worsen his situation, regardless of the momentary satisfaction it might bring.

"No, I've created another path to get what I want. You refused my first plan, so I have created another. You should be thanking me, Doorsal and his companions were there to get information from you about Lascrill, and after they were done, they would have killed you. I will still reward you with wealth and freedom, for both you and your family. Now that you know who I am, you should know I can deliver on that promise."

The Magistrate was calmer than he'd been in Shisnath, confident in the trap he'd unleashed.

"How?" Zornan exploded. "How are you going to fix this? By recanting your accusation? By casting a spell to clear my name? How? You've ruined my life! Regardless of whether I took your request, or if I even could, you are tearing me from my wife and children. You have ruined me! How dare you talk of your plans and your important request! Why would I help a man who has so little regard for me? I would rather attempt a flight to the Fire Moon than ever help you."

Zornan was sure he'd gone too far, but he didn't care. He hated Stethdel, and he had no desire to appease the man. Zornan turned his gaze back to his food and stuffed his mouth with a large bite of breakfast stew. Stethdel sat in silence, not responding to Zornan's tirade.

After a few moments, the High Magistrate's face softened for the first time. He frowned slightly and sat forward with his arms resting on the table.

"I do not want to tear you from your family, but my current choices are extremely limited. I promise that you will, at some point, understand all of this. You may still hate me, but what I am asking of you is vitally important to me personally, and it may very well change the course of the Empire."

Zornan looked into the Magistrate's eyes. The man was right, he would always hate him. But he had little choice but to hear him out. Change the course of the Empire? Zornan had no desire to be part of anything like that. He wanted to do his work and live happily with his family. If Stethdel could grant that, shouldn't he try to take it? Even if he wanted to take one of the tavern chairs and break it over the man's head?

"Why not approach me as Stethdel the High Magistrate instead of as a stranger? I would have believed you could deliver your promise if I had known who you were."

"Would you have believed that I was a High Magistrate?"

Zornan sat back in his chair and frowned. "No. I would have thought you a madman."

"Exactly. This accusation works for us. Crisdan confirms my identity, and now the seriousness of your situation makes fleeing your most attractive option."

"Fleeing? But now I *can't* flee."

"You can, and you must. What does it take to convict a High Tradesman of such a serious crime as murder?"

"A trial, likely in front of a High Magistrate."

"And if the High Tradesman isn't there at his trial? What then?"

Zornan paused. He had studied little of the law at the High Trade Initiatory School and had thought even less of it since then. "I don't know. I assume he would be tried and sentenced regardless."

"No," Stethdel replied, shaking his head. "A High Tradesman cannot ever be convicted if he cannot answer his accusation, except in the case of treason against the Empire. If you flee, you cannot be tried or sentenced, and the Peak Crosser Council cannot remove the stipend that would, in your absence, fall to your wife."

If Zornan had known this part of the law, he had long forgotten it. A High Tradesman could not be put on trial if he wasn't there? Calla and the girls could live very comfortably on his stipend, not as richly as his contract with the Priests of Cazdanth, but they would have what they needed. They would not be turned into a burden for Thandar and Caladria.

Stethdel smiled at him. Zornan did not return the gesture.

"So you want me to leave my family behind," Zornan replied. "You want me to desert them, and I assume they can know nothing of where I'm going."

"Not just that, you can tell them nothing at all. Not about this meeting, not about my offer. It will be safer for them the less they know."

Zornan considered the High Magistrate's words. Stethdel was obviously manipulating him, but what could be done about that? The Magistrate had artfully trapped him in a treacherous maze with only one way out. As much as he despised the man, the only exit was the path of the High Magistrate's making. Unless Zornan wanted to wait for the Emperor or the moons to grant him clemency.

"And if I accept your offer?"

"We meet the day after tomorrow, a couple hours before dawn. There's a clearing three miles from your home that used to be a farm many years ago. Are you familiar with the spot?"

Zornan nodded. He and Calla sometimes took the girls there to picnic. It was isolated, which was surely Stethdel's intention.

"Excellent. All you need to bring is yourself. I will take care of all supplies."

"And Silver? And my weapon?"

"Yes, Zornan. I will take care of all of it. All you have to do is be there and be ready to fly."

Zornan pondered the request. He did not want to trust his life and future to a man who so clearly only cared about whatever it was Zornan was to carry. This path was filled with uncertainty and danger, but any other path was filled with disastrous certainty. *Curse the man.*

"I agree to the terms, High Magistrate, but it better be as you say. If not, I will find you and make you pay."

"Very fair, Peak Crosser. Any other questions?"

Any other questions? Zornan had a thousand questions, chief among which was what he would be carrying. But Stethdel was not going to share that information, and in the end, the cargo was insignificant compared to everything else swirling around this situation. At this point, he was throwing his trust at this man, like a woman asking a hungry prairie cat to carry her newborn. It seemed insane and right at the same time.

"One question: what about the demon you or this Doorsal fellow sent to my home?"

"Demon?"

"Sorry." Zornan shook his head and almost laughed. "My Calla's parents are very superstitious, and it pollutes my language at times. Several nights ago, some dark figure was in my house, but I startled it, and it fled. I assumed it was there at your command. It was inhumanely fast. You probably think me insane."

Stethdel's face went white. All the poise and authority the man possessed melted. "A Baldra. They sent a Baldra and it found me."

"A Baldra? Now you're sounding like Calla's father."

"Is this naïveté an act?" The Magistrate searched Zornan with his eyes. "Baldra are Imperial assassins, creatures formed by the priestesses. They are fast and strong, among their other abilities. They must know what I have. They must know what I'm doing. I'm not prepared." Stethdel was not speaking to Zornan; his eyes vacantly stared into nothing.

The High Magistrate suddenly refocused and turned back to Zornan. "It is even more imperative that we hurry. Instead of the day after tomorrow, I need you at the clearing a couple hours after nightfall tonight. I'd ask you to leave now, but I cannot be ready that soon." Stethdel paused again and looked back into nothing. "We may be ruined."

If his own life didn't hang in the balance, Stethdel's sudden discomfort would have been amusing. A Baldra? Those creatures were real? And they were created by priestesses?

"Go, Zornan. Spend a few hours with your family. We must be ready to move soon."

9 | ESCAPE

ornan sat in a chair in the near-dark of his bedroom watching Calla sleep. Beautiful, wonderful Calla. Mother of his two children. Maybe his only true friend. How could he leave her without telling her where he was going, without assuring her that he wasn't fleeing and abandoning them to the fickle fate of the moons?

So against Stethdel's wishes, he wrote a letter detailing everything: the Baldra, Stethdel the High Magistrate, and the details of his interview with Crisdan.

That evening Zornan had tried his best to act as if nothing were really happening. He lied to Calla, Thandar, and Caladria, telling them Crisdan was sure that it had been a total misunderstanding and that the witness had been old lady Drastra, who ran a small sewing shop on Fallindra's main street. Something had woken her, and she had peered out her window. Her word as a witness would not stand against a High Tradesman. It was a believable lie that would hold up long enough for him to leave.

Thandar and Caladria seemed satisfied by this explanation, and the rest of the day had proceeded as usual, filled with food, happy conversation, and games with the girls in the field by the garden. Despite the weight hanging over him, Zornan had enjoyed it, especially the time with Windsa and Caldry. He asked Thandar and Caladria to stay the night, just in case Crisdan or Ninel needed him the next morning. They happily agreed.

Calla had not believed his story, but she said nothing. After the day was done, they made love and Calla fell into a deep sleep; Zornan's eyes had never closed. He lay next to Calla for a long time, staring at her face, wishing he could wake her and kiss her again.

Stethdel had commanded Zornan to tell Calla nothing, but Zornan did not have to do everything the cursed man asked. Calla deserved to know the truth. And the letter revealed nothing of his destination or what he was carrying, because he knew nothing of either.

He laid the letter down at the reading table near their bed. There was enough light in the room to make out the outline of Calla's face. He stood there for a few moments, observing her, and considered kissing her forehead. He decided against it. If he was going to leave, it had to be now. Stethdel and his wind-blown destiny were waiting for him in the darkness.

As he left their room, he fought the urge to check on the girls. Windsa and Caldry would likely sleep through the intrusion, but he couldn't risk it. He had said his mental farewell when he put them to bed; that would have to be sufficient. He wondered what on earth Calla would tell them. Probably just that he was on one of his typical trips. How many lies would she be forced to pile on this?

Zornan went out the back door and into the night. He was glad it was clear; his walk would have taken a lot longer on a cloudy night, and leaving the valley with Silver would have been treacherous. But two of the night's three moons were visible, and the entire small circle of stars was visible above the valley's peaks. The largest of the moons, Circlarl, was full tonight, in all its white glory. The smallest moon was also just barely visible, its orange light belying its name: Fire Moon or Thru'Cada in the ancient tongue. It waned and dangled dangerously close to the peaks; their jagged edges looked as if they might pop the orange sphere like a child's finger would a soap bubble. The third moon, the bluish Dithdee, hid behind the peaks, though, if Zornan had his days right, it was only a day or two past being new.

Zornan entered the woods at about the same place where he'd seen the Baldra a few nights before. This realization sent a sharp wave of fear through his body, which he suppressed as best he could. Worry about a supernatural assassin would do him no good. If that foul creature was on to Stethdel's plan, their arrangement was likely doomed anyway.

Zornan felt oddly peaceful after dispelling the thought of the Baldra. Was this what it would be like to walk to your own execution? This feeling of certainty, of direction, was in many ways preferable to the dread of the unknown that had plagued him for days.

As he reached the edge of the woods, he could see the field. Peering across it, Zornan could make out outlines of two creatures on the eastern edge of the farmland. One looked like Stethdel, though his features were indistinguishable in this light, even with Zornan's eyes. But the other outline was unmistakable: it was Silver. Zornan had no idea how Stethdel had arranged to get the mrakaro out of her keep in the middle of the night without waking a good section of Fallindra. Mistar or Giltar must have helped him, most likely the master keeper. What manner of treachery had the man used to force the former Peak Crosser to do his bidding?

Silver shifted nervously, and Zornan could almost feel her anticipation. Despite her obvious apprehension, she remained silent, as if the mrakaro knew noise was their enemy.

Zornan stepped into the field and began the walk toward Silver and Stethdel. He was glad Silver would be coming with him. He had no particular attachment to his hatari, though he knew many High Tradesmen were very fond of their particular weapon. But Silver was Zornan's companion, a friend as much as any man could have. If he was going on some crazy adventure, he was glad Silver would carry him, not some strange giant flyer.

The long grass brushed against Zornan's thighs. The night was cool but pleasant. Zornan would have considered it beautiful if not for the circumstances.

As he approached the High Magistrate, he saw a sword or its brastilia counterpart, a hatrindi, tied to the man's hip. Stethdel had his hand on its grip, his entire body flexed and ready. As Zornan got closer, the High Magistrate eased and took his hand off his weapon.

"Greeting, Peak Crosser."

Zornan simply nodded. Whatever peace he had felt on his walk melted as he looked at the man who was ripping him from Calla and the girls. He again felt the urge to strike him but suppressed it. Now was not the time to change course.

For the first time, Zornan noticed that Stethdel had nothing with him besides his weapon. No package or parcel, no pack with supplies, no hatari to arm Zornan. Was this some strange deception, or was Stethdel so paranoid that he had to keep his secrets until the last possible moment?

Stethdel noticed Zornan's searching eyes.

"What you carry is close, but I had to be sure it was you."

"Well, it's me. Let's not delay, especially with a Baldra on our trail." The mention of the creature sent a chill through Zornan, and it seemed to do the same to Stethdel.

"Yes, Peak Crosser, let's proceed." The man turned toward the woods behind him. "Come out, Mairie."

A young woman carrying two packs stepped from the tree line. Zornan could not have been more shocked than if Stethdel had summoned a Baldra or a talking duck. Surely Stethdel was not asking him to transport a *person*? Zornan hoped the young woman was merely a companion and that the second pack contained his cargo.

The young woman was likely in her seventeenth or eighteenth year. She was tall and thin, and her hair was light, probably blond, and extreme in its curls. How far the hair hung below her shoulders, Zornan could not see. She was dressed in tight leather clothing, similar to the clothing of an apprentice at the Initiatory School and very similar to that of his attacker from the night before. She gracefully crossed the short distance and stood next to Stethdel.

"Zornan, Peak Crosser, this is my daughter, Mairie."

His daughter? Stethdel's desperation finally came into focus. He had a forbidden daughter. Magistrates were forbidden to marry or have children. Having a child without authorization was high treason against the Empire. And standing before Zornan was proof that this High Magistrate had broken his covenant. If knowledge of Mairie's existence were made public, Stethdel's execution as a traitor would likely follow.

"Are you mad, Stethdel?" Zornan peered at the High Magistrate. "Carrying people is very difficult and strictly forbidden."

"I think we're both past worrying about what is forbidden, wouldn't you agree?"

Zornan was an accused murderer. Stethdel was a traitor against the Empire. Following lesser laws was not going to win either of them points with the High Magistrates. Their fates were, whether Zornan liked it or not, completely intertwined.

"Still, flying someone who is not a Peak Crosser is dangerous. The high altitude could kill her, Stethdel. She is not dressed well, and if the chill doesn't kill her, the lack of air might."

"You think me a fool, Zornan? I know the dangers of flight. We have come prepared." Stethdel looked at the girl, and she took something from her bag. In her hand quivered a malleable little blob; the nibrak was a small creature bred specifically to help those who weren't Peak Crossers breathe while flying. Zornan had not seen one since using them during his training flights before he had learned the skills of a Peak Crosser. Stethdel was prepared.

"Where are we going?"

"Mairie will tell you that after you've left the valley. There may be prying ears close by."

Zornan glanced around. He couldn't imagine anyone close enough to be listening, unless the Baldra also had that supernatural ability.

"Fine." Zornan looked over at Silver. "Then we should leave."

Zornan took the packs from the girl and prepared to load them onto Silver. The mrakaro continued to rock back and forth as much as the short tether that attached her to the ground would allow. Zornan attached one bag to one side of the saddle and walked around her to attach the other. The second pack had a hatari tied to it, and Zornan slipped the weapon from the pack and fingered the signature. It was not his, but it would do just as well. What High Tradesman had Stethdel killed or manipulated to get it?

After sheathing the weapon behind his back, he gently caressed Silver's neck.

"Easy, old friend. We will be gone soon." Silver stilled her feet and craned her neck so that one of her large black eyes was focused on Zornan. He smiled back at her and patted her beak as she reached down to nuzzle.

Stethdel and Mairie were engaged in an almost silent conversation as Zornan came back around the bird. The two looked nothing alike, at least not in the light of the moons, though maybe her height came from her father. As young as she looked, she was a good head taller than Calla and most women Zornan knew, though still a few inches shorter than he was.

Calla. He imagined her sleeping in their bed, the moonlight shining into lightly illuminate her delicate nose and long eyelashes.

"Zornan." The Peak Crosser's head snapped toward Stethdel. "Please help Mairie onto your mrakaro."

Mairie had said nothing, and her face was as long and pathetic as Zornan's had been when he thought of Calla. She was being torn from her father and taking a flight with a strange man on a giant creature. Zornan could hate Stethdel for involving him in all this, but as a father, he now understood why. And Mairie was as caught up in the circumstances as he was. Yes, he would continue to despise Stethdel, but he could not hate Mairie.

"Put one of your feet here, and I will lift you." Zornan intertwined his fingers and created a little basket for Mairie to step into just below his waist. Despite the darkness and the strangeness of this situation, the girl stepped easily into it, and Zornan lifted her toward the rear of the saddle. The saddle had an extra strap at the back for a passenger, which Zornan had not used since his academy days. Many Peak Crossers never carried a passenger; this would be Zornan's first time.

As he boosted the girl, she gracefully hooked her other leg over the saddle and was on the bird quickly. She removed the nibrak from a pouch at her waist and placed it over her nose and mouth. She looked like a small child trying to stuff too much frozen milk into her face at a festival day. But the rest of Mairie's face looked nothing like a child's during festival. Her eyes stared blankly ahead, and no smile turned up behind the small creature.

"Zornan," the High Magistrate whispered as he brought his mouth to Zornan's ear and gripped the Peak Crosser's shoulder. "The Baldra is here, in the woods opposite the bird." The fear that had gripped Zornan before returned, his body stiffening at Stethdel's revelation. "Listen closely. After I release you, begin to argue with me loudly about how you're not going to do this. I will eventually pull out my hatrindi to strike you. When I do, jump onto the mrakaro and be ready to leave. I will cut the tether with my weapon. Get to the air as quickly as you can."

Stethdel released his shoulder and stepped back into view of the Baldra. Zornan joined him, fighting the strong urge to turn around and look to where Stethdel said the Baldra would be. Stethdel pulled Zornan close again and whispered even quieter than before. "You are taking my daughter to her mother, and Mairie looks nothing like her mother. We blessed her to look nothing like either of us." Stethdel turned away, leaving no chance for further explanation.

"You should leave soon," Stethdel said, raising his voice to a normal level as he pulled away.

"I am not leaving. This is insane. I can't walk away from my family." Zornan's voice was solid, sharp. He did not need to fake this argument. "Everything I have is here. You're taking everything I hold dear; why should I now help you? I was a fool for coming here."

"But you agreed to this! If you do not mount that bird in the next few moments, I will take this ruined life of yours and make it a thousand times worse. You know who I am. You know what I can do!" Stethdel raised his voice to a fevered pitch and stepped close enough that Zornan could feel the High Magistrate's warm breath against the cool night.

"You bastard! How dare you continue to threaten me. Do you think you own me? I'm of the High Trade myself. I am not your servant to be pushed around as you will. By the towering peaks, I hate you!"

Zornan's words stunned Stethdel, to the point that he hesitated. Zornan wasn't sure if the hesitation was part of the act for the spying Baldra or if the true vitriol of Zornan's retort had confounded the High Magistrate.

After a moment, Stethdel placed his right hand on the grip of his sheathed hatrindi. He spoke in a much lower, intense voice. "Then let's finish this, right now."

As the High Magistrate pulled out his weapon, Zornan turned, crouched, and jumped. He grabbed the saddle's pommel and swung onto Silver, landing roughly. Silver responded with an annoyed screech. Zornan patted the bird with one hand as he strapped himself in with the other. He hadn't paid attention to see if Mairie had strapped in; he hoped she had.

The tether snapped from Stethdel's unseen blow, and Silver immediately took two steps back, spreading out her wings and screeching again in surprise. Zornan spared a glance to the southern tree line and saw a dark shape streaking toward them at incredible speed, swifter than a large prairie cat. The Baldra's arms ended in sharp points, as if it had sprouted claws.

Zornan squeezed with his knees and urged Silver with a shout. The mrakaro began trotting forward, gaining momentum for their flight, her wings extended. Her pace was slower with a second passenger, as the extra weight made her steps uneven. The Baldra closed quickly, less than thirty yards away, streaking with such fury that it was almost a blur.

Silver pushed into the air. Her belly and wings dipped dangerously close to the ground, her usual grace disrupted by the strange circumstances and weight. But with two powerful beats, she lifted into the air. Zornan sighed deeply. They were safe.

And then the Baldra jumped.

The creature's leap carried it high into the air. Zornan could see it better now as it floated toward them. It was human-like in form, dressed completely in black, and what had looked like strange claws were two short brastilia swords or long knives. For a moment he thought its supernatural jump was going to land it on Silver's back, dooming them all. As if sensing the danger, Silver increased the angle of their ascent, and Zornan lost sight of the Baldra as it passed below them. It came dangerously close, but fell harmlessly, landing deftly in the long grass.

The Baldra's face was illuminated by the moons as it peered skyward. Its skin was gray and milky and stretched over its bones like too little dough over a meat pie. Its deep-sunken eyes were dark, and its mouth was pulled into a sneer, bearing ghostly white teeth. Zornan shuddered again.

Zornan lost sight of the Baldra as Silver banked to the left and turned to head toward the eastern mountains and their escape. Looking to his left, Zornan picked out the Baldra again, this time streaking across the field toward Stethdel.

In the last few moments, Zornan had forgotten about the High Magistrate. Surely the assassin wouldn't kill a High Magistrate? But Stethdel had been legitimately frightened of the creature, and now that Zornan better understood the man's situation, maybe this all made sense somehow.

He pushed Silver in a circle, banking left again so he could keep an eye on the Baldra and Stethdel. Zornan's mind searched for some way he could help the High Magistrate. He could get lower again and try to attack the beast. He was armed now, the hatari in the holster on his back. But after seeing the Baldra leap, Zornan wasn't sure he could get close enough to throw the weapon without putting them in danger, and throwing it would leave Zornan unarmed for the rest of his journey. And as fast as that infernal creature moved, he was almost certain he couldn't hit it without an element of surprise or something to restrict its movements. He had neither. So he would stay high and observe, and hopefully he could think of some way to assist a man he did not actually want to help.

The Baldra reached Stethdel and stopped, but it did not put away its knives. Their mouths moved as if talking, but Zornan was too high to hear anything; the rushing air and the flaps of Silver's wings filled his ears. As they circled above, Zornan could alternately see Stethdel's face and then the Baldra's. The creature's expression was mostly obscured by its cowl, leaving its dead gray chin and ghostly teeth the only things visible against the blackness.

Stethdel had sheathed his sword as the Baldra approached. For now, the assassin seemed content to talk. Were those things even capable of reason?

Zornan looked back to see how Mairie was handling everything. She sat in the saddle, her legs tucked and strapped as if she had been trained or had done so before. She looked surprisingly comfortable. Had Stethdel smuggled her on a giant flyer previously? Possible. The nibrak was on her mouth and nose, and she seemed to be breathing easily. She was wearing flight glasses, which Zornan had not noticed. Without them, it would be almost impossible to see with the rushing air coming into her face. Zornan had become accustomed to it after years of riding, and he rarely wore the things.

She looked intently down toward her father, trying to peer around Silver's wings. Because Mairie sat farther back on Silver than he did, Zornan doubted she caught more than a fleeting glimpse of what was happening below. Even then Zornan doubted her eyes were good enough in this light and at this distance to be able to see anything at all on the ground. Her long, curly hair was pulled back tightly behind her head. Zornan hadn't noticed her do that either.

He suddenly became aware that they were drifting lower. Silver's curiosity must also have gotten the best of her, and their hovering circle was now only fifty feet or so above Stethdel and the Baldra. It was still probably too high for the Baldra to jump, but he had seen the creature's archery skills in the dark two nights before; he couldn't risk an arrow picking him off or hurting Silver.

As if thinking the same thing, Stethdel looked up at them and started waving wildly with his hands. At this distance Zornan could not hear his indistinguishable shouts, but he was clearly urging them to leave.

With Stethdel's eyes skyward and his arms in the air, the Baldra struck, thrusting its two knives into his chest. As Silver circled, moonlight glinted off the tips of the long knives emerging from Stethdel's back. A second later, the assassin pulled out the weapons, and the man who had woven Zornan into this plot sank into the long grass and disappeared from sight. Zornan looked away, his stomach turning at the image. Maybe Stethdel had been the demon's target all along.

The Baldra looked up and bared its teeth. As it stared, its cowl fell back, revealing a bald head the same sickly color as its face. The creature screamed, a high, piercing noise, and Zornan winced. It was like a wild dog howling after a kill. Zornan pulled on Silver's neck and edged her upward. It would take a few minutes, but they needed to get high enough to get out of the valley. He did not look back at the Baldra.

Mairie slipped her hands around his waist and laid her head in the middle of his back. His body recoiled at the contact and then relaxed. He thought maybe their ascent was too rapid and that she was feeling sick. This fear grew worse as she started to shake and spasm.

But she wasn't sick; she was weeping.

For the next several minutes, as Silver circled higher and higher, the young woman cried as deeply as anyone Zornan had ever witnessed. Her sobs were not really audible through the nibrak, but the intensity of her grip varied with the intensity of the sob. As they climbed, she buried her face as deeply as she could into the middle of Zornan's back, to the point that the Peak Crosser had to steady himself to keep from being pushed forward.

Of all the cargo or papers Zornan had transported in his years as a Peak Crosser, he rarely knew much about their contents, purpose, or importance. He was given a task and a destination. This time was no different: he had a task, and Mairie would tell him the destination. Zornan wasn't sure if she was really as important to the future of the Empire as Stethdel said, or if it was just matter of protecting her and keeping Stethdel's indiscretion a secret. Maybe he would never know. In the end, he didn't really care.

Zornan's body grew cold, and he fought back tears of his own. He was leaving behind Calla, leaving behind Windsa and Caldry. The man who would have helped him restore his life was now dead. Zornan worried that blame for Stethdel's death might fall on him as well. He had every reason to want the man dead, and Crisdan knew that. *Curse you, Stethdel!* Even as a dead man, he made Zornan's life more difficult.

Zornan pushed Silver higher, and the mrakaro's flight evened out as they crossed over the peaks and out of Fallindra.

10 | A GRAND MEETING

The lodging room was filled with more than Mizcarnon could ever need. The bed was large enough to fit six or seven men side by side. On the bed were richly-colored blankets, and thick, soft pillows. The entire room was decorated in a rich maroon with gold accents on the pillows, blankets, and drapes. A large chair sat in the corner next to the window, a richly carved table at its side.

The chair would be considered a throne by most. The armrests were carved to resemble the form of a mrakaro, with the legs carved to resemble its feet. Maybe this room had been chosen for him because he was a Peak Crosser, but the ornately carved mrakaros did not make the room feel more like home; it made it feel even more foreign and uncomfortable.

Despite the luxury, Mizcarnon missed the open sky and his usual bed in the Infinite Mountains. He missed feeling his mrakaro, Sunset, sleeping close by. His bed was the hard ground; his furnishings, the trees and bushes; and his fellow occupants, wild creatures. The overly large room, the gaudy furnishings, and the lack of natural light set him in a constant state of nervousness, as if he dangled dangerously off a cliff. Three days he'd sat in this room, sequestered until he could give his final report to the Emperor. The time had come.

During his brief time in the Imperial palace, he heard other guests outside, but he did not join them and none came to call. His fellow occupants were likely some of the most powerful men and women in the entirety of the Empire of the Peaks, visiting from all corners, calling on the Emperor and his attendants. His fellow lodgers would probably have been intrigued by the presence of a military Peak Crosser scout in their midst but not in a way that would make them want to drop by for a drink and conversation—they would rather gawk as if they were seeing a prairie cat or a Croxshinian monkey up close. Mizcarnon would be a curiosity to them, mainly because, unlike all the other guests, he would not leave the palace alive.

He finished straightening his shirt, making sure his dark brown military uniform was in place, then took a deep breath. He eyed his hatari, which was sitting on his bed. Should he bring it? Certainly they would search him before he gave his report to the Emperor and the High Counselor, and bringing weapons into an audience with the Emperor was treason. But why should treason bother him now? He was going to be executed, as was the Emperor's right when a scout returned with information that, if revealed broadly, could be damaging to the Empire. And the information he brought was definitely of that kind. According to General Chandish, Mizcarnon had been the only one of three scouts to return.

Duty had pulled Mizcarnon home, a force more powerful than the fear of death. The information he possessed needed to be told. Sharing this might doom him, but it might save the Empire.

He looked at his hatari one more time but left it there on his bed. There was no real chance of escape. The palace was filled with Imperial Guards. These elite fighters were the Emperor's to directly command and control. They were the most skilled fighters in the Empire, extremely loyal to the Emperor, dressed in brastilia armor. Even if he somehow concealed his weapon, his escape would be met by dozens of these dedicated guards, and his life would end at the points of their hatrindi. No, if he was going to die, it was going to be with honor, as a Peak Crosser and an Imperial scout, not as an attempted deserter.

Moments later, four Imperial Guards appeared at his door to escort him to his audience with the Emperor and the High Counselor.

The guards led Mizcarnon down a large and imposing hallway. The two in front of him walked with ceremonial hatari. The weapons were longer than a regular hatari, too unwieldy to use in battle, with a spear tip on top and a flat bottom which they struck upon the marble floors with every other step, sending sharp echoes through the great hall. All four guards wore hatrindi at their waists, the actual weapon of choice for their kind. Their armor was brastilia, the swirling ore covering everything but their eyes. The armor was a curiosity to Mizcarnon. It appeared to be hard like brastilia should be, but it flexed when the guards moved. It looked like it would make movements awkward, but the four guards walked naturally. He knew the Priests of Cazdanth could make brastilia do amazing things, but none of their other creations matched the amazing armor of the Imperial Guard.

Among the other High Trades, Imperial Guards were a mystery. They did not train at the High Trade Initiatory School, and they did not socialize with other High Tradesmen. They were forbidden to show their faces to anyone except the Emperor. The strange restrictions were meant to protect them from all influences outside of the Emperor himself. Mizcarnon's fellow Peak Crossers joked that the men must sleep in their armor and probably brought fruit to the Emperor on his command, like a servant or a pet. Though it was common among the High Trades to mock the complete devotion of the Imperial Guard, Mizcarnon respected it; if he hadn't been similarly loyal, he wouldn't be walking down this magnificent hallway to his death.

As they approached the massive doors of the Emperor's throne room, Mizcarnon glanced up to the roof, which was easily thirty feet from the floor; giant flyers would have been able to stay airborne in its expanse. The brastilia doors to the throne room stretched up twenty feet on the wall to his right, the edges shooting up parallel until the doors began to curve into a peak symbolic of the Infinite Mountains. Mizcarnon breathed deeply. Two guards standing watch joined with his escorts to pull open the large doors.

Mizcarnon was rarely apprehensive, but he had to focus to make sure he walked without shaking and that his hands didn't twitch.

The room was the size of a city square, and the ceiling was a good ten feet higher than the hallway. Four giant pillars formed an enclosure in the center, as round and as tall as the legendary trees of the Ice Mountains. The colors were cream, red, gold, and occasional accents of dark brown brastilia. Blood red drapes hung from the ceiling behind the throne, partially obscuring massive windows which stretched to the ceiling. The sun shined brightly behind the Emperor, creating a powerful silhouette.

Mizcarnon's eyes followed the sunlight to the throne, which was made of brastilia, the dark, milky brown a stark contrast to the brighter colors that dominated the rest of the room. It was situated in the middle of a circular section of floor, tiled with brastilia and extending twenty feet around the chair. The seat was elevated, ten feet from the ground.

Gradual steps led up to the throne, upon which sat Emperor Tothdarin, son of Gathrizdel. The young emperor looked a good ten years younger than Mizcarnon. His long, dark, curly hair hung nearly to his shoulders and was tied behind his head with a gold ribbon. The Emperor was said to be tall, but Mizcarnon found it hard to tell from ten feet below. He was dressed in fine, cream-colored robes with a sash the same blood red color of the drapes behind him. The Emperor sat straight, his arms comfortably on the throne's armrests. His long, pointed nose reminded Mizcarnon of a mrakaro's beak.

Mizcarnon bowed deeply. The Emperor responded with a slight nod.

Overcome with the majesty of the moment, Mizcarnon had hardly noticed Lanthia, the High Counselor, seated to the right of the Emperor. She sat in a golden chair just outside the brastilia circle. Her posture was formal. The chair's armrests were too high for her slight stature, so her hands rested in her lap. Many in the Empire spoke of Lanthia's beauty, but he did not see it. She was incredibly thin, like a young girl who had skipped too many meals. Tight dresses like the one she wore were the fashion in the capital, primarily because Lanthia wore garments like this. The black dress plunged deeply, almost to her navel.

Mizcarnon looked away and tried not to blush. He was glad that particular dress hadn't yet become the fashion.

He had to admit that her face, with her thin lips and deep cheek bones, was pretty, but she looked too much the girl and not enough the woman. Like the Emperor, the High Counselor looked ten years younger than Mizcarnon; he believed their ages were close to their looks, though no one knew for sure, especially when it came to the Emperor. He had spent his childhood in seclusion, separated from his parents and his seven siblings. Out of the eight, Tothdarin alone had survived to adulthood.

Mizcarnon focused his eyes on the Emperor and waited to be addressed.

"Welcome, honored Peak Crosser Mizcarnon." The Emperor's deep voice filled the massive chamber, a trick of magic or acoustics. "We anxiously await your report of Croxshine."

"Welcome greeting, Greatest Emperor of the Peaks, Tothdarin, son of Gathrizdel." Mizcarnon spoke loudly to ensure he was heard, but whatever had carried the Emperor's voice did the same to his. He bowed deeply again and spoke a little more softly. "I am honored to be in your great presence."

The Emperor nodded and smiled a bright smile like you might see on a man his age in any tavern throughout the Empire. It was a warm, happy expression, one that seemed at odds with everything Mizcarnon knew of the Emperor's tumultuous childhood. *Careful*, he chastised himself. *This is not a young man at a tavern; this is the Emperor, the most uncommon of men.*

"I wish I could offer you a seat after your long journey, but convention demands that only the High Counselor sit in the presence of the Emperor."

"Please do not apologize, Emperor. I am not worthy to sit in your presence."

The Emperor smiled again, and the Peak Crosser could not help but be warmed by it.

"Enough with the pleasantries, Peak Crosser." It was Lanthia speaking, spitting his title with disdain. "False compliments and idle chatter waste the great Emperor's time."

Mizcarnon blushed at the chastisement and lowered his eyes.

"Nonsense, Lanthia." The Emperor waved his hand. "The man is our guest, and one who has served the Empire honorably. He deserves courtesy." The Emperor stared at his High Counselor. "And you will find your place."

Mizcarnon fought to keep his mouth from gaping open in amazement. An open argument between the Emperor and his High Counselor in front of an inconsequential Peak Crosser scout? Lanthia glared angrily at Mizcarnon, her steel blue eyes cutting him in half. But she said no more.

"But the High Counselor has a point," the Emperor continued. "Tell us what you found in Croxshine. Were you able to gain audience with King Dichnire?"

"No, Great One. My reports indicated that King Dichnire is dead, and his entire family dead or scattered. The face of the land is embroiled in war, with an invading force having conquered more than half the continent."

If the Emperor was surprised at Mizcarnon's report, he hid it well. The smile had disappeared when he corrected Lanthia, and he retained a blank, emotionless expression.

"Preposterous!" Lanthia cried. "Croxshine is a mighty kingdom with stout warriors. No one could have conquered half the continent! It was free of war a year ago."

"Alas, High Counselor, I tell the truth. The Kingdom of Croxshine is but a memory of history now, extinguished by an aggressive conqueror. Some of the eastern provincial governments survive, but a couple of them fell even in the short time I was there."

The two most powerful people in the Empire sat silently for several moments, absorbing the disturbing detail.

"Who is the invader?" The Emperor's question was spoken as if he suspected the answer.

"They call themselves the Nansarta. Most of the conquerors claimed to be from the former kingdom of Boothdrinka."

"Former kingdom?" Lanthia asked.

"Yes," Mizcarnon replied. "They claimed that this Empire of Nansarta started when their Emperor conquered Boothdrinka. They worship this Emperor of theirs like a god, claiming he holds powers beyond that of any man, woman, or creature."

Lanthia turned to the Emperor. "Clearly this is a lie, Your Greatness. How could he have spoken to these agents of this imaginary empire? He is not trained in the language of Boothdrinka, and I can't imagine the invaders already speak the language of Croxshine."

"Excellent point," the Emperor agreed. "How were you able to speak with these invaders?"

"They spoke The Tongue of the Empire of the Peaks."

"Liar!" Lanthia stood as she shouted. "That is impossible! How could they know our language? And well enough to speak with you! And they just gave you all this information freely? To a spy? Your report smells of lies."

"Sit, Lanthia!" The Emperor did shout this time, his sonorous voice ringing through the throne room, ruffling the drapes behind him and shaking Mizcarnon to the core. "We must hear his complete report. And do not accuse him of lying again unless you have evidence to support your claim."

Rumors sometimes held that the Emperor and his High Counselor were lovers, while others claimed they were sworn enemies. Mizcarnon wasn't sure this conflict disproved either theory.

"Continue, Peak Crosser."

"I know that speaking our language seems strange, but it is true. They gave up the information quite freely, even though I suspect they knew I was a spy. They were proud of what their Emperor has done. They also claimed that their Emperor was a native of the Empire of the Peaks."

Lanthia stirred in her chair at his assertion but said nothing. Mizcarnon did not look in her direction. He kept his eyes locked with the Emperor. Tothdarin remained calm.

"Do you believe them?"

"I can't say, but they fought with brastilia weapons, Your Majesty. Their warriors were trained like Enforcers and Imperial Guards. They had Peak Crossers on giant flyers in the skies, and they had what I could best describe as Baldra fighting amongst them as well." Mizcarnon had not been sure he should mention the assassin High Trade class since officially they did not exist. But he had fought alongside the formidable creatures, and the Emperor and High Counselor surely knew of them, so pretense was unnecessary. He hoped.

"Baldra? They had the deformation and the Shindar?" The Emperor rested his hand on his chin.

"They were not deformed like Baldra, and I could not tell if Shindar were close by. They looked like normal humans, but they fought with the inhuman speed, strength, and ferocity of a Baldra, beyond even the abilities of the Imperial Guard, and they fought with hatnuthri."

For the first time since he began his report, Mizcarnon saw some worry creep onto the young Emperor's brow.

"How many of these Baldra-like warriors?"

"Hard to say. At least several hundred."

Lanthia gasped.

The Emperor erased the worry from his brow and sat back into his throne. He had leaned forward at the mention of the Nansarta Baldra, but he now returned to his imperial posture.

"That is why I believe the Emperor of Nansarta must be from the Empire of the Peaks," Mizcarnon continued. "They have been trained in our magic and the skills of the High Trades; they have our creatures, like mrakaros, and cosows; and they speak our language, though most of them not well. I can only assume that this Emperor with his godlike powers employs Bendathdrans and Cazdanthians, although I wouldn't have thought that likely before I visited Croxshine." Mizcarnon glanced at Lanthia; she sat stunned, her posture deflated, her arms gripping the armrests.

"But surely we're safe," the High Counselor said, almost as if to herself. "Surely they cannot cross the great ocean. And surely our army is greater than theirs."

"I do not know about their ability to cross the ocean, though they seemed to cross from Boothdrinka to Croxshine with little difficulty," Mizcarnon replied. "It's closer, for sure, but they moved a massive army. They have giant flyers they call miotop, lizard-like creatures that dwarf mrakaros. They can carry as many as twenty soldiers and fly great distances."

"They could not have moved an invading force over the ocean twenty at a time," the Emperor said. "The must have used boats."

"I thought so, too, Emperor. But the people on the western shore of Croxshine saw only the miotop before the invasion began in earnest.

They claim the remainder of the invaders seemed to spring out of the ground."

"Is their force sufficient to overcome ours?" the Emperor asked.

"I believe so, Your Majesty. Their army is twice the size of ours, maybe more, though they will have to leave a great number in Croxshine to maintain control there. Many of its people are not accepting the invasion and are fighting back, though they are hopelessly outclassed in every way."

The Emperor remained regal in his posture, and worry only adorned his brow for mere seconds before it was wiped away again. Seeing a man this composed, kind, and wise in the Empire's highest seat filled Mizcarnon with confidence.

"Anything else that we must know, Peak Crosser?"

"Yes, Emperor. Every soldier of Nansarta said the same thing: after Croxshine was secure, they had their eyes set on conquering the Empire of the Peaks."

For the remainder of his interview, Mizcarnon detailed the Nansarta. He elaborated on their capabilities, numbers, tactics, and magic. He was asked to repeat many of the details several times, as if the Emperor and especially the High Counselor were trying to catch him in lies or exaggerations. The Emperor was clearly disturbed by the report, and Lanthia was almost in tears when he left. Counselors were supposed to be emotionally strong, the voices of reason and perspective to leaders throughout the Empire. But the High Counselor advising the Greatest Emperor of the Peaks, Tothdarin, son of Gathrizdel, was a blubbering fool whose questions lacked depth and whose emotional control was similar to a petulant child. The faith he gained in the Emperor was equal to the disdain he felt for the High Counselor.

Four Imperial Guards (it was impossible to tell if they were the same ones from earlier) escorted the Peak Crosser back to his room. He eyed their weapons, wondering if he should try to overcome them and escape. He had fulfilled his duty. He had returned when none had. And he had given his report directly to the Emperor. Did he owe his life as well? Did duty require that? He might say he did not fear death, but he knew anyone who sought death was a fool; death would come to all, so there was no need to flirt with it.

Mizcarnon banished thoughts of escape. Even if he got a weapon from one of the guards, it wouldn't matter; they would easily kill him. Even if he bested these warriors, escape from the palace would be impossible. And even if he were to somehow escape the palace alive, he would be hunted for the rest of his life. He would be branded a traitor and bring immeasurable shame to his family and his High Trade. No, if execution was to be his fate, he would face it with honor, not like some coward, not like the others. He had no desire to die, but he would not disgrace himself in his final act.

To his astonishment, the two Imperial Guards escorted him through the great hall he had come through before, past the guest quarters, and to the same entrance he had entered days before. The two brastilia doors opened as he approached as if moved by some unseen hand. Brilliant, midday sunlight flooded his eyes, temporarily blinding him. Ten Imperial Guards stood outside the door, each one holding a ceremonial hatari and armed with a hatrindi. Mizcarnon stopped just short of the entrance, his surprise freezing him in place.

"You may go," said one of the guards, his words muffled by his helmet.

"Your things will be brought to the Peak Crosser keep," said another.

"The Emperor has requested that you not leave the capital until he gives you written permission," said the first. "After he is satisfied, you will report to General Chandish for your next assignment."

Mizcarnon turned to the two guards, disbelieving. He nodded and began to leave.

"Wait," the second guard said. Mizcarnon turned to face the guard at his left. "Welcome parting, Mizcarnon, Peak Crosser. You have brought great honor to the Empire. As the High General of the Imperial Guard of the Empire of the Peaks, I give you our thanks. You have earned our respect, and I do not give any measure of respect lightly." The man dropped to one knee and bowed to Mizcarnon. His companion and the ten Imperial Guard stationed at the entrance all did the same.

For a few moments Mizcarnon was too stunned to say anything. "Thank you, High General. Sad parting to you. I am immensely honored."

The twelve Imperial Guards returned to their feet, and the High General and his companion turned and walked back into the palace.

Mizcarnon descended the long stairway leading to the palace gate. He passed several more Imperial Guards, and each time, they knelt on one knee. He acknowledged each of them with a word of thanks.

Death most certainly did come to all. But somehow Mizcarnon had cheated it once again and had gained more honor than he thought possible.

11 | CONSEQUENCES

Calla sat in the chair next to their bed, staring at the disheveled blanket and rumpled pillows. She repeatedly creased Zornan's letter with her left hand to the point that the crease was now likely to tear if pulled. She felt colder than she should have. She was still dressed in her white night clothes, and her bare feet hung slightly above the floor—the chair had been made for a man Zornan's height. *I'm sitting in Zornan's chair,* she thought, *and he's gone. He's gone.*

This nightmare still felt unreal. The man she loved, her partner and greatest friend, was gone. She had no idea when, or if, he would return.

Last night she'd known something was hanging over him. He'd brushed away all questions about his interview with the Investigator, as if this were all a fantastic misunderstanding that would clear up within a day or two. They had a pleasant dinner with her parents and then played games with the girls. Zornan had insisted her parents stay the night, and they obliged. Then Zornan and Calla had spent time alone in their bed.

During that otherwise pleasant evening, she'd known he was haunted by something. She suspected the situation might be a lot worse than he was letting on. But she decided to let him be, to wait for him to share with her once he had collected his thoughts. She figured they might take a walk this morning, and she would learn everything in his heart and mind; instead she learned everything from a letter.

Calla had woken that morning with the faint sun, and when she turned over and didn't find Zornan there, she shot from bed, her heart racing. Her eyes scanned the room until they stopped at the parchment on the small reading table next to Zornan's chair. She hoped for a romantic note, that he was up early toiling in the garden. But somewhere within herself, she knew he was gone. She began to cry before she had even read the letter.

She'd slid across the bed and scooped up the letter and began to read. Through her muffled tears and occasional sobbing convulsions, she learned about his conversation with Crisdan and Stethdel's entrapment. At the words, *I'm so sorry my love, but it is best if I leave...*she fell onto her knees and buried her head into the chair, her violent sobs carrying across the house and likely beyond.

Moments later her mother had appeared at her side. Calla hadn't heard her approach above the sounds of her own grief. Mother hadn't even asked what was wrong; she simply hugged her daughter and caressed her hair. For a few small moments that hung like hours, Calla sobbed as her mother held her, often repeating the words, "I love you, dear. I'm here, dear." Calla could only assume that Father was taking care of Windsa and Caldry. She hoped her screams had not terrified her girls too much.

After Calla had regained a measure of composure, Mother propped her into Zornan's chair and returned downstairs. She came back a while later with some breakfast—fruit and a piece of bread. She told Calla that father and the girls were off for the farm and that she would be downstairs in the parlor or the kitchen if Calla should need anything. Calla mumbled a thank you and her mother left her alone again.

Calla had hardly moved since. She read the letter several times, each time barely crossing the words, *I'm so sorry my love, but it is best if I leave...* without returning to weeping. She learned in those repeat readings that Zornan planned on returning, that he believed Stethdel would honor his promise and restore Zornan's name. But he also alluded to the point in the law that said High Tradesmen could not be convicted in their absence, so if something happened to Stethdel or he turned out to be even more villainous than assumed, Zornan would have to stay away forever in order for Calla and the girls to maintain the money that came with his position.

Over the course of the hours since she'd woken, Calla had rotated between dueling emotions of anger and admiration. Anger, because she wished he had talked this over with her, that he would have trusted her to help him make the right decision. *Does he think I am so weak that I couldn't have helped?* She had cursed his name a dozen times that morning.

But she also admired him. He was still the selfless man she had married seven years before. He had carried the burden of his decision alone and had left to protect her and the girls. He entered into a deal with an unscrupulous man in the hopes that it would protect *them*.

She remembered that fateful meeting eight years before when she worked in The Howling Dog. His quiet gray eyes attracted her first, followed by his strong chin. His nose was broad, and his hair was light brown. He was unshaven after several days of flying, a look Calla loved, though Zornan rarely wore it. Though initially attracted by these features and his exotic role as a Peak Crosser, she married him for his kindness, sincerity, loyalty, and dedication.

And now that selfless man who dedicated his life to providing a comfortable life for them was in the clutches of a man who was using and manipulating that goodness. Calla had her doubts that Stethdel would ever actually help them. *Peaks help me, but if I see the man this morning, I will claw his eyes from his face!*

In the end, she had landed on admiration and love for her husband. Grief had a way of entangling emotions in unexpected ways. She couldn't imagine ever letting go of this dread pulling at her. She knew she must, but not yet.

She finally stopped crying when a loud knock shot through the quiet house. Her right hand clenched her night skirt. She had known they would come eventually, but she wasn't prepared to meet them yet. *They must know he's gone. Couldn't they leave me alone to grieve?*

"Good morning, mother of Calla." The voice of Crisdan Investigator carried from the foyer below. "I need to speak with the Peak Crosser, Zornan, or his wife."

"Zornan is not here, and Calla is not feeling well. May I help you?" Her mother's voice was amazingly calm.

"No, I am only interested in talking with Zornan and Calla. If they do not greet me soon," he said more loudly, "I will be forced to enter the house."

"You cannot do that! This is the home of a High Tradesman!"

"Yes, lady, and I am an Investigator of the High Trades, looking into some of the most serious charges imaginable. Trust me when I say the law gives me quite a bit of latitude."

A flash of movement caught Calla's eye, and she turned to the window to see two men dressed in loose-fitting, maroon leather clothes walking through her yard. A sword—or whatever High Tradesmen called their special weapons—hung at each man's waist. Enforcers.

"I'm coming, Mother." Her words were weaker and more choked than she hoped but loud enough that Mother would know to stop her resistance and Crisdan would know she was coming.

The night clothing lacked modesty, so Calla grabbed a shawl from her dresser. She cleared her tear-stained face and took a deep breath. She shouldn't keep Crisdan waiting any longer, because she didn't want him storming the house or hurting her mother. But she couldn't give away the source of her grief. She was still tightly gripping Zornan's letter, which he had told her to destroy after reading. She tucked it down her shirt and below her breasts. A chill ran through her as she wondered if that would keep it safe from a search by either the Investigator or his Enforcers. She prayed to the moons that it did not come to that.

Mother and Crisdan stood just inside the door, flanked by two more Enforcers and Ninel. Her mother's face was sympathetic and the Enforcers' glares were stern. Crisdan's expression was the only thing that surprised her: he seemed regretful, like Zornan often looked when he knew he had to discipline the girls but did not want to.

She brushed aside thoughts of her husband and curtsied slightly, her hands gripping the shawl to keep it in place.

"Greeting, Crisdan Investigator, and Ninel, and Enforcers. I apologize; I don't know your names." The two large men nodded slightly as Calla turned back to Crisdan. "How can I help you?"

"Where is your husband?"

"He's not here."

Crisdan's eyes drifted toward the stairs. "Where is he?"

"I don't know. He was gone when I awoke this morning. And before you ask the question, I have no idea where he went. He told me last night we were going on a walk alone this morning, that he had something important to discuss."

"May we look upstairs? I apologize for the inconvenience, but it is very important. We will be as discreet as we can."

"Discreet? Investigator, please, discretion is gone. You came to my home with four Enforcers and the constable. By now every home in Fallindra knows that you are here and something is wrong."

Crisdan frowned and curled his lips. "I am sorry. Under the circumstances, it was necessary."

"Why? May I ask what this is about?"

"May we search your home?" he asked again, brushing her question away. She nodded, and Crisdan shared a glance with one of the Enforcers, who moved quickly up the stairs. Ninel strode into the kitchen and then the parlor. The other Enforcer remained at Crisdan's side.

"Silver, your husband's mrakaro, is gone," Crisdan said, his voice flat. "And the man who accused your husband is also gone. He left the inn where he was staying in the middle of the night and has not returned."

"I don't know where he is." She hoped the statement was truthful enough to fool his piercing glare.

"I believe you. Your husband is too smart to leave the knowledge of his destination behind. It would endanger you and the girls." He paused. "The girls aren't here either. Where are they?"

"My husband took them to our farm," her mother answered.

"After I found that Zornan was not here this morning, I feared the worst," Calla added. "Father took them so they wouldn't have to see me so frantic and worried. We did not want to frighten them." Calla fought tears.

The Enforcer came back downstairs, circled behind the women and stopped.

"What is this door for?" the Enforcer asked.

"It is a cupboard. My husband uses it to store his hatari and his Peak Crosser things. It is locked to keep our girls away from his weapons and travel gear."

Without asking, the Enforcer slammed his fist down onto the small lock. The hinge detached from the wall and clanked to the floor. Both of the women stepped back at the sudden force.

"Stargarn." Crisdan's voice was firm. "That was unnecessary. I'm sure the lady Calla has a key."

The Enforcer eyed Crisdan curiously, as if he had said something unusual. The large man turned back around and opened the door. A man slumped from the cupboard onto the floor, his shirt blood-stained and his body completely limp.

"High Magistrate Stethdel," the Enforcer gasped. "He killed the High Magistrate."

She didn't know this man, but the Enforcer's words made something clear: she would never see her husband again. She screamed again, and her body went completely limp. Someone caught her, though she didn't know who. She heard her mother screaming, as if in the distance. She looked and saw Ninel gently holding Mother. Calla screamed a third time and buried her head into the chest of whomever had caught her.

Crisdan surveyed the chaos. It was bad. Bad for the women, bad for Zornan's chances at restoration, and bad for him as an Investigator. A High Magistrate had been murdered within a short distance of an Investigator and four Enforcers. Not only would Fallindra soon be filled with Investigators, Enforcers, Magistrates, Peak Crosser Warriors, Counselors, but Crisdan's incompetence would be part of the inquiry.

Ninel held the woman Caladria. She was her daughter's equal in beauty, though at the moment her wails and distorted expressions masked her beauty. Stargarn held Calla who was in an even more inconsolable state. Their screams rent the air like those of a startled mrakaro. Calla and her mother had been right in sending the children away. Regardless, Crisdan would need to send an Enforcer to the farm to make sure all this wasn't a ruse on Zornan's part to make everyone assume he had left when he was still concealed in the valley.

"Get them out of here," Crisdan commanded. "Ninel, take the mother upstairs to one of the bedrooms. Stargarn, take Calla into the kitchen. And for the love of the Emperor, please get them calmed down."

The men obeyed. Caladria took slow, cautious steps, guided by Ninel up the stairs. Calla hung limply on the Enforcer's arms, so he picked her up and carried her to the kitchen.

Crisdan had thought the morning could not get worse, but he had been wrong again. He had awoken to Ninel reporting that Silver was gone from the keep, and the man he had stationed there the night before had been found unharmed but bound in the mrakaro's stable. The keeper, Mistar, and his young apprentice, Giltar, both claimed ignorance about Silver's departure, but both men had lied. They would be questioned thoroughly later. *Confound it, I should have left an Enforcer there! Zornan would not have overpowered an Enforcer.*

He turned his attention to the body. The other two Enforcers joined him in the entry. No use guarding the backyard any longer. Zornan was not here, and he was probably miles from this valley.

Crisdan had already made his contact, the Secretary of the High Investigators, aware of Zornan's departure. He had been told that two atacikics were released to track down Zornan. Crisdan had no idea why Stethdel had involved the poor Peak Crosser in whatever was happening here. Even with his murder, Crisdan doubted whether the

High Investigators would ever allow him to dig deeper into the life of the mysterious High Magistrate.

He had no desire, however, to tell his superiors about the High Magistrate's death. How could he explain his incompetence at not foreseeing these events? He had not protected Stethdel or detained Zornan. Of course, he had no authority to do either, but he doubted that would clear his reputation among the High Investigators. Results would condemn him more than procedures or laws.

He should communicate Stethdel's demise soon, though; the Enforcers were likely communicating with the Council of Enforcers, and that information would pass to the High Investigators. He had only an hour, maybe less, before the knowledge of the murder of a High Magistrate spread throughout the leadership of the High Trades.

Crisdan refocused his attention on Stethdel's corpse. Two matching wounds dotted the High Magistrate's chest, the signature kill of a Baldra. The manner of Stethdel's death drained his spirits even further. Legally speaking, Baldra did not exist. Crisdan had encountered their work in several investigations over the years, but the High Investigators were clear on those occasions (and likely would be on this one) that assassination by Baldra was not a classification Crisdan could make.

Though most High Tradesmen knew they existed, and though many commoners assumed as much, the Empire did not recognize the Baldra's existence, which made them even better assassins. If you could not legally pin a murder on a Baldra, the Empire (or whoever controlled the foul beasts) could murder without detection. Most of Crisdan's investigations were straightforward, crimes of passion or greed. Clearly, this case was anything but straightforward. Crisdan realized it would probably consume years of his life and possibly destroy his standing among his peers.

The lack of a foul odor also indicated a Baldra kill. He picked up the slight scent of the incense that the Baldra used to cover the stench of their victims. Stethdel had also been carried into this house and placed in the cupboard without leaving any blood and without disturbing anything or anyone. Stethdel was a large man; only a Baldra or an Enforcer had the strength to do that. Even the newest Investigator would have seen that Zornan had not killed Stethdel, and he certainly could not have concealed his body here unless he'd had a Baldra accomplice. And even if Zornan possessed the strength, what kind of fool would hide the body here and not throw it into the woods to be devoured by animals?

None of that mattered because Baldra did not officially exist. And if you pretended they did not exist, the logical conclusion would be that Zornan killed Stethdel, had assistance in concealing his body here, and then fled the valley on his mrakaro. That was the accusation he would likely have to file with the High Investigators, the High Magistrates, the Council of the Peak Crossers, Trillia the Magistrate of Fallindra, and maybe with the Emperor himself. Only the least damning part of it was likely true: Zornan had fled after being ordered by an Investigator of the High Trades to remain in the valley.

"Find something in the house to wrap the body in."

The two Enforcers eyed him curiously. Enforcers hated taking orders from Investigators, and hated when it was an order that a man with lesser skills could accomplish. "And find someone in town who can preserve the body. It is evidence, and it will be some time before there is a trial."

The Enforcers exchanged another glance then disappeared upstairs to fulfill his request. Crisdan turned and walked into the kitchen, cursing the muscular morons he so frequently had to deal with. Most High Tradesmen viewed Peak Crossers as the lowest of the High Trades, but that was likely due to a lack of exposure to Enforcers.

Calla was sitting at the small prep table in the kitchen. She was still crying, but had calmed down to the point that the only noises she made were soft, periodic inhalations. Stargarn stood next to her, staunchly guarding against her escape. *Fool. She's not going anywhere.*

"Go help the other Enforcers," Crisdan said, entering the kitchen. The large man nodded and left the room. Crisdan pulled up a chair and sat across from Calla. Even in her disheveled state, she was beautiful. She was dressed in white night clothes, and a shawl hung loosely across her shoulders. The night dress dipped deeply down her chest. Crisdan stole a glance, then looked away, chastising himself. He couldn't help being attracted to her, but he had to maintain focus. His life was on the line as much as Zornan's.

She looked up at him. Her eyes were filled with tears, her face stained with their sorrowful streams. When recognition of whom he was flashed on her face, a warmth flowed through Crisdan. Seeing him changed her deep despair into flickering hope.

"My husband is doomed." She was trying to state a fact, but it also came out like a question.

"I do not know, Calla," Crisdan lied and hated himself for it. Investigators lied all the time in their attempts to get information from witnesses or the accused. The lying rarely bothered him, but this lie, at this moment, bothered him a great deal. He suspected it would be the same for other lies he would likely have to tell her.

"But a High Magistrate, he's lying dead…" She began to choke up again and broke eye contact with Crisdan, looking down. She quickly pulled the shawl back around herself, covering her exposed skin. A touch of shame ran through Crisdan. He hoped she hadn't noticed his glance.

"There could be other explanations for the High Magistrate's death." He left it at that. He had to lie to her, but he did not have to insult her intelligence with convoluted explanations.

"I can't imagine anyone will believe anything but what seems obvious. People rarely do."

"Maybe not, but I don't believe Zornan killed anyone." Usually this was a lie he told the family and friends of murderers to make them believe him an ally, even when he wasn't.

"Why? The man's body is in our house! And Zornan fled…" She began sobbing again, and Crisdan patiently waited until she regained herself.

"It is my job to find the truth, Calla, and my experience and skills tell me something else is going on here. I can't guarantee I will be able to uncover the real truth, but I can promise I will try."

Crisdan felt the hope well inside Calla, and her eyes softened as he stared into them. Deep, rich green eyes.

"Thank you, Investigator. That is all I could ask for."

"Call me Crisdan, Calla. May I offer one piece of advice?"

She nodded.

"Study the law. Learn the rights and privileges of the High Trades and their families. The law may be your friend in this case, even when I cannot be. The library here contains all of our written law, everything you need to be an advocate for Zornan in his absence. It may help you protect yourself and your daughters."

Calla's eyes moistened again and fresh tears escaped. "Why are you being so kind? Thank you…Crisdan."

Crisdan reached over with his right hand and grasped her fingers, squeezing them gently. He quickly stood, left the room, and left the house. He couldn't stay any longer without doing or saying something more that would only add to his ruin.

12 | IN THE MOUNTAINS

Zornan, Silver, and Mairie glided among the mountain peaks, headed southeast. The air was cold against Zornan's face, and occasional bursts of wind pushed against them, making for a bumpy ride. Silver used the bursts to her advantage, shifting her wings to maintain her course. Heading mostly east was to their advantage; the swirls of wind would grab them, but the wind currents were forcefully behind them, pushing them farther and farther away from Fallindra.

Mairie had been silent, almost motionless in the hours since they crossed out of Fallindra. After she stopped crying, Mairie sat as still as she could manage. Her curly blond hair was pulled tightly behind her head, and the wind tossed the long tail all around her face. Zornan couldn't imagine flying with so much hair. The few women Peak Crossers he had known all kept their hair short so they wouldn't have to deal with it while flying.

The rush of the wind and the nibrak covering Mairie's mouth and nose made verbal communication nearly impossible, so Zornan and Mairie had not spoken the entire flight. Zornan was accustomed to using hand signals to communicate with other Peak Crossers in flight, but Mairie would know nothing of that form of communication.

Zornan pointed Silver a little south now in order to fly directly at the sun. He kept his gaze a little off where they were going to avoid looking directly into the powerful light.

Flying toward the sun had its risks, but Zornan thought it was the best option. If someone was tracking them and approaching directly from the southeast, Zornan would be nearly blind to their approach. But there wasn't really much southeast of their current position, and any Peak Crossers who would be dispatched to find him would likely be coming from the south or the west. He weaved among the mountains to hide himself from northern or southern approaches, and the sun should protect him from a western approach. But their current path made them vulnerable to pursuers from the east. He hoped his choice wouldn't doom them.

He was flying purely for evasion. He did not know their destination yet. Zornan knew he might be flying in the completely wrong direction, but first he had to distance them from Fallindra. Only after he found them a safe place to land and rest could he find out from Mairie exactly where they were going. The sooner he was rid of the girl, the better, but he had to do it safely.

Dark, ominous peaks, wispy clouds, and the outline of the medium moon, Dithdee, hanging lightly in the southern sky, filled his sight. It was the one moon Zornan had not seen in the sky the night before, and now it hung like someone had placed a small, faded piece of fruit in the sky.

Zornan looked back at Mairie again, but she avoided his gaze. He wanted to reach out to her, help console her. But they couldn't even hear each other, and Zornan had no idea what he could say to help. So he turned his head forward and concentrated on flying.

A few moments later, Mairie startled him with a poke in his back. He turned to see her pointing directly behind them. He focused his eyes into the distance and saw what she was pointing at: they were being followed by two giant flyers, atacikics by the look of it.

Mrakaros were beautiful, majestic creatures who ruled and dominated the sky. Cosows were the other common giant flyers, which looked like their bat cousins with leathery wings, thick fur, and short, fanged faces. Cosows were not as beautiful as mrakaros, but they were intelligent and loyal.

And then there were atacikics. Zornan hated them. The atacikics were the smallest and fastest of the giant flyers and easily the ugliest and least graceful. They looked like the gods had taken a human, a butterfly, and a lizard, mixed them together in a celestial bowl, and pulled out a bizarre monstrosity. Their form was very human-looking, with legs and arms. But their hands ended in razor claws, and their feet mimicked the feet of the mrakaros, with sharp talons and the ability to grip a large branch or outcropping of rock. Their heads were bald, with a flat face and shallow-set, stone-black eyes. Their teeth were razor sharp, and atacikics often bore them to intimidate other flyers and humans. Their skin was tan-colored, and tight and rough like a lizard.

Atacikics flew with large wings that could not fold into their bodies neatly as a mrakaro's, but rather were held back when not in flight, like a moth or a butterfly, and like those insects, each wing separated into two sections which could flap independently. Besides being the fastest of the flyers, their wing structure also made them the most maneuverable; they could hover in the same place much more easily than a mrakaro or a cosow. When standing, Atacikics were only a foot or two taller than a man. They weighed less than half of even the smallest mrakaro. Peak Crossers who rode atacikics looked like children riding on the back of their fathers. Atacikics rarely had a rider though, a fact that pleased most Peak Crossers.

His gamble on flying toward the sun had paid off. He felt fairly certain that the atacikics had not seen them yet, even if their eyes were as resistant to the sun as a mrakaro's. But that advantage was going to last only a few more minutes. Zornan could not outfly them, especially with Mairie as an extra passenger. He needed to find a place to hide.

He scanned his memory for a safe location. There were many common Peak Crosser camps among these mountains, but the atacikics likely knew of those. And even if they didn't, atacikics were often used to quickly pursue and track, like hunters might use a dog or a falcon. Zornan had to assume that Peak Crossers were coming, and they would know these mountains as well as he did, some of them even better.

Zornan's memory landed on a small cave several miles away. There was no place for a giant flyer to comfortably land, the cave was just big enough for three people, and it was so short that Mairie and he would not be able to stand. This made it an illogical hiding place, which made it perfect for them. He knew another Peak Crosser might think of that possibility, but he had few choices. The atacikics would catch them soon, and then it would be difficult to lose them, even among the peaks. He needed them and the Peak Crossers who would follow to move on in their search. He also needed a chance to rest and find out exactly where they were going.

Zornan reached back, took Mairie's hands, and guided them around his waist. It was about to get rough, and he needed his passenger to be stable.

As soon as her arms were tightly wrapped around him, Zornan guided Silver into a steep and sudden bank to the left. They sank below the windstream, and the strong gusts swirling amongst the peaks pushed hard against them. Silver adjusted quickly, flying among the blasts of air. Zornan banked left again, below the mountain line and out of sight of the atacikics. If they hadn't seen Silver and her riders before, the foul creatures certainly had now. But that didn't matter; they would soon be hidden in a cave and safely out of sight.

The next half hour was spent weaving through the peaks, staying within a hundred yards of the mountains to provide better cover. The atacikics would be unable to follow them precisely, especially now that their course was on a weaving, northeasterly line. If the atacikics left the windstream, most of their speed advantage would be eliminated in the gusts swirling closer to the peaks. No creature was better at that than a powerful mrakaro like Silver.

Zornan could feel the targeted cave growing closer. He slowed Silver so they wouldn't shoot past it. He scanned the sky around them for any sign of the atacikics. Nothing. Unless the mid-morning sun, the wispy clouds, or the Infinite Mountains themselves betrayed them, no one would see them enter the small cave. As they approached it, Zornan guided Silver to a landing just above the cave that was just big enough for Silver's two giant feet. The bird hesitated. Zornan leaned forward, Mairie's arms slipping away.

"Easy now, great one. Land softly. It will only be for a moment."

Silver's hesitancy eased with his words, and she deftly landed on the small platform. She rested just above another small outcropping which led to the cave. He and Mairie would have to drop straight down from Silver's back about eight feet to the entrance to the cave.

The cave was located about halfway up the mountain. The air was thin and cold at this altitude, though not nearly as thin and cold as it had been during most their flight. The sharp inclines of two peaks, as if joined at the hip, formed a deep valley. There was nothing but rock below and only empty sky and a few peaks visible above.

Zornan unstrapped his legs and turned to face Mairie, one hand still firmly gripping Silver's saddle. He motioned with the other hand for Mairie to remove the nibrak from her mouth.

"This is our hiding place," Zornan whispered. Mairie looked down wearily to the landing below. "I know it looks precarious, but that's the point. I'll jump down first. Untie the packs and throw them to me. Then I will be there to catch you." The girl nodded.

Zornan slowly slid down Silver's back, repositioning himself on the saddle and around Mairie with each movement. As he reached Silver's tail, he could feel the mrakaro straining to maintain her balance. Zornan took a deep breath and let go.

The drop was quick, and Zornan landed on the larger outcropping below, steadying himself with a hand on the mountain wall. He turned to look into the cave. It was just as small as his mind said it would be. Between their packs and the two of them, it would be very tight. He stepped out of the cave and looked up to see Silver's tail, the only part of her visible from where he stood.

"Throw down the packs, one at a time," he shouted. The first pack dropped soon thereafter, with only Mairie's hands visible as she released it. He threw the pack into the cave. The second came a few moments later.

"Now, ease yourself down just like I did. Once you reach the bottom of the saddle, wait on my signal. When I say let go, let go. I will catch you."

Zornan knew this was the most difficult part of his plan. He was asking a young woman to make a drop from one cliff to another with almost no room for error. If she jumped too far, or if Zornan caught her off balance, either or both of them could end up tumbling from the cliff's edge and down the mountainside to almost certain death. But this risk was their protection. And surely only dangerous choices existed from now on.

Mairie's feet appeared and stopped. She was at the end of Silver's saddle and awaiting his signal. He positioned himself against the face of the mountain and steadied his feet.

"Let go!"

Mairie slid from Silver's back and began her fall. Zornan reached out to grab her, but she remained steady and landed softly right in front of him, her landing easier than his. She looked blankly at him and then entered the small cave. Her graceful landing would have made even the most agile High Tradesmen proud.

Zornan turned his thoughts to Silver.

"Fly away, old friend. Go find something for yourself to eat. Don't return until after nightfall."

His final word launched Silver off the outcropping and away from the mountain. She dipped more than fifty yards below Zornan, and angled herself even lower still, flying into the valley below.

If the atacikics or Peak Crossers captured or killed Silver, Zornan and Mairie would be trapped in this small cave until they died from want of food. There was no way to climb down from here, and there was no place to go nearby even if they could climb down. Silver's return was their only sure way to survive.

As Silver disappeared between the mountain to the north and

the mountain to the east, Zornan stepped into their small, hopefully temporary, home. Mairie was already situated on the ground of the cave. She chewed on some dried fruit and handed some to Zornan. He took the small meal and sat down next to her. They ate in silence.

One of the things most Peak Crossers hated about atacikics was the noise. The foul things were always making noise, screeching or mumbling in their strange language. But that was what alerted Zornan to their presence, and he was grateful, for the first time, that the things were so loud.

After their brief meal, Zornan angled himself in the cave where he could see much of the sky above them without exposing too much of himself. He sat that way for more than an hour, scanning the sky for signs of the atacikics or other Peak Crossers. Just when he was ready to give up looking and get some sorely needed sleep, he heard a faint screech echoing softly through the mountains. Moments later the two atacikics came into view. Riding behind them were two Peak Crossers, one on a dark brown mrakaro, the other on a similarly-colored cosow. The sight startled Zornan, and he retracted into the cave like a turtle into its shell. His hasty movement startled Mairie from her nap into sudden wakefulness. He put a finger to his mouth to keep her quiet, then slowly maneuvered his head to get another view.

The atacikics and Peak Crossers had crossed most of his narrow view by that point. They were not low enough to properly search the nearby valley or mountain crevices like the one where Zornan and Mairie were hidden. Their flight had a purpose, and they were flying quickly in a northeasterly direction. That fact gave Zornan comfort; it meant that the atacikics had lost their trail in the mountains thanks to Silver's evasive flying. So Silver was likely safe, and the Peak Crossers were not going to search each potential hideaway, not even the most obvious ones.

Zornan pulled back into the cave, committing to memory their purposeful flight path. Their course confused him. He assumed they were headed for a city or outpost of some kind. But their path, if followed directly, would take them near no such place. They would fly over uninhabitable valleys like this one and a few major Peak Crosser camping spots. Why this strange path with such purpose and speed? Where were they going?

"Where are we headed, Mairie?"

The girl looked at him. Her eyes were a deep blue, very different from the grayish eyes of her father, though they held some of his intensity. She hesitated before speaking.

"Bendathdra, the former home of the priests by the same name."

Zornan closed his eyes and imagined the location. Yes. It was a shelf high on a mountain, filled with crumbled, ancient buildings and small plants and trees, likely remnants of its former occupants, the mysterious priestesses of Bendathdra.

Did their pursuers know of the meeting place? The path they were flying would not take them directly over Bendathdra, but it would take them very close. It could be chance, or it could be that they were flying a favorable wind before ultimately ending at the same ruins where Zornan and Mairie were supposed to meet with her mother.

"When? When was your mother expecting us?"

Marie paused a moment before answering; she hadn't heard Stethdel tell him who they were meeting.

"The day after tomorrow."

The Peak Crossers had to be headed to Bendathdra. What other explanation was there? There was nothing else of note in that part of the Empire. They were either following what they believed to be the last general direction of Zornan and Silver, or they knew of the meeting place.

"We won't be there the day after tomorrow."

"What?" Mairie shouted the word in a panicked voice, tears welling in her eyes. "But we have to be there!"

"What's the backup plan, Mairie? Was there a second meeting point if we couldn't reach the first?"

Mairie sank, burying her legs in her chest and her face in her knees. After a moment and with tears now streaming down her face, Mairie looked up at Zornan. "There is, but it's not for another month." Mairie barely choked out the last word before burying her face in her knees again.

Zornan leaned his head against the cave wall. A month. What was he supposed to do with Mairie for a month?

They certainly couldn't stay here. Returning to Fallindra would be a disaster, as would showing themselves in any major city or any place with a Peak Crosser keep. There were some uninhabited valleys where they could hide themselves, but that would be the first place the Peak Crossers were likely to look. And what if Mairie's mother were captured or diverted because the Peak Crossers or others were at the first meeting place? And if the Empire knew of the first meeting place, who's to say they didn't know of the second one? Was there any scenario that did not end with Zornan captured and then tried for who knows what? Zornan had absolutely no idea where to go, and, worse yet, he wasn't sure it mattered. He saw only three outcomes: capture and a lifetime of imprisonment, death, or a life on the run which would end in capture or death. He couldn't conceive a scenario that landed him back with Calla and the girls.

13 | LANDING

Mairie slept awkwardly, her body wrapped around her pack on the hard cave floor. Zornan's thoughts drifted toward his own little girls. Like them, Mairie needed his protection. The Empire was intent on finding her, and after seeing what they did to her father, he wasn't about to let them have Mairie.

In the time since he awoke, he had decided where to go. There was a month until the next meeting time, and after thoroughly considering all the options, he could think of only one place to go, even though he was nearly certain that no place in the entire Empire of the Peaks was safe for them.

Mairie stirred a few moments later, unburying herself from under her mat of curly hair and stretching out of her compact position. Even after some rest, she wore the same expression of exhaustion she had worn earlier that day.

"Good afternoon," Zornan offered. Mairie smiled weakly in return. "You should eat. Silver should be back soon, and we'll need to fly at night again."

"Where are we going?" Mairie foraged in her pack.

"Skathall. Have you heard of it?"

Mairie raised her eyebrows. "Yes, everyone's heard of Skathall. Why there?"

"Many reasons. I am familiar with the valley, so we can find an isolated place to rest for a while. And it does not have a large Imperial presence, so it should be pretty safe." Zornan hoped he didn't sound as unsure as he felt.

"Why do you know it so well?" she mumbled through a mouth full of dried fruit.

"I was born there."

Mairie almost spit out her food. "What? We can't go to a place you lived! Stethdel said that if something went wrong, I should avoid any places I've lived or people who know me. The same goes for you. We're not going there."

Zornan sighed. "This isn't a discussion. I've made up my mind."

"What about a deserted valley?"

"There aren't many of those, Mairie, and the Empire, or whoever is looking for us, is likely to search those first."

"Okay," she said, her eyes scanning as if trying to find another solution. "What about another small valley like Skathall? But one where you don't know anyone?"

"Mairie," Zornan replied softly, repressing his frustration and fatigue. "I'm not familiar enough with any other valley like that. I could land us in the middle of a common hunting or grazing ground, or too close to a farm. I know the wilderness of Skathall, and little ever changes in that valley. I've spent a long time thinking about this, examining the same options you're considering. This is the best option out of a bunch of lousy ones."

"But what if someone recognizes you?"

"I doubt anyone will," he said, pulling out a dried piece of fruit for himself. "I haven't been there since I was a child, and we'll avoid people anyway. If it becomes a problem, we'll go someplace else."

"But the Empire is going to look there, and they'll probably look…"

"Enough!" The word came out harsher than Zornan intended, but he was exhausted, and she was being unreasonable. "Stethdel put you in my charge, and I have made a decision. I have explained all I can. Eat and rest, because it will be a very long night of flying."

Mairie's dark blue eyes cut into Zornan like a pair of hatnuthri.

"Fine," she sulked, folding her arms across her chest, "but when this goes poorly, it will be all your fault." She turned away and took a vicious bite.

Fortune favored them again with another clear night for flying. The two-hundred-forty-mile journey from their hiding place to Skathall would not have been doable in one night if the weather had been poor or the night overcast. Flying in the dark among the peaks was a dangerous proposition, but flying during the day would have been riskier. Silver had flown with him at night often enough that Zornan was accustomed to not being able to see everything. He trusted his instincts and Silver's abilities.

Mairie sat behind him, alert. The nibrak was in her mouth, which was just as well. She had muttered continued disagreement with his decision until Silver arrived and they mounted. Zornan was grateful for the relief from her verbal onslaught. Though she did not resemble her father physically, she had a few of his less desirable personality traits—stubbornness and an air of superiority. Zornan could have done without those.

She stopped sulking shortly after they got into the air. Mairie enjoyed flying, which seemed to confirm Zornan's earlier impression that her father had transported her by giant flyer before. She was so comfortable on Silver, so at ease hundreds of feet from the ground. No one was this comfortable on their second flight.

As they approached Skathall, Zornan's thoughts turned to his family: his father, Zortranc; his mother, Bastina; his older brother, Hisvan; his younger sister, Zandia; and his baby brother, Ballin. The decision to return to the valley of his birth rekindled emotions he thought had been blown away by time: his hatred of his father, his bitterness toward his mother, and his continuing affinity for his siblings. He knew nothing of what had happened to them in the past sixteen years. They could be dead, prosperous, or destitute—he had no idea. The family had been desperate when he left, which was why his father had decided to sell him into the High Trades. The farm had been unfruitful for three straight seasons, and Father had built up a lot of debt, some in trying to keep the farm running but most of it in gambling.

As morning approached, they entered Skathall Valley, the ground mostly indistinguishable from the sky. A few lights flickered in the distance, but there were none at the valley's edge. Using the moons' illumination, Zornan found a small clearing in the thick forest and guided Silver there.

After landing, Zornan and Mairie dismounted. He removed the packs from Silver's weary back. The clearing was surrounded by towering trees, and the ground was rough and rocky. It provided plenty of room for their camp and for Silver to stretch her wings before leaving again.

The first purple lights of dawn began to creep higher above the peaks. Light came easier to Skathall Valley than to Fallindra Valley; the mountains were not as tall here and the valley was twice as large. Zornan knew Silver only had a few minutes before the sun would make her departure easy to spot for miles around.

"Come here, Silver." Zornan gripped the mrakaro's head and pulled her beak toward his face. "We will meet you again, right here, in three nights. Come after nightfall, my friend. Be careful." With that, Zornan patted Silver and stepped away. The mrakaro also stepped back and began to trot. She launched herself into the air and flew above the dark tree line. After several minutes she disappeared against the darkness of the mountains.

Zornan felt lonely. Yes, Mairie was there, but he hardly knew her, and she was likely still upset about his decision to come here.

He turned back to his pack and began to make camp.

14 | SKATHALL

Zornan and Mairie sat in silence eating a small meal after spending several hours sleeping in the early morning sun. The dried food Stethdel had provided made fire unnecessary. Zornan might try a fire some night when the trees would conceal its light and darkness its smoke. It might also help to ward off the wolves who ventured out of the mountain foothills and into the valley when food was scarce. But now, during the day, a fire would have revealed their presence.

Zornan finished a piece of dried fruit and leaned against his pack. He needed something to occupy his mind, or this month was going to be more than he could bear.

"I'm sorry about your father." Zornan regretted the words as soon as they escaped his mouth. Conversation was so tiresome.

"No, you're not."

Marie looked up and met his eyes. Her face was blank, but her eyes held pain and anger.

"Not entirely true; I had no fondness for your father, but I am sorry that you lost someone you cared about."

"I hardly knew him."

Zornan had no idea how well she knew him, but her weeping two nights before surely indicated it affected her more than she let on. But he decided to leave it be.

"Do you like Skathall Valley?"

"You mean, do I like this small clearing?" She laughed at her own joke, a small break from her constant sulkiness. It was a short, high-pitched laugh, befitting a girl her age. Zornan could almost imagine Mairie like one of the girls on the streets of Fallindra, giggling as a boy walked by.

Almost. There was something different about her, a seriousness you rarely saw in someone her age, though maybe that was more the situation than her nature.

"Yes, I guess that was a ridiculous question."

"Can I ask you a question?"

"Of course."

"Why do you hate your family?"

"Hate my family?" Zornan replied, stunned. "How could you think that? I love my wife and my daughters."

"No, not them," Mairie said, shaking her mane of hair. "Your parents. Why do you hate them so much?"

"Because they sold me."

"But if they hadn't sold you, you would have never met your wife."

"They get no credit for my happiness." Zornan paused. "For the happiness I had."

Mairie paused as well and looked off into the trees.

"Don't you want to know what has become of them, your family here?"

The truth was, he did, especially his siblings. During their journey to Skathall and in the hours since they had arrived, he wondered what had become of them. Hisvan would be in his thirty-first year, likely married with children, possibly running the farm, as was his birthright as the firstborn. Zandia would be in her twenty-fifth year, likely married, maybe with children of her own. Could she have married his best friend Loothdram's younger brother Cathnar? They had been inseparable as children, just like he and Loothdram. And what of little Ballin? He was only five when Zornan had left (younger than Windsa was now), but he would be almost twenty-two. That was nearly marrying age, especially for a younger son who would need time to establish himself. What had happened to the precocious little boy who had followed Zandia wherever she went?

"Yes, I wonder about my siblings, but it would be too dangerous to search for them. If there are Investigators here looking for me, they would certainly be watching my family."

"How far is your family's farm from here?"

"Three miles southwest."

Mairie raised her eyebrows and laughed. "Pretty close for a guy who doesn't want to see it. Could we at least get a peek of the farm? You can tell almost everything about a farmer from the state of his land."

"How would you know that?"

"I grew up on a farm. My father...I mean, the man I thought was my father, used to always say that he could tell you how well a fellow farmer had done over the past ten harvests by walking his farm. And he was always right." Mairie's eyes lit up with excitement as she spoke of her other father.

"Where is your father—the one who raised you?"

Mairie shook her head. "I'm not sure. Probably at home. Stethdel took me quite suddenly. He made an agreement with my father years ago that he could take me when he wanted. My father refused, but, as you know, Stethdel can...could be very persuasive."

"So why don't I just take you home? I mean, to the home you know."

"I can't go home. You saw what follows us. I could not bear the thought of a Baldra..." Her eyes began to fill with tears, and she turned her gaze to the ground. She remained silent for some time before she spoke again. "So let's go see your family's farm."

"I told you, Mairie; it's not safe."

"Of course it's not safe, but neither is anything we do. Is there a safe place where we could see it from a distance? I want to see more of this valley than a rocky clearing."

Zornan looked intently at the young woman. She was sitting on the ground, lounging against her pack. Despite her emotional outburst after Stethdel's death, despite her reacting like one of his little girls to the idea of coming to Skathall, she was not a girl. She was handling this well, managing a strange situation like she had been in strange, stressful situations before. And if she had been hiding with Stethdel since leaving the parents who raised her, then what was strange for Zornan was now common for Mairie.

"You must get your powers of persuasion from Stethdel. We will go take a look at the farm, but then we return here. We'll be here for nearly a month; there will be plenty of time for exploring."

There was a small hill just east of Zornan's childhood farm that provided a perfect view of the southeastern part of the valley. Skathall Valley was shaped like a boot, with the foot jutting east. The capital, Skathall City, was almost in the 'boot's heel,' along the Skathall River. The river, which started in the western mountains, ran along the southern valley past Skathall City and into the Wuhiveyn River before the combined river emptied into Grizthall Lake. The city of Grizthall sat on the shores of the massive lake, between the valley's western heel and its eastern foot. The beautiful rivers and majestic lake made Skathall one of the prettiest places in the Empire by Zornan's estimation, and he had seen almost the entire Empire.

As he and Mairie climbed the eastern bank of the hill, he could imagine the farm in his mind: the small, three-room house; the fields of grain and vegetables; a few animals milling about; and maybe Hisvan and his unknown wife and children working the land. Mother could be there tending the grandchildren. And if Hisvan did indeed run the farm now, Zortranc would not be there; Hisvan's hate for their father had burned as bright as Zornan's, maybe even brighter.

Zornan's happy vision was wiped cleaned the moment the farm came into view.

He leaned on a tree to keep himself concealed and looked out at what had been his farm. The small wooden house was there, but it was in a state of disrepair, one corner of the roof ready to collapse. Low grass filled the former fields; no grains were visible, and only a few stubborn vegetable plants remained in the former garden. He couldn't see any animals, and there were no children playing anywhere nearby.

Zornan sank to his knees, no longer worried about concealment; there was no one to see him or Mairie. She stood behind him, silent.

Why had Zornan let himself imagine a happy ending for his family? His father was worse than a fool, a man whose passions for gambling, drink, and women humiliated and damaged the family. Apparently his vices had ultimately destroyed everything. Zortranc's gambling debts must have caught up to him, or maybe some rich merchant had caught Zortranc with his wife and claimed the farm as restitution. And what of Hisvan, Zandia, and Ballin? Had Father's sins destroyed them as well? Was everyone destitute and without standing, commoners scraping a living out of the bowels of Skathall City? For years Zornan had assumed that the portion of his Peak Crosser stipend given each year to his parents would have provided regular enough income to keep his family from complete disaster. He had underestimated his father.

Sudden movement at the edge of the barren fields broke him from his despair. A female deer walked slowly from the tree line, each step high over the tall grass. The doe's eyes scanned the tree line. She took a few more steps and then relaxed and grazed. Zornan and Mairie were upwind and out of sight.

Startled, the doe looked up toward the decrepit farmhouse. With a sudden violence, an arrow shot from somewhere near the house and pierced the animal right in its chest. The doe reacted too late, running toward Zornan and Mairie, wounded and dying. The arrow had struck perfectly, the vital organs pierced and bleeding. Zornan was not much of an archer or a hunter, but he had grown up with great hunters: his father and Hisvan. Whoever shot that arrow was either an expert shot or extremely lucky.

The doe collapsed in a heap less than twenty yards from Zornan and Mairie. Her head remained raised for a few moments, but soon the wounds were too much, and the doe's head disappeared into the grass.

Another movement caught Zornan's eye, and he and Mairie stepped back behind the tree. Someone dropped from the old oak next to the house. That tree had seemed so large when Zornan was a child, and it looked even larger now with years of growth. Mother had planted the tree to celebrate her marriage; instead the tree stood only as a reminder of pain and despair.

The hunter slowly crossed the field, his bow in hand and an arrow at the ready. About halfway across the field he put the arrow back in his quiver, slung the bow across his chest, and pulled a long knife from a sheath at his waist. As the hunter pulled the knife and his face became clear in the sunlight, recognition shot through Zornan.

It was Ballin.

The age looked about right. He stood thin and tall, with a narrow nose and a shaggy head of dark brown hair. Just as he had as a boy, the young man Ballin shared Mother's features.

Zornan's heart raced. Ballin would be able to tell him everything about what happened to his family, what happened to Hisvan, Zandia, Mother—what happened to ruin their lives and destroy the farm.

But Zornan did not move to greet his brother. He could not risk catching Ballin in the same whirlwinds which threatened Zornan.

Before Zornan could decide what to do, Mairie stepped from behind him and started walking toward Ballin.

"Hello there," she shouted as she slowly walked down the hill.

Ballin's eyes shot toward Mairie. He quickly sheathed the knife, pulled out his bow and cocked an arrow. He didn't aim it at Mairie, but if Ballin was anywhere near the hunter his father and eldest brother were, he could aim and shoot an arrow through Mairie's neck before she uttered another word. Zornan stepped out and began making his way down the hill, but kept his face down in a feeble attempt to shield his identity.

"Hold, woman. Do not take another step." The face was Mother's, but the voice was Father's deep, commanding tone. Hearing the similarity frightened Zornan. "Who are you? What are you doing on my land?"

"We're adventurers," Mairie said, gesturing toward Zornan, who stopped a few paces behind her. "We've come to explore beautiful Skathall. I thought a woodsman like yourself would know the most adventurous climbs and dangerous forests."

"I'm not a woodsman; I'm a farmer."

Mairie looked around. "Not much of a farm."

"Curse you, woman, get off my land, or by a demon's claws, you will find me about as hospitable as that doe found me." Ballin's eyes glared with the temper Zornan had seen so often in his father.

"Hold, Ballin." Zornan stepped next to Mairie and locked eyes with his brother. "She means no harm. She is here with me."

Ballin's eyes grew wide, and at first, his arms grew slack as if he would drop his bow. Then he assumed an archer's stance with the arrow clearly aimed between Zornan's eyes.

"Zornan!" He spat the word like a curse.

"Yes, it's me. Lower your arrow so we can talk."

"Why should I?" Ballin did not ease at all. "It's been sixteen years! You left our family to rot! Never a letter or a visit. A great Peak Crosser who has the freedom to visit any land in the Empire, and he never comes to see if his younger sister and brother are cared for. Never comes to rescue us from our monster of a father! And now you come, after disaster has run its course. I'd rather you'd stayed away." Tears were streaming down his face now, and his lower lip trembled with anger.

Zornan's eyes moistened at the accusation. Abandoning his family? He had been sent away. And until getting his own commission as a Peak Crosser ten years ago, he'd had no freedom to travel where he wanted to. But since he had started working for the Priests of Cazdanth, he could have visited. He had considered it, but he didn't want to confront his father, didn't want to see the potential ruin of his family. Didn't want to revisit the horrors of his childhood.

"I'm sorry, Ballin. I did not come back to help you; I did not come back to kill or stop Father as I should have. I'm sorry."

For a few moments more, Ballin held the bow tight, his fingers poised to loose the arrow. But after a deep breath, he lowered the weapon. "And what do you think of your former home?"

Zornan shook his head. "It makes me sad, but I'm not surprised. Father ruined everything he touched, including this beautiful place."

Ballin disarmed himself and began walking toward them. "I'm sorry, Zornan. I should not have reacted that way. There is too much of Father in me." He stopped five yards from them. "Come, help me dress this doe and then we can eat. The tale of our family will take some time to tell." He looked over at Mairie. "Hisvan said you got married. She looks a little young."

"I'm not married to him," Mairie said pointedly.

"She is a traveling companion, the reason I'm here actually. Our story may be as long."

Ballin raised his eyebrows. "Sounds like we have a lot to talk about."

Zornan and Mairie helped Ballin dress the doe. They took most of the meat to the old curing shed next to the house, saving some for lunch. They built a small fire behind the house to cook the meal. It was after midday now, and the sun hung at its zenith, pouring heat onto the valley floor.

Ballin insisted Zornan tell his tale first, so he told his younger brother briefly about his time in the High Trade Initiatory School and then in the Peak Crosser Academy. He told of his assignment to the Priests of Cazdanth and his relocation to Fallindra. Ballin was particularly interested in the story of Calla and the girls, asking details about his nieces and smiling at stories of their exploits, proud as an uncle should be.

Zornan then told the story of how he and Mairie had ended up in Skathall, leaving out any details that would attach them to a High Magistrate. He said that Mairie's father had hired him to help Mairie escape capture by evil rogues, and now Zornan was wanted by the Empire for things he hadn't done. Zornan hated leaving out some of the most important details, but the story was a dangerous one, and the less Ballin knew of some of the details the better.

"You shouldn't have come here," Ballin said as Zornan finished his story. The younger brother waved his hand as Zornan tried to speak. "Don't misunderstand. Despite the hateful things I said earlier, I'm glad to see you, Brother. But everyone you might have trusted as a child will now be your enemy."

"Even you?" Mairie asked accusingly.

"No, I'm no threat to anyone, but I'll be of little help. So much has changed since Zornan left." He turned back to Zornan. "If you are a fugitive from the Empire, then you will not find a more unfriendly place in the Empire except maybe Bristrinia."

"Skathall was never so loyal to the Empire," Zornan said.

"Historically, no, but the new Imperial Governor is a loyalist and has transformed this land into a different place than the one you knew."

"Who is this governor? An outsider?"

Ballin laughed. "No, Zornan, not an outsider. You know the governor well. It's our brother, Hisvan."

Zornan could not have been more surprised if Ballin had told him Hisvan was now a goose. The governor? His brother? "How could the son of Zortranc rise to prominence? How could a farmer become governor?"

Ballin leaned against the house. "Hisvan left us two years after you were sold into the High Trade. He ran from home and went to live in Skathall City, out of Father's reach. He met and married a woman there after getting her pregnant; their first son was born seven months after the wedding. His wife, Jojana, was the daughter of a rich merchant. After the marriage, Hisvan became an apprentice merchant and then a member of the Low Trade. His past was unknown, even to Jojana—so no one connected him to Father.

"His wife's father was a cruel man, from what I've heard, though in a very different way than ours. He adored Hisvan and his daughter, and he adored their three grandsons. But he hated those of lower station, and he aspired to greatness, wanting to become Imperial Governor. He envisioned Skathall as one of the most important valleys in the Empire, a center of trade and culture. But he had made too many enemies in his business dealings, so Hisvan became his tool to power. Everyone loved and trusted our brother. A few years ago, it looked like Hisvan was destined to be governor. He even came out to the farm and told me all about it, and about his life. His third son had been born, and he was excited. He even promised to help me find work and get away from Father.

"But somehow Father discovered Hisvan's new life, and he couldn't, being Father, let it be. He blackmailed Hisvan with threats of revealing him as the son of a drunk, womanizing gambler." Ballin twisted a piece of grass in his hands and tossed it to the ground. "Hisvan told his wife's father, Sodean, and the merchant became enraged. He was angry with Hisvan for lying about his past, but he was mostly angry with Father for tearing down his plans. I'm sure Sodean wanted to have Father killed to keep him quiet." Ballin smiled darkly. "That would have made things easier.

"But Hisvan was smarter than that. He came clean about everything. The revelation gained him respect with the Imperial power brokers and made him even more popular among the Low Trade. He completely distanced himself from us, publicly proclaiming that he was no longer a branch of the corrupted tree, that he was his own plant. With his bold declarations, he could never associate with us again, or he would risk being associated with Father.

"He became governor almost two years ago, the youngest Imperial Governor in the Empire. And we were left to rot. Sodean died of a fever about a year ago. So he saw his adopted son rise to power, but he won't see what Hisvan becomes or how he transforms the valley."

Zornan shook his head. Hisvan, the governor. As a child, all Hisvan wanted was Father gone and a chance to run the farm. He and Zornan daydreamed of that day when the farm would be theirs, when they'd be free of Father's tyranny. Instead Hisvan had ascended to heights they never could have imagined as boys.

"One of Hisvan's first acts was to move the capital to Grizthall," Ballin continued. "He built a governor's palace right on the water, and he's been transforming the city into what he says will be one of the finest in the Empire. He brought in immigrants to work in the mine. He built a university that has attracted scholars from around the Empire. He's paving the city's streets to make it look more like the other great cities. Hisvan continues to build Sodean's dream.

"Hisvan blamed Father for Sodean's death. He was convinced Father had somehow poisoned his wife's father. Father had been holed up in the house with Mother for months before that. Creditors came almost every day. The decay you see on this farm was well underway; Father saw no point in farming any longer when every ear of corn or pint of milk was claimed by a creditor before it even reached his lips or his pockets. They barely survived, and in this state, I can't imagine Father had the means to assassinate Sodean.

"Still, Hisvan believed it to be true. When a creditor from a different valley came looking for Father, Hisvan changed the law. If you owed debts because of gambling, you could become the payment. So Father was sold into indentured servitude after the Magistrate determined the new law was sound and Father's guilt was assured. So ten months ago he was sold to that creditor, and no one has heard from the wretched man since. I wouldn't be surprised if Hisvan paid the man to slit Father's throat the moment they reached the tunnel."

Zornan had dreamed of the day Father would die, more often than he would ever admit. But the news of Father's demise left him empty.

"But what of Mother? What of Zandia?" Zornan asked.

Ballin looked away. "Zandia is dead."

"Dead! How?"

"Father sold her into the High Trades three years after you were sold. We received a letter nine months later that she had been killed in training."

Zornan looked away from his brother and off into the mountains. So Zandia had followed him into the High Trades. It was much less common for women to be sold to the High Trades; giving up a son was honorable, but giving up a daughter was viewed as cowardice. Of course, courage had not been Father's hallmark.

Zandia had been only eight when Zornan was sold. She'd been so quiet, so reserved, her will broken by an angry and violent father. While a tiny Ballin had often followed Zornan or Hisvan when he wasn't following his sister, Zandia was always found at Mother's side, as if Zandia's presence might stop Father from taking out his drunken anger on Mother. But it had only worked a few times until Father took his anger out on both. Not even Zandia's sweet face could still the man's wrath. And now she was dead, killed by Father's avarice.

"And Mother?"

"She lives in the governor's palace."

"Hisvan took Mother in?"

Ballin shook his head. "Not exactly. Mother works as a maid in the palace, cleaning, from what I can tell. She took the job after Father was sold. I don't think she sees Hisvan much, or her grandchildren. Hisvan was clear that no one was to know who she was. She goes by the name Rithnia."

Rithnia: the name of Mother's mother. How could Hisvan be so cruel to their *mother*? Yes, she had never stood up for them; she even told them to submit to the beatings because Father was the master of the house and was to be obeyed. But Zornan had never blamed Mother; he pitied her. She had married a handsome, charming young farmer who came from a good family. How could she have envisioned what Father was or would become?

"And you, Ballin?"

"I'm just Ballin." The young man smiled, twisting another piece of grass in his hands. "Technically, Hisvan owns this land; he bought it from Father's creditors. Last time I saw him, which was just after Father was sold, he told me he had plans to build a cottage here so he and his family could get away from the city and the pressures of leadership. But I doubt he'll ever do that; too many memories.

"So I hunt here. I also work in the mines near Moztarn and pick up occasional work in Grizthall. I was an apprentice builder, but the Low Trade rejected me. Not sure if that was my connection to Father, or if Hisvan just doesn't want someone from his corrupt family rising above our current station." Ballin motioned with both arms, as if revealing the decrepit farm for the first time. He leaned against the house again, stretched out his legs, and put his hands behind his head. "I get by, live free. It's a much better life than what we grew up with, and it's a much better life than Hisvan with his shackles of power and fame."

"Wife?"

"Wife? Come now, Zornan. I have nothing to offer a wife except hunting skills, a bleak past, and a sharp wit. Most women only care about the last one if you are handsome or rich, and I am neither." Ballin shot a look at Mairie.

Something itched at the back of his mind, reminding him of his current predicament. Hisvan. Zornan and Hisvan had been close as children, confidants and defenders of the family. They often escaped together to the woods to find some solace among the trees. They played, laughed, cried, and fought: brothers and friends. Would that still mean something to Hisvan the Imperial Governor? If Zornan ever hoped to return to Calla and the girls, he needed a powerful ally.

"I'm going to Grizthall to meet with Hisvan," Zornan blurted.

"What?" Mairie and Ballin shouted.

"I'm going to meet with Hisvan. He's a powerful man, and he may be able to help me reunite with my family. He's our brother. He could help."

"You will not find the boy you knew in the man Hisvan." Ballin shook his head and lowered his eyes to the ground. "He may lack some of Father's nicest personality traits, but he has some of them. I've seen how he treats his boys: sharp, unkind words that echo Father. He treats his staff and subordinates in a similar fashion, not with physical violence, but with verbal lashes that cut just as deep. And the city is filled with rumors of his infidelity to his wife. If you are wanted by the Empire, he will give you to them and profit from it. You'd be better off marching into the Emperor's palace."

"I agree with Ballin," Mairie added. "That's a terrible idea."

"Ha! Everything is gone!" Zornan shouted, and then turned to Mairie. "You're just worried that you won't get where you need to be. I will try and get you there, but I have to take this chance to return to my family, even if it's a small one."

"I'll get her where she needs to be," Ballin responded before Mairie could. "I think this idea is doomed to fail, but I understand why you're trying. If you don't return, I can accompany Mairie wherever she needs to go. I have little to leave behind. I've been thinking of leaving Skathall and trying my hand somewhere else. By the Fire Moon, I need a fresh start."

Zornan stared at his brother. Their initial exchange had made Zornan fear that years of abuse had turned Ballin into his Father. But Ballin not only looked like Mother, he had her heart as well.

"You men are impossible!" Mairie stormed off and walked away from the shade of the farmhouse and into the field.

"She's a handful, Ballin."

"A beautiful handful." Ballin gazed at Mairie. "Don't worry Brother, I know she's young, but a man can make a decision to help his brother and to help a beautiful woman, can't he?" He winked.

"Yes he can," Zornan replied, smiling back.

"Regardless of what happens in Grizthall, I want to come with you and Mairie. There really is nothing here for me." The grin disappeared. "Living in the shadows of Father and Hisvan is too much. I need to find some sunlight."

"I'm not sure you can come with us. I can't carry three on my mrakaro, and tunnel travel is too slow and would expose us to the Empire."

Ballin looked away, frustrated. After several moments of silence, Ballin spoke again. "Two more things before you go. First, your friend Loothdram is now the Investigator of Skathall." Though Zornan and Loothdram entered the Initiatory School together, they had only met twice there, and only briefly. They had been placed in different cohorts and Zornan had never learned what trade Loothdram was placed in. Investigator did not seem to fit with the mischievous boy Zornan had known. "When Hisvan found out Loothdram was a prominent Investigator," Ballin continued, "he requested he be stationed here. Your old friend has been here for six months or so. He lives and works out of the governor's palace."

"Someone else to talk to, perhaps."

Ballin shook his head. "He's an Investigator, Zornan, a man sworn to bring justice to the enemies of the Empire. Even if Hisvan does not turn you into the Empire, certainly Loothdram will feel honor-bound to arrest you. I know you hope someone will help you get your life back, but I don't think either of these men will want to, even if they could."

Zornan sighed and looked toward the sky. Part of him knew Ballin was right; relying on the charity of a man who was blood but that he hadn't seen in so long was foolish. Despite Hisvan's power, he'd never tried to contact Zornan. Hisvan had distanced himself from the family. Why would those bonds hold true now?

But just like on the cliffs avoiding the atacikics, only terrible choices were available. Hisvan might be his only hope to right his course and find his way home.

"I have to try, Ballin," Zornan responded. "I have to get home."

"Amazing," Ballin said, locking eyes with Zornan. "Are you really nothing like Father or Hisvan? If only Mother and Father had sold Hisvan instead."

"No," Zornan said, shaking his head. "If I had stayed, who knows how I might have been warped by Father." Zornan paused and put a hand on his brother's shoulder. "What was the second thing you wanted to tell me?"

"Your clothes." Ballin looked Zornan up and down. "Your Peak Crosser clothes will give you away. We should switch before you go; my commoner garb will make you invisible in the city. Plus, I've always wanted to live the life of a High Tradesman; I'll be a Peak Crosser for a day."

15 | STRANGE HOME

I t was too late in the day to start the three-hour journey to Grizthall, so the three companions made camp back at the clearing where they had landed that morning. If Zornan did not return, Mairie and Ballin would meet Silver the next night and set her free. Then they would try to escape the valley and journey to the next meeting point by way of the tunnels.

Zornan left the next morning well before dawn, while Ballin and Mairie slept. They had spent the night listening to stories of Windsa and Caldry, of Zornan's travels as a Peak Crosser, and of their escape from Fallindra and pursuit by the atacikics. They avoided any further talk of Zornan's family. Mairie said little.

Before Zornan reached the city, the moons evaporated from the morning sky. The sun's light filled the valley, diffused by several billowing clouds. Zornan thought of Silver as he watched hawks soar through the sky outside the city. He hoped she had found food and a good place to hide herself on the other side of the mountain. A slight breeze off the lake filled the forest with a damp, cool air.

In order to avoid meeting any of the farm families who might recognize Zornan, he stayed off the road for the first two hours. These were the only people in Skathall who were likely to recognize his face, and he needed to avoid detection until he reached the governor's palace and hopefully gained audience with Hisvan and Loothdram.

As Zornan cleared the woods, the road opened to reveal Grizthall. A gleaming, sprawling city had replaced the town of his boyhood memory. It crawled across almost the entire southern shore of Grizthall Lake, and the new palace rose above everything else. Hisvan's home stood seven stories tall, dwarfing everything around it. Its reflection stretched deep into the choppy waters of the lake, waxing and waning with the waves. Bright granite walls sparkled in the morning light.

Zornan entered the city through its eastern gate, though it was a gate in name only, as the walls on either side were in different states of construction. Gates stood at the eastern, southern, and western sides. But the wall wasn't even half finished, and Zornan couldn't imagine why they needed it anyway. What dangers would it protect them from? No war or major conflict had threatened the valley in more than three hundred years. He had seen other cities across the Empire with walls, but these had been military targets in more recent conflicts or were set on plains without the natural walls the mountains provided. Either Hisvan foresaw a threat Zornan could not imagine, or his brother was using the wall as a symbol of Skathall's new prominence, mirroring some of the greatest cities in the Empire like Smagthan, Bristrinia, or Kandrinal. Zornan assumed the latter.

Seven men guarded the gate, including one Enforcer. They paid him no mind. They made little eye contact with those entering and leaving the city, and their conversation focused on the previous night, not their duties. Ballin's foresight in sending him in commoner clothes proved useful. He was among perhaps two dozen other commoners coming into the city at that moment, all headed for some work or commerce. As was common of the High Trade and the Low Trade, commoners were like a breeze or an insect; you might regard them, but you did not really see them.

The outer streets of the city were still dirt, dry from a lack of rain. Even at this early hour, the city was bustling with activity. He walked through the outer ring of streets, the shops and homes of the commoners. By Imperial law, all shop owners of any kind were supposed to be Low Trade shopkeepers, but it was tolerated in every city Zornan had ever been to for commoners to sell certain goods amongst themselves. Apparently Hisvan, for all Ballin's talk of strictness and severity, allowed this practice as well. With a little of the money Stethdel had provided in his pack, Zornan bought a piece of fruit from a girl selling it out of a basket on a street corner. He gave her twice what she asked. She was dirty, about seven years old, with long, unruly blond hair. She reminded him of his girls.

He passed through the common ring of the city and entered into the haven of the Low Trade. He had to keep reminding himself to look down and avoid getting in the way of the Low Tradesmen and a few High

Tradesmen. He had become accustomed to his station, but returning to the deference of a commoner came more easily than it should have.

He did not need to ask for directions to the palace; it dominated the skyline. He passed a Peak Crosser keep, which had originally been at the edge of Grizthall and now sat in the heart of the city. He could hear the screech of a mrakaro and the call of a cosow behind the walls of its courtyard. Unlike the keep in Fallindra, there was no open field for the giant flyers and Peak Crossers to land; here they landed behind the courtyard's high walls.

Zornan entered the final section of the city: the homes of the most prominent Low Trade and the High Trade. Large, stone homes lined the street, some as tall as three stories. There were still many commoners about, servants, couriers, and a few others. But this area was driven by status. Richly clothed Low Trade walked with heads high, trailed by a servant or two. These were the people who had benefited most from Grizthall's explosion. They had become rich through the expansion, rising from humble beginnings. But as Zornan noticed the richly dressed children, including a few taunting a young commoner boy who was acting as a courier, it was clear that whether these Low Trade came from humble beginnings or were a second generation of wealth, they were determined to maintain their position. An aristocracy had grown in Skathall.

Amongst all the Low Trade was an occasional High Tradesman. Zornan noticed a couple of young Magistrates. He saw two Peak Crossers, no one he knew. A group of three Enforcers, clearly on duty and alert, patrolled the street.

He saw a Counselor, a woman, walking alone, in her long Counselor robe and a veil that also indicated her position. All who noticed her kept clear, as if an invisible bubble surrounded her, pushing the sparse crowd away. Counselors served those in prominent positions, giving advice and providing insight into the human mind. Most believed they were witches who could read your mind and possibly even control your thoughts and emotions. Silly superstitions. But Zornan cleared her path as well, acting as any commoner would. She passed, her long, dark, curly red hair pulled up behind her head. She gave off an air of command and authority, similar to what Zornan had noticed in Stethdel. She didn't seem to notice the crowd parting around her. As it did, Zornan noticed two Enforcers walking closely behind her.

After passing the Counselor, Zornan stopped as the street ended in a 'T.' He faced the governor's palace. The structure was even more impressive up close, the sun's light reflecting off the granite crystals. Many large windows dotted the structure, light dancing off their colored glass. A large courtyard surrounded the building enclosed by a ten-foot stone wall. Perched on the wall at regular intervals were constable officers, all armed with bows and swords. Zornan faced a large, metal gate guarded by ten constable officers and two Enforcers. Everything about the building—the wall, the guards and their pristine, light gray uniforms— said this place was important. If Hisvan wanted Grizthall to look like one of the most prominent cities in the Empire, he had succeeded with his palace. Zornan had seen only a few buildings rival its beauty, and he had never seen a governor's palace guarded with such a show of force.

Zornan crossed the street and approached one of the Enforcers. He cursed himself silently as he realized he had made direct eye contact with the man. He quickly averted his gaze to the ground.

He felt very vulnerable. He, Ballin, and Mairie had debated the night before about whether he should bring his hatari. They had concluded that he should not, even if it could be cleverly hidden in Ballin's clothes. If he were searched and a hatari was discovered, he would be arrested on the spot. Commoners were never allowed to handle or carry High Trade weapons, even if they were employed by a High Tradesman.

They had also debated about what his story should be in order to reach Hisvan. They had concocted a number of elaborate tales, but Zornan decided a simple, direct deception would be the best and most likely to gain his brother's audience, and the least likely to raise suspicion.

"Hold." The Enforcer's voice was firm. "What brings you here, commoner?"

Without looking up, Zornan responded. "I am here to see the governor."

The Enforcer laughed, as did the guards within earshot. "And I would like an audience with the Emperor." The others laughed again.

"Pardon my presumption, Enforcer, sir, but I have urgent news that I must deliver to him personally. I am his brother, and I have news regarding our father." The men stopped laughing.

"What is your name?"

"Ballin, sir. My name is Ballin."

The guards searched Zornan, and though the amount of money he had with him was likely more than what was normal for a commoner, they said nothing. The one worry about his story was that someone at the gate would recognize Ballin and know that, despite Zornan's resemblance to Hisvan, he looked little like Ballin. But Ballin had never been inside the palace and had only talked with Hisvan a couple times since he became governor. So far, the ruse was working.

After the search, he was marched by the same Enforcer and three constables into the palace, through winding hallways and up several flights of stairs. The interior of the palace was not nearly as impressive as the outside, at least the part he saw. It was sparsely furnished, and work was still going on to finish some of the rooms and reinforce the structure. Hisvan had expended a massive amount of money, time, and effort on the building's exterior; its interior had been a lower priority.

On what Zornan thought was the fourth floor, they walked down a hallway and entered a large room with two desks. At one sat an Enforcer, who rose with their entry, and at the other was a young man who looked to be about Ballin's age. The new Enforcer walked over and glared intently at Zornan. He reached out and lifted Zornan's chin, staring directly into the Peak Crosser's eyes.

"I wish Counselor Gissa were here to talk with him before he met the governor," the Enforcer said to the young man at the other desk. "Have you ever met his brother?"

"No." The clerk stayed seated at his desk. "But he bears a striking resemblance to the governor, and his honor was insistent that we bring up his brother immediately."

The lie had worked. It had been Mairie's idea to say Zornan had information about their father. Hisvan's paranoia about his station and career would hasten the meeting. Ballin had no official standing that would have granted an audience with the governor, but even a hint of Father was enough for Hisvan to bring Zornan up without any delay.

"I don't like it," the Enforcer replied.

"Neither do I, but we need to bring him in." With that, the young man stood and opened one of the double doors leading into the next room.

The room was large. Shelves filled with books, scrolls, and decorations covered the walls. A wooden statue in the Bristrinian style sat high on a shelf to Zornan's left, a beautiful gold-gilded replica of the Emperor's palace. To his right there was a seer stone from Smagthan, a clear glass ball swirling with bright colors. The room looked like it belonged to a man who had traveled the Empire, collecting effects from its far reaches. It also felt like the room of a man who was trying very hard to impress whomever he met here.

Hisvan sat behind a large, brastilia-trimmed desk. He held some papers and read them intently, not looking up at Zornan or the young man who brought him in.

"Your Grace," the clerk said, "your brother, Ballin."

"Take a seat, Ballin," Hisvan said, without looking up.

"Would you like me to stay?" the Enforcer asked from the anteroom.

"Leave us."

The young man left and closed the door. Zornan did not sit.

Hisvan looked very much like an older version of the boy Zornan had known. He had a few lines on his face and some of the fat of youth was gone. That was one of the things that struck Zornan about his brother: how lean he was. Most politicians weighed their wealth on their bones. But Hisvan looked as fit as an Enforcer or a Peak Crosser. His hair was darker than Zornan's, maybe darker than it had been when they were younger. His face was frozen in concentration, a look Zornan had rarely seen on the roguish boy he grew up with.

Then Hisvan looked up from his papers, and his face went blank.

"Zornan."

"Greeting, Brother. Or should I say, Governor?"

Hisvan remained stunned for a few moments before he spoke again. "Welcome greeting, Peak Crosser. Please sit."

Hisvan set the papers aside and continued staring at Zornan as if a demon were sitting in the chair opposite him, only a few blinks breaking his gaze.

"What in the shadow of the Emperor are you doing here, Zornan?"

"I need help, Hisvan."

"Help?" Hisvan rifled through the papers on his desk and pulled one out. "I assume you need help from this?" Hisvan extended the paper toward Zornan's face. "You're an accused murderer, Zornan. How in the Empire could I help you?"

"You're a powerful man, Hisvan. You could help me prove my innocence."

Hisvan laughed, but the sound had no humor. "Help you? Are you mad? You're accused of killing an Enforcer, and you were accused by a High Magistrate. Then, the dead body of that same High Magistrate was found in your home after you fled. How could I possibly help you with that?"

Zornan's stomach sank. He hoped Calla or the girls had not found the body.

"But I am innocent, Hisvan; you must believe me. You've known me my entire life."

"I hardly know you." Hisvan's tone was firm, soft, and detached. "We have not seen each other in sixteen years, longer than we spent together on the farm. Now you are a wanted man, someone the entire Empire is looking for, and you drop into the palace pretending to be Ballin, bringing with you the shame and trouble of an accused murderer. You have put me, my family, and this entire valley at great risk. I can't help you. I can't even let you go. If someone found out you were here and that I let you go, I would lose everything."

Panic gripped Zornan. Ballin had been right; Hisvan was not the boy he knew. Maybe he wasn't as twisted as Father, but he certainly wasn't the caring older brother who defiantly stood in front of Father and took blows for the smaller Zornan.

"I thought you would help," Zornan said softly, desperately.

"Have you seen Ballin?"

"Only from a distance," Zornan lied. "I went by the farm and he was hunting there. I did not approach him." Zornan hoped Hisvan believed his lie.

"How did you learn about me?"

"I've kept track of our family, asking Peak Crossers I know to find out what they could while they were here in Skathall. What you've done with this city and this valley is truly remarkable."

For the first time in their brief conversation, Hisvan smiled, a true, deep smile. "Yes, it has taken years of work on my part and at the hands of my wife's father to transform Skathall into something great. You can understand why I can't risk it."

"It has become something great." Zornan continued to feed Hisvan's ego. "I had heard reports, but I wouldn't have believed it until I saw this great city with my own eyes. I have traveled all over the Empire, and few cities rival what you've built." He was flattering Hisvan like they used to do to Father; sometimes it worked, if only to buy them a few minutes away from his wrath.

"So you see why I cannot jeopardize this, even for my brother," Hisvan replied.

Zornan nodded.

"Good, I'm glad you understand." Hisvan stood and walked around the table, sitting on the edge of the desk just in front of Zornan. "I will tell you what I will do. If you walk out now, I will let you escape. You must move quickly; I will create a story about being overpowered or temporarily infected with familial love. But you must leave Skathall as soon as you can."

Zornan stood. Hisvan was not going to let him leave the palace, this much he was sure of. Zornan was a prize, something Hisvan could trade for more influence, a way to demonstrate his complete loyalty to the Empire. He had distanced himself from Father, from Mother, and even from Ballin, who was no real threat to his power. Why had Zornan believed he would be treated any differently? The offered escape was a ruse to get Zornan out of this room and away from the governor; Zornan was a trained High Tradesman after all. Hisvan was sending him away like the desperate animal he was, one that needed to be taken someplace else to be handled properly.

"Thank you, Brother. I owe you a great favor."

"You owe me nothing. Sad parting, Brother."

Zornan left the office and was guided down the hall by the Enforcer who had escorted him from the gate.

16 | AN OLD FRIEND

Zornan now had one, slim hope: Loothdram. His boyhood friend was probably more likely than Hisvan to turn him over to the Empire, but there was little risk now in seeking the man out.

The hallway was sparsely furnished, but Zornan and the Enforcer approached a small table with a large, empty vase on it. The Enforcer was walking in front of him, guiding them to his assured capture.

Zornan grabbed the large vase, lifted it high above his head, and brought it down as hard as he could on the Enforcer's head. The Enforcer slumped to the ground unconscious, the vase shattered in dozens of pieces on the floor.

Zornan froze and looked around. He had decided to act so quickly, he hadn't really thought about the next step. He was free of his escort, but he had no idea how to find Loothdram. He eyed the Enforcer's hatrindi, but dismissed it; if he escaped from the palace alive, it would be through deception and surprise, not through force. And he needed to move now.

He dropped the two small vase pieces in his hands and took to the stairs.

The stairway ended in a hallway, and Zornan sprinted down the empty space. He thought he heard voices yelling, but he couldn't tell from where. He could see another stairway at the end of this hall, and he moved as fast as he could toward it.

Zornan came to a sudden stop at the top of the stairs to keep himself from crashing into a man who was walking up them. He was an older man, dressed in servant's clothes.

"Pardon me, sir," Zornan exclaimed.

"Can I help you, young man?"

Zornan began to dismiss him, but stopped himself.

"Do you know where I can find Loothdram Investigator? I am the governor's brother, and he has asked me to take a message personally to him."

"Of course I do; follow me."

The servant led them back down the hallway from where Zornan had come, and the Peak Crosser almost abandoned the old man to escape down the stairs. But he heard more yelling and decided to stay with the man and get to Loothdram if he could. The man led them down a new hallway that curved and came to an end at a door. A gray-clad guard stood watch.

"Here you are, Brother of the governor."

"Thank you."

The servant left, and Zornan turned to the guard.

"I am here to see Loothdram. I am the governor's brother Ballin, and I bring an important message from the governor himself."

Before the guard could speak, a voice came from behind the partially-open door. "What kind of message?" Zornan could not be sure, but the voice sounded a lot like Loothdram, or what he thought he might sound like as a grown man.

"A message about our other brother, Zornan."

The door opened, and Loothdram's adult head appeared. He had the same, round, boyish face, his head covered in the same unruly blond hair which cursed him as a boy. He wore blue loose-fitting pants and a similarly-colored vest over a tight, lighter blue tunic.

His eyes grew wide when he saw Zornan. "Guard, I need you to leave the palace at once. Tell everyone you are on a special assignment from me. Go to your home and do not return until tomorrow. When you do, come directly to me."

The guard nodded at Loothdram's strange instructions and walked calmly down the hall.

"By the demon's teeth, Zornan, get in here." Loothdram opened the door wider, let Zornan in, and closed it behind them.

Loothdram's room was as large as Hisvan's but lacked the anteroom, the desk, or the books. Six comfortable chairs adorned the space, and the walls were covered with paintings of great battles and doomed heroes. Zornan recognized some of the scenes from stories he had heard or read, but the origins of most were lost on him. A fireplace in the wall opposite the door flooded the room with its warm, flickering light.

"Sit, Zornan."

Zornan sat in a large, upholstered red chair near the fire. Loothdram sat in an identical chair opposite.

"What in the Emperor's stockings brought you here?"

Zornan smiled despite himself. Dram's intensity, his flair, his dramatic speech, he seemed much like the boy Zornan had known.

"I am in trouble, old friend."

"Trouble?" Loothdram's eyes widened again, and he threw his arms into the air. "Trouble is when your wife notices you smile at another woman. You're sunk into a deep crevice with no light and little hope."

"So you know of my problems?"

"Of course, man!" Loothdram leaned forward, his eyes reflecting the dancing light of the fire. "Every single Investigator in the Empire, and likely most of the Enforcers, know of you and your escape from Fallindra. They know of the murder charge and the fact that a High Magistrate was found dead in your house. What I can't figure out is why you're here in this palace. Why did you risk everything to see me?"

"I actually came to see Hisvan."

"Hisvan!" Loothdram stood and threw up his arms again. "Please tell me you found your way here first."

"Unfortunately not, though Ballin warned me." Zornan regretted mentioning his younger brother, but something in this exchange blanketed him with trust in his old friend. "Ballin told me Hisvan would not help. Hisvan let me leave his office, but he wasn't going to let me out of the palace. So I knocked out an Enforcer, and a servant helped me find your room."

Loothdram slumped back into his chair. "Fathers of the Emperors, this is worse than I feared."

"So you will help me?" Zornan's hope rose again.

Loothdram looked at Zornan and then into the fire. "Of course, Zor, of course. I'm not sure I can fix your little trouble, but I can help you escape Skathall. But first you must answer me one question: did you kill Stethdel?" He looked back at Zornan, his eyes piercing Zornan's soul.

"Of course not." Zornan thought of the two men he had killed, and his conscious poked him with a memory of their faces.

Loothdram continued his stare for a moment, and then smiled broadly.

"I knew there was more to the story. Tell me everything."

Zornan told the entire story, including his exchange with Stethdel and his escape from the Baldra. He left Mairie out entirely, only mentioning that he carried something important for the High Magistrate and still needed to deliver it.

"We need to get you out of here soon. Can you call to your mrakaro? You should leave Skathall immediately."

"Call to her? She won't be able to hear me from here."

"Reach out to her, Zor. Tell her to come get you."

Zornan continued to stare incredulously at his old friend.

"You have no idea what I'm talking about, do you?"

Zornan shook his head.

"Lascrill kept you Peak Crossers in the dark about many things, but I thought you'd have learned since then."

"Learned what?"

"Oh Zornan, I wish we had more time. Where do your abilities as a Peak Crosser come from?"

What a strange question at a time like this, Zornan thought, but responded anyway. "Training and discipline."

"No," Loothdram said, shaking his head. "That's a piece, but a small one. Your abilities come from the Bendathdrans. They blessed you after you left the Initiatory School; those abilities come from their magical blessing."

"Impossible! What you're saying is silly superstition."

"Think about it, Zornan. You can breathe high in the mountains; you can live off only a few hours of sleep; you are stronger and faster than any common man and most High Tradesmen; you can see for miles farther and clearer than anyone else but other Peak Crossers. Do you think all of that came from *training*?"

Zornan thought about it, questioning everything he believed about himself. He recalled some of his cohort in the Initiatory School talking of magic, reverently referencing the Priestesses of Bendathdra. Many believed their skills would come from the blessings, not from discipline, focus, and training. But once Zornan reached the Peak Crosser Academy, Lascrill forced those thoughts from his young mind. Lascrill emphasized discipline and will. He never once mentioned magic and made only passing references to the priestesses. Under Lascrill's tutelage, Zornan and the other apprentice Peak Crossers learned and grew. Yes, they had received a blessing, but Zornan believed it to be ritual. Now he wasn't so sure.

"Haven't you communicated without words with your mrakaro?" Loothdram continued.

"No, Silver and I just know each other well. That's not the same."

"Fine. Then try something for me. Reach out to her. Quiet your mind. See if you can connect to her."

Zornan eyed his old friend curiously.

"Indulge me, Zor. Consider it my price for helping you escape. Close your eyes, and see if you can connect your mind to hers."

Zornan took a deep breath and closed his eyes. At first he could only think of how ridiculous this was, trying to communicate with a mrakaro who was a hundred miles from here. But he quieted his mind as best as he could and thought of Silver and what she might be doing. After several minutes, nothing happened. He thought maybe he felt something, maybe sensed her flight. But nothing more moved into his mind.

"This is ridiculous, Dram. You're talking nonsense."

"Relax. It may take a few minutes. But I think you two have been doing this for years on a lesser scale, unnoticed by your conscious mind. Open you mind and heart, Zor."

He calmed himself again, took a deep breath and spent several more minutes without anything happening.

Suddenly his mind flooded with overwhelming sensations. He could almost feel the wind whipping over Silver's back. He could feel her enthusiasm, her love of flying. He recognized these feelings, as he had shared them with her before, but had dismissed those as the natural feelings you have with those closest to you, animal or man. He couldn't see what she saw, he couldn't really feel what her body felt, but he felt a connection he couldn't really explain.

Silver, he thought. *Can you hear me?*

Yes, loyal rider. Silver hears you.

Zornan jumped in his chair, and his eyes shot open. He looked at Loothdram as his connection to Silver vanished. The Investigator grinned broadly.

"I guess believing in magic doesn't make me mad after all."

"But that's impossible!" Zornan shouted. "How could I not have known this all these years? Why didn't Lascrill teach us this?"

"You didn't believe, Zornan, so there was nothing to see. As to why Lascrill never taught you this, he didn't teach any of the Peak Crossers about this, trusting your emotional connection to your flyer would be enough. But most Peak Crossers I've met eventually figure all this out, despite Lascrill's attempts to keep many things hidden. Maybe it makes you stronger mentally, maybe not. That old bird has a lot of crazy ideas.

But here we are trying to harvest last year's crops. Call to Silver, and have her meet you tonight."

Zornan reached out to Silver. *I need you tonight, old friend. We need to leave Skathall now.*

I cannot be there. The sensation of her strange voice in his head startled Zornan again, even though he knew it was coming. It sounded much like his own voice, only more feminine and clipped. *I am too far away. I had to travel far to hunt, in order to stay out of little man's way.*

Little man? Zornan asked.

Your people, little rider. We call your people little men. Our small cousins call you big men. Zornan could feel Silver's amusement. Zornan smiled, despite not knowing what made it so funny.

Then stay safe, my old friend. I will call to you again soon.

You stay safe, little rider. Silver's words shot back into his head. *I am glad we speak now.*

"Silver is too far away," Zornan said aloud.

"Dammit. The Fire Moon does not shine on us." Loothdram paused. "Still, we must get you out of the palace. And we must find a way to get you, Ballin, and the girl out of Skathall."

"The girl?" Zornan stood up, glaring at Loothdram. "I said nothing of a girl." Zornan's heart began to race. How had he known?

"I apologize, Zor. You have been upfront with me, but I have not been with you. I know everything about Mairie. I am allies with Stethdel. He was a member of the Kuthraz, as am I."

The Kuthraz? The rumored rebels against the Empire? A High Magistrate and an Investigator? And possibly his Peak Crosser instructor Lascrill, if Crisdan's investigation was true? Had the entire world around him gone mad? First, he'd learned he could talk to Silver, and now the revelation that his childhood friend, his mentor, and the man who threw his world into chaos, were all connected through association with a treasonous group he hadn't even believed existed until a few days ago.

Zornan collapsed into the chair.

"I know this is a lot to absorb, Zor, but you must believe me. We are rebels, and Stethdel was an important member of our group."

"Stethdel is a fiend."

"Don't be too hard on him, especially now that he's dead," Loothdram said quietly. "I don't know why he chose to involve you, but he must have been desperate. Wouldn't you act rashly if it meant safeguarding your child?"

The same reasonable thought had tried to penetrate Zornan's thoughts since he had learned the cargo was Stethdel's daughter. Zornan would do anything to protect his girls, but there certainly had to have been other ways to ensure Mairie's safety. He understood Stethdel's motivations, but that did little to calm Zornan's burning hatred for the man.

The conversation was interrupted by a sudden, loud knock at the door. Zornan jumped, and Loothdram rose.

"Who is there?" Loothdram shouted, walking toward the door, his hand on his hatrindi.

"It's Natradni Enforcer, Investigator. Are you all right? The door is locked, and your guard is gone."

"I am fine, working on a delicate matter. Please leave me alone."

"I cannot, Investigator."

"And why in the name of Circlarl not?"

"A servant said he brought a fugitive to your room. I am under orders to search your room. My orders come from Hisvan, Investigator."

Loothdram leaned in closely to Zornan.

"Listen closely," Loothdram whispered. "Empty your mind again. I am going to reach out to you, but you must let me in." Turning slightly from Zornan, he continued, "I hope this works. Mindspeak does not always cross High Trades, but I hope our personal connection prevails. Fire Moon shine on us."

Loothdram turned toward the door. "One moment while I put away some of my private things," he shouted.

Zornan emptied his mind again. It was easier this time. Could he and Loothdram really talk the same way he had with Silver?

...hear me? Can you hear me? It was Loothdram's voice in his mind, but softer and hollower. Zornan snapped his eyes open and saw his friend. His lips were not moving. The Investigator smiled.

I can hear you, Loothdram.

Good. Adjacent to the fireplace is a secret door. Loothdram walked over to the fireplace and Zornan followed. The Investigator reached out to the wall and pushed a stone. A portion of the wall pushed back, revealing a dimly lit, narrow hallway. Zornan saw torchlight in the distance. *Follow this hall until it ends. It comes to a door in a servants' alley near the lake. My guard was instructed to meet you there. Go find Ballin, find Mairie, and get ready to leave. I will figure out a way to get you all out of Skathall.*

Zornan almost spoke his response, but focused inside his mind. *Your guard was instructed to meet me there? I thought you sent him home.*

He is Kuthraz as well. Go quickly, friend. I will speak to your mind later, when it's safe.

Zornan stepped inside the hallway, and Loothdram closed the door behind him.

17 | TWO MERCHANTS

Zornan navigated the dark, narrow hallway and arrived at a door similar to the one that led from Loothdram's room. He could see the outline of the door from the inside, just as he could from the hallway outside Loothdram's room: the doors were visible inside the hallway, but invisible on the outside.

As he pushed the door open, he raised his arm to shield his eyes from the blinding daylight. As soon as the door was open enough for him to fit through, someone yanked his other arm and pulled him from the passageway. The door shut behind him as he blinked against the brightness.

Standing next to Zornan was the guard he had seen at Loothdram's door. He wore a red cape draped over a gray guard's uniform. His head was adorned with a plain silver helmet, and a fierce looking wolf's head was emblazoned on his tunic. Zornan had noticed a similar symbol throughout the palace: his brother's gubernatorial seal. Dark hair sprouted from underneath his helmet, and his face wore the same blank expression Zornan had observed several minutes ago.

"We must move quickly, Peak Crosser," the man said.

"Thank you."

"I serve Loothdram. It is him you should thank. Follow me."

Zornan followed the guard through a servants' alley. He saw no other servants as they hurried down the path's narrow confines. The walls of the palace formed one side of the alley, and a ten-foot wall facing the lake formed the other. Smells of the water and fish filled the air. They passed several doors back into the palace as they approached a gate in the wall. The guard stopped short of the gate.

"Look ill," the guard said. Zornan wasn't sure what to make of the instructions, but he looked ill as best he could. The guard pushed the gate open.

The gate opened onto an almost empty street right next to the shore of Grizthall Lake. The blue water stretched out into an apparent eternity, only its southern shore visible. A few other servants milled about, and a small fishing boat floated away from the shore. Two guards stood on each side of the gate, all four armed with swords and dressed exactly like his guide.

"Greeting, Mayfran," one of the guards said to Loothdram's guard. "Who is this?"

"A sick servant Loothdram Investigator asked that I escort home. This one has a tendency to try and cure every ill with wine or liquor."

The other three guards chuckled. Zornan moaned.

"Very well. Loothdram is a strange one, sending a guard on this. Get back to your post as soon as you can, Mayfran."

"As you command, Master Guard."

Mayfran grabbed Zornan by his left arm and roughly pulled him away from the other guards. Zornan tried his best to look ill until they rounded the corner and were on one of the city's streets. At that point, Mayfran released his arm, and Zornan returned to health.

"Come. We have little time before they realize you've left the palace."

Zornan followed Mayfran out of the center of the city and into the Low Trade ring, keeping his eyes down as a commoner should. Everyone on the street cleared a path for the guard, and no one paid mind to the commoner or servant trailing behind him. They soon arrived at a tailor's shop, and Zornan followed Mayfran through the door.

The shop was small and filled with fine, Low Trade and High Trade clothes. The shopkeeper looked up from sewing a sleeve. A woman, maybe his wife, sat next to him hemming some trousers. The man was short and thin with a crest of white hair on his head. The woman was also short, but plump. She had matching white hair in a long braid down her back. They treated Mayfran's sudden appearance as commonplace, remaining in their seats and smiling. The guard scanned the shop for other patrons and did not speak until his eyes stopped moving.

"We need some clothes, Bandrank. And quickly. Make us look like merchants. Not too wealthy, but not too plain either."

The shopkeeper nodded and led the guard and Zornan into the back of his shop.

As soon as the curtain dividing the two rooms swung closed behind Zornan, Mayfran began to disrobe. Zornan followed his lead and began to remove Ballin's commoner clothes. Bandrank, the tailor, eyed Zornan, and then pulled out two sets of merchant clothes. Both outfits were mostly black, one with purple adornments, which the tailor handed to Zornan, and the other with red adornments, which he handed to Mayfran. Both had large, puffy sleeves and pants that stopped mid-calf. These might be the style of Skathall merchants, but that made them no less ridiculous, like a plum bird trying to catch a mate.

"It is the latest fashion," Bandrank said, noticing Zornan's apprehension. "I saw this style on my last trip to Bristrinia, and it's become very popular here in Skathall. It's certainly much nicer than the clothes you brought in with you."

"Fashion is not our concern today," Mayfran replied bluntly, as much to Zornan as to Bandrank.

The tailor shrugged.

The two men finished dressing, and Mayfran fastened his belt and sword over the new outfit.

"Most merchants are not wearing swords these days Mayfran," the tailor said, "even if it is legal."

"If we get into trouble, I can't fight a guard or an Enforcer with my fashion sense, Bandrank. I will risk the disapproving glares of other merchants."

The old man shrugged again.

When Zornan finished dressing, the tailor approached him with a small bag, folding Ballin's clothing into a careful pile and placing it inside. He handed the bag to Zornan as Mayfran passed by in a hurry toward the front door. The shop was still empty. The tailor's wife nodded and smiled to them as they left; Zornan returned the smile, thankful for their help, even if he had no idea why they had helped or what would happen next.

Mayfran said nothing as they weaved through the last of the Low Trade streets and into the commoner ring. In a few short minutes they approached the same gate through which Zornan had entered the city. A new set of guards watched the gate, these more attentive than the group from this morning. Mayfran's right hand edged close to his sword as they walked past the guards; apparently Mayfran was ready to fight his way through if it came to that. Zornan wasn't sure what a guard could do against a pair of Enforcers and six other guards.

But they passed through with little notice, making their way onto the eastern road. A few commoners passed, giving the two apparent merchants a wide berth. They reached the top of the hill and walked fifty yards into the woods before Mayfran stopped.

"I assume you know the way from here."

"Yes. Again, thank you."

The guard eyed Zornan curiously, nodded, and then walked back toward the city. Zornan watched him leave, then ran into the woods. He needed to hurry so he could get to their campsite before nightfall.

18 | A MONSTER

When Zornan reached the campsite, the sun was setting behind the peaks, and a few clouds moved slowly across the sky, reducing the light even further. It would be a dark, starless night which would make flying away even more daunting if it came to that.

The campsite was empty when he got there, just his own pack hidden under some brush behind a tree where he left it. He removed the silly merchant outfit and changed into his extra set of Peak Crosser clothes. Zornan sat down and ate a meal of dried fruit and meat.

It was more than an hour before he heard someone approach. Zornan slipped his hatari out of his pack and gripped it in his right hand, preparing for friend or foe. Ballin entered the clearing, his bow cocked. He sighed when he saw Zornan and lowered his weapon.

"I feared the worst, brother," the younger man said.

"As did I," Zornan replied.

"How is our brother?"

"As you described: he reaps as Father reaps. I had to get Loothdram's help to escape the palace."

"Loothdram?" Ballin questioned. "You went to see Loothdram? He didn't just arrest you on the spot?"

"No, Loothdram is actually a friend, unlike our brother. He helped me escape."

Ballin shook his head.

"Where is Mairie?"

"Hunting, I guess. Did you know she has a bow? She's quite a shot, too."

Zornan shook his head.

"Not as good as me, certainly, but good. She should be close; we were supposed to meet at sunset."

As time passed and the setting sun dipped below the mountains, Zornan told Ballin the details of his trip to Grizthall, though he left out the part about being able to speak to Silver and Loothdram with his mind; he wasn't sure Ballin would believe him. After that, they sat mostly in silence, hoping Mairie would return safely.

Where are you? Zornan jumped as Loothdram's voice intruded into his mind.

I'm at the old hunting grounds, the clearing where we played as boys.

Demon's teeth! They're headed straight for you!

Who is?

Fifteen mercenaries Hisvan hired to bring you in. He didn't want to use his own guard because he doesn't want the Empire to know you escaped the palace, and some of his guards are Imperial agents. He also did not approach me; I think he suspects I helped you. You must move now. Get around them, head for Moztarn.

Zornan looked over at Ballin. His sudden flinch and intense concentration probably looked quite strange; Zornan would have thought his behavior extremely odd just a few hours ago.

Zornan scanned their surroundings and listened for signs of their pursuers. Night stretched across the valley, only a few tendrils of twilight holding on to the day. He couldn't hear or see the attackers yet, but he trusted that Loothdram knew what he was talking about.

But Mairie has not returned, Dram. We have to wait for...

Confound you, Zor, get moving! They may already be close; I just learned of this, but they've been out of the city for hours. Mairie will have to take care of herself.

Distant voices broke his thoughts and he quickly rose to his feet. Ballin lay back against his pack, looking up at Zornan with a smirk. Two men were whispering in the distance, and he could hear faint footsteps on the soft, forest ground.

They're here, Dram. Zornan directed the thought to Loothdram.

Curse Hisvan! Try and get around them, Zor. Keep Ballin safe. I'm coming with help, but we're still miles away.

Zornan looked over at his brother.

"Grab your things. It's time to move," Zornan said quietly, firmly.

"What? Mairie's not here! We can't leave until she comes."

"Keep your voice down. A group of men are coming for us, and we'll be no help to Mairie if we're captured or dead. Move."

Ballin cursed under his breath, but got his pack together in a few seconds. Zornan packed as well and kept his hatari gripped in his right hand.

"This way," Zornan said, leading them out of the clearing and into the woods. The darkness had arrived. "Grab the back of my pack and don't let go. I'll lead you through the dark." Zornan hoped his eyes would be good enough; he saw better than most in the dark, but on a night with no moons, even his sight would be limited.

He made a straight line, as best as he could tell, toward the hill that overlooked their old home. From there they would head southwest toward Moztarn. He prayed to the moons that they weren't already surrounded.

After a few minutes, Zornan stopped, crouched down, and closed his eyes. He needed his ears to tell him if anyone was close. At first he heard nothing, but then he heard a slight groan, and then a thud, like someone had fallen. He heard it again but from a slightly different direction. And then a third time. The darkness made moving as difficult for their pursuers as it was for them. But three or four of them tripping at about the same time? Unless Hisvan hired the clumsiest group of mercenaries in the Empire, what he was hearing didn't make sense.

Silence came again for a few moments, but footsteps interrupted, the soft sound of someone stepping carefully through the woods. They were close, maybe within twenty yards. He cursed silently to himself. He examined their surroundings; he had inadvertently stopped in a small clearing, potentially exposing them. He silently cursed again.

A high-pitched call broke the silence. It was a good approximation of a deer sparrow, but deer sparrow didn't live this far south. And Zornan spent every day with a bird, even if it was a giant one; he knew a human bird call when he heard it.

A series of small clicks came next, and the forest awoke with the light of spark torches. One of the torches was only ten yards ahead of them, the mercenary holding it in his left hand and a sword in his right; he was standing at the edge of the clearing Zornan and Ballin were in. Zornan had not heard the man approach, so he had been waiting for them. They had surrounded the brothers, and Zornan had led them directly into their snare.

Zornan counted nine more men as they cautiously approached from all directions, four of them with lit spark torches. The light danced off their faces, each unshaven and snarling. Zornan commanded his hatari to grow into a full-sized spear, and Ballin unsheathed his sword.

An eleventh man stepped from the shadows and into the clearing. He had a dark, full beard. He was easily two or three inches taller than Zornan and fifty pounds heavier. He had two swords, one strapped to his left hip, the other in his left hand. He eyed the brothers lustily.

"Looks like we've found what we were looking for." The man's voice was deep and rough. "Give up your weapons. Even a Peak Crosser," he spoke the word with disdain, "can't best a dozen trained men. You're worth more alive, but the reward is sweet enough if you're dead."

Zornan knew the man was lying. They absolutely needed Zornan alive to collect any reward; no one was going to pay them for a dead High Tradesman. But Ballin probably wasn't even wanted, and he was a commoner, someone no one would care about if he was killed while these fools were trying to capture a fugitive High Tradesman. The bearded man was right about one thing: even if Ballin was good with the sword, they would lose to the eleven mercenaries, and Ballin would die. He needed to stall until Loothdram arrived with help.

"You lie, mercenary," Zornan replied. "You need me alive, and certainly the life of three or four of your men is worth something."

The man laughed. "Three or four? You boast, Peak Crosser. But, point taken; one or two of my men is worth something to me."

"Let this man go, and I will surrender willingly."

"No, Zornan!" Ballin shouted. "We die together!"

With a quick flick of his hatari, Zornan hit the butt of Ballin's sword and it flew out of his grasp and near the feet of one of the mercenaries.

"Zornan! You idiot! They're going to kill me!"

"Promise me he lives, and I surrender." Zornan avoided eye contact with his angry brother.

"You have my word," the man responded. His words were coated in grease, his honor as slippery as his tone, no doubt.

Zornan shrunk the hatari to its smaller size and tossed it to the man. The leader caught it and nodded to his men. Four of them approached, one on each side of the brothers. The mercenaries bound their hands with rope. The bearded man approached Zornan and stood close, waving the hatari in his face. His breath was foul, a mixture of liquor and raw meat. Up close and with the aid of torchlight, Zornan could see his right ear was mangled as if chewed by a dog.

"How do these work exactly, Peak Crosser? How do you get it to grow and shrink?"

"It's magic."

The man laughed heartily, and the rest of his crew joined the exuberant merriment.

"Now let this man go."

"I can't do that, Peak Crosser. Though he wasn't mentioned in our orders, he may be valuable." The man walked over to Ballin, eyeing him closely. "Maybe this commoner is wanted as well, or maybe he would make a good slave. Or maybe we'll kill him for sport. He has value, yes he does."

Ballin suddenly jetted forward and head-butted the leader just under the nose, the crack of bone echoing through the woods. One of the mercenaries holding him punched Ballin in the face. Ballin slumped momentarily from the blow but quickly stood straight.

The bearded man dropped Zornan's weapon and his own. He held his face and groaned. He pulled his hands away, blood saturating his beard. He reached down and picked up his sword.

"I'll kill you!" the man shouted wildly, his eyes crazed with anger. The two men next to Zornan gripped his shoulders tightly as he struggled fruitlessly against them. The lead mercenary charged Ballin with his sword outstretched.

A dark blur flew into the clearing, striking the bearded man in the chest and forcing him onto his back. The sword escaped his grasp and bounced into the darkness. The dark shape wore a hooded cloak, and claws grew from its hands. A Baldra. Somehow the Baldra had tracked them and found them, and like a prairie cat with a wolf, it was going to get the lesser predators out of the way before it claimed its prey.

The rest of the mercenaries stared at the apparition, glancing at each other in disbelief. Two of them were brave enough to charge the creature. The Baldra disarmed each in turn then thrust its short swords into each man's gut.

"Attack it, you fools, overwhelm it!" shouted the mercenary leader, who was still lying on his back in the middle of clearing. One hand gripped his face, the other his chest.

The remaining eight men charged chaotically; the five holding torches seemed unsure what to do with their lights. Each of the men who got close to the Baldra fell, as the two short swords connected with chests, stomachs, and necks. Its movements were a blur, its blows violent and decisive. After killing four of the men, including one with a torch, the remaining four torch holders froze and looked at each other. Their leader was still on the ground, unable to rise, but had managed to unsheathe his second sword.

One of the men dropped his torch and ran into the woods. The other three looked at their departing friend as if contemplating a similar, frenetic retreat, but the Baldra struck the nearest with a jab of one of its swords to the chest; the other sword swung and extinguished the torch. The darkness grew.

The other two men turned to run, and the Baldra flipped high into the air and blocked their escape. It swung and destroyed their torches, leaving the only light in the clearing coming from the torch that had been dropped moments before. In the near darkness, Zornan heard the remaining men groan and saw their bodies slump onto the forest floor.

The Baldra walked back into the light of the torch and toward the leader. He tried to stand, but whatever injury he had sustained from the first blow was too much. He propped himself up and raised his sword, which the creature flicked into the darkness with a swift kick. The man shook.

The hooded assassin knelt by the bearded man. One hand was empty and gripped the collar of his shirt. The other held its short sword at the man's neck.

"Does your life have any value?" The Baldra's voice was not what Zornan expected. He had imagined an animal-like voice, maybe even a foul language all its own. But the words were crisp, and clearly human. It was a high, feminine voice, and despite its ferocity and terror, it felt familiar.

"Yes, yes. I can give you money, or provide you with men, weapons, whatever you want!" Panic had replaced the mercenary's bravado.

"You threatened an innocent man with death."

"He struck me!"

Without another word, the Baldra flicked its sword, and blood poured from the man's throat. His body slumped lifelessly to the ground. The Baldra stepped away, its face still hidden from view.

Zornan looked over at the ground and saw his hatari's outline in the dancing light. Was he close enough to get it, free himself, and prepare to defend them? Did it matter? He had watched the creature almost catch a flying mrakaro. He had watched it kill ten trained and armed men in a battle measured in seconds. What other untold tricks did a Baldra know? So he stood there and looked over at his brother. The young man was completely calm, his face tinged with more sadness than fear.

The Baldra stood there for several moments then walked slowly out of the clearing and into the woods, evaporating into the night.

Zornan's heart sank. The creature wasn't here for Zornan and Ballin; it was here for Mairie, and it was looking for her.

But even that conclusion did not match the facts. If the mercenaries were a liability, weren't Zornan and Ballin as well? And what had it said about the bearded man threatening an innocent man? What did the Baldra care about justice? It had executed a High Magistrate. Now it was worried about how Ballin was treated?

Zornan stepped forward and grabbed his hatari. He held it with one end touching his bonds and created a sharp spear tip without growing the weapon. It easily cut through the rope and the remnants fell away. He turned to Ballin and did the same.

"We have to get out of here, Ballin. It may come back."

"She's no danger to us," came his brother's reply, his eyes staring at the point in space where the Baldra had disappeared into the woods.

"She? *It* is a killer and a monster, and it may come back for us, especially if it can't find Mairie."

Ballin stared at Zornan, his eyes narrowing, "What are you talking about?"

"The Baldra. That was the same Baldra that tried to keep us from leaving Fallindra!"

Before Ballin could respond, Zornan hushed him. He probed the silence and picked up the sound of approaching footsteps. He turned his eyes toward the sound and saw rapidly advancing torchlight.

He heard something else, something softer and closer than the on-coming light. He focused on the sound: someone was weeping, a girl or a young woman. It was Mairie, weeping like she had the night they'd escaped Fallindra, except this time there was no nibrak in her mouth to muffle the sound.

"Mairie!" Zornan shouted and turned to run.

"Wait!" Ballin called.

Zornan ran as fast as he could manage, but the thick forest slowed him. He could hear the weeping still, and he could see the torch approaching, its holder moving faster than he was. Zornan pushed harder, ignoring the sting of the branches that struck his arms and face.

He came into a small clearing at the same time as the torch, his hatari ready. Mairie was kneeling in the center of the clearing, her back toward Zornan. He looked up at the torch and saw Mayfran, the flame in his left hand and a hatrindi in the other.

"Mayfran!"

The man nodded. "Zornan. Are you safe?"

"I think so. Where's Loothdram?"

"Behind me. He could not keep up."

"You must go back to him! There's a Baldra here! He could be killed!"

"A Baldra? Are you sure?"

"Of course," came Zornan's frustrated reply. "I faced one of those monsters in Fallindra. You must help him. I will stay here with Mairie." The girl had stopped crying, but she didn't look up at Zornan.

"If there is a Baldra in the woods tonight, and it wants to kill Loothdram, there is nothing I can do to stop it."

"There's no Baldra in the forest tonight." Mairie's voice was soft and haggard. Zornan looked at her again. She was wearing a hooded cloak, part of her voluminous hair still contained within it. She stood and turned toward Zornan. In one of her hands was a dark, short sword. The front of her cloak was covered in a dark liquid, and red stained both her hands. "I am the only monster in the forest tonight."

Shock enveloped Zornan. Mairie was a Baldra? She had killed the mercenaries? *How could I have been so blind?* Ballin had known. Mayfran and Loothdram probably knew. And Zornan, again, proved ignorant. He had seen her mount a mrakaro as effortlessly as a veteran Peak Crosser. He had seen her land on the cliff's edge of their hideout cave. She was something more than just a young woman, and despite the clues, he'd missed it.

Mairie looked at him, her eyes still wet from weeping and her hands and cloak covered in the dark red of the blood she had spilt. Ballin stood next to him now, and she alternated her gaze between the two brothers. Zornan looked at his brother. Ballin smiled weakly at Mairie, and she returned the gesture even more weakly. Zornan locked eyes with her. Was she the same girl he had known the past few days? Did knowing she was an amazing warrior and killer change anything? Did she really even need his help? After what he had just seen, he didn't think she did. He clearly knew almost nothing about her.

Zornan turned away and walked into the woods. After a couple of minutes, he slumped to his knees and leaned against a tree.

I've lost everything to protect a monster.

Zornan knelt a long time in the darkness of the woods. No one approached him, and the only thing he'd heard after leaving the group was more weeping from Mairie and hushed conversation between Ballin and Mayfran. It had been silent for several minutes now.

Someone approached, soft footsteps growing closer. He remained where he was, not turning to face whoever came. He knew he couldn't face Mairie yet; he was scared of her now and ashamed of his fear. And he wasn't sure he could face the others.

"Hello, old friend." It was Loothdram. "We need to be going. We need to reach Moztarn by morning. I have a plan to get you, Ballin, and Mairie out of the valley, but we must move quickly. By morning Hisvan will know his bounty hunters failed, and he will be forced to move his soldiers out here to search for you."

"Why does Mairie need me?" Zornan asked bitterly. "She's a Baldra, a ruthless killer. What good is a Peak Crosser if I'm not flying her out of here?" The thought of sharing Silver with her again turned his stomach.

"She's not a Baldra, Zor. She has many similar abilities, but her blessing is very different."

"You mean her curse."

"Stand up and face me, Zornan."

Zornan stood and faced his friend. In the near darkness, he could not make out Loothdram's expression. He was sure his friend was disappointed in him, and he couldn't blame him.

"Baldra are not created like the other High Trade. They are usually orphans babies or young street urchins whom the Empire steal and transform into something very different. They are deformed; they have no free will. They are controlled by another secret High Trade called Shindar. Mairie was blessed as an infant by her mother with abilities like a Baldra but without their disfigured faces and white skin. And her will is her own, not subject to a Shindar or anyone else. She is not a Baldra, and she is not a monster."

"You didn't see her, Loothdram."

Speak to me with your mind, Zor. She can hear our conversation, if she wants to.

You didn't see her, Dram. She's a magnificent killer, like nothing I have ever seen. She slit the throat of the lead mercenary. He was unarmed and terrified. She slit his throat in cold blood.

She saved your lives, Zor. Now you question how she did it? That mercenary would have killed Ballin, and he would have sold you to your brother, who would have turned you into me. I would have been forced to send you, with Enforcers watching you the entire way, to Fallindra to be tried for your crimes. You would have been convicted by the local Magistrate, or sent to the High Magistrates and convicted there. Then your family would be left destitute without your stipend and shamed forever. You should be thanking her, not insulting her.

Zornan knew what Loothdram said was true, but he couldn't escape his fear and loathing for Mairie. He had always mocked Calla's father for his superstitions, but now he found himself in an unknown world of magic, assassins, and rebels. He didn't know what to think of this new reality, even if it had always existed just outside his view.

I know this is a lot to take in, Zor, but you have to understand. That ferocity you saw is part of her blessing, and she has paid a high price for it.

What price? She's unstoppable.

Did she tell you about her father, the man who raised her?

Zornan nodded.

That was her second family. Her first family was in a small village near the Ice Mountains. She learned to walk at six months, and she could do flips and acrobatics before she was a year old. She also attacked other children in the village, almost killing a five-year-old boy after he pulled her hair. Before she was two years old, Stethdel moved her to a man named Liven, a widower raising a small daughter in a village near Bastanda. He was a farmer and lived an isolated life. He taught Mairie to be calm, how to control her emotions and keep her blessing from turning her into a ruthless person. You have seen the fruits. She is a caring, thoughtful young woman, not the monster you portray her to be.

You didn't see it, Dram, Zornan repeated. He felt drained, tired from the extremity of his situation. Loothdram was right, but he couldn't get the vision of Mairie's ruthless killing out of his mind. And he couldn't reconcile that with the girl he had come to know in the last few days. And while he had been alone, he had made another troubling connection. Ballin had told him Mairie was a good archer. What if Doorsal hadn't been killed by the Baldra, but by Mairie? If Stethdel really saw what happened that night in Fallindra, then it couldn't have been the Baldra, it must have been Mairie with her Baldra-like skills. So she had not been an innocent bystander to Zornan's predicament; she had been a confederate.

I did not see it, Zor. The Investigator spoke into his mind, the voice turning sad. *But she grieves for what she did, even though I believe she did what had to be done. Do monsters grieve? Would a monster care what a Peak Crosser she barely knows thinks of her?*

Zornan closed his eyes and tried to calm himself. His goal was to stay alive and reunite with Calla and the girls. He could not do that by standing in these woods and waiting for Hisvan's soldiers to apprehend them. He also felt responsible for Ballin. He had pulled his brother into all of this despite the younger man's advice not to get involved with Hisvan. Now Ballin was going to be branded a criminal—but without the protections afforded a High Tradesman. Zornan owed it to his brother to help him find a life outside Skathall.

"You are right," Zornan replied out loud. "Helping Mairie and Ballin is the right thing to do." Zornan wanted to add that it might be his only hope at recovering the life he'd left behind, but speaking that hope out loud might reinforce its unlikelihood.

Loothdram stepped up close to his friend and grabbed his shoulders, Loothdram's eyes wet with tears.

"I hope, old friend, that we might be able to restore you to your family. You deserve that. After Mairie is delivered, we will see what we can do."

Zornan's eyes moistened as well, Loothdram's words fanning the embers of his hopes.

Zornan embraced his old friend and began to sob.

19 | THE EMPEROR'S REQUEST

n the four days since his audience with the Emperor, Mizcarnon remained in the Peak Crosser keep awaiting orders from General Chandish. He spent his time reading and playing a solitaire dice game he'd learned from his father. The other Peak Crossers in the keep were friendly, but they avoided deep conversations with him. Military Peak Crossers were viewed with suspicion by the rest of his kind. Peak Crossers relished freedom above all else, and Mizcarnon's life looked stifling to them in comparison.

But Mizcarnon valued honor over freedom, and his assignment, especially this last one, brought much honor. And he still enjoyed a lot of freedom traveling across the Empire and beyond; the other Crossers gained little honor by carrying messages and parcels.

That morning as he ate breakfast in the common room, two Imperial Guards arrived and asked him to return with them to the palace. The appearance of the Emperor's soldiers unsettled the other Peak Crossers, and, truth be told, worried Mizcarnon. Had the Emperor changed his mind? Was the knowledge he possessed too sensitive? The threat of a foreign invasion could destabilize the entire Empire, and this information might be just the kind of thing an emperor would want to keep secret no matter the cost.

He quickly dismissed the thought. The Emperor was known as a decisive man; if he were truly concerned, he would not have allowed Mizcarnon to return to the keep. The Emperor knew that if Mizcarnon leaked the information, his fellow Peak Crossers could carry it across the expanse of the Empire in a matter of days. If the Emperor hadn't trusted him, he would already be dead.

He settled on a more likely scenario: the Emperor or the High Counselor wanted to ask him more questions regarding what he'd seen in Croxshine. After mulling over the surprising and discomforting revelations, maybe they wanted to pose questions they had not thought of in the first interview, or maybe the High Counselor hoped to discredit him. He hoped he would not have to face that woman alone.

Upon arriving at the palace, the two Imperial Guards escorted him to a room he had not been in before, a library of incredible size. It was not as majestic as the throne room, but it was still larger than any room he had ever seen in his life besides the throne room. Books and scrolls covered every inch of wall. Most of the floor space contained shelves for more books. There were no windows, but brastilia-infused glow globes kept the room comfortably lit. The only way into the room appeared to be through the door he had entered. The Imperial Guards left him there alone with his thoughts and worries. And a lot of books.

Mizcarnon loved books. He resisted the urge to begin hunting through them. He could become lost in books like a merchant counting his money. But Mizcarnon was in this room for a purpose, and he couldn't imagine that purpose was to read.

So he paced the room for a while, casually looking at book and scroll titles. Most of the texts were historical, and much of the section he perused housed works about the Empire's early history. He saw titles like, "Conquering the Bendathdrans" and "The Subjugation of the Crazdar."

The next section was more to his interests, containing titles like, "Mrakaros: A Study of the Giant Hawks" and "The Discovery of the Great Prairie Cats of the Plains of Fandrill." Maybe because of his bond with Sunset, he was fascinated by animals, how they interacted with each other and how they interacted with men. He pulled out the mrakaro book and flipped through pages. It was a long book, more than seven hundred pages, with colored illustrations of mrakaros in flight, of mrakaros with Peak Crosser riders, and one of a riderless mrakaro fighting three atacikics.

The door opened, interrupting Mizcarnon's reading. He put the book back and walked out from among the shelves.

The Emperor stood alone just inside the door. Mizcarnon immediately fell to his knees and bowed his head almost to the floor. According to Imperial law, no one except the High Counselor, the High General of the Imperial Guard, or the Emperor's spouse (and he had none) should stand on the same level of floor as the Emperor. Mizcarnon broke Imperial law even with his kneeling bow, though the Emperor gave him no choice.

"Stand, Mizcarnon Peak Crosser." The Emperor's voice was as deep and powerful here as it had been in the throne room. "You have done nothing wrong. I am the law, and I decree that you may stand at my level."

Mizcarnon stood slowly. The Emperor was, of course, correct. He was the living embodiment of the law, and it bent to his will, except for some items that stood within the control of the Grand Council of the High Trades.

"Please sit, Peak Crosser." The Emperor motioned to a small sitting area nestled between bookshelves containing a table and two lush chairs. The Emperor sat opposite him.

The Emperor was dressed in similar robes to those he'd worn during their first visit, the same blood red on his sash, the rest of the robes a light orange. His dark, curly hair was pulled back as before by a thin gold band. Mizcarnon could properly judge his height now; the Emperor was very tall, several inches taller than Mizcarnon. Besides a full-grown Shantierd, the Emperor must be the tallest man Mizcarnon had ever met.

The Emperor took a deep breath and met Mizcarnon's eyes. "I need your help, Mizcarnon."

"Anything, my Lord, anything."

"The assignment I'm going to give you is a difficult one, possibly more difficult than your scouting trip to Croxshine."

Mizcarnon nodded, wondering what could possibly be more difficult than flying across an ocean and prying information from your enemies.

"The difficulty of the mission is of no consequence, Your Highness," Mizcarnon responded, bowing his head awkwardly. Honoring the Emperor was much easier when you were standing.

"Have you ever met a Peak Crosser named Zornan?"

"I only know his name, Emperor."

"He has been accused of murder, including killing a High Magistrate."

Mizcarnon flinched. How could one of his kind, even if it was a lower Peak Crosser, dishonor their High Trade by killing a High Magistrate? The shame shadowed them all.

"But," the Emperor continued, "I believe he is falsely accused and that there is something behind the base facts. I have read the report of the Investigator, a man named Crisdan, and this esteemed Investigator has significant doubts as to Zornan Peak Crosser's guilt. I believe this unwitting Peak Crosser may have been caught up in a nefarious plot. Have you ever heard of the Kuthraz?"

"Of course, Emperor. They are rebels."

"Yes, they hope to create an Empire where the High Trades are free and not servants of the Empire, one that is led by the aristocracy and the High Trades, not a hereditary emperor. They are dangerous, and we believe they have followers at every level of the High Trades and throughout the Low Trades and local governments. Have you heard of the Dundraz?"

Mizcarnon furrowed his brow. He had heard the word before but couldn't recall its meaning. He could remember something about an ancient order of the High Trade, maybe a group or person before the High Trade laws were codified two millennia ago.

"No, Your Grace, I do not know of the Dundraz."

"They are rebels as well, many times more dangerous than the Kuthraz. They operate in complete secrecy; outside their own ranks, very few in the Empire even know of their existence. Even the leadership of the Kuthraz know little, if anything, of their rival. The Dundraz seek to destroy me and to replace me with a ruling body of High Tradesmen or with a new emperor chosen from their midst. They are not content with someone like myself, unblessed by the power of the Bendathdrans, ruling the people. They believe that my ancestors were High Trade and that the Imperial line and law have been corrupted. They are biding their time, waiting for the right opportunity to overthrow the Empire and grasp its power for themselves. As patient as the Kuthraz have been, maneuvering for centuries to mold the Empire, the Dundraz are as impatient, looking for a way to quickly transform the Empire of the Peaks to their vision.

"The Dundraz do not value life, especially the lives of the Low Trade and commoners; this is what makes them so dangerous. The Kuthraz are piously devoted to keeping innocent commoners and the Low Trade out of the fray, but the Dundraz have no such moral convictions. They despise the aristocracy and would love nothing more than a complete revolt by the High Trades to dethrone me and take control of the Empire. And if tens of thousands die in the process, it is a sacrifice they are willing to force."

High Tradesmen plotting to overthrow the government? A secret sect bent on destroying the Greatest Emperor of the Peaks, Tothdarin, son of Gathrizdel? Mizcarnon shuddered. Both of these groups brought dishonor to all High Tradesmen and to the entire Empire.

"What I don't understand is how Zornan Peak Crosser is involved in these plots," the Emperor continued. "I believe the Kuthraz are growing more aware of the Dundraz and somehow this Peak Crosser is caught between the arrows of these adversaries."

The Emperor paused, looking away from Mizcarnon, his eyes focused on some distant point. "Both of these groups would destroy the peace, would kill me to get what they want. But I fear the Dundraz most. They are violent and immoral, and I have reason to believe they have members within my very court and within the highest councils of the High Trades. There are very few people I can trust. And you, Mizcarnon Peak Crosser, are one of those few."

Mizcarnon stared back at the Emperor. "Me, My Lord? I am an Imperial scout, a lowly Peak Crosser."

"How many scouts were sent to Croxshine?" the Emperor asked.

"Three, Your Grace."

"And how many returned?"

"I believe only I did."

"Yes, you were the only one to return. Did you know the other two men? Their names were Nundril and Beeldrat."

Mizcarnon knew Nudril well. The young Peak Crosser was very talented, one of the best flyers under the three moons. Mizcarnon had been a mentor to Nundril when he joined the military out of the academy. They'd flown scouting missions together beyond the Ice Mountains, traveling to some of the most remote and dangerous parts of the Empire.

He did not know Beeldrat well. The man had a reputation as a womanizer and a gambler. He was several years younger than Mizcarnon, and they had never been assigned to scout together. He had been suspected of deserting once before but then appeared months later in Junnidra, some five hundred miles from his scouting assignment. He claimed he had lost his cosow to foul weather and had been stranded in the mountains, pursued by wild beasts and wild men. His story of survival was legendary, but Mizcarnon had always suspected it was an elaborate story to cover his indiscretion. Regardless, he was a legend among Peak Crossers.

"I knew of them both, Greatest Emperor. Nundril, well and Beeldrat, less so."

"Neither returned. Either they died a glorious death fulfilling a mission of the Empire or they deserted and are now living in secret in the Empire or beyond. Why do you think they would not return, Mizcarnon?"

He hesitated. Was this a trap of some kind? Mizcarnon had been sucked in by the Emperor's nonchalance, but he began to worry that he was missing the man's intent. He needed to choose his words carefully. "I would not know, Your Grace."

"Come now, Mizcarnon, I know you know."

"Because," he replied with a deep sigh, "they thought they would be executed after the mission, especially if they saw anything the Empire might want to keep secret." Mizcarnon felt ashamed for suggesting such a thing to the Emperor.

"Precisely." The Emperor flashed a pleasant smile. "And in the past, we have done just that. But it was folly, an old custom that does more harm than good. Why would an emperor kill loyal men, the best of their kind? All to keep something secret that was likely to spread anyway?"

Mizcarnon remained silent as the Emperor gazed into the library.

"I have amended that law recently," the Emperor continued after a few moments, "but your fellow scouts don't know that, and many would not believe the change even if I signed an official decree out in a public courtyard. And yet, you came back. Why?"

Mizcarnon looked into the eyes of the Emperor. Was it possible that the Emperor was as sincere as he portrayed himself to be? Was it possible he was now protecting Peak Crosser scouts in a way they had not been protected in centuries? Mizcarnon had imagined the courts of the Emperor to be filled with scheming men and women with no regard for anything but their own power, the Empire held together despite the intrigue. Mizcarnon served the Empire faithfully, but he had never served the Emperor, not in his heart. He respected General Chandish, and felt loyalty to him. But his loyalty had been tied to the Empire and its people, not to those who led it.

Either the Emperor was acting in order to earn Mizcarnon's loyalty or he was sincere and fully engaged in the future of the Empire and its people. The Peak Crosser chose to believe the latter.

"Honor, Your Grace. And loyalty to the Empire of the Peaks."

"Where did you learn this sense of honor?"

"From my father. He taught me that living with honor is demanded by the gods and that living with dishonor will not only damn you but can also taint your family and your friends."

"Yes," the Emperor said, smiling warmly again. "And your father is Carnon the merchant, correct?"

"Yes, my Lord."

"And you have stayed in contact with your family? Most High Tradesmen I meet stay apart from their original families. Are you not taught in the Initiatory School that your old family is gone, and that your High Trade is your new family?"

The Emperor was challenging him again, and again Mizcarnon worried about a verbal trap. Perhaps the Emperor had changed the law about executing Peak Crosser scouts but might be looking for a way to justify Mizcarnon's imprisonment or execution anyway.

Mizcarnon decided to trust the Emperor at his word. *If this man wants you dead,* he thought, *he doesn't need to play games to make it happen.*

"Most High Tradesmen are sold into the High Trades by desperate or cruel parents. Many of them are orphans or come from families broken by death or financial ruin. I volunteered to join the High Trades to lift my family out of poverty."

"And your parents agreed with your decision?"

"No, they did not know of it. I forged my father's signature and hired a man I knew, another merchant, to pose as my father when I was sold. My parents only knew after I had a friend deliver a letter explaining what I had done. At that point it was too late to stop me.

"My father was a merchant, trying to establish himself in Bristrinia. But he could never get the capital necessary to begin the trade he hoped to establish. My family struggled under the weight of financial uncertainty, living day-to-day with whatever work my father and grandfather could attain. My stipend gave my parents the money they needed to establish themselves."

"They are successful now, yes?"

"Very much so, My Lord."

"And you see them often?"

"Every month or so. As often as I can."

"You are a singular man, Mizcarnon Peak Crosser. There are only a few men or women like you in the entire Empire of the Peaks."

"You honor me too deeply, Greatest Emperor of the Peaks, Tothdarin, son of Gathrizdel."

"No, Mizcarnon Peak Crosser, I don't think we honor you enough."

The Emperor paused. His eyes glistened with moisture, and his mouth tightened. Mizcarnon looked away; he had no right to see the Emperor cry. The moment brought immense honor to Mizcarnon and his family, even though he knew he would never tell a single soul. But the gods knew.

"Will you accept an assignment to track down Zornan Peak Crosser and find him before the agents of the Kuthraz or Dundraz do?"

"I am yours to command, Emperor. I will give this task all that I have."

"I know you will." The Emperor smiled, though it did not pierce the worry around his eyes. "The Imperial Guard will provide papers summarizing everything we know about Zornan and his situation. You should leave today. We believe, through a report that came in this morning, that he was in Skathall, his boyhood home. But he is likely out of that valley now, and hopefully safe. Do you know Skathall?"

"Yes, Your Grace. My father was born there, though his family left for Bristrinia when he was a child."

"Have you ever been?"

"No, Your Grace. My grandfather hates the place, and I have avoided it because it would dishonor him for me to go. I have never been assigned to go there."

The Emperor stood, and Mizcarnon rose from his chair and quickly sank into a bow. He kept his forehead nearly touching the floor, waiting for the Emperor to speak.

"Rise, Mizcarnon Peak Crosser."

He stood and looked up into the man's eyes. They were a brilliant, almost unnatural, blue. Mizcarnon knew the Emperor did not have the blessings of an Investigator or a Counselor, but those eyes seemed to be just as effective at weighing a person's soul.

"Welcome parting, Peak Crosser. Tell no one of our meeting, and remember this: if you are caught in this effort, you will be labeled a traitor and confederate of Zornan, and I may, for good reason, need to disavow you. No one can know your assignment came from me. The rebels must believe I do nothing to stop their plots."

The Emperor's words seized Mizcarnon's heart, similar to the fear which gripped him when General Chandish told him of his scouting mission to Croxshine or when he marched to the Emperor's throne room. But he pushed the fear aside and replaced it with the pride of being so honored with a personal request from the Emperor, an honorable man who was worthy of all the adulation he received.

"Of course, My Lord. Sad parting, Greatest Emperor of the Peaks, Tothdarin, son of Gathrizdel. I will not fail you."

20 | WHAT ONE MUST

alla adjusted her shawl. She rarely wore this shirt, as the style was too revealing for sleepy Fallindra. She looked down at the plunging neckline; yes, much too revealing. Zornan had purchased it in Bristrinia where the styles were far less conservative. She adjusted the shawl one more time then untied it and tossed it aside. If she was going to wear this shirt to flirt with Crisdan, she just needed to wear the shirt, not water it down with the shawl. He was waiting downstairs, and she needed to present herself soon.

"I did not realize you were courting." Caladria stood in the doorway, her eyes judging Calla more with each second.

"Mother." Calla breathed the word more like an exasperation than a name. Mother had been so kind in staying with her, in allowing Father to watch the girls and give Calla time to think and to study. She didn't want to fight, so she held her tongue.

"I raised you better than this." Mother wasn't going to let it go. "Your husband is away, potentially fighting for his life, and you sit here flirting with the man who wants to lock him away forever."

Calla inhaled, calming herself.

"It's not like that, Mother."

"It's not?" Mother walked into the room and sat on the bed, next to the discarded shawl. "I see how his eyes hunger; I see your smiles. I may be an old woman, Calla, but I'm not dead. I know flirtation when I see it."

"Of course you do. I learned it all observing you." Calla regretted the words, but they were true. Calla had seen Mother smile at Thistid, Father's friend. She'd seen mother laugh too loudly at the jokes of Bark, the owner of The Water's Edge. She didn't need to be lectured by the woman who'd shown her how to manipulate men.

"Calla." Mother stood and gently placed a hand on Calla's shoulder, her touch matching her kinder tone. "I know I'm the last person who should lecture on this, but a harmless smile or touch is one thing—what you are doing is different. Can't you see that? Your husband is not here. You can't return to his arms after a harmless exchange."

Calla closed her eyes and breathed deeply again. Those words stung worse than anything.

"Thank you for reminding me, Mother, that Zornan is not here." Caladria did not deserve her icy reply, but the emotion poured out, her heart unable to contain it. Mother had been nothing but giving since Zornan left, but Calla could bear no more. "I am doing everything I do to bring him home." Calla stood, facing her mother. "I spend almost every waking hour pouring through High Trade law, and I spend the other hours courting favor with a man who might have influence on Zornan's lawful return. I will do what I must." She kept her voice low, partially out of respect for her mother but also in case Investigator ears were as blessed as those of her husband.

Mother's face formed into a stony anger, but she kept her emotions in check. "As you wish, Calla. I will be in my room." Mother turned and walked out.

Calla slumped back into the chair. She regretted the tone but not the message. Didn't Mother understand what was at stake?

Her long hours at the library drained her. The dense language of the law was beyond her meager education. The work was slow as she constantly looked up words she didn't know or discussed points of confusion with the kindly librarian, Doothban, who had been extremely patient with her constant barrage of questions.

Much of what she found was encouraging. The High Trades were protected by the law unlike anyone else in the Empire besides the Emperor himself. Accusations against High Tradesmen from commoners or Low Tradesmen carried little weight with Magistrates. The witnesses in such cases would need corroborating witnesses and heavy, indisputable evidence. The result was that High Tradesmen were almost never punished for any offense against commoners and only slightly more often for offenses against Low Tradesmen and their families.

The charges against Zornan had one major weakness: Stethdel never officially spoke against Zornan. If she could prove, or if she could at least throw enough doubt on Crisdan's account of Stethdel's charge, everything would unravel. Without Stethdel's testimony, there were no grounds for prosecuting Zornan for the murder of Doorsal. And if she could convince the High Magistrate hearing the case that Zornan never believed the accusation, his motivation for killing Stethdel disappeared. The reason, then, for Stethdel's body being placed in their cupboard would be put into question.

Another option was to find Stethdel's actual murderer. The only way she could come up with using that defense was confessing to the murder of the High Magistrate herself since she had no idea who killed him or who his enemies might be. Even as the wife of High Tradesman, her punishment would be death. Zornan would hate her for that, and she couldn't imagine abandoning her girls. Still it seemed an easier path than trying to convince a High Magistrate that an Investigator of the High Trades was a liar, corrupt, or incompetent. But accepting her own death would not be easy, and her confession would taint Zornan and the girls for the rest of their lives.

She hoped it would not come to that.

Calla composed herself and descended the stairs. Crisdan stood at the bottom. The Investigator was tall, even taller than Zornan. He had his back to Calla, gazing out the window onto the street beyond. His thin arms were folded behind him, his Investigator uniform fitting loosely. He turned as she descended. He smiled and bowed his head slightly. His skin was dark, which made him stick out even more in fair-skinned Fallindra than his uniform did. His eyes were dark as well, and his straight black hair hung over his ears to his collar.

"Greeting, Lady Calla."

"Welcome greeting, Crisdan Investigator."

Crisdan's eyes drifted slightly toward her blouse then snapped back to her eyes. She hoped he didn't feel a flash of guilt or shame, focusing more on her warm feelings toward Crisdan. That might not actually fool an Investigator, but she'd do what she must.

"Please sit, Investigator."

"Thank you."

They sat opposite each other, too far apart for proper flirting. Crisdan's posture held nervousness, though Calla did not know its source.

"You have news of my husband?"

"Yes, my lady..."

"Please just call me Calla, Investigator."

"Of course," he said, nodding, and he blushed. "Your husband has been found, but he escaped again."

"Where?" Her heart raced, thinking of Zornan on the run from a focused effort by the forces of the Empire. *Take care, Zornan. Stay hidden until I figure out a way to save you.*

"Skathall."

Calla did not know what to do with that information. As a Peak Crosser, he could have visited his boyhood home a dozen times since she married him, but he had avoided it like the girls avoided spiders. Only after several years of marriage did Zornan finally confide in her that his father had been a vicious and violent man. Zornan's heart held nothing of his father's temper.

"He attempted to visit his brother, Hisvan," Crisdan continued, "who is the governor of Skathall."

"His brother is the governor?" For a moment, Calla wondered if Crisdan was lying to her. Zornan's family was common, and commoners did not usually jump station like that. Was this some sort of test? "How on earth did his brother become a governor?"

"I do not know the history, but Hisvan is the governor of Skathall, and Zornan attempted to visit him. He fled the palace when he was discovered."

"Did he visit his brother?"

"That is unclear, but his brother was the one who alerted the local Investigator."

"I can't believe a brother would do that." Calla could not imagine turning any of her family over to the Imperial vultures.

"It was his duty, Calla, as an officer of the Empire. He was bound to report the appearance of a wanted murderer. It's possible that Hisvan allowed him to escape before reporting it, which, if proven, would be a criminal offense in and of itself. I wouldn't judge him too harshly, my lady, especially if he allowed your husband a few moments to avoid the Enforcers."

"Is duty the highest law, Crisdan?" For the first time in the conversation, she used just his name without his title. She looked at him, finding it easy to summon the anger she needed. She burned with hatred for Hisvan for turning his brother in. She did not have a sibling, but she couldn't imagine betraying blood.

"The highest law, my lady?"

"Calla," she reiterated. "Yes, the highest law. My husband is innocent of everything he has been charged with, and I believe you know that. Hisvan is his brother. Does duty to the Empire trump justice? Does it overshadow familial love?"

"Duty may not supersede everything, my lady, but it is a good and strong path when the way gets murky and hard to follow." His words straightened his posture. Crisdan hung his apron on duty, the central tenet of his High Trade.

"That sounds like justification for cowardice." Again she struck at kindness with fierce words. These dark days pulled her into dark places she did not like to see herself in.

But Crisdan did not flinch. He sat straight up as he had before, not breaking eye contact. He let silence hang between them for several moments before responding. "Calla," he said her name softly, kindly. "Duty binds the Empire together. Is it not duty to your husband that drives you to the library every day?"

"You know of that?"

"I'm an Investigator; I am supposed to know everything." He smiled, and she couldn't help but smile in return; his smile was beautiful. "It is duty to Zornan and duty to your girls that drives you. Please understand that my marriage is to the Empire, so my duty lies there. Do not condemn us for placing our allegiance with the Empire; there are worse places one could direct it. And besides, searching for justice and being faithful to the Empire are, in my experience, usually one in the same."

Since childhood, she'd been taught that the High Trades were filled with greedy and manipulative men and women, people who would toss commoners and Low Tradesmen aside to satisfy even the smallest of needs. Even Trillia Magistrate, who was well respected here, was viewed by Calla's parents with suspicion. Her parents were not alone in their prejudice—the entire valley was united in its hatred and distrust for strange High Tradesmen and their peculiar abilities.

Then she'd met Zornan. He wasn't like what she had been taught at all. He was kind and sincere, and he wasn't interested in anything beyond fulfilling his duty as a Peak Crosser and living a simple life. She had fallen for him almost immediately, not because of his position and the comfort it could bring her but because of the fine man he was. When they began their romantic relationship, she assumed it would be temporary, or if it was more permanent, that it would rob her of her dreams of having a family. But she was willing to give up her dreams to be with a man like Zornan, even if it would have marked her as a promiscuous outcast.

And now she met Crisdan, another man of principle and heart. Was it possible that High Tradesmen were not that different than commoners? That many were corrupt or evil, but that most were good and kind? She had thought, when she met Zornan, she was meeting a singular High Tradesman. But he might not have been as unique among his kind as she'd thought.

"Thank you, Crisdan."

"You should not be quick to thank me. I may be the one responsible for ruining your husband's, and ultimately your own, life."

"If our lives are ruined, it will be the doing of Stethdel and whoever killed him. You are not responsible for the law, and you're not responsible for those actions any more than I am."

"You are too kind, Calla."

"Calla," came her mother's voice from the kitchen. "I need your help with something as soon as you are able."

Calla smiled. Despite how cruelly she'd treated Mother, the woman continued her protective watch.

"Is there anything else I should know about Zornan's situation, Investigator?" She returned to his formal title for Mother's listening ears.

"No, my lady, only that the Investigator who is in charge in Skathall is a man named Loothdram. Have you heard of him?"

"No, Investigator. Should I have?"

"I thought your husband may have mentioned him. Loothdram was also raised in Skathall, and from what I understand, was a friend of Zornan's before both were placed in the Initiatory School."

"I don't know of him," she replied. "I hope, for Zornan's sake, he's not as good an Investigator as you."

"Unfortunately, my lady, his reputation is quite good," he said, looking away for a moment. "But it appears Zornan escaped him. I will return with news as soon as I have it."

Crisdan stood to leave, and Calla stood and walked the Investigator to the door. He opened the door and paused, looking down at her.

"Sad parting, Lady Calla."

"Sad parting, Crisdan Investigator."

21 | ALLIES

Crisdan walked away from the Peak Crosser's home, pulling at his smile to keep it from blossoming. His interactions with Calla were intoxicating. Every time he learned something new about Zornan, a strong desire to share it with Calla overwhelmed him. Her beauty was beyond compare, and her spirit was as strong as any person he'd ever met. With her husband likely headed to ruin or a permanent exile, and with her entire world crashing down around her, she kept her head. Crisdan knew enough about human nature to know how rare her reaction was.

Crisdan knew he was being manipulated to a certain extent. Calla did not feel for him what he felt for her. Yes, she smiled a lot and warmed with his presence, but he was nothing more to her than a tool to get her husband back, even if she was fond of him.

He cursed himself for spending so much of his mental energy on this unrequited relationship. If Karzdiff Investigator caught even a sniff of this romantic distraction, it would be the tide which drowned Crisdan's career.

Despite all that, Crisdan basked in his feelings toward Calla, as dangerous as they were. His station forced him to keep his emotions hidden from others with similar abilities—Investigators or Counselors. Karzdiff would have to use more traditional means to prove Crisdan's incompetence, and Crisdan doubted the man capable of finding anything of the sort. Karzdiff was a lazy Investigator who leaned too heavily on his abilities and ignored the basic principles of investigation.

He shook himself from these thoughts as he approached the home of Trillia Magistrate. He was due to give her an update on the investigation.

The judgment for Zornan, if any was to come, now sat in the hands of the High Magistrates. His visits to Trillia were a matter of courtesy as he was not bound to report to her. But she was a Magistrate, a highly respected one, and Crisdan needed all the allies he could get.

Trillia's servant greeted him at the door and led him to her judgment room. It was a medium-sized chamber on the first floor, covered with the most beautiful woodwork Crisdan had seen outside of the capital. The walls perpendicular to the door were divided into panels, expertly carved into murals of various nature scenes. He recognized one as the Plains of Fandrill, with a prairie cat hunting in the long grass. Another was a mrakaro gliding riderless above the Ice Mountains. On the opposite wall was a large, menacing lizard of some kind in the Jungles of Crazdar. The last scene was a wolf climbing among ancient ruins.

Behind four rows of chairs, Trillia sat at a desk. Another large chair sat immediately to her right, and two more sat along her left, the furniture arranged for trial. Most Magistrates Crisdan worked with did not use the judgment room as a work space. But Crisdan admired Trillia's choice; seeing everyone in this room reminded all who visited of the power Trillia wielded.

Trillia looked up at the sound of the door closing behind Crisdan and motioned for the Investigator to take a seat opposite her desk. The diminutive Magistrate sat in a small chair behind a small desk that made her appear regular size by their proportions. But she was more than a foot shorter than Crisdan, and her frail frame made her look even smaller. Crisdan estimated that she was in her fifty-fifth year or so; her hair was mostly silver, with some of its original dark brown sparingly mixed in. She kept her hair short, which was not the style anywhere in the Empire except among the women of Crazdar and women Peak Crossers. It was shorter than Crisdan's hair, but long enough that it reached her eyebrows and covered her ears. She wore an elegantly simple black dress with a high collar and a flowing skirt that almost entirely filled the space under her open desk.

Crisdan took his seat and waited for the woman to address him.

"News of Zornan?" she asked after several moments, only then looking up from whatever she was reading.

"Yes, Trillia Magistrate. Zornan was spotted in Skathall but slipped through the hands of the local authorities."

"You mean to say his brother Hisvan botched his capture."

"I can't say, Magistrate. I have no details beyond the fact that he tried to visit the local Investigator, a man named Loothdram, and was spotted by an Enforcer and fled. As to the vigorousness of Hisvan's pursuit, I can't say."

"From what I know of the man, Hisvan would sell his own children to find greater favor in the Emperor's eyes." She shook her head. "I'm shocked that naive, innocent Zornan has been able to escape twice now." She raised one eyebrow. "No offense, Investigator."

"None taken, Magistrate. I underestimated the Peak Crosser, and perhaps so did his brother."

"Perhaps." She looked back down at what she had been reading and back at Crisdan. "Tell me what you know of the High Magistrate, Stethdel."

Crisdan paused before answering. In his previous two visits, they had only discussed the High Magistrate as a witness and a victim. High Magistrates were not to be discussed casually, especially with a Magistrate.

"I know very little of him, Magistrate, besides what is widely known."

"Do not treat me the fool, Crisdan." Trillia snorted. "He accused a Peak Crosser of murder, witnessing this strange occurrence in the middle of the night. Why was a High Magistrate out in the middle of the night watching a deserted street? And why was he in Fallindra to begin with, when he was supposed to be vacationing in Skathall?"

Crisdan wasn't sure if Trillia was asking him or speaking rhetorically, so he remained quiet.

"You Investigators are blessed to be curious; surely your mind has pondered similar questions."

"Indeed," he replied, measuring his words carefully. "But it is not my place, even as an Investigator of the High Trades, to question a High Magistrate."

"But that's the point, Crisdan Investigator. He is no longer a High Magistrate, just a memory of one."

Crisdan continued to hold his tongue.

"Very well, I will make you a promise: I give you my word as a Magistrate that anything we discuss here remains in this room of judgment and within the confines of my mind. I will repeat it to no one."

"Very well," Crisdan replied, still wary of the net she cast.

"What did you think of his accusation?"

"I believe it was false, Magistrate."

"And why?"

"Because I could tell he lied. His emotions betrayed him." Most High

Tradesmen distrusted Investigators and Counselors for their abilities to probe emotions and the mind. If Trillia was bothered, there was no indication. "In addition, it made no sense. Zornan had no motive, and his life was a clean one. It would seem strange to murder an Enforcer in cold blood in the middle of the night when the two men seemingly had no connection with one another."

"Precisely. I believe Stethdel lied. And do you believe Zornan killed Stethdel?"

"No, Magistrate."

"Why?"

"He had motive this time, but the murder was done by hatnuthri, which would be very difficult for Zornan to acquire. It has all the markings of a Baldra assassination. But, as you know, none of this can go in my report. The word of a High Magistrate is truth in the law, even if there is evidence to the contrary. And Baldra are not recognized by the Empire, so I can hardly tell the High Investigators and the Emperor that the assassin class was responsible."

"Then we must find a way to make the charges against Zornan disappear."

Crisdan leaned back, stunned. Why was Trillia so interested? This case would be decided by the highest courts and councils of the Empire, far above the heads of Crisdan and Trillia. Though she was respected and had been a Magistrate for almost thirty years, her influence was minor when considered on an Imperial scale.

"With all due respect, Magistrate, I cannot see how we could do that."

"Easily, Investigator. We prove that Stethdel was a liar and possibly a traitor."

An uneasy laugh escaped Crisdan, but he choked it immediately. Trillia was serious, her expression hard and her emotions harder. The desire to prove Zornan's innocence burned in her. And so did a hatred of Stethdel.

"Stop searching my emotions Investigator."

Crisdan blinked and withdrew his mind from her emotions. "Of course, Magistrate, I'm sorry." Holding back his ability was like a like asking a fish to stop breathing water.

"Are you going to help me or not?"

"I'm not sure what you hope to accomplish, Magistrate. I think it's possible to find another explanation for both murders, but not by discrediting Stethdel. Though you would know more than I, I can't imagine the High Magistrates would take kindly to having one of their own besmirched in a public trial."

"It is the only way to save Zornan and his family," she replied. "A High Magistrate is dead. If we leave him on his pedestal, then the High Magistrates and the High Investigators will demand a conviction and likely an execution—of someone, anyone. No phantom murderer will do, and all the circumstances point at the otherwise innocent Peak Crosser."

"But this would mean investigating a High Magistrate," Crisdan responded cautiously. "I have no authority to do that, and, pardon me, Magistrate, but neither do you."

For the first time since Crisdan met the woman, Trillia smiled. It was a deep, full smile, showing her straight white teeth. The smile creased her face with new lines, indicating her smile was not a frequent event. "Do you know why I'm the Magistrate of Fallindra?"

Crisdan shook his head.

"Because I am not trusted by my own kind. Other Magistrates dislike me, Investigator, because I look for justice.

"The Magistrate High Trade has become corrupted, possibly beyond repair. We have become legislators, aristocrats, advisers—everything except what we're supposed to be: judges. We exist to help the truth prevail, to punish the wrongdoer, and to protect and vindicate the innocent. I've been in Fallindra for nearly twenty-five years. I'm well-respected, which means I don't take bribes and I don't tell Fallindrans how to live their lives. And I'm an outspoken critic of my own High Trade.

"I know neither of us technically has authority," she said, leaning over her desk. "But I think the law helps us. There are thirteen High Magistrates, never more or less. Stethdel's death necessitated another be lifted to High Magistrate, which happened yesterday. The protection of the law, and I've read this closely, applies only to the thirteen. Stethdel is no longer part of that thirteen, and therefore, your investigation of him is perfectly legal, though, to be completely honest, politically unwise. So tell me now, young man, what are you here to do? Find justice? Or find favor in the eyes of the High Investigators and High Magistrates?"

Crisdan admired the woman's passion. He knew what she said of Magistrates as a whole was true, that corruption and power-mongering were more common than not among their kind. Sometimes he felt Investigators were the only group in the Empire still worried about justice, and even many of the Investigators were corrupt or uninterested. It was possible Crisdan had found his first true Magistrate ally, an obscure and respected woman who apparently had been banished to an inconsequential valley in the middle of the Empire.

"I would like to find justice for Zornan, Trillia Magistrate."

"Good. Neither of us has much to lose, do we? We both had a High Magistrate killed under our watch, and my ascent to the highest courts of my High Trade was halted decades ago. Do you have a working theory about Stethdel, about what he was doing here in Fallindra and why he would accuse Zornan of murder?"

"Not exactly, Magistrate. But I have some reason to believe he may have been associated with the rebel group, Kuthraz."

"Kuthraz?" Trillia folded her arms and sat up straight in her chair. "Now that would be interesting. What would lead you to believe that?"

"The accused Kuthraz ringleader, Lascrill Peak Crosser, and Stethdel have a pattern of being in the same city or valley at the same time. There are dozens of such occasions over the past decade. No official contact, but I don't believe in coincidences, not at that frequency."

"Stethdel in confederation with Lascrill? Now, if we could prove that, it would discredit him and make his actions against Zornan some kind of rebel conspiracy." She smiled again, but this time with a gleam of mischief in her eyes. "Let's find this connection, Crisdan, and let's bring Zornan home a free man."

22 | LEAVING AGAIN

Even with the gravity of his situation, Zornan felt ridiculous being fitted for new clothing in the middle of the woods. But strange flights led to strange navigation. He, Loothdram, Mayfran, Ballin, and Mairie had journeyed all night to arrive just east of Moztarn near the southern tunnel. Zornan wondered how the tailor and his wife were tangled into this mess.

Loothdram gave each of them a new identity to use while traveling. Ballin would be Nagtorn, the son of a prominent merchant from the city of Coothree in the Rinderel Valley. Ballin's character visited Skathall for several weeks, looking for new trade opportunities. Mairie would play the part of young Nagtorn's wife, Hannata. Zornan would be their personal guard, Doftil. Loothdram had allies in Rinderel who would house the three fugitives until it was time to meet Mairie's mother.

So, here Zornan stood in the middle of the woods, dressed in plain guard's clothing, and was being waited on by a tailor. The scene would have been the height of comedy if their lives didn't hang in the balance. He wore Ballin's sword on his left hip, and his hatari was cleverly hidden in a holster on his thigh which looked like it held a knife. Merchants typically did not wear arms themselves, especially in the eastern Empire where fighting was seen as beneath the Low Trade and aristocracy, so Zornan would carry both of their arms.

Of course, if it came to fighting, Zornan didn't believe he and Ballin would do any more than get in the way. Mairie, or Hannata, had been the first to be fitted in a sensible blue traveling dress made of thick, durable wool. The skirt was wide and pleated so she could move quickly and fight if needed. The skirt also held her two hatnuthri, the strangest weapons

Zornan had ever seen. They were blocks of brastilia with grooves for her hands. Like his hatari, the hatnuthri grew at her command from small rectangles into beautifully crafted short swords. Loothdram said most Baldra carried the weapons in the sleeves of their cloaks, the reason why legend said claws grew from their hands.

Besides the dress she wore, two more were packed in her bag: one a formal, frilly light blue thing, the other a green traveling dress almost identical to the one she was wearing. She had whined for some time upon learning that she would not be wearing pants, but the wife of an apprentice merchant (and a wealthy one at that) did not wear pants. For the first time since their attempted escape last night, Zornan smiled at Loothdram. Ballin and Galla, the tailor's wife, calmed her down. Despite her lethal abilities, she was still a young woman with strong opinions and childish reactions when she didn't get her way. She finally gave in when Galla showed her that the dress had been specially designed with her abilities in mind and was even more comfortable than the High Trade clothing her father had provided.

Since last night, Zornan had only exchanged a few uncomfortable glances with Mairie. He wasn't sure how she felt about him, and he was still struggling with what to make of her. He had called her a monster, had thought worse, and part of him still saw her that way. Her participation in setting him up for the murder of Doorsal still angered him. Maybe she had been forced to or manipulated by her father, but she'd played a part in Stethdel's wicked manipulation.

Ballin did not feel the same. He spent much of the night cleaning blood from Mairie's cloak and helped clean her hands. Despite seeing the same ferocity Zornan had seen, his younger brother was reacting with warmth, kindness, and understanding. Zornan wasn't sure if he admired his brother for it or if he should chastise him for his credulity.

After finishing with Mairie, Galla turned to help Ballin. The younger man did not take well to being dressed as a merchant. He wore a tight-fitting black and blue suit, with a jacket and a high-collared shirt. He was also wearing a ridiculous hat: a blue feathered thing that looked like some strange bird had taken up occupancy on his head. Ballin kept stretching and pulling at his collar.

"Stop moving, young man," Galla chastised. "If you're not careful, I will stick you with my needle."

"The prick of the needle would be better than wearing these street performer's clothes," Ballin responded sullenly.

"But it has to be done," Mairie shot at him with a deep smile. "Isn't that what you told me?"

Ballin just frowned.

"All done, young man." Galla rose to her feet and examined the younger brother. "Now stop acting so uncomfortable, or every Enforcer and guard between here and Rinderel will know you are not whom you pretend to be." She reached up and pulled Ballin's hands away from his collar. "You're acting as if this is the first time you've ever worn clothes like this."

"It is the first time I've ever worn clothes like this!"

"Ballin," Loothdram said, placing his hand on the younger man's arm, "please. You must play the part of a merchant and play it well. This is a risky plan, and its success very much depends on convincing everyone you meet between here and there that you are whom you claim to be."

"Fine." Ballin raised his hand but stopped before tugging at his collar again. "But you should have had Zornan play the part of the merchant; he has never had any problems acting a fool."

"As true as that may be, Ballin," Loothdram said with a smile, "they'll be looking for your brother. He has a much greater chance of going unnoticed if he's a nondescript guard than an extravagant merchant."

Galla approached Mairie and hugged the girl. At first, the younger woman recoiled from the unwanted embrace. But after a moment, Mairie wrapped her arms around the older woman's back.

"Take care of yourself, Mairie," Galla said, backing away. "I knew your father. He was a great man. And I know your mother. She will be very proud of the woman you've become." Galla's eyes filled with tears.

"Thank you," Mairie replied, grabbing Galla's hand. "Thank you for everything." Mairie let go of the seamstress's hand and showed her thanks by twirling in the dress.

Galla smiled, laughed, and clapped her hands.

"Come, love, we are due in Moztarn." Bandrank put his arm around Galla, and they walked through the thick green woods toward the road and their horse-drawn carriage.

"They are some of the best people I know," Loothdram said after they'd left.

"True words, old friend," Mayfran added.

"They were High Trade," Zornan said, a statement more than a question.

"Yes," Loothdram replied. "Galla was a Counselor and Bandrank was an Investigator. They fell in love and deserted the High Trade. I found them years ago, hidden here in Skathall. They have been loyal Kuthraz ever since.

"Come," he said, walking in the direction of the tunnel entrance. "We must be getting on our way. The sooner we get you out of this valley, the better I will feel."

An hour later, the group stood on a small hill overlooking the tunnel entrance, which was a large cave at the base of one of the valley's most southern peaks. Zornan's memory flooded with the first and only time he'd traveled through this tunnel, the day he was sold into the High Trade. He and Loothdram had traveled with several Imperial officials, collecting other initiates along the way. Entering this dark cave had been one of the most frightening moments of Zornan's young life; he felt only slightly more comfortable today.

The tunnel entrance stretched for thirty yards across and up even farther. A small guardhouse sat at the west side of the tunnel. Peering around a tree, Zornan saw two Enforcers, armed and dressed in their maroon uniforms. Both men were large, as Enforcers tended to be. Zornan also counted at least eight uniformed guards dressed in Hisvan's gray. Ten men. Under different circumstances, Zornan would have advised them all to turn around, that the risk was too great. But with Mairie, ten men seemed nothing more than a slight headwind.

Are you ready, Zornan?

Zornan wasn't sure he'd ever become used to Loothdram speaking directly into his mind. It was harder to ignore than spoken words.

Are you ever ready for something like this?

Of course not. But you are a good man, Zor. I can think of no one better to escort Mairie to safety. She is important to the Kuthraz, but more importantly, she's the daughter of my good friend.

Do you know her mother?

Not really. Loothdram looked past Zornan toward the mountains. *I have met her, but she's not really Kuthraz, only a sympathizer because of her love for Stethdel and the protection we've given her daughter. I don't trust her entirely, but I think she will be very grateful for your service.*

Who will meet us in Rinderel?

"You will be met by an Enforcer named Vacks," Loothdram responded out loud. "He is Kuthraz as well, and he will escort you to a remote farm we have outside of Coothree. It should provide you with a safe haven until your meeting with Mairie's mother."

"Is there any chance I can meet my mother sooner?" Mairie asked. Her eyes sparkled with hope.

"I cannot say, Mairie. Your mother's connection to our group was mainly through your father. I have sent a message to her, but I have to be extremely careful or I risk exposing her. If we can move up the meeting, I will get a message to Vacks or to Zornan."

The girl nodded appreciatively but frowned and looked at the ground.

Girls her age should be happy, Zornan thought to himself. *They should be thinking about boys and gossip, not about Empires and rebels.* At that moment, Mairie seemed fragile and small, worry and fear written across her face. Echoing Loothdram's words from the night before he thought, *Would a monster really feel like that?*

"We must get moving to meet our schedule, Doftil," Ballin said in a commanding voice. "Come, Hannata. Doftil, get our bags and let's be on our way." He held out his arm and Mairie slipped hers into his.

"Of course, dear husband," Mairie responded, smiling brightly, the pain from moments before wiped away. Ballin broke character for a just a moment and blushed but quickly returned to his assumed regal air.

"Farewell, friends," Loothdram said. "Mayfran and I will watch from here. If there is trouble, Mayfran will join in the fight. I hope it doesn't come to that."

In the short time it took to reach the tunnel entrance, Zornan grew sick of Ballin's merchant act. He ordered Zornan around obnoxiously, including a request to tie a loose shoelace. Ballin took too much pleasure in his temporary role.

One of the Enforcers would be an ally of Loothdram's, but the Investigator had not told them which one. He wanted it to appear that Ballin (Nagtorn) knew no one and was a first-time visitor to Skathall. Recognition of an insignificant Enforcer might raise suspicion. Zornan wasn't sure all of these precautions were necessary, but almost every decision he'd made since leaving Fallindra had been the wrong one, so he deferred to Loothdram's judgment.

As the group of three approached the tunnel entrance, they were met by the two Enforcers and three of the guards. One of the guards held a roll of parchment.

"Greeting, sir," said one of the Enforcers to Ballin. "Greeting, lady." He did not even look at Zornan. "What brings you to our tunnel today? Leaving the valley?"

"Welcome greeting, Enforcer," Ballin replied. "I am Nagtorn, and this is my wife Hannata. We are looking to get on this afternoon's tunnel ferry."

"Where are you headed?" asked the second Enforcer, a massive man with multiple scars crossing his face and another on the back of his left hand, disappearing into the sleeve of his uniform.

"Rinderel. We're returning home to Coothree."

"You are not on the schedule, sir," said the guard holding the parchment.

"No, I am not," Ballin replied calmly. He maintained his merchant act with casual responses. "I was scheduled for next week, but our business here is done, and my new bride misses home."

"Skathall is a beautiful place," Mairie added. "But it is not home."

The first Enforcer looked at the guard who was checking the future schedule. After a few moments, the guard looked up and shook his head.

"I'm sorry, master merchant," replied the first Enforcer, "but we need to check our records. I apologize for the inconvenience, but Governor Hisvan has ordered just this morning that all departures must be verified on our records."

"This is outrageous!" Ballin shouted, maybe a little too strongly. "I will not be delayed by this."

"It is all right, master merchant," the second Enforcer said. "I was here the day you and your wife arrived." He turned to the other Enforcer. "They came in two weeks ago, under the same names."

The first Enforcer nodded nonchalantly. "Of course, I apologize for the delay. The guards will escort you to the tunnel ferry."

After the exchange with the guards and Enforcers, the three fugitives walked to the guard house where Mairie wrote their names on the log sheet and Ballin paid their fare to Rinderel. The Enforcers and guards began to ignore them as soon as the second Enforcer had vouched for their identity, turning their attention to other travelers.

"I hate tunnels," Zornan muttered as they approached the cave. "Too dark and too confining." Zornan shuddered at the cool breeze escaping the tunnel.

"I thought you could see well in the dark," Ballin replied, taking care not to mention Zornan's station.

"I can see in the dark, even pitch black," Mairie said, her mouth twitching nervously.

"Really?" Ballin beamed.

"Yes, since I was a child. I close my eyes and I can see people in a green sort of light, their heat radiating in vibrant color."

Two days ago, Zornan would have thought her comments to be a deranged joke. But since he'd just learned to speak to Silver and Loothdram using his mind, he thought better of ruling out the possibility.

As they walked deeper into the cave entrance and into the tunnel, brastilia glow globes provided a dim light, like the diffused illumination of a stormy afternoon. Toward the back of the cave sat the tunnel ferry, a flat barge made mostly of brastilia. Most of the ferry contained a passenger seating area surrounded by high fences with long wooden benches lined parallel to the ferry's edges. The passengers of highest rank got the benches (High Trade, aristocracy, and Low Trade first), and commoners typically sat on the hard brastilia floor. Zornan would likely spend the two-day journey there.

The cargo section at the back of the ferry was much like the passenger section only smaller and without benches. It was already half full with several boxes and crates. A guard and a servant inside the cargo enclosure stood at the larger cargo gate and checked the contents against writings on a scroll.

The Ferry Guides, a captain and a pilot, stood toward the front of the ferry near a compartment which was separated from the passenger area by a tall, brastilia wall.

Zornan had limited experience with the reclusive High Trade of Ferry Guides. They were not considered lowly like Peak Crossers, neither were they considered leaders like Magistrates or Counselors. In many respects, they were not considered at all.

Zornan looked over at Ballin and saw him fidgeting with his collar again. Ballin nervously eyed both the ferry and the Ferry Guides. Zornan hoped it wasn't as clear to them that this was his brother's first time in a cave or on a ferry.

Mairie continued to play her part, at ease in the confines of the tunnel. She looked over at Ballin and smiled at his obvious discomfort. "Calm yourself, husband. I know you dislike tunnel ferry travel, but it surely agrees with you more than getting on the back of a giant flyer."

"Of course," Ballin replied, smiling weakly. "I would just prefer having my two feet always planted firmly on the ground."

Mairie laughed a little and stood closer to her supposed husband, grasping his hand. They shared a warm smile.

Zornan sighed. He'd suspected it before, but the truth was as clear now as the three moons on a cloudless night: Ballin was smitten. Zornan could understand why, at least on the surface; the girl was pretty and usually charming, when she wasn't ruthlessly killing a dozen bounty hunters. She was several years younger than Ballin, but she was old enough to be considered an adult in most of the Empire.

Not only was he dealing with escorting a supernatural assassin through terrifying tunnels, his brother might be opening his heart to a young woman who was more monster than maiden. Zornan could not imagine a happy ending.

"Passengers, please form a line near the ferry gate." The voice came from one of the Ferry Guides, a short man with a well-trimmed black beard that matched his hair and uniform. The other Ferry Guide, who must have been the Pilot, climbed into the front section and disappeared behind the wall that separated the passengers from the Guides. "Watch your step."

First to board the ferry was an Enforcer. He was likely there as a guard against tunnel pirates. Zornan entered next. Despite the two-foot base of brastilia, Zornan deftly climbed in, taking both the bags with him, and quickly cursed himself for a physical maneuver that exceeded the dexterity of the commoner he pretended to be. He looked back at the Ferry Guide, but the man was uninterested, his eyes lazily scanning the cave for other passengers, or maybe he just didn't care. The Enforcer was already in his seat, also paying no mind, stowing his bag underneath the bench.

Zornan offered his hand and helped Ballin onto the ferry. Mairie came next, and Zornan worried she would make the same mistake he had made, using her supernatural dexterity in a revealing fashion. But she played the part of a young merchant wife well, struggling with the large step and pulling heavily on Zornan's arm. His brother took her hand, and the group turned to find a seat toward the back of the passenger hold, away from the eyes of the Enforcer and the Ferry Guides. Though it was likely that a description of only Zornan was being widely distributed, it was prudent to avoid close examination. Loothdram said the official warrant for Zornan's arrest only mentioned the Peak Crosser, so their existence as a group acted as identity camouflage. And, as a Peak Crosser traveling by tunnel was like a fish traveling by wagon, they were unlikely to search for him here.

Three other passengers boarded the ferry, all men and, judging by their dress, merchants. Each one carried a small bag and dressed in a similar style to the ostentatious outfit Zornan had been forced to wear the day before. They sat separately, none seeming to be familiar with any of the others. They all nodded politely to each other and to Ballin, their equal, and smiled and nodded at Mairie. As Loothdram predicted, everyone continued to ignore Zornan.

Zornan took a seat a few feet away from the couple, welcome on the bench since no passengers of higher rank had boarded at this station. Ballin and Mairie sat close together, marking them as the newlyweds they pretended to be. Zornan shook his head and looked away.

The passengers sat in silence for several minutes as the Ferry Guide Captain closed the gate, checked on the cargo, and then disappeared into the front of the ferry to join the Pilot.

Zornan turned his attention to the other passengers. The Enforcer was lounging lazily on his bench near the front, leaning against the Pilot's wall. He ate an apple and occasionally looked back, but only at Mairie, eyeing her lustily and looking away whenever Mairie or Ballin looked in his direction.

The first merchant was examining a scroll, looking up occasionally into space as if calculating profits or imagining shipments. He was a small man, short and skinny, the baggy merchant clothes accentuating his tiny stature. The second one was a large, fat man, his clothing struggling to contain him. He had an oily mustache that was sculpted into large circles and painted gold, the mark of a Kandrinalli. He stuffed a cream-filled pastry into his bulbous mouth.

The third merchant sat as still as an Imperial Guard. His clothing was brand new, recently purchased. He did not have the opulent air of the other two merchants. If you ignored the fancy clothes, he sat like a soldier. Maybe it was paranoia, but he made Zornan very nervous.

Without warning, the ferry rose from the ground, and Zornan's examination of the other passengers ended as his stomach churned with the sudden movement. He glanced over at Ballin. His younger brother leaned forward, breathing heavily. Mairie did not flinch, nor did the first two merchants or the Enforcer. The third merchant, the one Zornan suspected was not a merchant at all, paled and steadied his head in his hands, leaning his elbows against his knees. His discomfort with ferry travel only added to Zornan's apprehension.

Zornan was sure he was a soldier, possibly placed on the ferry to watch for his escape, even though a Peak Crosser would be unlikely to leave by tunnel.

Slowly the ferry entered the tunnel, hovering only a few feet from the floor, quickly leaving Skathall behind. For the second time in his life,

Zornan left the valley this way. And like last time, he doubted he'd ever return.

23 | THROUGH THE TUNNELS

The bright sunlight faded as they sank deeper under the mountain. The passengers and the ferry would be at the mercy of the Ferry Guides from here on out, and the only light would be the passing light of brastilia glow globes.

Their first stop would be a day's ride, an exchange called Nabfryn. Loothdram warned them to be particularly cautious at the tunnel exchange. Once Hisvan discovered the dead mercenaries and feared Zornan gone, he'd know they had escaped by tunnel, especially if he suspected Ballin had come with him. The Enforcers stationed at the tunnel exchange would know to look for them, and an Investigator could get involved if one was close. As panic-inducing as getting into the tunnel had been, the tunnel exchange held far more risk.

Zornan focused on the passing globes. Glimpses of the tunnel walls, with weaving patterns of black and brown sedimentary rock, came and went with the light of the globes. He looked away and back at his feet as the movement continued to spin his stomach.

In order to free his mind from the confining tunnel and the upcoming tunnel exchange, Zornan decided to reach out to Silver. He hadn't had time to ask Loothdram whether distance or depths of hundreds of feet of earth would dampen their ability to communicate.

As he closed his eyes and calmed his mind, he could sense Silver. He recognized the feeling from other long journeys, but he'd never known it had meant more than the physical bond between rider and animal. Through the connection, he felt her exhilaration of flight. She followed their path thousands of feet above them. Zornan wished he could join her.

How are you, friend? Zornan projected the thought at Silver.

Excited to be moving with purpose, little rider.

Zornan could feel the excitement, and it made him smile despite his melancholy.

You should be up here with me, and not down there with the rats and worse. I will catch up with you soon. Those tunnel boats do not move as swiftly as I do.

I need to be with Mairie and Ballin. I need to protect them.

As you wish, little rider.

Zornan broke the connection, though he could still feel her in the back of his mind. Despite the chaos of the past several days, the revelation of these abilities, of his blessing at the hands of a priestess of Bendathdra, provided some comfort and eased his loneliness. It was the one good sapling among a small forest of bad ones.

He looked back up at Mairie and Ballin. His younger brother was asleep, leaning up against Marie. Mairie's eyes were wide open, looking intently at the other passengers. Zornan still did not know how to feel about her, but it was comforting to have her on his side.

Knowing the most fearsome of their group was on careful watch, Zornan leaned up against the two bags and let his exhaustion overcome him.

"Doftil, wake up."

Zornan sat up quickly and reflexively grabbed at his back where his hatari was usually holstered. Ballin hovered over him. The ferry was still moving swiftly through the tunnel. Without the sun or the stars to mark the passage of time, Zornan had no idea how long he'd slept. He stood and straightened himself, playing the part of the faithful servant.

"Sorry, master. I must have fallen asleep for a moment."

"Longer than a moment."

Zornan almost smiled at the rebuke but held his act together. None of the other passengers appeared to be paying attention to them, but they had to be diligent.

"We need to talk, master."

"About what?"

"Not here where others could hear."

They stepped to the back of the ferry.

"You can talk openly, Zornan."

The Peak Crosser looked skeptical and peered up at the other passengers.

"Mairie and I tried it out. I whispered back here, and she stood near the passengers. Even with her hearing, she could hardly hear me; the rushing wind is too disruptive."

Zornan looked up at Mairie, who was sleeping on the bench. He was more worried about her ears than even the other passengers, but he wasn't sure he'd get this opportunity again.

"You cannot fall in love with Mairie."

"What?" Ballin said indignantly, blushing. "I'm not falling in love with her."

"I admit I don't know you that well, but seeing who a young man's heart belongs to is not a hard thing to see. So either you need to go to Bristrinia and audition for the Emperor's Theater or you are smitten by our little assassin over there."

"Stop calling her things like that!"

"That's what she is, Ballin. That's why I'm so worried."

"Worried?" Ballin shook his head. His eyes and face tightened with tension. "You haven't worried about me in ten years! Why worry now?"

Zornan stopped at that rebuke. His brother was right, and though he had hoped they had buried this with their conversation outside their childhood home the other day, he knew better than that. Hurt like this couldn't be erased by a simple conversation.

"I know, I have no right…"

"No, you don't have any right!"

Zornan looked up and saw that two of the merchants, the soldier-looking one and the fat one, observed them closely now. A master getting angry with his servant was mild entertainment, but it was all they had on this journey.

"Please calm down, master. Your anger has attracted the attention of the others."

Ballin looked back, and the two merchants quickly averted their gaze.

"Doesn't matter," he said, turning back. "This conversation is over." He turned to leave.

"Master." Zornan's voice was as calm as he could make it. His brother paused but did not look back. "Please be careful. Everything about this situation is dangerous, including your feelings."

Ballin peered over his shoulder, his face softening but still creased with annoyance. He walked back and took his seat next to Mairie.

Zornan returned to his seat as well. The conversation could have gone better, but he had given his warning. Of course, men in love rarely heeded any advice to the contrary.

Some hours later they arrived at the exchange, though it was impossible to know the time of day. He reached out to Silver, and she informed him that the sun was setting in the unseen skies above. Mairie had been awake half an hour or so, and they were all on the alert. They looked far too tense for a simple tunnel ferry-exchange, and Zornan noticed that the merchant who carried himself like a soldier paid particular attention. Their pretended facades were fraying under the constant stress of potential discovery.

The ferry entered a massive cavern with seven tunnels shooting off in all directions. The cavern looked large enough to fit the entirety of the Emperor's palace inside it. Their ferry joined three others in a flat area near the tunnel they'd exited.

Beyond the other ferries stood a large building, three times as big as his home in Fallindra. Dozens of people milled about: merchants, Enforcers, guards, and commoners. It was like a small, bustling town hidden hundreds of feet below the ground. Even though the cavern's ceiling floated hundreds of feet above them, Zornan still felt confined, as if the cavern were a third its size. He reached out to Silver and was calmed by her mental embrace.

The ferry touched down with a slight bump. After a moment, the passenger gate opened, and the two Ferry Guides greeted the passengers with stern expressions.

"Welcome to Nabfryn. Journey well." The Pilot spoke this time. He was younger than the Captain but looked almost identical, with the the same dark hair and a close-cropped beard. He stood next to his partner, their arms locked behind their backs.

The three fugitives exited the ferry and waited in line behind the other passengers for a servant who would ensure passage on the next leg of their journey. The dark cavern bustled with activity. The central building contained two shops, one selling food, the other selling a variety of goods. A third entrance led to a small inn and tavern, the words "Hidden Tavern" written above the door.

As the officer questioned the other passengers, Zornan looked around and saw that no one, including the soldierly merchant, paid them attention. Mairie made idle chatter with Ballin about being amazed at the size of the Nabfryn cavern each and every time she visited, as if she had been here a dozen times. Ballin responded absentmindedly; he was scanning the landing spot, same as Zornan. But no one approached. If they were to be confronted, it wasn't going to be right here.

After the fat merchant finished with the servant and walked away toward the tavern, their group approached.

"Greeting, travelers," the servant said.

"Welcome greeting," Ballin replied.

"Where are you headed, fine sir, young miss?" The servant was older, likely approaching his seventh decade. He was bald with willowy hair on the sides of his head, yellow and decaying teeth.

"Rinderel. We need the next ferry to the eastern Empire."

"Of course, sir. You are in luck. The next ferry leaves in just a few minutes, and it has room for three." The servant looked over at Zornan and back at Ballin. "Is this all you have, sir?"

"Yes, my guard, and the two bags."

"Excellent. The ferry to the eastern Empire is just over there." The man pointed to the ferry farthest from them on the other side of the large building. "I would not delay. They are loading passengers and cargo as we speak; the Captain is rather punctual." The man bowed his head and quickly moved on to his other duties.

"That was easy enough," Ballin said after the man disappeared.

"Maybe," Zornan said. "We'll see who greets us at the other ferry."

They walked across the landing area and toward their new ferry. They passed dozens of other passengers, mostly merchants, some commoners, and a few aristocracy. There were also High Trade of almost every kind: Enforcers, Investigators, Magistrates, and Tunnelers, all dressed in the clothing of their trade, but no Peak Crossers.

In this tumult, no one paid their group any mind; they were background to all these travelers, and not even that interesting. A young merchant, his wife, and a guard. There were a dozen other parties just like theirs within his sight. Loothdram had picked the ideal disguise.

They slowed as they approached the new ferry. The Captain stood there, flanked by an Investigator and two Enforcers. All three of them stopped short as they noticed the Investigator. Part of Zornan's mind demanded flight, to turn and run away. But where would they go?

"Greeting, sir, lady," the Investigator spoke, not the Captain. "Are you looking for passage to the eastern Empire?"

"Yes, Investigator," Ballin replied calmly, calmer than Zornan thought he could have. "We're not usually met with Investigators at the ferry gate.

Is there something wrong?"

"No," the man said, shaking his head. He had voluminous blond hair, and like Crisdan and Loothdram, his manner was friendly and engaging. Zornan was beginning to think that friendliness was part of their training. "Just a routine passenger check. Nothing to be concerned about. What is your name, sir, and where are you from?"

"Nagtorn Merchant, Investigator. This is my wife Hannata. We hail from Rinderel."

The Investigator nodded politely to Mairie and turned his gaze onto Zornan. "And your servant's name?"

Ballin laughed, but cut it short when the Investigator turned to him without a smile. "Sorry, Investigator, not many ask for my guard's name. He is Doftil."

"Just one moment, sir."

The Investigator walked a few feet away, joined by one of the Enforcers; the other stayed with the Captain and glared at Ballin. Now that Zornan knew about mindspeak, he suspected the Investigator was checking with someone or discussing it secretly with the other Enforcer. Mindspeak wasn't as comforting now as it had been when he'd reached out to Silver.

Mairie slipped her hand into Ballin's. It was an innocent maneuver, but Zornan saw it for what it was: fear. Her other hand was pulled up tensely in a fist, very near the place in her dress where she could extract her weapon.

After what seemed like a relative eternity, the Investigator turned around and walked back without speaking to the Enforcers. His friendly demeanor was unchanged, and he smiled brightly at Ballin and Mairie.

"I apologize for the wait, Nagtorn Merchant. You are free to board the tunnel ferry when you wish. Travel well."

The Investigator and the two Enforcers walked away, leaving the ferry to its Captain. Ballin, Mairie, and Zornan each took deep breaths and exchanged surprised glances.

The Ferry Guide Captain gestured for them to go aboard. This time Zornan acted more awkward, and Ballin and Mairie repeated their act. Zornan wasn't sure how, but they had fooled the Investigator and were headed to Rinderel. There were only minor exchanges between Nabfryn and their destination, no stops where they would have to leave the ferry or be checked again by servants or others. If that Investigator had indeed been fooled, they were likely safe. At least for now.

The ferry was much larger than the one that carried them from Skathall to Nabfryn, half again as large in the passenger area and close to twice as long in the cargo section. It was also jammed with passengers. There was hardly room for Ballin and Mairie to squeeze between some others on a bench. Zornan found a small space on the floor for himself and their bags. The floor was crowded with other servants and commoners. Zornan would not only spend the two-day journey stuck in a lightless tunnel, he'd spend it on a hard floor, crammed between sweaty bodies and luggage.

After seating himself next to a young servant, Zornan took inventory of their surroundings. Again, they drew little attention from their fellow passengers, and he found no obvious threats. Four Enforcers sat on the bench against the wall between the passengers and the Ferry Guides, but they were engaged in loud banter with each other, ignoring everyone else. Everything seemed routine, and no one stuck out as an obvious agent of the Empire trying to figure out if the fugitives were aboard this ferry or not.

Even so, none of that eased Zornan's nerves.

The hours passed slowly. Zornan stayed awake, diligently watching their possessions. At this point, he was as worried about theft as he was about being discovered. The passenger hold was crowded, and it would be easy for another servant to slip his hands in their bags and remove something without drawing attention.

They passed a small exchange where they lost several passengers and gained only one. It freed up some space on the benches, which allowed the Low Trade, aristocracy, and High Trade to spread out a little; none of the servants or commoners dared make a move for a more comfortable seat.

According to Silver, they were still more than a day away from Rinderel, but safety was nearing, and Zornan's comfort was slowly growing. His biggest source of worry at this point was Ballin, who cuddled closely to Mairie.

Zornan leaned back against the bags and felt himself slipping into rest. He knew he should stay awake, but exhaustion pulled at him until he drifted to sleep.

He shot awake some time later with a sudden feeling of deceleration. They'd slowed before, but this felt more intense than previous curves or turns. The four Enforcers seemed to notice as well; one of them was sleeping, and another hit him to wake him up. They looked at each other like they were speaking, but their lips didn't move: mindspeak. One of them peered back against the wall behind him as if he might be speaking to the Ferry Guides as well.

The ferry sped up again, and Zornan leaned back, trying to act as if the commotion was of no concern to him. He wanted to rush over to Ballin and Mairie and alert them, but he couldn't do that without raising suspicion. He wasn't even sure there was something to be worried about.

Over the next ten minutes, the Enforcers continued to exchange glances but did not speak. Mindspeak was clumsy, Loothdram had told him, in that only two people could communicate at a time. So their exchanges were likely the awkward passing of information, but judging by their alertness and stern expressions, they were discussing something. Gone was their light conversation from before. Two of them visually examined the passengers, including one who locked eyes with Zornan before they both quickly looked away.

After another few minutes passed, the ferry slowed again, this time almost to the point of stopping. The sudden change startled all the passengers, with many sitting up straighter and looking forward. Ballin and Mairie sat up; Mairie's hand drifted to her skirt. Ballin reached over and calmed her hands. As the ferry came to a complete stop, the four Enforcers stood and walked into the passenger hold. Three broke off toward Ballin and Mairie, one toward Zornan.

They sent three after an unarmed young man and a young woman, which could mean only one thing: they knew about Mairie, about who posed the greatest threat. But if she decided to let loose, Zornan did not believe three Enforcers would be able to hold her back.

Zornan looked around; innocent bystanders filled the passenger hold. If Mairie fought the Enforcers she would win, but at what cost? How many innocent people might be injured or killed in their ferocious battle? And then what would they do? Force the Ferry Guides to take them somewhere? And then what?

"Stand up," the Enforcer said as he reached Zornan.

"What's going on?"

"Stand up," the man repeated, drawing his hatrindi from its sheath. "Move slowly, or I will kill you, despite my orders. And hand over your sword."

Zornan stood slowly, and he handed the sword over to the Enforcer. Without taking his eyes off Zornan, the Enforcer sheathed the sword with his left hand.

"Come with me."

"I don't understand."

"Come with me, Zornan Peak Crosser. Now."

They knew everything. They knew who he was, who Ballin was, and who Mairie was and what she was capable of. The young woman looked at him, awaiting instructions. He shook his head as he followed the Enforcer. Ballin, Mairie, and the other three Enforcers followed closely behind. The ferry gate opened as they approached. The Ferry Captain stood there at the tunnel floor.

"Step out," another of the Enforcers commanded them.

"This is outrageous," Ballin said. "I'm a merchant heading home…"

"You're no such thing!" shouted the Enforcer. "You're killers and fugitives. Your names are Zornan Peak Crosser and Ballin Maggot. I don't know the girl's name, but she's as likely to be my wife as she is yours. Now step out." The man's voice was forceful, but he eyed Mairie warily. Zornan wasn't sure what they knew of Mairie, but they knew enough not to press the issue.

Mairie looked again at Zornan, her body tense. He looked back at the innocent passengers and shook his head. Even though he didn't like Enforcers, they were following orders; no one here deserved to die.

As they stepped off the ferry, Zornan looked at their surroundings. They had landed on a small platform that connected to a tunnel too small for ferry travel, one of the walking tunnels which were rarely used.

The three fugitives exited the ferry, this time with Mairie and Zornan making no attempt to hide their enhanced dexterity. The Ferry Captain shut the gate and quickly re-boarded. None of the Enforcers had followed them.

"Why are you leaving us here?" Zornan questioned. "What are we to do?"

"Wait to die!" yelled one of the Enforcers as the ferry pulled away, leaving them in the dim light of a few glow globes.

24 | CONFINED

"Why didn't you let me do something?" Mairie shouted as the tunnel ferry disappeared into the darkness.

"Because it would have cost lives, Mairie." Zornan kept his calm, though he wanted to shout back. "They were lives we had no right to take. In that confined space, you couldn't have helped but kill innocent people."

"Yes, I could have! You don't know…"

"Mairie." Ballin's voice was calm, and he gripped her hand. "Zornan is right. It was too dangerous."

She pulled away from Ballin. "More dangerous than waiting here for a couple of Baldra or a legion of Enforcers to come and kill us all?"

"Yes," Zornan replied, stepping close to her, his face growing intense. "Ballin and I may have died in the fight, and there were women and children who could have been caught in it. This is our fight, not theirs. We have no right to involve people who shouldn't be involved."

Mairie's eyes continued to burn with anger, but her body eased a little.

"Now what?" she asked, her tone still angry.

"We start walking."

Zornan reached out to Silver as soon as they started walking through the much narrower tunnel. Unlike the ferry tunnels, which were easily forty yards floor to ceiling (enough room to accommodate two large ferries passing each other), the walking tunnel was only about ten yards top to bottom. Certainly not small, as it was more than three times taller than the tallest man. But it felt a thousand times more confining to Zornan.

Do you know the walking tunnels, Silver? he asked after explaining their situation.

That's a silly question, little rider. I would know as much about those as I would the bottom of the sea. She seemed amused at herself.

Can you contact Loothdram?

I can, but I would have to fly far away, far enough that you and I could not think together.

Do it, Silver. He needs to know. I'm not sure if he can help, but it's our only hope. He paused for a moment. *Can you tell me where this tunnel is pointed, at least if we continue in this direction?*

Yes, she responded. *It's pointed toward Dagtarna.*

Tell Loothdram that as well, old friend. Fly well.

Travel well, little rider... Her presence lessened as she flew away.

"It looks like this tunnel is headed toward Dagtarna."

"A lawless community?" Mairie asked.

"Yes, a lawless community."

That seemed a strange destination. He had dismissed the lawless valleys as places of refuge for them when he had chosen Skathall, but now he welcomed it. Anything to be out of the Empire's watchful eye.

Ballin and Mairie responded with silence, as they'd likely reached the same conclusion he had. Dagtarna would offer a thousand dangers, but nothing more dangerous than what was likely looking for them in these tunnels.

They walked for several hours, Ballin tiring much faster than Zornan or Mairie. He started to look weak and mumbled about wanting water. Zornan eased the pace.

Darkness lurked between the sparsely spaced glow globes. Slight variations in the rocks, swirling black, red, and brown, provided the only scenery.

They approached what seemed to be the last working globe in the tunnel. Darkness seemed to envelop them. When they got closer to the darkness, they saw the source of it: a wall. The tunnel looked as if continued onward at some point, but a flat wall of brastilia separated them from the rest of the tunnel. Dagtarna had been cut off from the rest of the Empire.

"Still think we're safer here?" Mairie shot at Zornan.

"I never said we were safer, only that it was the right decision."

Mairie snorted in disgust, walked a few feet away, and slumped against the tunnel wall, sliding into a seated position.

"You made the right decision," Ballin said, placing his hand on Zornan's arm. Mairie glared at him. "We will make our final stand here."

"But you don't even have a sword."

"Do you really think that makes a difference, Zornan?"

Zornan and Ballin embraced.

The sudden sound of moving rock rumbled in the darkness behind them. Zornan also heard faint footsteps, though they sounded like they came from a different direction, maybe even the other side of the wall. But the first sound came from behind, from the darkness.

Mairie shot up as well, her two hatnuthri pulled from her skirt and extended out like claws. After Ballin stepped away and backed against the wall, Zornan removed his hatari and extended it into a spear. Even with Mairie, they weren't likely to survive whatever was coming, but Zornan would try. For Calla and the girls, for Ballin, he would try.

Out of the darkness walked a lone, hooded creature, moving slowing and smoothly toward them, its tell-tale hatnuthri extending out of its arms past its cloak.

"Surrender now, little girl," the creature hissed, its voice high and shrill, as if its sound had been ripped from a nightmare.

"Never."

"Then I will be forced to kill your friends."

Mairie stepped into the middle of the tunnel. "You'll have to kill me first."

"No, child, you will not die today. They have need of you. But your friends will die. The Enforcers should have killed them as instructed. They feared the half-Baldra instead." The creature stopped walking four or five feet from Mairie. "I give you one last chance. Surrender, or I will kill your friends."

Mairie responded quickly, jumping through the air and thrusting her weapons at the Baldra's chest. The creature easily blocked her blow and jumped back like a spider, covering several feet with ease. The only thing Zornan could see of its features was its mouth, illuminated by the glow globe near the ceiling. The Baldra smiled.

"Just as well, child."

The speed and intensity of the fight made it hard to track. Their unnatural momentum, dexterity, and strength made each action more fantastic than the last. They exchanged blows, evading or blocking with their matched weapons. It was more like fist-to-fist combat because of the shortness of the hatnuthri, not the elegant fight of a hatari or hatrindi. Zornan occasionally saw the Baldra's pale hands flash out of its long-sleeved cloak. The garment made sense when he'd seen it before, as it allowed the creature to disappear completely in the darkness, but it was clumsy for fighting, the sleeves and length of it flapping constantly. Zornan would have been annoyed by it, but the Baldra hardly seemed to notice; the cloak seemed to struggle to keep pace with the Baldra's body.

The two assassins continued for several minutes, even using the walls to gain the advantage, flipping from them in the semi-darkness. Mairie made a short jab, and the Baldra blocked and kicked Mairie in the stomach. The young woman gasped for air and slumped to her knees. The Baldra's next blow was to the back of Mairie's head; she fell to the ground with a thump, and her two hatnuthri slipped from her hands and to the ground, returning to their square shape.

"Mairie!" It was Ballin's voice from behind him. The young man lunged forward, but Zornan blocked him with his body.

"Get back, Ballin."

The Baldra approached them. "I think someone cares for this bastard child."

"Shut your mouth, monster!" Ballin hissed.

"Come dance with me, brash young man. Let's see if you can do any better than your lady."

Mairie sprung to her feet, grabbed one of her hatnuthri and shoved it toward the back of the Baldra's head as the weapon extended into its full shape. As if sensing the movement from behind, the creature moved its head to the side, but Mairie's thrust connected with its cloak and ripped the flesh along its cheek. The Baldra's deep crimson blood shot through the air, and it bellowed a scream, swiping its left hand backward toward Mairie. The girl easily dodged the defensive blow and stepped back.

The creature turned toward Mairie, its back facing Zornan for the first time. He wondered if he should attack from behind, but after watching it dodge Mairie's blow, he feared he'd do nothing but get in the way. The power these two held scared Zornan to the point that his feet and hands were frozen with fear. The feeling was so overpowering that he wasn't sure he could even raise his hands to defend himself or his brother.

The Baldra's hood had been knocked loose by Mairie's strike, revealing a bald head and more sickly white skin. This time the Baldra did not speak, but struck at Mairie with a renewed ferocity.

The Baldra's moves grew faster and stronger than before. Mairie defended herself, but she was falling back, and for the first time, Zornan could see fear in the girl's intense eyes. *The Baldra had been holding back*, he thought to himself, as impossible as that seemed. And now it was not.

The Baldra aggressively struck with both swords right at Mairie's chest. The young woman parried, trying to deflect downward. The Baldra brought its legs together in a kick toward Mairie's hands, hovering for a moment in the air in what should have been an impossible attack. Its feet struck Mairie's hands, forcing them, and the weapons in her grip, together. The young woman dropped her weapons and cried out in pain. The Baldra landed deftly and struck Mairie in the head again with the butt of its hatnuthri, harder than before. The young woman slumped to the ground again.

The creature bent down and checked Mairie for consciousness. Satisfied, it turned to Zornan and Ballin, its face contorted in a hateful scowl.

The Baldra's face struck Zornan as strangely familiar. Maybe it had haunted him in recent nightmares. But with its face contorted with anger, and with the imminent realization of his own death hanging in the air, Zornan knew it didn't really matter if he had seen its face in a dream or somewhere else.

"Zandia." Their sister's name slipped from Ballin's mouth, an echoing whisper.

Zandia? Why would he invoke our sister's name at a time like this? Then Zornan looked at the Baldra again and saw what Ballin saw. He had seen that face, not in a nightmare, not in an acquaintance, but as a child. It was Zandia.

She had been nine when he'd left and twelve when Ballin said she was sold into the High Trade. But Zornan could see it now. The slight nose, the soft features, the brown eyes. All of these belonged to Zandia, or had before the Empire molded her into something entirely different.

"Zandia." It was Ballin again. "Oh, Zandia. What have they done to you?"

The fierce anger left the Baldra's face, replaced by an uncomfortable confusion. The expression seemed strange, as if her face were rejecting anything but a hateful scowl.

"Zornan. Ballin." Her voice was less shrill this time, more human.

"It's us!" Ballin said excitedly, trying to push past Zornan, but Zornan held strong. Zandia or not, she was still a Baldra. "Please Zandia, help us."

"I am not Zandia," she replied, replacing any sympathy that may have invaded her face with a cold gaze. "My name is Tha'Strukra. Zandia has been dead for some time. Zandia would never do what Tha'Strukra must do."

"But Zandia, you can choose to help us," Ballin pleaded. "You can save Mairie. You can save us."

Zandia looked back at Mairie and shook her head. "Baldra have no free will, Ballin. Please know as I kill you that Zandia takes no pleasure in it. Zandia would never do something like that to you. But Zandia is dead, and Tha'Strukra will do what must be done."

Their once-sister restarted her approach, crouched in an attack position. Zornan brought his hatari up, ready to put up a likely futile defense. Fear still gripped him tightly, but he fought it back. He would not die a coward. He would defend himself and Ballin, even if it was useless.

Light suddenly flooded the cavern as a section of the wall to Zornan's right opened. He heard dozens of shouting voices and saw a band of armed men streaming into the tunnel. The Baldra looked over, confused. Her hatnuthri disappeared, and she pulled her tattered hood back over her head. Without a word, she leapt against the opposite wall, using it to launch herself into the darkness. As quickly as she came, she was gone.

Dozens of men stormed into the tunnel brandishing swords and hatrindis. The first ones through the door looked disbelieving into the darkness, their minds processing the vanished Baldra phantom. One man, his hatrindi now sheathed, stepped from the crowd toward Zornan and Ballin.

Zornan turned to the newcomer, his hatari still raised.

"Check if the girl lives," the lead man said to another behind him. The second man sheathed his sword and stepped toward Mairie.

"Don't touch her," Ballin spat.

Zornan flinched at his brother's aggressive tone.

"We just saved your life," the man said. "I would expect a little more courtesy."

"She's alive, Dashnal," said the man checking Mairie.

"Good. Bind her with the strongest cords you can find. And make it tight. If Matha is right, that one is almost as fierce as a Baldra."

"Now, what to do with you two?" Dashnal said, turning to Ballin and Zornan. The man was older than Zornan, likely by fifteen years or more. Gray dominated his dark hair, and deep lines creased his forehead and around his eyes. He was fit and strong, almost as muscled as an Enforcer. And his intense blue eyes dug at the brothers like those of an Investigator or Magistrate. His face was covered in a full, well-trimmed beard.

"Set us free," Zornan said.

"Not likely," Dashnal responded flatly. "You're clearly fugitives of the Empire. We can profit from something like this."

A woman burst into the tunnel, brushing passed the armed bandits. She was short, not much taller than a child. Her presence was amplified by curly, voluminous red hair. She was pretty, with a nose that was a little too big and round cheeks, rosy from exertion. She was dressed in a plain brown dress, and she held a short sword that may have been considered a knife in a man's hands.

"Where is the Baldra!" the slight woman shouted as she neared them. "I have the curse to stop it!" She held up a string of beads in her left hand.

"What are you going to do with those beads, Matha? Strangle the Baldra?" The mocking comment came from a man in the crowd, and most of the men laughed. Matha scowled, and it looked more like a child's expression than an adult's.

"Silence," Dashnal commanded. "If it hadn't been for Matha's diligence, we'd have missed this opportunity. These men would be dead and the prize would be gone." He glanced at Mairie. "She deserves your respect, not your scorn." Some of the men looked down at the chastisement, while others glared defiantly.

"What will it cost to set us free?" Zornan asked. "Both of us, and the girl."

"Cost?" Dashnal responded, laughing. "I'd bet that hatari and the girl's hatnuthri are the only items you could barter with, and we'll have those soon enough. Unless you can prove you have great wealth to trade, I'd say the cost of freedom is well beyond your reach. Until I determine your fate, I would suggest you remain quiet and give me your hatari." The man held out his hand. As he did so, a dozen of his men stepped forward, swords drawn.

Zornan shrunk the hatari and handed it over. If Mairie had been conscious, this would have been over in seconds. But an unarmed man who was not used to fighting and a Peak Crosser who wasn't a great fighter were no match for two dozen armed men.

"Good," Dashnal said, handing Zornan's hatari to another man. He turned toward the man who bound Mairie. "Bind them as well, only at the hands."

They traveled through a smaller walking tunnel, this one only ten feet high and three men wide, even narrower at some points. Zornan began to breathe rapidly, and his limbs tingled, the confinement preying on his mind. He wanted to stop, crawl, or close his eyes. But he kept moving, prodded by the armed man behind him.

One man guided Zornan, another escorted Ballin, and a third carried Mairie over his shoulder. Dashnal and Matha, as well as some of the others, were at the lead, though Zornan couldn't see them clearly through the winding tunnel. Several armed men formed a rear guard.

Just as Zornan thought he might collapse, the tunnel opened into a large cavern. It wasn't as large as Nabfryn, but it was high enough that the ceiling was hardly visible, and it stretched hundreds of yards in each direction. It also was not as well-lit as Nabfryn, with only half as many glow globes placed throughout, leaving the cavern's corners and crevices in darkness.

"Welcome to The Bowels," said the man behind him.

Though the buildings were crude and darkness hung between fading glow globes, it was like nothing Zornan had seen before. A small town sitting hundreds of feet below ground, a community he'd never even known existed. Several hundred people milled about, men, women, and children. The homes on the edge of town were built of discarded lumber and held together loosely with rusting nails. Families sat around cook fires, seated outside on rocks. The people were dressed shabbily, but they played, ate, and spoke like folks might do in Fallindra or Skathall.

A large building rose above the others in the center of the cave, similar to the one at Nabfryn. There were also carts scattered about with a few merchants selling food and wares. The cavern was damp and musty, a dank smell of clothes being washed combined with food being prepared. Zornan had lost track of time in the tunnels, but it was definitely mealtime in The Bowels.

Most of the people stopped and stared at the group as they entered, and the few people in their path parted. As they approached the largest building, they were met by a group of six older men all into their sixth decade or more, and what hair they had was wispy and white. Zornan had imagined Dashnal as his own man, but he bowed deeply to the six men.

"What do you bring into our home, Dashnal?" asked the largest of the six men, his voice stern and accusatory. He was bearded like Dashnal, though his was not as well-trimmed. The beard was the only hair on his head, and it was a dirty gray. He was fat, with a large belly and arms and legs like the trunks of healthy trees. His clothes were that of a merchant, once fine, but now dirty and stretched.

"Great prizes, Pagton," the thief responded.

"I'll judge that." The man walked around and looked at Mairie, bound and now slumped on the floor. He examined Zornan and Ballin next. Pagton moved with great difficulty, as if each step were a monumental achievement, his heavy legs barely bending at the knees.

"The girl is a Destroyer," Dashnal said.

Pagton's thick eyebrows, which matched his beard in color, shot up at the word. "Destroyer? Those are only legends, Dashnal. The priestesses don't make Destroyers anymore; it's treason."

"She is! She is!" Matha bounced as she shouted.

Dashnal silenced her with a glance. "Matha saw her fight a Baldra, almost to a standstill," Dashnal replied. "If she is a Destroyer, the Empire or the Dundraz will pay a lot for her."

"Baldra, Destroyers." Pagton exhaled, the air released with great effort. "You should know better than to trust the little whore, Dashnal."

Matha's face reddened to match her hair, but she held her tongue.

"She's a good scout, Pagton, and not prone to exaggeration. You know that."

"Unless it's about her skills in bed," one of Dashnal's men joked, and many of them laughed. Matha looked down and folded her arms over her chest.

"The rest of you, get out of here!" Pagton bellowed. Dashnal's men scattered (as did Matha), leaving only Dashnal, two of his men, the six older men, and the three fugitives.

"We will take it from here, Dashnal," Pagton continued after the others left.

"But sir, she is a prize, and I would like…"

"I don't care what you would like!" Pagton bellowed. "If Matha is telling the truth, a Baldra will be close by and looking for these three. You may have brought the vengeance of the Empire or the Dundraz down upon us, Dashnal."

"I am sorry, Lord Pagton," the thief replied demurely. "I thought the reward was worth the risk."

"That is why you don't sit among us," another of The Bowels' leaders said. "You think too much about today's gain and forget tomorrow's price."

"Monton is correct," Pagton continued. "I let your group operate from here, but your light is dimming."

Several very large men approached, all armed. All six of them carried themselves like Enforcers, and two of them had hatrindi to match.

"Leave us, Dashnal," Pagton commanded. "If any reward is to be had, you will get your share."

Dashnal bowed deeply again. His face flashed with anger, but he left without another word.

"What should we do with these three?" Monton asked.

"I don't know, Brother," Pagton replied. He turned to the six large guards. "Hold them in the pit until we decide."

25 | LAWLESS

The pit was a small cave about the size of the common room at The Water's Edge, with only one entrance. It contained no glow globes, so darkness prevailed. As the guards pushed Zornan and Ballin inside and laid Mairie's body on the floor, Zornan started to breathe rapidly again; he could feel his chest tighten. He could not fight the feeling that they'd entered their tomb.

His fears heightened when the men rolled a large rock over the doorway, extinguishing all light. Zornan's eyes were great at night or in a poorly lit room, but in complete darkness, he was as blind as anyone else. He fought back his growing trepidation and tried to remain calm by drawing several long breaths.

"What shall we do?" Ballin asked.

Zornan had no idea. They were completely at the mercy of Pagton, and he wasn't sure what to make of the man. He housed thieves, but he also led a community of some kind, and he feared that Mairie's presence put his community in danger. There was no telling what the man would do with Mairie, or with them.

"I don't know. I don't know."

Zornan sat and closed his eyes. What a strange sensation; eyes opened or closed, made no difference. His stomach grumbled audibly as he considered their seemingly hopeless situation, hunger making its claim alongside his fear. Another emotion also yearned to break free: anger. Torn from his family, stuffed in a cave, and seemingly without hope, Zornan's rage burned.

The brothers remained silent for some time, though Zornan could not say for how long. He reached out to Silver but could not connect with her. He could still feel her in some way, like a forgotten thought trapped in the back of his mind, but he could not talk with her.

"Zornan? Ballin?" Mairie's weak and raspy voice echoed in the small cave.

"Mairie," came Ballin's reply.

"Where are we? What happened?"

Ballin explained what had happened to them.

"So we're alone? Good," she replied, her voice stronger. Moments later, a loud snap echoed through the small cave.

"What was that?" Zornan asked.

"It was me, setting myself free," Mairie replied.

Setting herself free? He had watched the man bind her. He had done a thorough job with very strong cords, and she had snapped them like he might with twine. He felt a surge of confidence; there was no reason to abandon hope yet, not as long as Mairie was alive and with them.

"The door is too heavy for me to move," Mairie said, frustrated.

"How can you be sure you're trying to move the door and not just the wall?" Zornan questioned.

"Because I can see in the dark," she replied.

"There are too many people outside, Mairie. Even you can't fight your way out."

"We'll see," she replied defiantly.

They sat together in silence for a few minutes before the door began moving.

"It's not me," Mairie said, answering their unspoken question.

"What do we do?" Ballin asked.

"I kill whomever opens that door," Mairie replied coldly.

Zornan did not have time to argue as the door slid open to reveal a lone man standing in the blinding light. Before his eyes could adjust, he saw a blur of motion and heard the man gasp. Blinking to clear his vision, he saw Mairie's outline standing near the doorway, a hatrindi in hand. She had the man pinned to the ground, her foot on his chest, his weapon pointed at his throat. Two armed men stood in the doorway, their swords drawn.

"Please," said the man on the ground. It was Dashnal. "I'm here to help you. Pagton and the Elders are planning to execute you. They want to pretend I never brought you here."

"Why should we believe you, Dashnal?" Zornan asked. "You captured us and brought us here. You wanted to sell her to the highest bidder."

"I can get you out of here," Dashnal choked, struggling to speak and breathe with Mairie's foot pressing down on his chest. "The Elders do not want to profit by it, and they believe the Baldra will show mercy. But if they find out we killed you, the Baldra is more likely to kill most of us as retribution. Profit can still be made in this."

"How do we know you haven't arranged to hand us over?" Zornan demanded.

"You don't. But your fate is written in stone if you stay in this cave. Once outside, we can make a deal."

Zornan considered the man's words and looked at Ballin and Mairie. Ballin shrugged.

"I will kill them all if they betray us," Mairie said, glaring down at Dashnal. "Painfully."

Zornan shivered at the girl's fierce intensity. "How do we get out of here?" Zornan asked the thief.

"I can show you the walking tunnel to Dagtarna. You should be able to go anywhere in the Empire from there."

"We'll need weapons and food," Zornan commanded. "*Our* weapons. Hatnuthri for the girl, hatari for me. And a sword for my brother."

"We brought those with us." He looked up at his guards. "Give them their weapons." The men hesitated. "Now, you fools, before she makes sure I never breathe again."

"What are you hoping to get out of this?" Zornan asked as the men slid the two hatnuthri, the hatari, and a sheathed sword into the cave.

"Financial consideration after you leave or a future favor."

"You're in no place to haggle," Mairie snarled. "If we get out of this alive and free, you live. If not, you and these men die."

"A bargain indeed," he said, breathing deeply.

Though telling time in The Bowels was impossible, the lack of activity in the village signaled nighttime, or at least the equivalent rest period for the underground community. The pit was several hundred yards from the village, and Zornan saw only a few people milling about in the semi-darkness. No one looked in their direction as they moved away from the village.

"Where are the guards?" Ballin asked.

"They were relieved of their duties," Dashnal replied coyly.

The group quickly made their way away from the village and toward a rocky staircase. Standing at the top were four men, all armed. The men snapped to attention, hands on their swords.

"Where are you going with them, Dashnal?" One of the men asked, his voice quivering and his eyes focusing on Mairie. Apparently the legend of her abilities had spread throughout The Bowels.

"Does it matter, Nam?" Dashnal asked. "She will kill you if you don't let us pass or if you raise alarm. Play the martyr and fool or hand over your weapons. I know you're a smart man; you'll know what to do."

The three other men looked at Nam. He bowed his head and withdrew his sword, placing it on the ground. The other three followed him.

"Very smart, Nam." Dashnal turned to his guards. "Bind them and gag them."

"What now?" Zornan asked.

"Follow me, Peak Crosser."

Zornan grabbed Dashnal by the collar and brought his face in close to the thief's. He drew his hatari but did not ready it. "How do you know I'm a Peak Crosser?"

"Well..." Dashnal started.

"No lies, thief. Or I will let the girl finish you. We have no time for games."

"Okay," Dashnal said, pulling away. "I was sent a message and payment to rescue you. I don't know from whom, but someone who has contacts in The Bowels wants you alive. I was paid richly. The message I received referred to you as Zornan Peak Crosser. That's all I know."

Mairie took a step toward Dashnal.

"Honestly, that's all I know. I did not get what the girl would have fetched from the Empire, but it was a rich sum, more than I was going to get if the Elders killed all of you."

"I don't trust him," Ballin said. "He could be leading us into a trap."

"Better than that pit," Zornan replied. "And if he does lead us into a trap, I'm sure Mairie will kill him first."

Mairie glared at Dashnal and the man shivered.

"Lead the way, Dashnal," Zornan commanded, and he and his two companions led them into a walking tunnel very similar to the one they'd followed before entering The Bowels. Zornan and Mairie stopped the group periodically so they could listen for followers, but they heard nothing. Binding the guards had worked, and fortune had favored their escape.

He reached out to Silver with his mind as soon as they started down the tunnel, but she was still too far away. Now that his panic was receding, he realized he could not only feel her but could sense where she was in the Empire—as if he could see her upon a map in his mind's eye. If these thoughts were correct, Silver was headed away from Skathall and back toward the spot where they had last connected. Zornan yearned to travel with her again and leave these accursed tunnels behind.

After traveling for several hours, they came around a curve and entered an open cavern. Six armed men crowded the space. The man at the front was armed with a hatrindi and was as large as an Enforcer, though dressed more like a merchant. Unlike the guards on the other end of the tunnel, no one here was surprised to see them.

"Hello, Dashnal," the former Enforcer said, his speech slurred and hard to understand.

"Hello, Finthon," the thief replied. "We are looking to get into Dagtarna."

"Of course you are." Finthon looked over their group. "Your crew isn't the usual." Finthon eyed Mairie hungrily. "Introduce me."

"We don't have time for this," Mairie said impatiently.

"You'll have time for whatever I'd like, girl," Finthon shot back.

"Trust me, old friend, you want no part of her." Dashnal approached and handed a small bundle to Finthon. "I think our quick and unquestioned passage can be arranged, no?"

Finthon looked into the bag and then smiled, revealing a mouth full of silver teeth. "Yes," he mumbled. "Yes, welcome to Dagtarna. You left The Bowels under duress, no?"

"Yes, friend. We will be followed."

"Then they will need a lot of coin to pass."

"That's what I'm counting on."

The band of guards parted at Finthon's command, and Dashnal's group passed through. Finthon continued to stare at Mairie.

"Come back anytime, little girl," he said as they reached the passage above ground. Mairie stared back, her eyes filled with anger and hate. Zornan feared she might kill the greasy man on the spot.

"The girl is with me," Ballin said in reply.

Finthon's laugh rent the air as they walked out into the daylight.

Dagtarna was not what Zornan expected. He had always steered clear of both Dagtarna and Manmandoo, the other lawless community. Rumors persisted of deserter Peak Crossers who patrolled the sky looking for legitimate Peak Crossers to rob. And though fraternizing with the lawless wasn't forbidden by High Trade law, it was frowned upon by High Trade leadership. Zornan was sure his Peak Crosser contract holders, the Priests of Cazdanth, would have terminated his contract if they ever found out he had gone to Manmandoo or Dagtarna seeking adventure or pleasure.

Dagtarna looked like almost any other city he had visited, except for the terrain. Unlike most of the valleys of the Empire, Dagtarna was not heavily wooded. The ground was barren and rocky. The mountains formed a tight circle around the small valley, towering high above the city, which covered almost the entire valley floor.

During these first moments, he would not have been able to guess this was a lawless community. Merchants, commoners, and even some High Tradesmen bustled about the city. He even saw a Peak Crosser keep on the edge of town, marked by the shrill cry of a cosow. Children scampered about, smiling and running. The place seemed bland and common compared to The Bowels.

But as Dashnal led them into the city, the differences between Dagtarna and the Empire proper increased. Every single man was armed—commoner or merchant, High or Low Trade. Most cities forbade commoners to wear weapons in public, but that was not enforced here. Even many of the women carried knives and swords.

Even referring to the people here as commoners was a misnomer. They were dressed as such, certainly, but they did not defer to the merchants and Low Trade. He saw a merchant and a commoner bump into each other on the busy street, and both grumbled and cursed, locking eyes violently for a moment before deciding better of an open conflict over something so small. Commoners throughout the Empire would never behave that way, as it could lead to incarceration, embarrassment, and possibly death. The balance of power in Dagtarna differed from most other places.

Deference was still paid to the High Trade though, as people gave them wide berth and avoided eye contact. He saw a few Enforcers, a Peak Crosser, and a couple of Investigators, at least, if they were all dressed in the correct uniforms.

"Where are you taking us?" Ballin asked, as they continued deeper into the city.

"A tavern called The Galloping Hen," Dashnal replied. "It's in the Center Circle. I know a woman who usually does business there, and I think she's just the person to get you out of Dagtarna and on your way to wherever you'd like to go."

"We still don't trust you, Dashnal," Mairie warned. "So step carefully."

"Of course you don't," he said, smiling, and leading them on. "But this is a foreign and dangerous place. I think it's better to have a guide than walk alone, no?"

"He's right," Zornan said. "But be careful, Dashnal. You survived your betrayal of Pagton; you won't survive betraying us."

Dashnal stopped, his eyes locking with Zornan's.

"I have survived a long time in situations when most men die. I know how to survive, Peak Crosser, and nothing I do today is going to endanger that." The thief spun and walked a little faster toward their destination.

People and tightly spaced buildings filled the chaotic city. Street merchants sold food, clothing, and a thousand other things. Women dressed in shirts with deep necklines and skirts with slits above the knees. They smiled at every man as they passed, and one even approached Ballin. She was rebuffed by a cool look from Mairie. Prostitution was not uncommon in the Empire's largest cities, but Zornan had never seen it flaunted like this. The more time he spent in this city, the more he realized that his initial assessment was wrong: Dagtarna was unlike any other place in the Empire.

The streets in the city's outer section were mostly laid out straight, a grid-like system that was common throughout the Empire. But the city changed as they reached its center. The four innermost streets circled around each other, each getting smaller until the last street formed a circle around a collection of buildings. Each building in the circle was distinct, both in purpose, architecture, and size. Some were made from wood, others from brick or stone. Some had as many as five stories, but most were one or two. Some looked like they had been there for hundreds of years, and others looked new.

"Welcome to the Center Circle of Dagtarna," Dashnal said, motioning with his arms like a street performer. "Home of the three most powerful men in this city. And at the center of most of this less-than-lawful activity, The Galloping Hen."

The tavern was one of the smaller buildings, only a story tall and made of wood. It looked as though it had been here for a long time, the outside worn and faded. The tavern's name and a white hen were carved into the building above the doorframe, the paint on the hen chipped and faded. The front door was propped open, revealing a hallway which stretched back from the building's facade.

"Are we sure this is a good idea?" Ballin asked sardonically.

"No," Zornan replied with an equal tone. "I'm not very sure of anything anymore."

As they stepped inside, the smells overwhelmed Zornan's senses. Smoke rose from pipes in almost every mouth, and even more hands swung half-mugs. A dozen young women carried food to eager and boisterous patrons. The maids were young, and all seemed equally miserable, with tired smiles greeting the rowdy guests. The tavern was overwhelmingly loud. Card or dice games were active on many of the tables, creating the only punctuation in the constant din of noise as winners and losers called out in staccato.

"Come with me, Zornan," Dashnal said. Turning to his two guards he said, "Take the happy couple to a table and find them something to eat." Dashnal smiled playfully at Mairie, and she shot a deathly glare back at him.

"I don't think she likes me," Dashnal said, as they weaved deeper into the narrow, long room.

"She hasn't killed you yet," Zornan replied. "That's something."

Dashnal laughed heartily. Zornan wasn't sure why he joked with the man who was likely to betray them if it profited him even a little, but Dashnal was likable despite his villainy. And Zornan needed to release the tension building inside him. He had never considered himself a humorous man, but maybe in these dire circumstances, it was time to find that part of himself. If not, the anxiety and stress might break him apart.

As they approached the back wall, Zornan stopped suddenly, his eyes resting on an all-too-familiar face.

"Come, Zornan," Dashnal said, looking back at him. The thief's eyes followed Zornan's and landed on the same person. "You know her?"

"Yes, I know her."

"Good, that will make introductions easier. That is who I'm taking you to see."

Zornan continued to stare, still unable to move or believe what he saw. The woman they were supposed to meet, the one who was going to help them escape the dangers chasing them, was Maeltha: his first and only love before Calla.

"I don't think it is going to make the introduction any easier," he said, slowly approaching the table with Dashnal.

26 | CLUES

Mizcarnon walked out of the Grizthall Peak Crosser keep into a dreary rain. The strong weather met him and Sunset several miles before they reached Skathall Valley, and it hampered not only their flight but also his assignment from the Emperor. Mizcarnon had been honored by the Emperor's request, but during the flight to Skathall, he doubted his ability to fulfill it. He was not an Investigator; neither his training nor his blessing gave him the skills he needed to track down the missing Peak Crosser. These feelings were new to Mizcarnon; as a scout, he knew his purpose and knew how to do his job well. Now he felt like a magician on a stage with a series of tricks to perform but no idea how to do them.

As he walked toward the governor's palace, he cursed the rain. He was dressed in his traveling Peak Crosser clothes, the usual brown and tan Peak Crosser uniform. He had left his gray military uniform in Bristrinia, as he was not really here on military business, at least not officially, and the gray uniform would bring unwanted attention. The story he had concocted for himself was that he was an old friend of Zornan's from the Initiatory School and Peak Crosser Academy. He was trying to find and help Zornan. He was using the name Nundril, the Peak Crosser he had trained who disappeared on the same scouting mission Mizcarnon had returned from not long ago.

The rain made the air colder, and few people were out. Mizcarnon had arrived the day before and spent an afternoon looking at Zornan's childhood home, which the report said had been his hiding place when he was in Skathall Valley. What he found there had discouraged him even further; the small farmhouse had been burned to the ground.

When Mizcarnon visited the nearest farm to ask about it, the man reluctantly told him it had burned down just the day before, likely local youth messing around and doing what they shouldn't. The home had been abandoned for some time, though the youngest child of the family, Ballin, sometimes hunted on the land, the neighbor said.

Mizcarnon didn't need to be an Investigator to know the man was lying and frightened. He might have seen more, but the Peak Crosser didn't push further; the remains of the house told him all he needed to know. The rain had begun washing soot away and revealing the remains. Most of what Mizcarnon discovered was innocuous: an old cooking pan, a rusted sword. But as he and Sunset dug more, they discovered more than that: human bones, and a lot of them. The house had been used as a burial ground for as many as a dozen men, and then burned to keep it from becoming too attractive to wolves or other scavengers and from revealing what had been done there. Mizcarnon worried that Zornan and his younger brother might be among the dead.

Now he approached the governor's palace to speak with Loothdram Investigator. After making his request of the Enforcer at the palace's gate, he was escorted into the thankfully dry building and to Loothdram's office. After having spent some time in the Emperor's palace, nothing was going to compare, but it was a fine building. The handiwork was good, and it was an impressive display for a valley that was relatively inconsequential to the rest of the Empire.

When they reached Loothdram's office, the open door revealed a hum of activity. An Investigator sat in a chair in the corner reading some papers. Another Investigator stood in the middle of room talking with several guards and an Enforcer. This was the man his guide took him to.

"Loothdram Investigator," the Enforcer guiding him said, "someone is here to see you."

Loothdram stopped his conversation and turned toward them. "I am impossibly busy, Vankran. Tell the man to wait."

"But sir, he is a friend of the fugitive."

Loothdram eyed Mizcarnon suspiciously, likely using his abilities to search the Peak Crosser's soul. Such silent interrogation no longer made Mizcarnon nervous. He had been subjected to it dozens of times and had been trained to deflect it. Unless Loothdram's skills were beyond that of the average Investigator, the man would get very little information from Mizcarnon.

"Leave us," Loothdram commanded.

The guards and Enforcers stood to leave. The other Investigator stopped looking at his papers and eyed Mizcarnon curiously as well.

"You too, Motpar," Loothdram said to the other Investigator.

"I would like to hear what the man has to say," the younger Investigator said, crossing his legs.

"And I will ask you again to leave. Investigator of the High Trades or not, you are not here to investigate me, and I am still your senior."

The younger Investigator stood, though his short height made him close to the same size, sitting or standing. He nodded to Loothdram and left the room, closing the door behind him.

"Sit," Loothdram commanded as soon as the door shut. Mizcarnon complied, choosing the seat Motpar had vacated. Loothdram sat as well behind a small desk. "And let's drop the pretense of your friendship with Zornan."

The sudden statement surprised Mizcarnon, but he'd prepared for anyone's disbelief about his pretended connection to Zornan. "But I am his friend. My name is Nundril and I…"

"Stop." Loothdram glared at Mizcarnon. "If you maintain this pretense any longer, I will throw you out of this palace and out of this valley. Zornan had only one close associate among the Peak Crossers, and it was not this Nundril character. So who are you, and why are you here?"

Loothdram was good, better than Mizcarnon had been led to believe. That made this situation all the more dangerous.

"My name is Mizcarnon. I am a Peak Crosser serving in the Emperor's Army. I am dispatched to find and contain the damage done by wayward Peak Crossers. I am trying to find Zornan and stop any further damage to the reputation of the Peak Crossers. I can say no more than that."

It was a clever lie, his secondary plan if his ruse as Nundril failed to convince. The Peak Crossers were a very insular bunch, more worried about their reputation as a whole than any other High Trade besides the Magistrates. Mizcarnon knew of no special individual or group within the Peak Crossers who did what he claimed to be doing, but the High Trade's insecurity was enough to make it believable.

"Curious," Loothdram responded. "And what would you do if you found Zornan before the Investigators did?"

Mizcarnon did not respond.

"Interesting indeed." Loothdram eased a little, but Mizcarnon knew better than to trust an Investigator's body language; they were master manipulators. "And what did you hope to discover here, Investigator Peak Crosser?"

"Zornan's next destination."

"Ha!" the Investigator shouted, slapping his desk and startling Mizcarnon. "As if any of us knows that."

"Also, I want to understand his motivation. Do you believe he killed the men he's accused of killing?"

"Have you read Crisdan Investigator's report?" Loothdram asked.

Mizcarnon nodded.

"Then what do you think his motivation is?"

"I have no idea. It makes no sense. I can see no clear motive."

"Exactly. Which only means we don't have all our facts straight—or Zornan is mad. Crisdan is one of the best Investigators in the entire Empire, and if he hasn't been able to uncover what is really going on, what hope do you or I have?"

Mizcarnon sensed some sarcasm, but couldn't be sure. "But he did come to his brother seeking help."

"Yes, but he told his brother little. The only useful information Hisvan gained was that their youngest brother Ballin may have been helping him, and Ballin hasn't been seen since Zornan escaped from the palace."

"How did Zornan escape a heavily guarded palace? Did the governor assist him?"

Loothdram smiled and shook his head. "His escape is curious. Hisvan doesn't have a merciful bone in his body, so I can't imagine he helped. He must have concocted an escape plan before entering the building. The Master Guard may have seen him leaving through the servants' entrance with the help of a guard. That guard has not returned to the palace either. All very curious."

Loothdram was lost in thought now, clearly working through the puzzle in his head.

"Where on earth would he go from here?"

Loothdram shook his head. "I wish I knew. To tell you the truth, Peak Crosser, I believe him innocent of the first killing and likely only somewhat connected to the death of the High Magistrate. Guilty or innocent, I figure he would find a spot in the far corner of the Empire to hide in."

There were many such spots Mizcarnon could think of, and it would take months, if not years, for Mizcarnon to search them all. And he knew that other Peak Crossers were involved in the official search, so he'd be tripping over his kind at almost every turn. His task seemed more impossible by the moment.

"I wish I had a Peak Crosser as part of my investigative team," Loothdram said absently.

"Why is that, Investigator?"

"Because a Peak Crosser with a mrakaro might be able to use it to connect with Zornan's mrakaro. The giant birds are so trusting of each other. What an advantage that would be to approach it that way, especially if you believed the man to be innocent and could convince his bird of that."

Loothdram was looking directly at Mizcarnon now, his gaze intense. The man was giving Mizcarnon instructions on how to track Zornan down, a method he should have considered. *Curse the moons, I didn't even think of asking Sunset to help me!*

But why was Loothdram helping? Why was he giving this piece of advice to a man he hardly knew, who wasn't really involved with the search for the fugitive?

"That would be an advantage, Investigator."

Loothdram stood, and walked over to Mizcarnon's chair. The Peak Crosser stood as well.

"Good hunting, Mizcarnon Peak Crosser."

"To you as well, Loothdram Investigator."

Mizcarnon hurried from the palace to the keep, mentally altering his plans as he cut through the steady rain. What he had learned was not what he had expected, but it was more than he'd known before. Zornan had escaped from the governor's palace, possibly with help from a guardsman or Loothdram himself. A band of mercenaries had been sent to hunt Zornan and Ballin down in the woods (by whom, he did not know), and that group had been killed.

This was the most curious fact: how could a non-warrior Peak Crosser and a farmer take down a band of trained fighters—even poor fighters? Numbers alone should have overwhelmed the brothers. Maybe Zornan had more help than Mizcarnon knew of. And if Loothdram was involved, maybe this was part of a bigger picture. The two rebel groups, the revolutionary Kuthraz or the mysterious Dundraz, might be involved, just as the Emperor worried.

He rushed through the streets, the rain battering his face. Mizcarnon tasted hope for the first time since departing Bristrinia. Loothdram had given him a way to locate Zornan, a way that he had never heard used but made perfect sense. As much as Peak Crossers loved their giant flyers (unless, of course, the Peak Crosser rode an atacikic), they were viewed as animals, even if most Peak Crossers had learned they could mindspeak with them. But the creatures were much more than that, and Mizcarnon cursed himself again for having to be reminded by an Investigator.

He reached the keep and rushed through to the courtyard. Sunset and another mrakaro huddled close together in a corner of the yard. A cosow milled around the yard, more comfortable with the rain. Through his connection to his giant flyer, he could feel Sunset's distaste for the dreary weather.

Sunset, old friend, I need your help.

I am too cold to help, little flyer. Come back when I am dry. Bad weather makes Sunset especially temperamental.

One simple question: Do you know the mrakaro of the man we're chasing, Zornan Peak Crosser?

Of course, foolish little man. I know all mrakaros. There are not many of us. There is Peak Dagger, he and I met as hatchlings while training...

No time, Sunset. Mizcarnon could feel the mrakaro's annoyance at being cut off. Sunset loved to tell stories. *How well do you know Zornan Peak Crosser's mrakaro?*

Very well, came the bird's reply. *We are mates. Or were mates, depending on your perspective.*

Mates? Mizcarnon had never considered that Sunset might have a mate. When did he have time to have a mate?

We have created no eggs, came the bird's annoyed reply, likely sensing Mizcarnon's doubt. *Humans are not the only creatures with needs and feelings.*

Mizcarnon needed to be careful. Sunset was physically the most resilient mrakaro he had ever known, but he could become quite petulant when offended.

My apologies, great friend. I should not have doubted you. The words seemed to soothe Sunset a little. *What is her name? Have you spoken to her recently?*

Silver is the beautiful one's name, which matches the stunning color of her every feather. And I spoke with her last year when we were scouting near the Priests of Cazdanth.

So you can mindspeak with the other mrakaros?

Of course! Sunset shouted into his mind. *And cosows, though we avoid that. They are very moody creatures. Take this one, just moments ago...*

Mizcarnon stifled a laugh and let Sunset continue his story. He didn't want to annoy the bird again.

...so you can see why we, the noble creatures of the sky, get quite annoyed by those furry things.

Of course, Sunset. How close would we need to be to Silver for you to reach out to her?

Twice the distance of you and me, little flyer. I actually felt her on this trip, but said nothing to her. She was headed away from here as we entered Skathall.

Mizcarnon controlled his anger. Sunset felt the mrakaro of the fugitive and did not mention it? He masked it as best he could, but some of it seeped through to Sunset. Mizcarnon could feel his companion withdraw.

I'm sorry, old friend. I do not mean to be angry. Humans are prone to fits of temper.

So true.

We need to fly soon, and I need you to reach out to Silver as soon as we get close to her. Do you know what direction she was headed?

Northeast, little flyer.

I am going to get my things. Eat up. We leave within the hour.

Mizcarnon rushed again, back into the keep to his room to gather his things. Mizcarnon felt like he was playing the common Bristrinian children's game hidden box. It used a small box that opened and closed and had little holes all around it. The object was to put three strings into the right holes and thread them to the other side. If you had the three strings in the right holes and pulled, the box opened, revealing its prize. If not, nothing happened.

He was trying to find the right holes, and he felt closer now, with at least one string in the right place. But in this game of hidden box, he might need a dozen more strings to discover what he searched for.

27 | SOMETHING HIDDEN

Crisdan sat across from Karzdiff, Investigator of the High Trades, in the constable's small office. Crisdan tapped his foot on the dusty floor, a rare show of nervous energy he couldn't seem to stop without conscious thought. Karzdiff was here to finish this, to tie a ribbon on this embarrassing case, and he'd waste no time doing it. Crisdan couldn't imagine a scenario in which the man's inquiry did not put Crisdan under heavy scrutiny or under investigation for negligence.

"She's hiding something." Karzdiff frowned. He'd just returned from interrogating Calla.

Karzdiff and Crisdan had much in common. They both came from the same seaside Koofpashi village in the southern Jungle of Crazdar. The other Investigator was a decade older than Crisdan, so they had not known each other before their High Trade lives began, but Crisdan remembered Karzdiff's parents and a younger brother who'd been his own age.

Their similarities stopped there. Ambition acted as Karzdiff's guiding light, not justice. For Karzdiff, justice was just something to be found if convenient.

"What do you think she's hiding?" Crisdan asked.

Karzdiff did not answer his question, his eyes distant and his mind deep in thought. "Why do you think Zornan married?"

Crisdan sat back in his chair, confused by the change in subject. "I'm not sure what you mean."

Karzdiff looked up at Crisdan. "Marriage is the end of a High Tradesmen's career. He'll never advance, never teach at his academy, never be considered for his High Trade's council. And children are even more of a snare."

Crisdan shrugged. "The man lacks ambition." Crisdan wondered if he were talking of Zornan or himself. "His priorities include family and diligence. It doesn't seem that strange to me."

"Calla is attractive."

Crisdan maintained a blank facial expression and buried his feelings deep within himself, safely locked away from Karzdiff's probing. "Certainly. At least in a classic way. What constitutes female beauty seems to be changing these days."

"I think his desires locked him into marriage. Women can rule your world if you let them."

Crisdan let the comment pass without response. He refocused the conversation. "What could she be hiding?"

"I don't know," Karzdiff said, shaking his head. "She's spending a lot of time at the library researching High Trade law. She's looking for ways to free her husband from his accusations, of that I'm sure. But I don't think she's intelligent enough to have come up with that idea on her own."

More intelligent than you, Karzdiff.

"I suspect Trillia has guided her," the older man continued. "I cannot prove it, but I do not trust that woman. She has about the same political sense as Zornan—by which I mean to say, none at all. But she's not unintelligent."

"What of it? So she's hiding that she's trying to find a way to help her husband? And a local Magistrate pointed her to it? Why would she hide that?"

Karzdiff frowned again. He'd done a lot of frowning the past few days. "No, that's not it. There's something else. She's terrified about something we could uncover. I don't think she was directly involved, but she may know more than she's told us. And it may be the key to all this, the key to convicting Zornan, exonerating you, and getting out of this backward valley."

With those words, Crisdan knew he was doomed. Karzdiff was not going to give up until he understood what Calla was hiding, which would lead him to Calla's manipulation of Crisdan's affections. Crisdan knew Karzdiff would keep digging until the whole truth was exposed because that's exactly what Crisdan would have done. Their motivations were different, but Karzdiff was no less diligent.

"What should we do, then?" Crisdan meant the question more for himself than for the other Investigator.

"I would like you to go question the woman again," the older Investigator continued, "but this time you must press harder. If that fails to unearth whatever she's hiding, then we might need to bring her here and press on her together."

The thought of bringing Calla in front of Karzdiff's intense questioning made Crisdan shudder. She was strong, but no man or woman could resist a full attack by an Investigator. Whatever she was hiding, he would find it. Crisdan had to come up with something to keep Calla away from Karzdiff's jaws.

"I will go immediately, Investigator."

"Yes." Karzdiff eyes went distant again, and he spoke more to himself than to Crisdan. "Your arrival shortly after mine may be disconcerting enough for you to pry loose what I could not."

"Is that all?"

"Yes," Karzdiff said, motioning for Crisdan to leave. As Crisdan turned for the door, the other Investigator of the High Trades spoke again. "I feel we're close, Crisdan. I hope this investigation ends soon."

"As do I, Investigator."

Crisdan walked through the door and closed it behind him. He wanted to shake with fear, to shout a curse into the air. But he remained calm, both on the surface and as far beneath it as he could muster; Karzdiff was likely still probing him. There would be plenty of time later for fear and cursing, especially if this ended as he feared it might.

Calla sat in the sitting room, still shaken by her encounter with Karzdiff. She felt comfortable around Crisdan; he had an easy manner, and though she knew it was his job to pry the truth from her, he did it in a way that was completely unthreatening.

Karzdiff was entirely different. He was like a force of nature, a relentless wind beating on your emotional walls until they finally fell over. She held firm against his attacks, but she wasn't sure she could endure another visit if he chose to come back. The man was too strong, and unlike Crisdan, he cared nothing for her feelings and well-being. He showed outward respect to the wife of a High Tradesman, but truth was his objective, not her comfort.

Zornan had almost convinced her in their years together that High Tradesmen had no unnatural abilities, that what appeared as magic to commoners and Low Trade was merely an intense focus and training that enhanced natural abilities. But he'd never completely extinguished the beliefs her father had instilled in her. This short encounter with Karzdiff proved Zornan wrong and Father right; the man wielded an unseen power, she was sure of it.

She wished at that moment that the girls had stayed at the farm, but on her mother's insistence, Windsa and Caldry had returned that morning. Mother was adamant that the children needed to be with their mother, that grandparents were no substitute for her love and affection.

Calla envied their youthful ignorance. To the two girls, Zornan was gone on one of his adventures with Silver. They missed their father dearly when he was gone, but they innocently believed he would return. Calla and her parents would let them believe that as long as they could.

Calla feared she could not be both mother to two active little girls and Zornan's legal savior. High Trade law had become her obsession, and at this point, she likely knew more about it than most High Tradesmen. But temporarily ignoring her motherly duties had to be for now. She could not bear the thought of losing Zornan because she didn't uncover the piece of law that would free him.

Guilt overwhelmed her as the girls ran into the sitting room. They deserved a fully-committed mother, the mother she had been just a week ago. The mother who wiped away their tears, who played games with them, who fixed their meals and mended their clothes. The mother who spent almost every waking moment with them on her mind. She could not be that mother right now.

A giggling Caldry leapt into her lap, barely avoiding the clutches of her older sister. Calla grabbed her youngest and squeezed her tight. The little girl returned the embrace, and Calla breathed deeply. She buried her face in her youngest child's unruly hair, her tears dripping onto Caldry's head.

Windsa stopped short of her pursuit, and looked up at her mother. Deep concern laced her young eyes, which had turned in the last few years into the bright green common in Calla's family. Caldry still had the grayish eyes of her father.

"What is wrong, Mama?" Windsa asked, her words dipped in sincerity.

"Oh, don't worry about me," Calla replied, trying to regain control of her emotions. "Sometimes I just miss your father when he's gone."

Windsa smiled. "You know what I do when I miss Father?"

"What do you do?"

"I pretend I'm on my mrakaro, who I named Gold. I pretend I'm flying behind Father on one of his adventures."

Calla smiled and fought back another surge of tears. "That's a great idea," Calla choked. "I will try that." She pulled the older girl close and embraced them both. "Thank you, Windsa."

"You're welcome, Mama."

And with that, Caldry pulled free from Calla's embrace and darted out of the room, Windsa following with a loud squeal.

Calla had her own way of feeling close to Zornan. Instead of imagining herself flying behind her husband, she pulled his letter from the top of her dress. Part of her knew she should burn it, that it contained details that could make things worse for Zornan, especially his accusation that Stethdel was having Zornan fly something out of Fallindra. Accusing a High Magistrate of a crime was a serious thing, and though his letter was not a formal accusation submitted through an Investigator of the High Trades, it was a written account which closely mirrored an official accusation. And if an accusation against a High Magistrate was not proven correct, the accusation itself was considered treasonous. So even if Calla somehow found a way to free Zornan from the murder charges, the words of the letter could damn him to another charge.

But the physical presence of the letter brought her comfort. When she ached for Zornan, the feel of the paper against her breasts soothed her. She knew it was silly, but sometimes the simple things were the most helpful, like the feel of a letter or the hug of a child.

She pulled out the letter and began reading it again. She'd read it dozens of times. Though she was still angry at him for leaving, most of her heart filled with pride and admiration. He put himself at great risk to protect their family. She wasn't sure the risk was necessary or wise, but he believed it was, and that was enough.

A knock at the door startled her, and she quickly folded the letter and tucked it back into her dress. She wiped the tears from her face, took a deep breath, and rose to answer the door.

She pulled the door open to reveal Crisdan. She breathed deeply again to keep from crying.

"May I come in?"

She nodded, guiding him into the parlor. She took her usual seat, but Crisdan broke with their short tradition, and sat in the chair nearest her. Only a small table separated them.

"Karzdiff believes you are hiding something," Crisdan said, forgoing his usual pleasantries.

Calla gasped. Did Karzdiff know of the letter? Or did he only know she was hiding something, but not what?

"What are you hiding, Calla? Please tell me. Whatever it is, Karzdiff will dig until he finds it. Please share it with me, and we'll find a way to protect you."

"So he doesn't know what I'm hiding?" she asked, hope rekindling inside her.

"No, but I believe I do."

"You do?" she responded, confused. *Have I been that easy to read?*

Seemingly sensing her confusion, Crisdan eyed her curiously. "Your secret is not a flirtatious manipulation of one certain Investigator?" The man smiled.

Calla felt color fill her cheeks as she blushed. She knew Crisdan knew the game they were playing, and she certainly was aware of his feelings toward her. But it somehow seemed more real and dangerous spoken aloud.

"I'm sorry, Calla," Crisdan said, reaching out his hand and grasping hers.

She started to pull back, but didn't. His affection felt good, and she needed him as an ally.

"So if you weren't worried about disclosing that," he continued, "what were you worried about?"

Calla became aware again of the letter nestled against her skin. She had trusted this man since the day Zornan disappeared, and he had led her to paths which would help Zornan. His motivations were strange, since reuniting with Zornan would mean an end to their relationship. But she had never doubted his sincerity in helping her.

But maybe she should have. The more she read of Investigators, the more she feared them. In many cases, Investigators manipulated the accused or witnesses to uncover the truth. They were masters at finding weak points and exploiting them. Idealistically, this was done in the spirit of uncovering truth and bringing justice. But she knew better now. Sometimes the Investigators brought their skills and powers to bear for political or personal purposes. If Crisdan was one of those men, he had played this game perfectly and left her with no choice but to trust him.

"This is my secret," Calla said, reaching back into her dress and pulling out the letter. "Zornan left me a letter. It details much of his interaction with Stethdel, and it contains information that could destroy my husband."

Crisdan pulled his hand away. He looked at the letter with his usual, curious eyes.

"May I read it?"

Calla took a deep breath, and then held it out to him. "Yes."

Crisdan spent the next few minutes reading and then re-reading Zornan's letter. After he finished it for the fourth time, most of it memorized, he let the paper fall into his lap.

All this time Crisdan assumed Zornan went to the Peak Crosser keep and freed Silver out from under the noses of the guards and Ninel the constable. But, if this letter was to be believed, Stethdel made the arrangements to get the giant bird from the keep to their meeting place in the field the locals called Winthral.

Crisdan had not questioned Mistar, the Peak Crosser Keeper, or his young apprentice, Giltar since they'd found Stethdel's body. Why check an empty net a second time?

But Stethdel would have needed help to get Silver to the field. The mrakaro would not have gone with a stranger to the location; only Zornan, Mistar, Giltar, or possibly another Peak Crosser could have gained the bird's trust. The keeper and the apprentice would need to be questioned further.

And the field. No one had mentioned it, and it had not been searched. There might be clues there to Stethdel's intentions, or maybe evidence that he had been murdered far from Zornan's home. It had rained once since all of this happened, so some evidence might have washed away. But there could be something there, something to change the course of his investigation.

Poor, sweet Calla, Crisdan thought. *You held this thinking it damned your husband, but this letter is his salvation!*

"I must go," Crisdan said, standing and dropping the letter on the table between them.

Calla stood and picked up the letter. "What is it?"

"I have much work to do. This letter holds a lot of new information, and some of it may help us prove Zornan's innocence."

Crisdan started to leave but turned back and almost ran into Calla.

She had moved to follow him, and now they stood close to each other. Too close. Crisdan felt his desire for the woman surge, almost overpowering him. It took every bit of self-control he had not to kiss her or stroke her auburn hair. Calla stood still and did not recoil. Crisdan gently placed his right hand on her arm. She did not jump, and his emotions surged again. Even this small touch was dangerous.

"But you must burn the letter."

Calla's eyes sank. "But why?"

"Because I'm going to lie, and there must be no evidence of my deception. I see a clear path to free Zornan from his charges, but I need to know this letter is destroyed. If my lie is uncovered, it could discredit anything I discover."

Calla nodded. "Thank you, Crisdan."

For the first time, pure affection emanated from Calla toward Crisdan. It wasn't the confused mixed feelings he'd felt from her at other times, or the reluctant deception she used with her eyes and face to go beyond what she felt inside. It was a strong, warm, positive feeling, stronger than anything he'd sensed from her before.

Crisdan's hand lingered on Calla's arm, and he knew he had to remove it. He caressed her arm briefly with his fingers and lowered it.

"Promise me you'll burn the letter today."

"I promise," she replied placing her hands on his shoulders. Because of the height difference, she stood on her toes and gave Crisdan a light kiss on his chin.

"Good day, Calla," he said, as he turned away from her. He quickly walked through the door and into the late afternoon sun.

He had to get away from her. He had wanted to feel her lips on his skin, and now that he had, deep sadness emerged where he thought he'd find exhilaration. Calla had played him, using his feelings to get what she wanted. And when Crisdan helped Zornan return, he would be assigned somewhere else and Calla wouldn't need him anymore. His actions and emotions were as foolish as a High Trade initiate falling for his instructor at school.

He cursed himself, angrily banishing all the romantic feelings swirling inside him.

Zornan was an innocent man, and Crisdan was close to proving it. That would need to be enough. Winning Calla's heart was not part of this. It couldn't be. Restoring a man's freedom would be pointless if you then stole all else he held dear.

Calla stood in the window of the parlor watching Crisdan retreat into the city. She tried to revel in the joy that keeping this letter, something she had chastised herself for every day since Zornan had gone, was actually going to help. She would burn it as soon as she could get to the kitchen without Mother or Father asking too many questions. She owed Crisdan that.

Crisdan. She should have been more excited, but guilt muted her emotions. The man was falling in love, and the proper thing was to be cold to him and rebuff his attentions. He was a good man, and he was trying to restore her family. She couldn't be sure he would continue fighting for Zornan without the possibility of winning her affection, so she continued playing the game.

But her guilt wasn't just for manipulating this man. It was also for feeling something for him. When he touched her arm, it thrilled her. When he caressed her with his fingers, emotions burned inside her. And before he left, she wanted to kiss him on the lips, but controlled herself and kissed his chin.

How can I betray Zornan? Especially now?

She had not behaved this way since they were married. She had been a flirt before that, especially in her short time working at the tavern. Men would tip better if you smiled and winked some, and the innkeeper and his wife instructed all the girls to act that way. It came naturally to Calla, and she was good at it.

But since marriage, she had been completely faithful, physically and emotionally. Yes, she occasionally noticed a fine looking man in town, and she and her mother or her friends would say something to each other. But that was fleeting. She wasn't just flirting with Crisdan; she was feeling something for him. She wanted to be close to him again, not just to learn more of Zornan's situation but to be with him. And she was beginning to hate herself for feeling that way.

Hurry home, Zornan. Hurry home.

28 | A FAMILIAR FACE

ornan sat in silence, barely drinking his beer and letting the food Dashnal ordered go cold. Maeltha avoided eye contact, drinking a second ale. They sat alone. Dashnal had excused himself when it became clear there was a history between the two Peak Crossers.

"I'll go converse with the *happy* couple," Dashnal said, heading toward the table where his men were seated with Ballin and Mairie.

Zornan and Maeltha said nothing to each other. When he had approached, she met his eyes, and a dark look stretched across her face before her gaze quickly darted to her drink. She was seated alone, and Zornan was sure he wasn't the person she was expecting or wanting to see.

Zornan understood her reticence. Their parting almost ten years ago had not gone well. They met at the Peak Crosser Academy when they were both in their sixteenth year. Zornan was smitten from the start. Maeltha was tall, only an inch or two shorter than he was. Zornan had never met a woman like her in Skathall. Besides her unusual height, her skin was dark, a stark contrast to the light skin so prevalent in his community and in most of the Empire. Her hair had been long during those first days in the Academy, but she'd cut it short as almost all Peak Crossers do; long hair was a burden in the sky.

Maeltha's hair was still short, though a little longer than it had been when he had seen her last. And she was just as beautiful, maybe more so. Her face was a lighter color than her black hair, but only by a few shades. Her features were soft, not the chapped and worn look of most Peak Crossers. She had not smiled yet during this reunion, but Zornan clearly remembered how bright and infectious her smile had been. Her eyes were a light brown, and Zornan remembered when he could light them up with a joke or a smile of his own. That light was gone.

At their last meeting, Zornan had confessed his love for her. Zornan was awkward, even after three years in the Initiatory School, uncertain of his place in a new, strange world. Maeltha was confident almost to the point of arrogance. In his first days at the Academy, she defended him in front of some older bullies. They became inseparable after that, best friends. They ate together, trained together, and shared stories of their lives. She knew of his terrible father, and he knew of her life with her uncle after she lost both of her parents to a devastating illness. They came from different worlds, him at the center of the Empire, and her from Smagthan, a city at the Empire's edge many times more populous than the entirety of Skathall Valley. And yet they fit perfectly together as friends.

Until he ruined it all by confessing his love.

She had walked away, calling him a fool. She had accepted a commission as a courier stationed in Koofpash. His first assignment was in Kandrinal, about as far away as they could be from each other and still be in the Empire. He had suggested they take their mrakaros and disappear together, creating a new life. She looked at him sadly, as if she wanted to say yes, but stalked away muttering curses as she went.

Now they sat together, and all he could think of was how beautiful she was. The rejection had pained him for a long time, but Calla had soothed those wounds to the point that he thought they were gone. Seeing Maeltha opened them anew, and Zornan felt guilty for betraying his wife with such thoughts.

"You should not have come here," Maeltha finally said, her tone as cold as it had been the last time they had been together. "This is a dangerous place for a fugitive." She also kept her voice low, slightly above a whisper. Without his Peak Crosser hearing, he would not have been able to make out her words.

"How do you know I'm a fugitive?"

Maeltha's eyes widened, and one side of her face curled into an almost-smile. "Still as naïve as ever, Zor?"

Zornan wanted the banter to be like it was a decade ago, but despite her familiar words, it felt forced. And he had never really liked her mocking him for being naïve.

"I don't know what you mean."

"You are a wanted man, a deserter Peak Crosser. I know in your version of the Empire, they would never lean on criminals to catch a criminal, but every half-wit in this tavern knows your name now, though luckily I'm the only one who would know your face. And they know the reward they will get if they turn you over to the Empire."

Zoran stared back into his drink. So there was no escape, no safe haven anywhere in the Empire, even among criminals. Where could they go? Where could they be safe?

Have you learned to mindspeak? Maeltha's voice slipped into his head.

Only recently, he said, wondering how she spoke into his mind. Loothdram made it sound like it was impossible to mindspeak with someone without making some sort of connection first. Maybe that was only the first time, or maybe he and Maeltha had connected all that time ago without knowing it, like his connection to Silver. *Did you know about mindspeak at the Academy?*

No, that idiot Lascrill kept most of reality from us.

Her venom toward their one-time mentor surprised Zornan. Both of them had idolized him at the Academy, as had most of the students. He was a dynamic teacher. But he had left much of their powers and the realities of the High Trades out of his teaching. Zornan couldn't help but feel some of the same bitterness.

Well, we can do it now, Zornan replied.

We need to go someplace quiet where we can talk, she thought to him, standing up. *I hate mindspeak, and we can't talk here. Too many listening ears.*

Zornan thought her paranoid; it was so loud in The Galloping Hen, he couldn't imagine even magically blessed High Tradesmen could hear any conversation besides that at their own table.

"Where to?" he asked out loud.

"Follow me."

Zornan walked behind her as she weaved among the tables. She was dressed in a Peak Crosser uniform, but it was a light blue color instead of the customary light brown. He could see two hatari holsters on her back, each holding a weapon in its shortened form.

They weaved into the center of the tavern until they reached the table where Dashnal and his men sat with Ballin and Mairie.

"Stay here, worm," Maeltha said to Dashnal. "And get them more suitable clothes. Those merchant outfits are going to get them robbed or worse."

"Whatever you say, my flying flower," Dashnal replied with a large smile. "When do I get paid?"

"When I decide if what you brought is worth payment," she replied coldly, wiping the smile off the man's face.

"I didn't know all Peak Crossers were so moody," Dashnal mumbled as they walked away.

Zornan glanced back at Ballin and Mairie who shot him nervous glances.

"Don't worry," Maeltha said. "Dashnal is more capable than he lets on."

Zornan wasn't sure that was true, but he knew Mairie could handle almost anything that came her way. He hoped she wouldn't have to.

Instead of leaving The Galloping Hen, Maeltha turned before they reached the door and went up a staircase. Judging by where it was situated in the building, it led into a different building, out of the one-story tavern. He followed her to the second story of the adjoining building, down a narrow hallway with doors on each side every twenty feet. She stopped at the last door on the left, opening it after looking behind them.

The room was small, with two beds and a night table between. Lying in one of the beds was the largest human being Zornan had even seen. He was so tall that he had to curl up to fit. When he rose, Zornan realized he wasn't even human. He stood so tall that he was forced to stoop beneath the eight-foot ceiling. He wore baggy brown clothes that were plain and ill-tailored. Though Zornan had only seen one at a distance, he knew it must be a Shantierd, giant men who were said to come from beyond the Ice Mountains.

What set Shantierd apart, besides their size, were their inhuman faces. The man had two eyes, evenly spaced like most humans. But his nose was almost non-existent, a small ridge ending in two slits which pulsed as he breathed. His head was bald, and there were no eyebrows or evidence of facial hair. His mouth was disproportionately small, and he had no ears, only two small holes where his ears should have been.

He growled after he stood, a loud, guttural sound that shook the pitcher sitting on the bedside table. The growl revealed a mouth full of massive, flat teeth.

Maeltha said nothing, only locked eyes with the creature. His grimace disappeared, though he continued to eye Zornan. He walked past Zornan and miraculously squeezed through the door. Maeltha shut it behind him.

"What was that?" Zornan asked, still staring at the door.

"*His* name is Grad'Nusetoi; I call him Setoi."

"It's a Shantierd."

"*He* is a person, just like you or me. The blessing he got from the Priestesses of Bendathdra was not as pleasant as the ones we received."

"I thought those things came from north of the Ice Mountains."

Maeltha stepped close to Zornan, a menacing look in her eyes. "Listen here, Zor. He's not a thing or an it, he's a person. He was blessed as a child, changed into a Shantierd. After training, he was sold to a group of despicable bandits. He saved my life. Treat him with respect." She turned and slumped into her bed. "Sit," she shot at him, pointing to Setoi's unkempt bed.

Zornan sat. His sister a Baldra. Young children turned into giants by the same priestesses who blessed him to become a Crosser. The world he had known was not the world he actually lived in.

"Why are you here, Zor?"

"Dashnal helped us escape The Bowels, and he said you might…"

"No, Zor," she interrupted. She used his short name. Only his mother, Loothdram, Maeltha, and Calla had really ever called him that. "How did you end up a fugitive? Did you really kill a High Magistrate?"

"Of course not!" Zornan shot back at her. "How could you even ask that? You know I'm not capable of something like that."

"People change," she replied, looking down at her feet. "You probably never thought we'd meet again in a lawless valley."

"I never thought we'd meet again at all," he said, locking eyes. "I never thought you'd want to see me again."

"You are an idiot, Zornan Peak Crosser." Her face softened, and she almost smiled.

"That's nothing new."

"How did you get here? What is going on?"

The entire story spilled out. He told her about Stethdel and his strange appearance in Fallindra. He told her about leaving Fallindra, and even told her all about Mairie. He related the story of his ill-conceived return to Skathall and his encounter with Hisvan. He told of their escape, including Loothdram's help and his alliance with the Kuthraz. It all poured out. He finished with the tale of their capture and escape from The Bowels, including what Dashnal had said about some mysterious benefactor paying for their escape.

"And," he said finishing, "my little sister Zandia is a Baldra. She tried to kill us before Dashnal captured us."

Maeltha sat silently, listening to his story. She sat for some time after his story was done, her elbows resting on her knees and her hands propping up her chin.

"I can help you, Zornan," she finally said.

"You can? Can you find a place for us to hide until we have to meet Mairie's mother?"

"I can do better than that, Zor. I can get you to Mairie's mother sooner. I'm a member of the Kuthraz."

29 | DAGTARNA

ornan could not find peace, even in the dark as he tried to sleep. The image of Maeltha's beautiful face interrupted thoughts of home or worries about their journey.

Another face interrupted his thoughts—Zandia's. In the rush of excitement in The Bowels, he'd had little time to process that his presumed dead sister was alive, but maybe not truly living. If he'd branded Mairie as a terrible monster, how much worse was Zandia, a true Baldra full of violence and terror? Zornan tried to imagine her nine-year-old face, but it was always overcome by the chalky white one of a childhood nightmare.

Zornan closed his eyes, not to find sleep, but to contain tears.

What did they do to you, Zandia? What did Father allow to happen to you?

Mairie and Ballin slept in the room's two beds. Both had been exhausted. Mairie was excited to hear that her reunion with her mother might come sooner, and everyone's spirits were lightened by the prospect of their journey coming to a successful conclusion. Of course, Zornan would still be a fugitive, and Ballin would need to forge a new life outside of Skathall. But at least one of them would find harmony, and Ballin would find the fresh start he so needed.

"Zornan, you awake?" Ballin's whisper broke the silence.

"Yes. I can't sleep."

"I fell asleep, but I couldn't stay there. I keep thinking of Zandia."

"I know. Me, too."

"Do you think there's any way to save her?"

Ballin's voice reminded Zornan of the time when the farm dog they'd had died when they were children. Zornan had found the body, mangled by wolves in a glen near their home. When Mother arrived moments later, Zornan desperately pleaded with Mother to help the dog, to bring him back to life. Ballin's voice echoed that desperate hope.

"I don't know, Ballin," Zornan replied. "Despite being a High Tradesman, I know very little about the High Trades and even less about the Baldra. Loothdram said they don't technically exist: the Empire uses them as assassins, but the law doesn't recognize them. He said they are also controlled by a master, someone called a Shindar. I didn't know any of this until a few days ago."

"Do you remember anything about your blessing from the priestess?"

"Yes, I remember it. It came during my last weeks at the Initiatory School. I lay on a table made of brastilia, and the priestess, dressed in a deep purple robe, spoke in some ancient language I couldn't understand and waved a staff over my body."

"Did you feel anything?"

Zornan paused, pulling out as much of the memory as he could. "No, I don't remember feeling anything. I thought it was all ceremony, not magic. I didn't feel a thing. But apparently it changed me."

Ballin's questions stopped, and the brothers lapsed into silence for several minutes. Zornan began to feel sleep creep toward him.

"Zornan?"

"Yes, Ballin."

"Can you mindspeak with Mairie?"

"Why do you care about that?" Zornan smiled in the darkness. He knew why a man smitten by Mairie might ask that question.

"Oh, I thought it could be useful, but it doesn't seem that you two can."

"Mairie cannot mindspeak. Loothdram said it wasn't part of her blessing from her mother. Not sure why. I don't really understand any of this." Zornan paused for few moments before speaking again. "Go to sleep, Ballin. We have a big day tomorrow. You're going to have your first ride on a giant flyer."

Ballin groaned quietly. "I'm not looking forward to that. The tunnel ferry made me sick enough. I can't imagine what flying on one of those things will do."

Zornan laughed quietly. "It's not so bad, little brother."

"Yeah, not for you magic types," Ballin shot back. "I think it might be a little harder for me."

"Yes, probably. And harder still if you don't get some rest."

"That's the first smart thing you've said since landing in Skathall."
This time Ballin laughed.

Zornan laughed, relishing the brotherly banter. He clung to that
feeling and sleep quickly overcame him.

Early the next morning they sat in the common area of another
of Dagtarna's taverns, The Faithful Call, the only patrons in a large
common room.

Maeltha sat at the table with Zornan, Ballin, and Mairie. The younger
woman still did not trust Maeltha, and after a night's sleep found it too
convenient that the woman Dashnal brought them to was an old friend
of Zornan's and Kuthraz.

"The Empire is not that small," she complained on their walk over
from The Galloping Hen.

"But it's not that big, either," was all Zornan could say in reply.

After a night's sleep, he found it curious as well. He had not had the
chance to ask Dashnal about Maeltha's reputation or why he had chosen
her to help them escape. And their exchange about payment was even
more curious. But Maeltha was one of his oldest friends, so he wanted
to trust her. Even though his experience with Hisvan had soured him, he
had to trust her. He didn't see any other option.

"I was able to connect with my friends in the Kuthraz," Maeltha
began. The Shantierd giant, Setoi, stood at Maeltha's side. Because of the
tavern's high ceilings, he was able to stand without stooping. He eyed
everyone in the room suspiciously, including Zornan, Ballin, and Mairie.
"They were able to arrange a meeting with Mairie's mother sooner than
expected. We're to meet them in two days at an old military fort north of
Mandmandoo. Mairie should be safe after that."

"How long have you been a part of the Kuthraz?" Mairie asked
casually.

Maeltha's eyes narrowed as she looked at the younger woman. "Not
long. I was unjustly stripped of my title as a Peak Crosser two years ago,
and I've flown independently since then. The Kuthraz reached out to me
a year ago to join their cause. I have no love for the Empire, so I joined."

"Funny, my father never mentioned you," Mairie replied, smiling.

"I never met Stethdel or Loothdram. My connection came through
Lascrill, my old mentor. I work through a man named Bandrick, if
that's even his name. They are an insular group; they aren't about to

let a criminal like me into their fold without testing my faithfulness. Delivering you to your mother will demonstrate that."

Zornan looked back at Mairie; it was clear that she was not satisfied with Maeltha's explanation, but she held her peace.

"So how do we get out of here?" Zornan asked.

"There's an access tunnel two miles north that opens into a narrow, rocky valley," Maeltha replied. "Your mrakaro and the cosow I've acquired will meet us there."

"You don't have your own giant flyer?" Ballin asked.

"I lost my mrakaro when I left the High Trade. It's complicated and expensive to find another."

"So did you leave the Peak Crossers or were you forced out?" Mairie accused. "Now you've said both."

"I don't think your brother and his girlfriend trust me, Zor," Maeltha said, turning toward him.

"He's not my boyfriend," Mairie shot back, and Ballin frowned.

"You may want to let him know that." Maeltha raised her eyebrows. "I think he believes otherwise."

"Stop it, all of you," Zornan demanded. "We have to trust Maeltha," he said to Ballin and Mairie. "Or give this up and try and find another way."

"But there is no other way," Ballin replied.

"So we need to trust her."

The group sat in silence for a few moments. Maeltha's plan and explanation had not satisfied Ballin and Mairie, and now Ballin looked angry about Mairie's dismissal of their relationship. Still, they both nodded at Zornan and looked at Maeltha.

"What are we going to do with him?" Maeltha asked, looking at Ballin. "He won't survive on a giant flyer."

"We have a nibrak," Zornan replied.

"What about the sky sickness?"

"We'll just have to hope he can handle it."

Everyone looked at Ballin, and he smiled weakly. "At least if I get sick and pass out, I won't be as scared."

"But you might fall to your death," Zornan replied, and Ballin responded with a half-hearted shrug.

After gathering the needed supplies, the group left the city and headed for the north tunnel. Rocky foothills obscured their destination. Light brown colored the entire valley, with the loose soil clinging to everyone and everything. Most of the buildings in the town were unimaginatively built with wood and colored with paint and stone of that same color. Only the yellow brush on the outskirts of the city and the colorful clothing of the city's inhabitants broke up the bleak palette.

Zornan had reconnected with Silver the night before. The mrakaro had delivered Zornan's message to Loothdram. Loothdram's message was to get to Dagtarna and he would have an agent of the Kuthraz find them there. Maeltha was likely that contact, and now they were in the safe hands of Loothdram's group, closing in on completing the task of delivering Mairie.

We should be there in a couple hours, Zornan said to Silver. *Can you be there?*

I'm almost there already, little one. I can move so much faster than legs can carry.

Of course you can.

Do we really have to travel with a cosow? Silver's annoyance flooded Zornan's mind.

Better than an atacikic.

Flying underwater would be better than with an atacikic. I just don't understand how a Peak Crosser who flew on mrakaros could ever fly on a cosow.

Zornan looked at Maeltha. She led the group through the foothills toward the tunnel entrance. She looked very much the same as when he had known her, but something had changed in her demeanor. Like most mrakaro riders, she had made fun of cosow riders in the Academy. It was a common rivalry among Peak Crossers, and one that usually continued through life. But then, he didn't really know the Maeltha walking ahead of him; he'd known a different version, a dedicated Peak Crosser, not a criminal living most of her life tethered to the ground.

Setoi accompanied them, walking close to Maeltha. He was only coming as far as the tunnel entrance; even the largest mrakaro would buckle under his massive weight. And they only had two giant flyers anyway, Silver and the cosow.

He didn't know much about Shantierd, but Setoi was not what he'd expected. He was very gentle with Maeltha and acted more like a brother to her than a guard or a servant. And he had warmed to Mairie and Ballin. Though he could only speak with his mind, Maeltha spoke for him. He really liked Mairie's hair and said, through Maeltha, that he wished he could grow hair like that.

Zornan almost ran into Setoi as the Shantierd stopped. Maeltha raised her hand for the group to stop. Zornan looked ahead and saw a short man and a dozen others step from behind a series of boulders.

"Where are we going, my pretty little Peak Crosser?" The short man at their lead twirled a knife in his left hand. All of his companions were armed, and they stood between them and the tunnel entrance.

"None of your concern, Nmarid," Maeltha replied. "I don't work for your boss anymore."

"He disagrees," the man replied. Nmarid was powerfully built, like an Enforcer in a shorter man's body. He wore merchant clothes, bright red and accented with a sash of pink. He also wore a large-brimmed hat that was a darker red than his tunic. He looked like he hadn't shaved in several days, and by the smell of him, he hadn't bathed in twice as long.

"Dashnal said you had some precious cargo you were transporting. I didn't think it would be a girl." Nmarid eyed Mairie hungrily. "Hello, little girl."

"Don't look at me that way," Mairie replied defiantly.

"Feisty one," the man replied.

"Leave her alone," Zornan barked, tired of these bullies.

Nmarid stepped close to Zornan and looked up at him. "You don't know your place. I am second in command to Mazthain. We fear no one, not even the Empire. And I can certainly handle a girl, in more ways than one." His men laughed.

Zornan almost gagged at the strong combination of the man's breath and odor.

"What do you want, Nmarid?" Maeltha's voice and stance were calm and casual. While Zornan and Mairie's hands drifted toward their weapons, Maeltha's were still.

"Payment for safe passage," the man replied, stepping away from Zornan.

"No." Maeltha folded her arms and glared at the man. "I won't pay you a thing."

"You won't?" he snarled. "Do you think your awkward giant will save you? There are thirteen of us, dear; not even that ugly brute can take all of us."

"Ugly?" Maeltha replied. "On his worst day, Setoi is a hundred times better looking than you, little boy."

Nmarid moved quickly, firming the grip on his knife and lunging at Maeltha's gut.

But Mairie moved faster. She removed and extended one hatnuthri and quickly struck Nmarid in the arm before he reached his target. The man screamed in pain, dropped his knife and fell to his knees.

Two of his men reacted immediately, both going for Mairie. The first lunged with his sword, which she kicked away; it clanged harmlessly against a rock. She turned, and with the other leg, kicked the first attacker in the neck. He collapsed onto the ground, gasping for breath.

At the same time as Mairie's defense, Setoi grabbed the second man by the head, as if he were picking up a child's toy. Before the man could turn his attack on the giant, Setoi flung him into the air more than fifteen feet away. The second attacker disappeared with a thump behind the boulder Nmarid had emerged from.

Maeltha stood over the gang leader now, her hatari fully extended, and one of its sharp points touching his neck. Blood trickled down from where Maeltha applied pressure with her weapon. The rest of his men stood ready, but none made a move to help, their eyes darting between their fallen leader, Mairie, and Setoi.

"Here's what you're going to do," Maeltha said. "You're going to return to Mazthain and let him know that I work for myself. He's to leave me and Setoi alone. I paid my debt."

"You can never step foot in Dagtarna again," Nmarid replied weakly. "Mazthain will not stand for this humiliation."

"Don't worry, I don't plan on coming back." Maeltha kicked the gang leader in the face, and he slumped to the ground. His men flinched, but did not move.

"Take this little tit-sucker back to your master," Maeltha said loudly to his crew. "Make sure my message is delivered. No one is to follow us, or the giant will remove some of your heads, and the girl will remove the rest of your crew's guts."

Each of the gang sheathed his weapon and cleared the path for them. Maeltha led the way, followed by Ballin and Zornan, with Setoid and Mairie coming last, glaring at the crew to reinforce Maeltha's threats.

After a few moments, Zornan looked back and saw one of the larger men carrying Nmarid over his shoulders as the entire group made their way back to the city.

"I think you've just made a powerful enemy," Zornan said to Maeltha.

"Maybe," she said, shrugging. "Mazthain respects power and honors it. He may actually respect me more now."

"I wasn't talking about him. I was talking about Nmarid. He'll hunt you till his dying day."

"He'll have to get in line."

30 | PREY

Tha'Strukra crouched in the southern foothills of Dagtarna, watching the setting sun's light slowly recede from the valley. She had arrived the night before, but her command was to wait for Dres'Dargpa. She'd spent an entire day crouched in the same spot, only breaking from her statuesque stance to eat. She snarled at the thought of being joined by another Baldra. She was strong. She was Baldra. She needed no help. She could have gone into the poorly guarded criminal city last night. She could have killed Zornan and Ballin and captured the other prey. She had already defeated the girl in battle. This was *her* mission, and she seethed at the thought of another Baldra sharing the glory. Especially Dres'Dargpa. If the old fool had done what he was supposed to and captured the girl in Fallindra, they wouldn't even need to be here.

But failure's scent hung over everything. She had failed to kill Lascrill, and Dres'Dargpa had allowed the girl to escape.

Zornan and Ballin. Seeing them distracted her more than she would ever admit to anyone besides her all-knowing Shindar. No Baldra expected to see their pre-birth kin ever again and certainly did not expect to be assigned to kill them. But Zandia lived no longer; only Tha'Strukra remained, and she would do as she had been commanded. She had no other choice.

She enjoyed the time alone with her own thoughts. Her Shindar was occupied elsewhere with another Baldra, so Tha'Strukra could think as she wished without anything leaking to her master. She could still feel the Shindar's commands like constant, distant drum beats in her head. But she could think freely without any chastisement for her hate of Dres'Dargpa or for her affection for Nin'Kindo.

She missed Nin. If she had a friend, it was Nin. Connected through the same Shindar, they could mindspeak no matter the geographic distance, which they often did. Since becoming Baldra, she'd only shared any part of herself with her Shindar, because she must, and with Nin, because she wanted to.

"Good afternoon, Dres'Dargpa." Tha'Strukra stood.

"Good afternoon, young one." The cloaked figure stepped into view.

He was getting old and careless; Tha'Strukra had heard his approach minutes ago.

"For once, you obey." It was a Baldra joke, of sorts; they always had to obey.

"Has your Shindar given new commands?" Tha'Strukra asked. "Mine is silent, occupied elsewhere."

"Yes," the older Baldra replied. "We are to wait until nightfall. A scout will come with the location of a thief named Dashnal. He is our prey now."

"What of the other prey?"

"My command only mentioned Dashnal. I am assuming the other prey are hunted by others or maybe already disposed of."

"You mean pursued by a different Baldra."

"Perhaps." The older Baldra paused, the end of the word lingering. "Or perhaps they've already been captured. We've failed, which means we may never know the end."

"We will be punished for that failure."

"You, perhaps. I killed one of my prey in Fallindra."

"Yes, but you let the bigger target slip through your fingers," Tha'Strukra said, smiling broadly.

"Watch your tongue," Dres'Dargpa hissed. "I am not the one who let my human weakness stop me from killing my brothers. You are weak, Tha'Strukra, and you will always be."

They stood facing each other, each poised to strike, their hatnuthri out and ready. This was why Baldra were rarely placed together; they had a way of maiming or killing each other.

Tha'Strukra! It was the voice of her Shindar. *What are you doing?*

Preparing to kill Dres'Dargpa, my master.

Stop that. You are not to kill Dres'Dargpa on this mission. The command was precise, and Tha'Strukra felt her free will melt as she sheathed her hatnuthri. But her Shindar had not commanded her to never kill Dres'Dargpa. She yearned for the day she could. *You are to kill the thief*

Dashnal and his associates. No trace of the Destroyer girl or her companions is to be found.

As you command, Shindar.

Dres'Dargpa also sheathed his weapons, a similar command from his Shindar likely cooling his hatred for her. The commands did not keep them from glaring at one another.

"It appears we will be working together for now, weak one," the older Baldra said through closed teeth.

Tha'Strukra smiled again. "For now, old one."

Mizcarnon glided high above the peaks, Sunset turning toward Dagtarna. Though Zornan's trail ran cold in Skathall, Loothdram's clue about connecting with Zornan's mrakaro had already proved useful.

Sunset had reached out to Zornan's mrakaro, Silver, and confirmed that they were in Dagtarna but likely leaving soon. Silver had weaved an exciting tale of an escape from Skathall and also from The Bowels. Zornan was accompanied by his brother Ballin and another person, a girl. Silver would not share with Sunset who the person was or why she was with Zornan, which annoyed Sunset immensely. As former mates, he felt he had the right to know whatever she knew. All of this amused Mizcarnon, but he hid those feelings from his moody mrakaro.

Something felt wrong about using the mrakaros to gather information about Zornan. He was almost sure that neither Sunset nor Silver really knew the purpose of Mizcarnon's manipulation. He wondered if Investigators knew this trick, as it would be a simple way to track and gather information about any Peak Crosser. They were likely ignorant of it, just as he had been. All except Loothdram.

Regardless of his qualms, he had found the man, and he was getting closer. But certain details of Silver's story worried him. Zornan's mrakaro claimed Baldra were involved, both in Skathall and in the tunnels outside The Bowels. Apparently the creatures were tracking and trying to kill Zornan and his companions. At first, Mizcarnon worried that this signaled duplicity on the Emperor's part, but in the last few minutes of contemplating, he'd come to a different conclusion.

In theory, all Baldra and their guiding Shindar were under the command of the Emperor or one of his generals. But what if the Kuthraz or Dundraz contracted with the Priestesses of Bendathdra to get their own Baldra and Shindar? Greedy Bendathdrans and Cazdarians were known to create Shantierd, giant flyers, and brastilia weapons for the underbelly of Imperial society. It was treason to do so, but greed was a powerful motivator, and criminals or rebels would pay an incredible sum for a Shindar and a pair of Baldra.

Maybe even more harrowing was the thought that generals or others betrayed their Emperor and joined with these groups. Baldra, weapons, Enforcers—endless resources could be positioned against the Empire, even from within its tightest ranks.

Mizcarnon shuddered at the thought of Baldra being in control of those who strived to overthrow the Empire. But it all made sense. If the High Magistrate Stethdel had indeed been killed by a Baldra (which Crisdan Investigator's report hinted but wisely never claimed), this Baldra had turned his attention to Zornan and whatever cargo he carried.

Mizcarnon pushed Sunset hard, knowing the mrakaro could rest as soon as they reached Dagtarna. They would be there a few hours after dark, and Mizcarnon wanted to find Zornan tonight.

Any other word from Silver? Mizcarnon asked Sunset.

No, the bird replied in a pouting voice. *She refuses to talk with me.*

No matter, old friend. You will see her tonight, and we'll be back in Bristrinia within a couple days. Our honor will be increased and our mission complete.

Sunset screeched in response and flew faster. The mrakaro cared little for the honor Mizcarnon found so important, but his desire to see Silver pushed the giant bird to fly as fast as the winds would allow.

The scout who had been dispatched to find their prey arrived at their hiding place just after nightfall, approaching the two Baldra carefully. The man stammered his information, informing them that the thief Dashnal was staying with his two men in a room at The Faithful Call, an inn and tavern on Dagtarna's third circle. The scout overheard Dashnal tell his companions that they would be retiring early tonight before leaving for Manmandoo early the next day.

Good, Tha'Strukra thought to herself. *It is time for the kill.*

The scout scurried away, and the two assassins waited an hour and then weaved their way into the city. Lawless cities were unguarded on their perimeter but were still tricky to infiltrate. Prostitutes, gamblers, and criminals worked all night, and though it was a lot less busy than during the day, there were still dozens of people to avoid. The Baldra wouldn't be the only ones sneaking around in Dagtarna at night, and likely not even the only people wearing hoods and cloaks. But they would be the only ones with the tell-tale chalky white skin of a Baldra. So they avoided contact, and it took them most of the next two hours to approach the inn without drawing attention.

They entered the building through the cook's door in the back. The tavern room was still partially filled with drinkers and gamblers, but they weren't serving food anymore, and the kitchen was empty and dark.

As they approached the door that the scout had said would lead up to the rooms, it swung open, a man stumbling through it. He wore merchant clothes and blundered about, drunken and confused. He was likely searching for his room, his drunken stupor leading him the wrong direction.

Before the man even saw them, Dres'Dargpa slipped up behind him and grabbed his head, twisting it until a familiar crack signaled the man's neck was broken. It was a bloodless, silent kill.

Help me get his body into the stone oven, the older Baldra commanded.

Tha'Strukra quickly grabbed the man's feet and helped Dres'Dargpa carry him toward the large stone oven. She deftly opened it with her foot, and they silently slid the dead man into it, closing it behind him. Some cook would have a rude awakening the next morning as she prepared breakfast. Either that, or a careless cook would fire up the oven without checking it first and roast the corpse. Tha'Strukra couldn't decide which would be more amusing.

With one unexpected obstacle eliminated, the pair crept back toward the door and climbed the stairs.

A pair of lamps lit the dark hallway. Dashnal and his men were in the third room on the right, and, according to the scout, his companions were large men, possibly former Enforcers and definitely trained fighters. Tha'Strukra enjoyed killing Enforcers the most of any humans. They were arrogant bullies who believed their blessed strength was unequaled. She had even heard of Enforcers bragging about taking on a Baldra by themselves. That was, of course, impossible. Baldra were immeasurably stronger and faster than Enforcers; a half dozen Enforcers would be lucky to land even a blow against a trained and experienced Baldra. Dres'Dargpa and Tha'Strukra were both carefully trained and experienced.

The two Baldra closed their eyes and let their minds absorb the things only they could sense. It was difficult with the wall, but after a few moments of concentration, Tha'Strukra could see into the room. The heat of three men hung clearly in her mind. The smallest man, likely Dashnal, slept in a bed. The two larger men slept on the floor near each other. The only weapons she was able to sense with this kind of sight were brastilian ones, and one of the thief's companions had a hatrindi lying near him. Dashnal had a hatrindi as well, lying next to his bed. The third one certainly had a sword, even if she couldn't see it. Weapons or no weapons, these kills were going to be easy.

Ready?

Tha'Strukra glared at her companion, wishing it was him she had been ordered to kill. *Of course, Dres'Dargpa.*

The older Baldra reached for the door and turned the knob, which moved easily. He quietly opened it. The fools had not even been smart enough to lock it.

The two Baldra moved quickly, Tha'Strukra leaping onto Dashnal's bed, and Dres'Dargpa going for the two guards. She landed on the bed, straddling her prey just as she heard Dres'Dargpa slit the throat of the first, and then the second. Both men were dead, and neither had made a sound.

As she pulled back her hatnuthri to plunge it into Dashnal's chest, the man's eyes opened and filled with terror. She slipped one hand over his mouth and pulled back her other arm to ram her hatnuthri into his chest. But something held her. Never before had she delayed an order. She must do her duty. But something else pulled at her. Not morality, as she never felt remorse. But a desire burned within in to know what happened to Zornan and Ballin.

"Where are the three you helped escape The Bowels?" she hissed. "If you cry out for help, I will kill you." She slowly moved her left hand away from the thief's mouth.

"Good merciful gods of the peaks," Dashnal whispered.

"Where are they?" she demanded, pressing one of her knees into his ribs.

What are you doing? Dres'Dargpa asked.

Out of my mind, she replied. *I have other orders.* She was incapable of lying to her Shindar, but the woman wasn't in her head at the moment. There had been no order to be honest with Dres'Dargpa.

"I delivered them to a woman named Maeltha. I don't know where they went."

"Why did you help them out of The Bowels?"

We are not Investigators, Dres'Dargpa intruded. *Finish him.*

Leave me alone!

"I was paid to help them escape."

"By whom?"

"I don't know. It was anonymous, but whoever it was has far-reaching eyes and even deeper pockets."

Without another word, she slit the man's throat, and his head turned to its side, gasping for a moment before his eyes went lifeless. She pulled out her other hatnuthri with her left hand, extended it, and then plunged both into his chest, marking him as the target of their fury.

What was that? Dres'Dargpa demanded as they slipped from the room, closing the door behind them. They scanned the hall and returned to the stairwell from which they'd come.

None of your concern, old man. They slipped down the stairs and quickly dashed through the kitchen and into the alleyway. Their exit went undetected.

As the two Baldra slipped out of Dagtarna and headed to the tunnel, Tha'Strukra's thoughts turned toward her brothers. Why this sudden affection for them? Her home life had been a horror, not much better than the one she lived now. Zornan had not come to rescue his little sister, and Ballin had watched the night Father had become enraged enough to beat young Zandia close to death. None of her brothers deserved her sympathy. Maybe they weren't the monsters Father was, but they weren't heroes, either. They were weak, pathetic men. She was strong now, stronger than them. She was Baldra.

The thoughts of her father filled her with the familiar hate which burned like a glow globe deep within her soul. Someday, she would kill the man. She'd been close once, only a few feet away. But her hunt had ended prematurely. Someday soon she would hunt down the man and show him what kind of monster he had spawned.

Mizcarnon and Sunset reached the Peak Crosser keep in Dagtarna just after midnight. After turning his mrakaro over to the unctuous, sleepy keeper, he headed toward a tavern in the city that the keeper had suggested. The tavern keep at The Faithful Call was known as someone who could provide information—for a reasonable fee, of course.

At this time of night, almost any city in the Empire would have been completely deserted, but not Dagtarna. Even in the middle of the night, the city crawled with prostitutes, rogues, and those selling what could not be safely sold—even here—during the day. Mizcarnon ignored it all. He had to find Zornan and hoped he was still in the city. The fugitive Peak Crosser had escaped a Baldra in Fallindra, a rogue attack in Skathall, and who knew what other dangers along the way. His path should not end in a despicable place like Dagtarna.

Sunset had reached out to Silver again just before they reached the city, but Zornan's mrakaro had refused to speak to her former mate. Sunset became insufferable after that. He filled his rider's mind with a tirade against female mrakaros and their moody and unpredictable nature. Mizcarnon did not cut him off because he knew they were close to their destination.

When Mizcarnon reached The Faithful Call, he was unsurprised to find it about a quarter full. A couple of card games were still going on, and a few lonely souls drowned their pain with a healthy measure of alcohol. As he entered, a pretty young barmaid approached him.

"What can I do for you?" Her eyes were a striking, bright blue, and her hair was long and blond and pulled up behind her head. She looked tired. Mizcarnon could see several food stains on her skirt where a man or two had tried to lift it.

"Is the tavern keep awake and about?"

"He's over there," she said, the smile disappearing from her face. "Watching the game of nine fingers."

The tavern keep was a small man, at least half a foot shorter than Mizcarnon. He was younger than expected, likely only a year or two older than the Peak Crosser. He was lean and fit, not like most tavern keeps Mizcarnon had met in his journeys, who were all too fond of their own food and drink.

"Greeting, tavern keep," Mizcarnon said, probably too formally for the occasion.

"Welcome greeting, Peak Crosser," the man said without taking his eyes off the card game. "If you need food or drink, any of the barmaids can help you."

"Maybe later. I need information."

The man finally looked at Mizcarnon. "Information? What kind of information?"

"The location of some new arrivals. I will pay, if the information is useful."

"Come." The tavern keep walked away from the card game table and offered Mizcarnon a seat at an empty, secluded table. The Peak Crosser sat, and the tavern keep sat opposite him. The man motioned with his hand, and the same barmaid who had greeted Mizcarnon approached. "Bring us two drinks." He turned back to Mizcarnon as the woman walked away. "My name is Bith. I know most everything that goes on around here, and if I don't, I can point you in the right direction. The only thing I don't talk about is specifics of the lives of the three gang leaders. No one lives long who tells their tales."

"My name is Beeldrat," Mizcarnon replied with a nod. "Not here to discuss the gangs. Looking for an old friend of mine. Would have come out of The Bowels in the last day or so. Traveling with another man, maybe some others. Any idea where I might find this man?"

"As a matter of fact, I believe the one you're looking for was here in my room this very morning." The man stopped and stared at Mizcarnon.

The Peak Crosser pulled money from his pocket and slapped down three gold Imperial coins.

The tavern keep continued: "They were escorted out of The Bowels by a man named Dashnal, and he's staying here tonight. He's in the seventh room on your left up those stairs. I would knock softly; he's got two guards, and they're fierce men from what I hear."

"I'm not interested in this man, just in whom he brought out."

"He brought out two men and a young woman. They were here this morning with a woman named Maeltha, a former Peak Crosser who hunts down those Mazthain wants found. They set out from here this morning, but I don't know where they went. Dashnal will know. The group looked ready for a journey, like they were going to be leaving Dagtarna."

Mizcarnon threw another coin on the table and headed for the stairs. So the brother Ballin was likely with Zornan, and there was someone else, the young woman Silver mentioned to Sunset. Possibly a friend or lover of Ballin's from Skathall? Neither the Emperor nor Crisdan Investigator's report had mentioned anything about a young woman.

And they were being helped by Maeltha. Mizcarnon knew the woman. She had been expelled from the Peak Crossers a couple of years ago for taking extra, unapproved work. But more damning, she was also wanted for murder after using her mrakaro to kill one of her accusers.

Her mrakaro had betrayed her and flown her to Bristrinia for trial. The tale was well known among most Peak Crossers. She had escaped and been tracked to Kandrinal, where the Investigator and Enforcers who were sent after her were found dead, their heads crushed like fruit smashed against a stone. She was dangerous and unscrupulous. Whatever her involvement with Zornan, it complicated things. Either the Peak Crosser was more of a criminal than the Emperor or Crisdan Investigator believed, or he had just been forced into using such a person due to the desperation of his situation. Either way, Mizcarnon needed to find Zornan and his companions before Maeltha profited by them.

Mizcarnon reached the seventh door and paused; waking a group of armed men in the middle of the night was rarely a good idea. But he could not wait until morning to get the information. If Zornan and his group had left Dagtarna this morning, he needed to know where they went and what they were doing with Maeltha.

The Peak Crosser knocked softly on the door and stepped back, his hand on his hatari. But he heard nothing, not even Dashnal or one of his men turning over. So he knocked again, this time more forcefully. He stepped back again, ready to be greeted by angry, groggy men. But again, only silence greeted him.

Mizcarnon withdrew his hatari, keeping it in its short form. He approached the door slowly and gripped the handle. It turned easily. He nudged the door open, flooding the small room with the hallway's dim light.

The room was in chaos. The two men on the floor lay in unnatural positions, blood pooling around each of their heads. They had been killed in their sleep. A man lay on the room's only bed, likely the thief Dashnal, in a gruesome posture. His neck was slit open, and his chest had two dark red holes. These men had been killed by a Baldra or by expert killers who were trying to leave the sign of a Baldra.

Mizcarnon withdrew and closed the door behind him. There was no more information to be discovered in that grisly scene. He slipped out of The Faithful Call without drawing any more attention and walked back toward the Peak Crosser keep.

Zornan was likely gone from Dagtarna, and his only lead was a moody mrakaro communicating with another moody mrakaro. Zornan was in the company of an untrustworthy murderer who would likely sell them out at her earliest convenience. And, if Dashnal's murder was any indication, they were still being tracked by a Baldra.

Mizcarnon walked into the keep and headed straight for the courtyard. He knew he was going to annoy Sunset with the command to leave, and even more so with a request to reach out to Silver again. But he had to fulfill his duty, even if it meant bothering his temperamental companion. Time was running out before Zornan's trail would go cold again.

Sunset, he thought gently, in case his mrakaro was sleeping.

What is it? The bird was particularly annoyed. Either he had been sleeping or was close to sleep.

We need to leave now. Silver's rider is in great danger, and they've already left the valley.

I know, came the bird's reply. *Please wait while I finish my conversation with Silver.*

The Peak Crosser took the stairs two at a time, going to his room and collecting his things before heading to the small yard Sunset shared with two cosows. He passed the keeper on his way to the yard, gave the man a gold coin, and told him they wouldn't be staying after all. In any other keep in the Empire, arriving and leaving in the middle of the night would have been cause for alarm. This keeper simply shrugged and tucked the coin in his pocket.

When Mizcarnon reached the yard, Sunset was stretching his wings and prancing in his pre-flight ritual. The two rodent-like cosows were in a corner of the yard, huddled together, eyeing the pretentious bird.

What did you learn, faithful friend?

They left earlier today, headed someplace west of here, though Silver does not know where yet. She carries Zornan and a young woman. She follows a cosow, which is an indignity in and of itself; mrakaros should never follow cosows. Sunset glanced in the direction of the two cosows in the yard. *The rodent carries a woman Peak Crosser and the brother of Silver's rider. They have stopped in the mountains west of here as the brother is quite sick with the flying sickness. Weak humans. They plan on moving again in the morning.*

Excellent work, Sunset. We must follow them.

Of course, my little rider. I will fly faster than the wind.

Mizcarnon jumped onto the saddle and secured his pack.

Why did she answer you this time, Sunset? Mizcarnon asked tentatively, hoping not to send the bird into a fit.

She is worried about the brother, came his reply, *and she does not trust the Peak Crosser they ride with.*

Sunset was calm and happy as they lifted out of the yard and climbed into the star-filled sky, away from Dagtarna. They were close now, if only they could reach Zornan before something else happened to him.

I should tell you stories of Silver the beautiful, Sunset said excitedly. *She is the most graceful flyer I've ever seen. Her patterns of flight are like a great painting coloring the sky with…*

Mizcarnon let his thoughts drift as Sunset mindspoke poetically about his love.

31 | EVIDENCE

The morning sky was filled with clouds, the largest moon, Circlarl, still hanging stubbornly in the sky. Crisdan walked toward Winthral Field, accompanied by a sleepy Ninel. They'd spent the early morning at the Peak Crosser keep interviewing Giltar and Mistar, and now it was time to find out if Winthral Field held as much new information as the keeper had.

The day before, Crisdan had revealed many of the details of Zornan's letter to Karzdiff, insinuating that the specifics came from an intense interrogation of lady Calla. He included the detail of Stethdel's command to Zornan to meet in Winthral Field where the cargo and his mrakaro would be waiting. The revelation stirred Karzdiff into an agitated state. It took Crisdan more than an hour to convince the stubborn man not to ignore Calla and just continue their investigation as if this new information was nothing more than the imaginings of a desperate wife. Karzdiff wanted this to be clean, for Zornan to be a murderer and fiend. The other Investigator had no desire to drag a dead High Magistrate through the muck. But Crisdan had prevailed on the more experienced Investigator, and they spent the rest of the evening coming up with their plan.

As Karzdiff was officially there to oversee Crisdan and ensure he did things properly, he agreed to let the younger Investigator handle the interviews with the Peak Crosser keeper and his apprentice; Crisdan would also examine the field for evidence. Two Enforcers were dispatched that evening to stay the night in the field to keep anyone out.

Within a matter of seconds, Mistar had revealed himself as Stethdel's confederate. He denied it, of course, but his heart and mind betrayed him. He was the one who had snuck Silver out of the keep and to the field. He had done it for Stethdel, and his denial that he had been paid seemed genuine. Which meant the dead High Magistrate and Peak Crosser Keeper were confederates of some kind, maybe Kuthraz. How deep did Lascrill's talons go into the flesh of the Empire?

As soon as the interview with Mistar was done, Crisdan ordered the Enforcer to escort Mistar to the constable's office and place him under arrest. His charges included lying to a constable, lying to an Investigator, and theft of a mrakaro. The older man accepted the arrest calmly and without protest. He seemed relieved to not have to lie anymore. More questioning would be needed, since Mistar had not admitted to anything and there were no witnesses to verify he had indeed helped Stethdel, but that would come in time. The old man would wilt under his or Karzdiff's questioning, of that Crisdan was certain.

He moved on to the young apprentice. Giltar denied knowing anything about Mistar's plan to get Silver into the field and said he'd never seen Stethdel before. All of his statements were verified by Crisdan's senses. His heart raced because he was nervous under the watchful eye of an Investigator, but it fit normal patterns.

However, when asked if he had been awakened when Mistar retrieved the mrakaro, the boy's mind went blank, and his heart started beating at a slow, deliberate pace, almost as if he were asleep. Crisdan could feel nothing of the boy's emotions; not apathy, not confusion at the question, just nothing. Giltar sat in silence for several moments, and then asked for Crisdan to repeat the question. When he repeated it, the boy reacted in the same way, never answering the question. When Crisdan changed the line of questioning and asked about his history with Zornan, the boy snapped back and answered the questions honestly, his emotions and body returning to their prior state.

In his years as an Investigator, he had never experienced anything like it. It was as if part of the boy's memory was blocked, even from his own recollection. It was not like he was blessed with the ability or training to evade an Investigator—Crisdan had experienced that—this was something else entirely. Some magic Crisdan didn't understand was at work. After he proved the deceased High Magistrate's malfeasance, he would need to return to this mystery. If someone was secretly altering the mind and memories of the Empire's citizens, this could prove to be as dangerous as rebel factions. Or maybe it was the tool the rebels used to undermine the Empire.

As Crisdan and Ninel entered Winthral Field, Crisdan shuddered. Almost everything about this investigation was unnerving. Each turn revealed a new and almost unimaginable scene; it made Crisdan extremely wary of this fallow farm field and what it could be hiding. He wanted justice for Zornan. He always wanted the truth. But what if by pulling this one thread, the entire net holding the Empire together came unraveled?

He and Ninel spent the next few hours combing the field, joined after an hour by the Enforcer who'd taken Mistar to the constable's office. During these first few hours they found nothing. If there had been a struggle between Stethdel and a Baldra, or if Silver had been here, the evidence had washed away in the rain. Frustrated by their lack of progress, Crisdan split them up, sending the Enforcer to walk between the field and Zornan's home and Ninel into the woods west of the field. Crisdan took the woods to the north.

It was a relief to be alone. Crisdan was sure that Karzdiff had instructed the Enforcer to keep an eye on him. The relentless man was likely in contact with the muscle-bound fool at this very moment. Crisdan sent him in the direction he thought least likely to reveal anything. And even if it did, that mindless brute would probably walk right over it.

Ninel was a stark contrast to the Enforcer; he was a good man, and a good constable. For someone who lacked the blessings of an Investigator, he was good at judging the character and intentions of people. Yes, he had missed Mistar's lie, but Crisdan did not blame him for that. The constable was diligently working with the abilities the gods bestowed upon him; that was to be respected.

Crisdan passed into another clearing and saw what he'd been looking for: a sign that someone had been here recently. The charred remains of the fire were nearly washed away, and there was an outline where someone had slept.

Crisdan stared at the extinguished fire and slowly circled the clearing, looking for any other signs of who had been there. The outline of the bed was telling; in order for it to have lasted through the rain, someone would have slept there several days. It wasn't Stethdel; he had stayed every night in Fallindra. He couldn't imagine the Baldra had been this careless in concealing its camp. The outline was also not tall enough for Stethdel, though it was likely a man or maybe a tall woman.

As he continued his circle, he saw some brush near the roots of a tree that looked out of place. A closer look revealed it to be branches piled together to look like a small plant. But it hadn't been done well, and whoever had been in this campsite was not experienced enough to cover their tracks. That eliminated the Baldra or a well-traveled High Tradesman.

Crisdan pulled the branches away and uncovered a large green bag matching the one Stethdel had been seen carrying when he arrived in Fallindra. Originally, Crisdan had assumed the bag contained whatever Stethdel wanted Zornan to carry, but here it was, sitting in the woods seemingly untouched. What had Zornan been asked to carry if not this bag?

Crisdan's natural inclination was to reach out in mindspeak to Karzdiff and reveal this discovery. But he hesitated. Karzdiff's motivations were not the same as his. Crisdan wanted justice, wanted the truth. Karzdiff, for all his words about finding the truth, wanted nothing more than to finish this investigation, condemn Zornan, and move on. If this bag revealed Stethdel to be a traitor or in any way confirmed Zornan's initial story, this investigation would transform into something very different: the discrediting of a dead High Magistrate and the wounding of the reputation of the entire Magistrate High Trade.

This was exactly the type of entanglement Karzdiff would try to avoid. If it came to it, Crisdan feared the other Investigator would destroy evidence or hide the truth to protect Imperial politics. Crisdan had been shocked the day before by Karzdiff's refusal to listen to Calla's new story, by how long it took to convince him to do anything but ignore it. By the end of their conversation, Crisdan worried that Karzdiff had agreed only to shut Crisdan up, still hoping their search turned up nothing but air and ghosts.

But Trillia would want to know about this. The woman seemed intent on uncovering the truth, on proving Zornan's innocence and discrediting Stethdel. She would see this as an opportunity, not a stone hung around a mrakaro's neck.

Trillia, it is I, Crisdan. He reached out to the Magistrate, repeating the phrase a dozen times. They had not yet connected via mindspeak, so this might not work. Many High Tradesmen protected their minds to the point that the only new people they let in were ones standing right in front of them.

This is highly unconventional, Investigator, she finally responded. *Why do you bother my mind?* Her emotions emanated extreme annoyance.

I found something: Stethdel's bag. And it looks like he was accompanied by someone else. I may be close to exonerating Zornan.

And discrediting the Magistrates. Her mind voice echoed with glee. *Bring the bag here, Crisdan. I need to see it and speak to you about another matter that is important to your investigation.*

I must bring it to Karzdiff, my lady.

No! she shouted. *Come to me, Crisdan, before him. He will only destroy it. He's the puppet of the High Investigators, and they are closely tied to the High Magistrates. If that bag reveals anything incriminating about Stethdel or his High Trade, Karzdiff will make sure no one ever sees it.*

Her concerns echoed his own: Karzdiff was not going to let this out. An important piece of evidence like this, the belongings of a High Magistrate, was only to be opened in the presence of two Investigators of the High Trades or by one member of the High Investigators. Because Crisdan was under investigation himself, he would not be chosen to look through it. Karzdiff or the High Investigators could claim it held nothing more than some clothes, and that would be that.

You are right, Lady Magistrate. It will take me some time to get it discreetly to your house—tonight after dark.

Excellent. You are doing the right thing, Crisdan Investigator.

Crisdan cut off his connection with Trillia and stared at the bag. He wasn't going to wait for her, either; he needed to know now what Stethdel had been hiding.

Crisdan carefully opened the bag and his heart sank. It *was* filled with clothes. Yes, there was a High Magistrate uniform, which confirmed it was likely Stethdel's bag, but that was hardly damning. If it only contained personal effects, any number of circumstances could explain the bag's placement, and no explanation would be enough to incriminate Stethdel or free Zornan. If it was just some personal effects, he might as well just bring it to Karzdiff and be done with it.

His heart sank further when he emptied the back and found nothing but clothes, a dried loaf of bread, and a few pieces of dried fruit. The bag was waterproof, so everything in it was dry, but it was nothing more than a bag packed for a long journey. No indication of why Stethdel came to Fallindra, of what he asked Zornan to carry for him, or of who was with him in the woods. Was Crisdan wrong about everything? Had he been fooled by Zornan's naïve act and Calla's manipulation? Was Stethdel merely a High Magistrate who yearned for an obscure vacation and got caught in a murderous plot? Crisdan's mind strained to accept that based on the other facts, but his ability to prove otherwise was dwindling.

As he removed the food, he felt something at the bottom of the bag.

As he touched it again, he heard paper crunching under his touch, but saw nothing. He pulled at the cloth on the bottom of the bag, revealing a pouch containing dozens of papers.

He pulled out each one carefully, examining them. A quick scan revealed no names, but it didn't matter: the letters were about the Kuthraz. He recognized their code, and even more importantly, he recognized the script of the writer of most of the correspondence: Lascrill. These were letters from Lascrill to Stethdel, arguments about what to do and how to carry out actions among their group and against the Empire. Much of it was in coded language, so it made little sense, but it would after they examined it. This series of letters was a treasure. Only a few Kuthraz items were found in Lascrill's home; most of what they found was innocent writing between him and dozens of former Peak Crosser pupils. None of the letters indicated that Lascrill or Stethdel was the leader, but they referred to a third person who might be.

The last of the letters was written in a woman's hand, possibly to Stethdel. Crisdan had scanned the other letters, but this one he examined closely. It was not addressed to anyone, and it was only signed, "Your Love." He began to read.

My Dearest and Sweetest Love,

It has been so many years since those days we spent together. We were much younger, and naïve enough to believe our love stronger than the forces that would keep us apart. Only one thing remains from those days, and she is in your tender care. I am comforted to know you will treat her with all the tenderness you've always shown to me.

I have sent the information on the reunion location in a separate correspondence because I know you're a sentimental fool and will want to keep this letter. I wish I could claim less sentimentality—that I burned each of your letters after reading them—but they are precious to me. So I cling to them, as I cling to the vain hope that someday we may all be reunited—you, me, and the result of our love—living together as families should. But I know this is impossible, so I try not to think of it too often. If I think of it too much, the sadness overcomes me like a storm in the Ice Mountains, freezing me for days.

I wish you could deliver her, but I know that would not be wise. I also hope you can find someone outside of your little band to bring her. I trust them only slightly more than the forces you fight against. They would use her as a weapon in their fight. I know you trust them and think this fear paranoia, but the youngest of you three is ruthless. I am convinced he would watch his own mother die if it helped your cause.

Sometimes I believe the blessing I gave her was too much, but I will say no more about that. Please find someone trustworthy, someone who can protect her. Not from physical harm but from corruption by all the forces in this world striving for chaos. Like any mother, I wish for a simple life for my child. But her blessing and her parentage make that impossible.

Travel safely, my love. If you feel neither of the reunions will be safe, send word by our normal channel. It breaks my heart to think I might not see her soon, but I realize how dangerous this endeavor is, even for someone with your authority and abilities. Please be careful, not just for her sake, but for yours. I can't bear to think that something would happen to you, especially since I was the reason we had to pluck her from her tranquil life.

Crisdan read the letter through a dozen times; he needed to commit it to memory. After he was sure it was memorized, he put all the letters back in the pouch and repacked the bag as best he could, hiding it under the same pile of brush. It was a risk to leave it out here, but he couldn't carry it back into town. He would have to come back after dark to retrieve it and take it to Trillia. She would be very pleased; the correspondence from Lascrill was a dagger, especially in light of the fact that the old Peak Crosser trainer and Stethdel had been in the same place consistently over the years for no official reason. That, in and of itself, could be coincidence. But when combined with these letters from his fellow Kuthraz conspirator, it would be enough to open a full investigation into Stethdel. That is, if any of this evidence was ever presented to the High Investigators.

The revelation in these letters that tied everything together was simple: Stethdel had a child. Crisdan knew this law was often broken, but the child was usually killed shortly after birth. It was a harsh law, but history demanded the cruel justice. The children of the High Trades sometimes grew up to have blessings, even without the magical touch of a priestess, powerful blessings that made them as dangerous as Baldra but without the control of a Shindar. These children of the High Trades had caused civil wars and countless deaths in the past. The more powerful High Trades were completely restricted from having children; only Peak Crossers, Tunnelers, and Imperial Traders were allowed by law to have children because their children rarely exhibited any blessed abilities. Even then, as regulated by the Grand Council of the High Trades, these High Tradesmen could only marry and have children with those not of the High Trade. The kin of two High Tradesmen were the most dangerous kind, and that's why the blessings of most High Tradesmen took away the ability to even have children.

For a High Tradesman to not reveal a child was considered treason, and the punishment was execution. So Stethdel had rightly feared having his secret discovered. That's why he had manipulated Zornan—he needed someone to carry the child to her mother, probably to a meeting spot only a Peak Crosser could reach. Unfortunately, in the Empire of the Peaks, that did not narrow down the meeting spots much.

The mother. If he was to believe the letter, the mother was a priestess of Bendathdra. That seemed impossible. The priestesses were isolated in a location known to few. They were bound by law to remain in their isolated home, except when they were brought to the Initiatory School to bless the initiates as they were separated into their academies, or to oversee special High Trade or Imperial events. How could she and Stethdel ever have connected? Bendathdrans were trained by their own, not at the Initiatory School. And to Crisdan's understanding, the priestesses were guarded, both for their protection and to keep something like this from happening. Rumor said they were all sterile, so even if a priest and priestess gave in to the temptation of their isolation, children would not be the result.

But if Crisdan understood the letter correctly, the mother of Stethdel's child was indeed a priestess. What kind of power would the child of a High Magistrate and a priestess hold? Crisdan wasn't sure, but it sounded as if her mother had blessed her beyond that. This explained everything— Stethdel's impulsive actions, the campsite, Zornan's willingness to do what Stethdel asked. Zornan was an honorable man and a father; he would see the girl to her destination before trying to return to his family.

Crisdan turned to finish his search of the woods. He would reunite with Ninel in a few hours, call off the search for today, and return after dark to get the bag. Then he would visit Trillia.

32 | MIND GAMES

The night was blessedly dark, with spots of clouds covering most of the stars and one of the visible moons. Crisdan appreciated the darkness as he crept through Fallindra, toward Trillia's home in the center of the small city. Though it provided excellent cover, the darkness made his walk through the city slow. Crisdan wished at the moment for the better night vision of a Peak Crosser. But if he couldn't see anything, then likely no one could see him.

The last few hours had tested Crisdan's nerves. When he'd returned to report to Karzdiff about their fruitless search, the man became paranoid to the point that his emotional walls fell, and Crisdan could momentarily feel his fear. Karzdiff quickly regained his composure and hid his emotions again, but not before it became clear that the possibility of finding something incriminating about Stethdel frightened him. That made Crisdan even surer of his decision not to involve his fellow Investigator. Had he brought the bag to Karzdiff, the veteran Investigator would have found a way to make it disappear. The man was a disgrace to their High Trade; he wasn't interested in justice, only in his career and the political ramifications of the situation. Investigators were supposed to be above that. Crisdan's ideals had never left him feeling so isolated.

Yet he was not alone. He had an ally in Trillia.

After Karzdiff's uncharacteristic display of emotion, he ordered all the available Enforcers to guard the field and wanted a massive search of the area the next day. The guards had complicated retrieving the bag, but Enforcers weren't any better at seeing in the dark than he was, and he knew where they were stationed. And they were lazy. Several had grouped together to talk or play cards under the light of a torch. A cosow could have walked past them unseen.

Still, it took longer to retrieve the bag than it otherwise would have, and as he crept toward Trillia's house, he was sure it was after midnight. Time was running out. He would have to be back at the constable's office by daybreak or Karzdiff would grow suspicious.

Trillia's house was across the street now, only a few yards away, in the part of the city that contained all the homes of the Low Trade. Before Stethdel's murder, the Low Tradesmen of Fallindra worried little about their safety, but now many of them hired a guard or two to watch their homes at night. If a High Magistrate wasn't safe, who could be?

After several moments of scanning the street, looking for any signs of movement, Crisdan sprinted across the street toward her door. The door opened slowly as he made it halfway. He slipped through the door, and it closed behind himself. How had she seen him from across the street in the dark?

"You are late, Investigator." It was Trillia's voice in the darkness, coming from several yards in front of him. As she spoke, she lit a small lamp in her hand, lighting the hallway.

Crisdan gasped when the light revealed a giant man standing closely beside him, so close that Crisdan could feel his breath on the top of his head. He was at least a half a foot taller than Crisdan, who was taller than most, and was almost as wide as he was tall. He had the size of a Shantierd, but lacked its inhuman features. Everything about him was big: massive hands, a large nose, and long auburn hair. He looked down on Crisdan with a blank, cold expression.

"Come, Crisdan. Let us see what Stethdel's bag has to tell us."

Trillia led the way to her office. Crisdan hoped the giant would not follow, but he did. At least he wasn't so close now, his heavy feet echoing eerily through the hallway, drowning out any sound Crisdan or the Magistrate made.

Trillia's judgment room was set up as before, except for a second table set up behind her desk with no chairs surrounding it. Several glow globes lit the room, an extravagance Crisdan had not noticed on his first visit.

"Place the bag on my desk and have a seat," the woman said as she sat in her chair. Crisdan did as he was told and sat in a chair in front of her. She did not move to open the bag, and they sat in silence for several minutes as she stared at him, her expression and emotions unreadable. The large guard stopped by the door to the room and stood there motionless.

"You are causing me some problems, Crisdan Investigator," she finally said.

"What? I thought this is what you wanted? This bag will give us what we need to prove Zornan's innocence and embarrass Stethdel and the High Magistrates. Isn't that what you wanted?"

"I'm not speaking about this," she replied, waving at Stethdel's bag. "I'm speaking of you questioning my citizens without talking to me first."

Her citizens? he thought. *Since when did they become her citizens?* "That is not required by law, your grace. After learning from Calla that Stethdel retrieved Zornan's mrakaro, I knew that either the Peak Crosser keep..."

"You misunderstand," she interrupted. "I am not speaking about law. I'm speaking about wisdom. I thought a man as perceptive as you would understand that I could guide your investigation and keep you from trouble. But now you've uncovered something you shouldn't have, and that makes every decision I make now very complicated. I thought our alliance was going to be simple."

"I do not understand, Magistrate."

"Of course not. You have no reason to connect me to it, but it is knowledge that cannot leave this town. There are those of your kind who would know exactly what had happened the moment you explained it to them."

Crisdan's brow furrowed as he struggled to understand her meaning. "The boy. You're speaking about my interview with Giltar, the Peak Crosser keep apprentice."

"Ah," she smiled, her eyes glowing in the dim light of the glow globes. "You are such a good Investigator, not just with the proper sense of justice, but your mental skills exceed your blessing. That makes this all the more difficult."

"I'm sorry, Magistrate, but you overestimate me. I know you speak of the boy, but I don't know how you would be connected to that. What is wrong with him? Who did that to him?"

"I did."

The tone was simple and direct, and its implications left Crisdan wrestling for an explanation. A Magistrate's power did not extend to whatever had happened to the boy, unless Magistrates were hiding abilities from the other High Trades. That seemed unlikely; hiding a blessing for centuries would have been a singularly monumental task.

So there was only one explanation that made sense, and Crisdan knew how to verify it. If he was correct, the implications were staggering for him and the entire Empire. If one of them had been hiding in plain sight for decades outside of their sanctuary, it could mean war. So he reached out to probe Trillia's emotions and mind, pushing as hard as he could and as fast as he was able. His attack would have crippled a commoner or Low Tradesman and stunned and overwhelmed even a High Tradesman trained in resisting Investigator pressure. The act of doing this against another High Tradesman was punishable by expulsion from the High Trades, and a lifetime of imprisonment. If he was wrong, this action was a thousand times more damning than anything he'd done so far.

Trillia didn't flinch at the emotional attack. Crisdan felt nothing from her, as if she had no emotions or soul. It wasn't the confused blankness of the boy, but a void of emotion and thought. And that meant only one thing: she was a priestess of Bendathdra or had the power of one. They were the only people he knew of whose emotions existed entirely out of an Investigator's probing.

"See, Crisdan," she said as Crisdan's heart raced and his mouth grew dry. "I knew you'd figure it out. I am not what I appear, Investigator. I am not some idiot Magistrate, blessed with only a decent mind. I am something else entirely. Something much more complete."

"A priestess."

"Not exactly, though my blessing is similar to theirs. No, I am beyond them as well. The Bendathdrans have become weak, complacent, and happy to live in their little mountain and allow lesser creatures like the Magistrates to rule the Empire–even happy to support the rule of an unblessed Emperor. I represent an old guard of Bendathdrans."

"You're Dundraz," Crisdan said. "The High Tradesmen who want to rule the Empire."

"No, Crisdan, I am not Dundraz. The Kuthraz and Dundraz are cowards, simple minds who desire small change. I would reform the entire Empire into what existed millennia ago, where the Blessed ruled and everyone else bowed. Now the Blessed are nothing more than puppets for an unblessed Emperor. And the Magistrates are the worst of the lot. The least blessed of the High Trades, yet somehow they sit at the top of the stairs, casting scraps down on the other High Trades. Were it up to me, I would march in and kill the whole lot of them. Having to hide myself among them over these decades has been infuriating and is one of the reasons I isolated myself out here.

"I have been here for years before the gods revealed why I was drawn to this town. It was Zornan. Yes, the Peak Crosser," Trillia continued, waving aside Crisdan's disbelief. "His core is filled with power, but the current Bendathdrans have lost their ability to see the core. They see only the surface and send many of the most powerfully blessed into menial High Trades, like Peak Crosser. If they knew Zornan's potential, he would be an Imperial Guard or an Investigator or an Enforcer, not some courier moving packages from one valley to another.

"And so I took command of Giltar, my little pet, to watch Zornan's comings and goings, to tell me everything he could about this man of untapped potential. I was stunned to find the man was exactly whom he appeared to be: simple, honest, and completely unaware that he possessed magical abilities."

"So that's why you want him free," Crisdan replied. "You want him to join your cause."

"No, Crisdan." Trillia shook her head, and motioned for her guard to approach. He walked over and hovered next to Crisdan's chair. "The one I serve has no need of a man like Zornan. He can bestow powers beyond anything Zornan could achieve. No, we just need him to not fall into the wrong hands, not be manipulated by the Kuthraz or the Empire to fight against us when the time comes. We need him to remain a simple man so he will stay out of the affairs swirling around the Empire. Unfortunately, Stethdel's foolish actions may have forced Zornan's life into a very different path."

Crisdan sat stunned, his mind racing. He had both admired and mocked Zornan's childlike knowledge of the Empire, but, as it turned out, he himself had seen as little as the Peak Crosser. So much of the reality of his world had been completely obscured. A priestess posing as a Magistrate and controlling minds? A lowly Peak Crosser having more magical potential than most? And some unseen force, far beyond the Kuthraz and Dundraz, pulling strings throughout the Empire? All of these statements would have seemed mere fantasy moments ago, but now they stood as facts, binding him to their will and moving his life into unforeseen and unwanted territory. His existence had been a search for truth, and now he'd uncovered a tunnel ferry's load of it, and yet he yearned for his prior ignorance.

"So now you kill me."

Trillia's dark laugh echoed through the chamber. "Oh no, dear boy. You are much too valuable. Your relationship with Calla will allow me to watch Zornan more closely, and I can always use the abilities of an Investigator."

"I will not serve you," Crisdan said. "I serve the Empire, even with all its flaws."

"I know, Crisdan, that's what makes this so hard. It would be easier if, like Mabhif here, you were a willing servant. But I cannot trust you, so I will own you another way."

The guard seized Crisdan, lifted him into the air, and pinned Crisdan's arms to his side. He tried to resist and reach for his hatrindi, but the guard's strong hands restricted his movements. So Crisdan kicked Mabhif as hard as he could in both thighs, but his blows didn't even cause a flinch or a grunt. The giant man carried Crisdan over to the table behind Trillia's desk and pinned him to it. Trillia brought over thick cords, and the two of them tied Crisdan to the brastilia table. The bindings were so tight and complete that he could only move his head and his feet. Mabhif unsheathed Crisdan's hatrindi and tossed it across the room. Crisdan struggled with everything he had, but it was useless. He was completely at the will of this witch.

"I am truly sorry, Crisdan." Trillia stood in his view now, holding a hadbindhi, the sacred tool of the Bendathdrans. The brastilia staff, though half Crisdan's height, looked like a full staff in the hands of the tiny Magistrate. He had only seen one once before, at his blessing day more than fourteen years before. "You are too good a man to be treated like this, and I hope someday you are grateful that I gave you this life rather than killed you. Some Investigators search the Empire for people like me, people with power beyond their blessed calling. I cannot be uncovered yet; my work is too important."

Crisdan spat at her but missed. He screamed as loud as he could, but it was just a verbalization of his anger; he knew no one would hear him.

"Calm yourself," she said, stroking his shoulder. "One way or another, it will be over soon."

"But this is impossible," he said, trying to remove the panic from his voice. "Blessing a mature man will kill him. You're going to kill me anyway."

"Perhaps," she replied, her eyes tinged with a sadness Crisdan did not believe or feel. "Blessing a fully mature creature can have very bad results. The blessing, as it tries to tie itself to your soul, may very well overwhelm and kill you. I have watched it happen—it is a gruesome, slow way to die. But it is more likely that you will come out unscathed and completely obedient to my commands, like a Baldra with its Shindar. Or perhaps the intrusion into your mind drives you mad. Whatever happens, we'll know soon enough. Pray for the last option. Do not seek out death."

Crisdan struggled and screamed again, but the cords bound him as tightly as a school of fish wrapped in a fisher's net. His scream echoed through the chamber, bouncing off the walls and back to him, silent to the world beyond. Karzdiff and the Enforcers might be able to save him, but no one knew he was here. He had not trusted his own kind. Trusting his life to just one fishing spot would be his undoing.

"Hold still, Crisdan. This will hurt less if you relax and let the spell work its way through your body."

Trillia stood next to him now and began to swing the hadbindhi above her head. She muttered in the ancient Bendathdran tongue. Crisdan could only pick up a few words, the words "power" and "mind," the remainder of the meaning lost in her fast-speaking gibberish.

Crisdan yearned for death. He did not want to be like the boy Giltar and have holes in his memories and his soul. This was a fate worse than death, imprisonment, or anything else he could imagine. If what Trillia said was true, his will and freedom were about to evaporate.

Then the pain began. It started as a dull sensation in his chest then spread through his entire body, as if the blood carried the pain to each cell and organ. He screamed again, this time uncontrollably, cursing every god he could think of and shouting obscenities at the priestess and her guard. Trillia did not seem to notice, her eyes closed and her countenance pale. She was straining, as if Crisdan's body were rejecting the blessing and she was struggling to keep it in.

The pain intensified to the point that he began to drift between reality and dream, his body struggling with the magical intrusion. He looked up at Trillia again; her face was contorted, and she was shouting the spell and twirling her hadbindhi as fast as she could. Blackness began to overcome his sight, and he hoped she was wrong, hoped that he would die. He hoped that when he next awoke, he would find all his ancient ancestors gathered to greet him back on the shores of Koofpash. Since his boyhood days, he'd rejected the religion of his father, discounting it as pure superstition. Now he hoped it was true, that his ancestors would take his soul and free him from this. As the darkness overwhelmed him, he hoped this final prayer was not the last free action of his life.

33 | DREAMS AND REALITY

Calla sat up in bed, her forehead beaded with sweat, jolted out of sleep by the second intense dream of the night. She didn't often remember her dreams, but these two scenes burned in her mind.

In the first, she saw the world as if she were Zornan. He was in some remote valley mounting Silver. A young, blond woman rode with him on his giant bird. Another woman, her skin dark and her hair short, mounted what looked like a giant rat with wings; Calla couldn't remember what those giant flyers were called. A nervous young man sat behind her. Somehow, Calla knew the other Peak Crosser was Maeltha, an old friend of Zornan's whom he had mentioned once or twice. The young man was Zornan's younger brother Ballin, and the girl's name was Mairie. Calla saw the brief scene through Zornan's eyes and felt his emotions. He was worried about his brother, who had something stuffed in his mouth to help him breathe while flying. He was frightened of Mairie, which Calla thought odd. Why would he be frightened of a young woman, a girl? And his heart burned when he thought of Maeltha.

Calla turned jealous as she thought back on that and cursed herself for it. She had been flirting for weeks with a man she hardly knew; certainly she could forgive Zornan some old emotions about someone he'd loved many years ago. And her jealousy was even more ridiculous, since this was only a dream. She could not be angry at Zornan for feeling something he wasn't actually feeling. She was not sure how she had conjured up the brief scene of this group getting on two giant flyers and launching into the air. The dream had ended with Zornan's exhilaration at being back in the air and on Silver.

The second dream was longer and a true nightmare. She was Crisdan in that dream, and he was tied to a strange table. Trillia, the Magistrate of Fallindra, stood above him waving a strange staff and shouting something in an unknown language. Crisdan felt intense fear as pain coursed through his body. And he screamed. Oh, how that scream still rang hauntingly in her ears even though she was awake.

Her first instinct when she awoke was to run to Trillia's house, but reason kept her in bed. These were dreams, nothing more. If Zornan had been here, he would have told her that they were not omens or visions, just her mind trying to deal with the intense stress she was under. If she ran to Trillia's house in the middle of the night and accused her of some strange ritual involving Crisdan, she would be locked away as a madwoman.

She lay back down and tried to dismiss the dreams, but she could not. She could still feel Zornan's longing for Maeltha, could still hear Crisdan's terrifying scream. She finally sat up and lit the lamp in her room and took out paper and some ink. She wrote down the details of each dream, as well as she could recall them. She'd never written down a dream before, but it felt right to record the details. She wrote down everything, replaying the dreams as they continued to float through her mind. When she finished both tales, she felt better. Exhaustion overtook her, and she soon drifted into a dreamless sleep.

Crisdan sat up, the cords which held him were gone. Mabhif stood guard by the front door. Crisdan rubbed his eyes, trying to decide if the events of this night had been real or imagined. As he tried to move, his body screamed in pain, especially his head, as if he'd been knocked out or had too much to drink. He put his head in his hands and steadied himself. After a few moments, the intensity of the pain decreased, and he was able to stand. If Crisdan's movement worried the large guard, it did not show.

Crisdan looked around the windowless room. How long had he been out? Had the blessing worked? Was he now under Trillia's control? Besides the pain and some dizziness, he felt no different. He also did not feel mad, though he wondered if madmen felt mad at all. Despite himself, he laughed at the thought.

He looked around the room, hoping to find his hatrindi, but it was not on the floor where Mabhif had thrown it. As he stood, he realized that the weapon was at his side, sheathed. Mabhif was large and powerful, as Crisdan had felt before, but maybe if he surprised him, pretended to be under Trillia's control, he could escape.

Do not hurt Mabhif, ever. As Trillia's voice filled his mind, he knew he could no longer attempt to hurt the man. *This is my first command to you. There will be many more.*

Where are you? Crisdan thought back, anger filling him.

Relax, Crisdan. With her thought, he relaxed, the tension falling from him. Her control was complete. The blessing had worked.

Curse the ancestors! he thought to himself, though he couldn't be sure that any of his thoughts were his own anymore.

I have a few more commands. You can never tell anyone what I've done to you, who I truly am, or anything about me except what you knew before you came to Fallindra and what I instruct in the future. And you cannot kill yourself or take foolish risks with your life. You are too valuable to me now.

I appreciate your concern.

Sarcasm does not become you, Investigator. That was not a command, and he felt as though he could still be sarcastic. But he held his bitter thoughts to himself anyway.

You can also tell no one anything of our conversation last night, except if I give you permission. And even then, you can only tell the specific details I authorize.

What time is it?

It's just after sunrise. I have many tasks for you today. First, I hid Stethdel's bag in the woods where you found it. Now we need Ninel to find it. Send him to search where you searched yesterday. He will bring it to me, and once it's in my official possession, I can reveal its contents to the Magistrates. I will do so publicly to ensure it is not buried. Stethdel's reputation will be destroyed, and Zornan's will be restored.

Is Ninel under your control as well? Crisdan asked, wondering just how deep her talons dug into this town.

No, it is only safe to control two at a time. Ninel views me as the authority of this valley, and he and I already have an understanding that he'll bring what he finds to me. He already guessed that Mistar had helped Stethdel get Silver from the keep, but he only shared that with me and not you.

Crisdan grimaced. Trillia controlled everything in this valley. Years before, she had expelled the Enforcers who had been stationed here and had dismissed the last Investigator to work here as well. Now those actions made more sense; not only did it ingratiate her to the people of

Fallindra, but it kept curious eyes away from anything she might do.

What other commands do you have for me?

Only one more: after Ninel has brought the bag to me, visit Calla and let her know what's been discovered and that Zornan, if he can be found, will be a free man. Let her know that I will help free him. Use her feelings for you. Be affectionate, kind, and loving. I want her feelings for you to grow.

Why?

I have my reasons. Now go and do as I've commanded. And don't do anything that will raise suspicion of you. Act as you normally would outside of these commands. It's important that you maintain your status as an Investigator. I have so many wonderful plans for you. Trillia's glee at the thought made Crisdan sick.

Free of her voice, he stood and wobbled toward the door. His legs were weak, his head hurt, and his chest ached. Couldn't she have at least commanded him not to feel like this?

As he passed Mabhif, the large man smiled. "Welcome." It was the first word he'd heard the giant say, and Crisdan wanted to take his hantrindi and ram it through him. But the thought was washed away as soon as he formed it, his angry desire dissipating into nothing.

His free will was gone, absorbed by Trillia's wicked blessing. He was her tool now, forced to do her bidding. At that moment, he did not feel angry or sad, did not feel like crying or screaming. He felt numb. The feeling which overwhelmed all others was to go and do exactly as Trillia commanded.

34 | TROUBLED FLIGHT

Today could be the day Zornan could be free. Not completely free to return to his family, but free from the burden of Mairie, free from the forces throughout the Empire swirling around her. It felt as if the entire world was searching for her, some to protect her, others to destroy her, and Zornan and Ballin were caught like a scavenging wild dog pinned between two dueling prairie cats: the battle wasn't theirs, but it could still kill them.

They flew among the Infinite Mountains, their peaks forming their path. They traveled low to avoid detection but also because cosows were not comfortable flying as high as mrakaros, a fact Silver used to reinforce the inferiority of cosows.

Despite the low altitude, Ballin had been battling flying sickness almost since the moment they'd taken to the air. He had looked better this morning after a night's rest, but whatever recovery he'd made was short-lived; Zornan could see Ballin's discomfort even at a distance. Zornan flew with Mairie on Silver, and they glided behind Maeltha's cosow. Ballin was coughing and shaking. Twice the nibrak had come out of his mouth during a particularly violent coughing spell, and Ballin had barely caught it to keep it from falling into one of the narrow mountain valleys below.

"He's not going to make it," Mairie shouted into Zornan's ear, her eyes focused on his brother. "This flight is going to kill him."

Zornan looked back at the girl and nodded. He wanted to fly with his brother, both to keep an eye on him and to get away from Mairie. What had been a fairly warm relationship between Zornan and Mairie at the beginning had devolved into an icy tolerance since that night in Skathall Valley. Zornan could not erase the ferocity he'd seen as she easily killed the mercenaries. She was violence. It might stay hidden most of the time, but that's what she was inside, wound up, looking for release.

But Mairie frightened Maeltha even more. His old friend refused to have Mairie fly with her, insisting that she take Ballin or she would not escort them at all. Zornan had reluctantly agreed. So here they were, flying in an awkward combination, with Zornan wishing he was flying with Ballin or Maeltha, Ballin wishing to be flying with Mairie, Mairie desperately wishing to be with her unknown mother, and Silver just wishing she was flying with another mrakaro and not, as she put it, a flying rodent.

Zornan's thoughts were interrupted by another coughing fit from Ballin, his body violently convulsing against Maeltha. His arms were wrapped around the former Peak Crosser's slender waist.

We're being followed. Silver's thought slammed into Zornan's mind, forcing out his worry for his brother.

What? How can that be?

Because I told them where to find us.

You did what? Told who?

Do not be angry, little rider. We're being followed by my love, Sunset, and his rider Mizcarnon. They are both honorable. Sunset says they want to help us. He says his rider was sent by the Emperor himself to help you and take you home.

Zornan shook his head at Silver's trusting nature. If this Mizcarnon had been sent by the Emperor, Zornan was sure it was to kill them and capture Mairie. There was no Imperial savior waiting to take Zornan home.

He looked behind and saw the outline of a giant flyer in the distance. As a lone rider on a mrakaro, he would catch them before they reached their destination.

Zornan turned his thoughts toward Maeltha. *We're being followed.*

What? came her frantic reply, as she looked back and saw the same distant outline he had seen. *How? Who?*

Silver says that it's a man named Mizcarnon. Do you know him?

How does she know that?

I guess his mrakaro is her love, or some nonsense.

By the three moons, mrakaros are an incestuous bunch.

Do you know of Mizcarnon? I can't place the name.

Yes, I have met him, once very briefly. He's a Peak Crosser scout in the Imperial Army.

A scout? This was getting worse. He and his mrakaro would be some of the best flyers in the Empire. Scouts were also highly trained fighters, both in the air and on the ground. He wouldn't be able to match Mairie on the ground, but in the air he would be able to take them down; Zornan and Silver hadn't practiced any aerial battle techniques since leaving the Academy. And cosows weren't usually used in battle because they were smaller and poor aerial fighters with few natural weapons.

We can't outrun him, Maeltha. He's going to get within range of his bow, and then he'll pick us off.

I know, I know, she replied hastily. *I'm trying to think of a way out of this. But we're flying in the middle of nowhere. There is nothing close by.*

They were meeting Mairie's mother at an abandoned military outpost called Doorie just outside the plains of Fandrill, a desolate place with no populated valley within one hundred miles. A few villages sat to the north and west of Doorie, and Manmandoo was not that far to the south, but that was the direction from which the Peak Crosser scout was tracking them. They were being chased through one of the bleakest regions of the Empire.

We have to ditch your brother, Maeltha thought.

What? We're not just dropping Ballin to his death!

Not dropping him to his death, you idiot. We'll find a suitable valley or cave, leave him provisions, and come back for him after we deliver Mairie. He's slowing us down. And if we fly how we need to fly, it's going to kill him.

Zornan sighed, but he knew she was right. The only solution was to try and lose Mizcarnon in the mountains, weaving low and tight. That kind of flying sometimes made even Peak Crossers lose the contents of their stomachs; in Ballin's condition, it would do much worse than that.

Okay, he agreed. *Do you have a spot in mind?*

I think so. Follow me…if you can. With that, her cosow banked hard to the right and cut into a small valley. He saw Ballin grip Maeltha with all his might as they dived lower among the peaks.

Zornan and Silver followed, flying low and close to the mountain's face. Zornan glanced behind and could no longer see the outline of the scout and his mrakaro; their maneuver had temporarily removed them from his sight. He would be pushing his bird now, too, trying hard to catch a view of them.

They cut between two mountains separated by, at the most, thirty yards. In another time and place, Zornan would have been thrilled to fly like this. Mairie desperately gripped him, even her strength and courage waning. Zornan glanced toward Ballin just in time to see him disgorge himself. He couldn't be sure if Ballin had removed the nibrak in time; if not, they'd have to find another before they came back for him.

The cosow slowed, and Silver angled upward, using the motion to slow herself. The agile cosow dropped almost straight down and landed in a tiny, narrow valley. Zornan could see a small cave near where the giant bat had landed, its opening barely big enough for a man to walk through. Silver flapped her wings and lowered them slowly, landing behind the other giant flyer. The entire jagged valley floor was no bigger than the foundation of Zornan's home in Fallindra.

Ballin jumped off the cosow and collapsed on the ground, his shirt and face still covered in vomit. His skin was pale, and his clothes were drenched in sweat despite the cold. His face was contorted in pain.

"Hurry," Maeltha said, sliding off her flyer. "We need to get him into the cave and get out of here. If that scout finds us here on the ground, we're dead."

Mairie slid off Silver, and quickly untied her quiver from the saddle. She pulled out an arrow, notched it, and turned to scan the sky.

"If he arrives, he's in for a surprise," the young woman snarled.

Maeltha raised an eyebrow.

"I've seen her hit a man in the neck in the dark from more than one hundred feet," Zornan whispered to Maeltha. "She can provide cover."

Maeltha shrugged as she and Zornan each grabbed Ballin under one arm and lifted him off the ground.

"Can you walk, Brother?"

"I think so," Ballin whispered, his voice rough and weak. Ballin took small steps, most of his weight distributed between the two Peak Crossers. As they passed the cosow on the way to the cave, the creature screeched at them, waving its vomit-covered wing.

"Leave him alone, you rat," Zornan snapped. "Or I will let Silver make a meal of you."

Silver screeched at the cosow and spread her wings, almost knocking Mairie over. The smaller cosow sank toward the ground and went silent.

The cave was small, similar to the one Zornan and Mairie had stayed in after fleeing Fallindra. There were no signs that any animal occupied it, which was not a surprise. There was no visible plant life in this valley, nothing to provide food for anything big enough to bother Ballin. It was a dead crevice in a dead valley, a safe hiding place. The only thing in the cave was a small puddle of water in the corner, evidence of a recent rain.

"Stay in the cave," Maeltha instructed, setting Ballin's pack and sword next to him. "There's little danger, but wild giant mrakaros sometimes fly these skies, and if they see a meal your size, they may come after you. There's plenty of food and water in the pack when you need it."

Maeltha left the mouth of the cave and jumped back on her cosow.

"No need to worry about me, Brother," Ballin said, his sickly voice betraying his confident words. "I've survived worse."

Zornan tried to smile. "Take care. We will return as soon as we can. Mournful parting, Brother. Mournful parting."

"Mournful partings make for the best reunions."

Zornan smiled, despite the danger and the nagging feeling that they could be leaving his brother to a slow, painful death. If something went wrong, they had imprisoned Ballin in a valley tomb.

As Zornan exited the cave and mounted Silver, Mairie walked over to speak with Ballin. Zornan spoke encouraging words softly to Silver to avoid hearing their conversation. He knew they were both fond of each other, and they deserved some privacy in their conversation, even if Zornan wished their relationship had not grown as it had.

"Come on, girl," Maeltha called. "This lovers' parting is growing tedious and dangerous."

Mairie wheeled around, drew out her bow and fired a shot toward Maeltha. The arrow flew fast, just missing Maeltha's head, shattering against the mountain wall. Maeltha and Zornan stared at Mairie. The power and precise aim of the sudden shot was like nothing Zornan had ever seen. Or maybe he had seen once in the dark of night not so long ago.

"Keep your mouth shut!" Mairie hissed. "I will say my goodbye. If that Peak Crosser arrives, I will shoot him and his bird out of the sky. So hold your tongue, and remember we have no need of you now that the meeting has been arranged."

Maeltha stared back at Mairie, her expression blank and unreadable.

Mairie turned to finish her conversation with Ballin, and Zornan spoke to Silver again, easing the mrakaro's tension after the brief and sudden violence. He looked up only once to see Maeltha staring at the back of Mairie's head, her eyes now cold and filled with anger.

After a few moments, Mairie leaned into the cave and gave Ballin a kiss on the head. She turned back toward Silver, her eyes glistening with tears. She slung the quiver over her shoulder and leapt onto the giant bird, landing softly in her seat. She strapped in her legs and sat tall. Without any more words, Silver and the cosow launched into the air, climbing back into the sky.

Mizcarnon cursed himself for losing them. They must have seen him in the distance and maneuvered out of view. Tracking them was going to be difficult since he did not know their destination. They were flying toward the Plains of Fandrill, or perhaps they would fly beyond to the Ice Mountains. Sunset said he was still in contact with Zornan's mrakaro, but he was only sharing some things with Mizcarnon now, claiming that sharing everything was unbecoming of a member of his race, a betrayal of their bond.

They weaved tightly into the mountains, going lower toward the valley and crevice floors, imagining a route he might pick if he were being chased. It seemed his best bet unless Sunset could ascertain their location again.

They abandoned the brother of Silver's rider, Sunset thought to Mizcarnon. *He's in a small cave, not two hundred yards from here. He's suffering from the human sickness of flight.*

Take us to the spot, Mizcarnon commanded. If Mizcarnon could explain to the younger brother that he was here to help and protect Zornan, maybe the young man would see the wisdom in telling Mizcarnon where they were going and why. The boy would not likely talk easily, but it was a better plan than flying aimlessly among these desolate mountains.

Sunset weaved between the towering peaks and lowered them into a small crevice valley. Before the mrakaro's feet touched ground, Mizcarnon flung himself from his saddle, landing in a low crouch, his hatari withdrawn, growing as he dismounted. He didn't think the brother would be much of a threat, especially if he was sick enough for them to leave him here, but it paid to be wary.

Mizcarnon approached the cave slowly, its mouth revealing Zornan's brother slumped against a pack, a sword lying across his lap. His eyes were closed, and his breathing was deep and labored. His shirt and pants were covered in vomit and sweat, and the cave reeked of the rancid combination. The cave was too small for open combat, so Mizcarnon reduced his hatari, but kept it in his left hand. With his free hand, he picked up the sword and laid it to the side, out of reach.

"Are you awake?" Mizcarnon spoke in a normal tone, trying to avoid startling the young man. But the commoner did not stir, remaining unconscious despite the movement and noise. Mizcarnon spoke again, louder, his voice echoing through the cave and the crevice valley. Still nothing. The boy was alive, but he was very sick, and Mizcarnon decided against violently waking him. The Peak Crosser backed away slowly and quickly remounted Sunset.

Where to now? Mizcarnon thought at his companion.

They fly to a place called Doorie, Sunset thought back. *They are meeting the girl's mother there.*

Mizcarnon leaned back as he considered this sliver of information leaking from Zornan's mrakaro, to Sunset, to him. What a strange way to track someone, flying blind most of the time, but getting clearly lit views every once in a while, like navigating a deep, dark wood during a lightning storm.

Doorie made sense as a meeting place. The forgotten military post was a relic of the ancient conflict between the Fandrillans and the Crazdarians, a time when the two flatland kingdoms fought for supremacy of the Infinite Mountains. It had also served, for a time, as a Bristrinian outpost after the second great Emperor of the Peaks had conquered the Fandrillans and the northwestern valleys. To Mizcarnon's knowledge, it had been abandoned for centuries, a remote reminder of long-forgotten conflicts.

Then let us not delay, Mizcarnon thought to Sunset. The bird took a couple of steps and launched them into the air, leaving Zornan's brother in the cave below.

One more question. How do you know where Silver is?

I can feel her location, Sunset replied. *Much like we can feel each other. My bond to her is that strong.*

That won't tell you where she's going, Sunset. Did she tell you more?

Yes. The bird's thoughts were hesitant and faint. *She told me everything she knows.*

Mizcarnon hesitated. Though Sunset could be temperamental and prideful, he was the strongest mrakaro Mizcarnon had ever known. His communication with Silver was something he held as sacred, and he knew Sunset was sharing it because of the honor this assignment could bring to Mizcarnon. He did not want to denigrate his closest friend, but they could not fail the Emperor.

Then you must tell me what you know, Sunset. We are here to help

Zornan and Silver. We may be their only hope of survival. I know it pains you to break that trust, but you must. I have to know what we're getting into.

I cannot tell you everything, came Sunset's melancholy reply. *But I will tell you what we need to know to help them. That is all I can promise, loyal rider. And that is more than I should. It is more difficult for me than you'll ever know.* Sunset banked to the left and took them into another narrow pass, angling toward Doorie.

35 | COMPULSION

The darkness hanging over Crisdan would not leave. He'd hoped that somehow he would awake from this terrible nightmare, that his will would become his own again. But each morning he awoke to the same pollution tainting his soul. Trillia's voice rang through his mind, and her commands bound him a thousand times tighter than an Imperial decree.

Ninel had Stethdel's bag, and Trillia now had her cudgel with which to destroy the reputation of a dead High Magistrate and exonerate Zornan. If only she'd let Crisdan stop there.

He stood at Calla's door, Trillia's command moving his arm to knock, even as his mind screamed to stop. But he had no power to stop, no power to resist. He would be forced to wound the only decent person in this entire fiasco.

Calla answered the door, her eyes lighting up. He could feel her desire for him, even if she tried to bury it. Her shame burned along with the affection, dueling waves roiling together in an unpredictable tide.

"Crisdan." She didn't use his title. "This is a surprise."

He smiled, but he hoped his eyes betrayed him. Could Trillia's commands change his eyes, the windows to his soul? He hoped some part of him could stay true, could testify of his true intentions.

Use her affection, Trillia had commanded. *You will be the wedge to divide Calla and Zornan.*

Why? Crisdan had pleaded. *What purpose could that serve?*

A higher purpose you wouldn't understand even if I shared it. You will kiss and hold her, let her feelings free. You might even enjoy it yourself.

Crisdan hated Trillia. Crisdan hated himself.

"I had not planned to visit you today," Crisdan said truthfully.

"Do you have news? Has the letter opened a new road home for Zornan?" Her hope surged, overpowering the feelings she'd flashed about him. This was not going to work. She desired Crisdan, but she loved Zornan.

"I have no news." His words hung between them.

Calla's emotions quickly shifted to nervousness, and she glanced around, as if her mother might appear.

"Where is your mother?"

"Out." Her desires swirled again, a yearning for Crisdan, but twisted and dashed by guilt and love for Zornan.

He reached forward and put his hand against Calla's bare arm. She shivered but did not recoil.

"I have not been completely honest with you." *Run, Calla! I am not myself.* "My motives have not been pure." *I don't want to do this.* "I think you know, but I have developed deep feelings for you. You are unlike any woman I've ever met." The words were true, but out of his mouth at this moment they came as the worst kind of lie.

Calla stepped back, her scrambled feelings cresting and crashing. "Crisdan, I..."

Before she could speak again, he gently held her arms and kissed her. For an ever-brief moment, she kissed him back, the desire burning in her as brightly as he had fantasized it might. But a new emotional tide erupted: anger, distrust, guilt, and horror.

She stepped back, tears erupting, her eyes unwilling to meet his. "Get out."

"Calla, please..."

"Get out!" The force of her scream came like a blow to his face. "You are not the man I thought you were. Please never return here again."

It was over. The one bright star in his miserable new universe had been extinguished.

What now? he asked Trillia, her presence hanging in the back on his mind.

Leave. We've done enough damage. I underestimated her love of her husband. You made a worthy attempt. We still might be able to use this in the future.

The only thing this attempt was worthy of was scorn.

"I am truly sorry, Calla."

"Please address me as Lady Calla, wife of Zornan Peak Crosser."

Her eyes met his now, her sadness transforming into fierce anger and resolve. "Leave."

The force of her command felt nearly as powerful as Trillia's compulsion. Tears stung his eyes the moment he reached the street.

36 | UNEXPECTED

As the sun began to hug the peaks, descending to its daily disappearance, Doorie came into view. It was a mostly flat plateau extending from a slightly taller mountain peak. Doorie's mountain was located in the middle of a desolate, rock-filled valley about the size of the city of Fallindra. Taller mountains obscured the place until you were close, so airborne travelers could easily miss the old military post if they didn't know it was there.

Human additions dotted the lonely, shorter peak. Zornan could see a door carved into the mountain wall where the peak rose out of the plateau, and on the peak itself he saw two windows, posts for scouts to scan the sky. But the structure lacked any visible human presence, as if Doorie were still the same ghost-inhabited structure it had been for centuries.

As Zornan scanned the valley floor, he saw signs of non-human life. Small shrubs covered the valley floor, and small animals scurried about. A hawk circled below them, scanning for an opportunity to grab a meal.

Despite the valley's bleak appearance, they were not alone. On the peaks immediately to the west and east of Doorie were two well-covered outcroppings. Standing in each of them were archers with brastilia longbows at the ready, weapons similar to the one Mairie held in her hand. She saw the archers and notched an arrow. She remained still and calm, not raising her bow. The archers stood menacingly but did not aim arrows at the flyers or their riders.

Nice welcome party, Zornan shot at Maeltha.

The archers? Normal precautions. And we are being followed.

We lost him hours ago, Maeltha. There's no way he could know where we are going. Our earlier course left a hundred destinations open to us, all of them more likely than here.

Of course, that was a lie. Mizcarnon could know exactly where they were going; there was no telling what Silver may have shared with her mrakaro friend. During the journey from Ballin's cave, Zornan had asked Silver if she told Sunset everything, but she ignored the question, filling his mind with another tirade on the uselessness of cosows. So it was possible Mizcarnon still followed them and knew where they were going and why. Zornan didn't push the issue with Silver. If Mizcarnon was close by, there was nothing they could do about it. Soon Mairie would be with her mother, and Zornan could go get Ballin and figure out a way to get back home.

We're going to circle the plateau, Zornan thought to Maeltha.

Why? We have nothing to fear here, and if the scout is on our tail feathers, we need to hurry.

I wasn't asking, Maeltha. We're going to circle Doorie and get a view of the place before we land. You're free to do as you will.

Zornan felt Maeltha's frustration, but she pushed her cosow to the east, beginning a wide circle around the structure; Silver followed. It took several minutes to circle, and the maneuver revealed nothing. Doorie appeared abandoned, the archers the only evidence of human life.

Can we land now please?

Zornan grimaced but tried to hide his growing worry before he replied, *Yes, but let's land near the edge, away from the door.* Maeltha angled her giant flyer toward the far edge of the plateau.

Worry grew in Zornan's mind and body. Maybe Mairie's doubts of Maeltha's intentions were rubbing off on him, or maybe it was his concern over what was next after he was rid of Mairie. Regardless, he'd begun to sweat despite the chill.

Maeltha and the cosow landed first, with Silver, Zornan, and Mairie landing next to them. The cosow laid itself flat and tucked in its wings, allowing Maeltha to step directly onto the ground.

If you could do that, Zornan thought to Silver, eying the prostrated bat-like creature, *getting off would be a lot easier.*

If I could do that, came Silver's defiant reply, *I would also eat the kills of other creatures and play in my own excrement.*

Zornan laughed as he hopped off Silver.

"What's so funny?" Mairie asked.

"Mrakaros have a sharp sense of humor."

Mairie eyed him curiously and shrugged. Silver stretched out her wing and nudged him playfully.

The plateau was unnaturally smooth and flat. If there had been any other structures on its surface, wind and weather had long since destroyed them. The wind at this height was constant, and it swirled in frequent gusts, causing Mairie's hair to dance around the back of her head where she had it pulled back. It was very cold, but their blessed bodies felt little of the biting mountain wind.

I need you to fly away from here, Zornan thought to Silver.

I cannot abandon you, little rider!

It is not abandoning me. I need a scout to circle the valley. Keep an eye on those archers, and let me know if the Peak Crosser scout gets here.

But you may need my help here if this is a trap.

Mairie can defend us, Silver. But only you can patrol the skies. If something happens to us, you have to go back for Ballin. He's alone and will die in that valley if we don't go back for him.

Nothing will happen to you! I will not allow it!

Please, Silver. I need you in the air. And promise me you will do nothing foolish if this meeting goes wrong.

I never do anything foolish, she shot back obstinately, *and I cannot promise I will not try to help you.* With her thought finished, Silver stretched her wings, turned, and launched herself into the air.

"Where's she going?" Mairie asked.

"She'll keep an eye out for the Peak Crosser scout and an eye on those archers."

For the next several minutes, they stood there waiting for the Kuthraz and Mairie's mother to reveal themselves. Mairie wore the bow around her chest, the quiver just visible over her shoulder. She tugged at her long, broad sleeves where she kept her hatnuthri. Her face was anxious, like Windsa's when she asked to play another few minutes before bedtime, filled with an expectant, fearful hope.

A hooded figure emerged from the door, followed by two others in similar attire. The robes were the deep purple of the priestesses of Bendathdra. Circular patterns of brastilia adorned the sleeves and chests. The lead figure was shorter than the other two, but all other details were obscured by their voluminous robes that reached to the ground, hiding even their feet. Their faces were almost entirely covered, showing only a hint of chin. They walked in a quick, measured pace, and their heavy robes swayed lightly in the wind. The three figures stopped just ten feet from where Maeltha, Zornan, and Mairie stood, the lead one still a few paces ahead of the other two. For several moments the figures stood there, motionless.

Movement caught Zornan's eye, and he looked toward the door to see three more robed figures emerging. They walked about twenty feet and stopped, remaining outside the encounter.

Maeltha stood nonchalantly, lacking the rigid tension Zornan felt in himself and could see in Mairie's posture. Whatever today's outcome, his former love was much more confident than he was.

Have the archers moved? he thought at Silver.

No, Zornan. They are in the same position.

The lead Bendathdran finally looked up, revealing a thin, feminine face. She pulled back her hood, unleashing a curly head of blond hair, which whipped violently in the wind. Her hair was identical to Mairie's, and her thin face was similar. She looked like she could be Mairie's mother. She was attractive and pleasant, and after a moment, she smiled at Mairie, her eyes brightening.

"Mairie. My daughter." The Bendathdran reached out her arms.

"Mother," Mairie whispered, and she stepped forward.

Zornan reached out his arm and blocked Mairie's path, Stethdel's final words ringing in his mind: *Mairie looks nothing like her mother. We blessed her to look nothing like either of us.* His parting words had been strange at the time. With a Baldra breathing down their necks, the manipulative High Magistrate had told him a seemingly meaningless bit of family history, and at the time, he hadn't even realized what the man meant by blessing.

But it all made sense now. In order to make Mairie's parentage even more difficult to ascertain, she had been changed to look nothing like her parents. If Bendathdrans could make a human baby into a Shantierd, or create mrakaros from hawks and cosows from bats, surely they could make a girl grow up to bear no resemblance to her parents. And Zornan was one of only a handful of people in the entire Empire who knew about these secret Bendathdran abilities. Deceivers would pick someone who looked the part to pose as the mother; even Mairie would be fooled.

"What are you doing, Zornan? That's my mother." Mairie's voice was strained, and her eyes filled with tears.

"No, it is not," Zornan replied firmly. "Your father told me about your mother. She does not look like this woman. This woman is an impostor. I don't know who she is or why she's impersonating your mother, but I

259

know she's not who she's pretending to be."

"That is ridiculous," the impostor shot back. "I am Mairie's mother. I am Stethdel's lover."

Zornan could tell Mairie still wasn't sure and glanced between the two of them, but she had stopped moving, and he lowered his arm. He tried to think of something Mairie's mother would know, something he hadn't told Maeltha. *Oh Maeltha*, he thought to himself. *How could you betray me like this?*

"Where was Mairie living?" Zornan demanded. "If you are her mother, you'd know where she had been concealed all these years."

"I don't know," came the woman's hesitant reply. "Stethdel kept that secret. It was for her safety. The fewer people who knew, the better…"

"No!" Mairie shouted, the tears streaming down her cheek, the hatnuthri appearing in her hands. "Father said you knew…that my mother knew. That she came to see me once, came to our valley for just a day. Liar!"

The impostor nervously eyed Mairie's hatnuthri. "No, Stethdel was mistaken, I never knew…"

"Shut your mouth, demon woman!" Mairie shouted back. "Or I will cut out that lying tongue!"

The woman's two companions disrobed suddenly, and one pulled out and extended a hatari, while the other pulled out a hatrindi. Zornan saw the other three robbed figures approaching quickly from behind.

"Do you think you can defeat me?" Mairie screamed, tears pouring in streams down her face. "I will kill you all. I will hand you your own hearts while they're still warm! What have you done with my mother? Tell me now, or you all die!"

One of the approaching figures pulled back its hood, revealing a feminine face and long, dark hair. She walked up and stood next to the impostor. She pulled her hands from her robe and started clapping, a smile lighting up her pale face and dark eyes.

"Well done, Zornan Peak Crosser," the newcomer said. "We had been led to believe," she looked over at Maeltha, "that you were a fool, or worse. But you are smart and cautious. In other circumstances, this would serve you well, but it will be your undoing today. We were going to take Mairie and let you leave, as we have no need of you. That was Maeltha's bargain with us. But that will have to be amended now."

Zornan turned toward Maeltha. She stood there as before, but her posture was more erect and she had pulled out her hatari.

"How could you, Maeltha? How could you?"

"You said it yourself," she said, fingering her hatari. "The girl is a monster. These people will take care of her in the way she deserves."

Mairie hissed at Maeltha.

"Don't blame me, girl. Blame your father and mother, and blame Zornan for trusting me. Blaming me is like blaming the wind."

"No, it's not," Zornan replied quietly. "The wind has no choice. You had a choice."

"And you would have survived, Zornan! We could have finally disappeared together, and you ruined it!"

Zornan shook his head. "I ruined nothing." He turned toward Mairie. "I'm sorry, Mairie. I failed you."

Mairie shrugged and placed her hand on his arm.

"As much as I'm enjoying this," interrupted the dark haired woman, "we must get inside. Rumor has it a Peak Crosser scout might be tracking you. So Mairie and Zornan, you will come with us now. Give your weapons to these two men."

"I told you before," Mairie said, her eyes returning to cold rage. "I am going to kill every one of you."

"No, you will not," the woman replied. "You are hopelessly outclassed here, girl."

As the woman finished her statement, the two remaining hooded figures, who were now standing behind the guards, pulled back their hoods as well. Zornan hadn't noticed until that moment that their robes were black, not the purple markings of the Bendathdrans. Their faces bore the sickly white skin of the Baldra. One of them was Zandia.

Mairie leapt high into the air, above everyone's heads, jumping toward the dark haired woman and the impostor. She extended one arm, ready to strike. But before she reached her target, Zandia leapt, crashing into Mairie with a kick to her midsection. The impact sent the girl tumbling to the ground. Zandia landed in a crouch in front of Zornan, her hatnuthri pointing at him.

Zornan pulled out his hatari and extended it, ready to parry if he could. Mairie slammed into Zandia's side, the two rolling together toward the plateau's edge, locked in a powerful struggle. The two women ran for the entrance to the fortress, while the other Baldra stood back, watching the fray. Zornan turned to the two guards, who were standing between him and the Baldra.

A sudden, sharp pain erupted at the back of Zornan's head, and he collapsed to his knees. He could feel a trickle of blood coming from his skull and flowing down the back of his neck. Dancing, blurry lights filled his vision. He struggled to get on his feet but fell back to his knees, the plateau rocking back and forth.

Fly away, Silver! he shouted through his mind. *Save Ballin. Leave us here. Tell Loothdram what happened.*

Zornan looked back, Maeltha looming above him, her hatari touched with a bit of his blood.

"I'm sorry, Zor."

Another blow came down, and Zornan's vision blackened in a surge of pain.

Mizcarnon cursed every god and moon he could think of as he watched the short battle on Doorie's plateau. Zornan lay on the ground, subdued by Maeltha. The girl was also down, defeated by one of the Baldra. The other assassin stood guard, never entering the fight. Zornan and the girl were captured or dead, and there was nothing he could do. Archers guarded the air, and even if he could get close, he and Sunset were no match for two Baldra.

He was perched on a mountain ledge with a clear view of Doorie. Two guards carried the girl. If he hadn't seen the short battle, he would not have believed the young woman's ferocity, her abilities rivaling a Baldra.

Mizcarnon scanned the sky for Silver, but saw nothing. Zornan's mrakaro had been circling the valley moments before, but she'd disappeared from sight. As soon as he deemed it safe, he and Sunset would track down Zornan's mrakaro.

What would he tell the Emperor? Mizcarnon had learned nothing about their captors, and he'd been too late to save them. He had failed them and failed the Emperor. Honor was lost.

Honor is not lost, came Sunset's reply to his unspoken despondence. *Silver is still here.*

Mizcarnon exhaled. *It does not matter, friend. We cannot overcome this. Even with Silver, they're back in their fortress now. And we don't know if Zornan even lives.*

Zornan lives, came Sunset's reply, *Silver can still feel him.*

But we can't rescue him. If we leave, we'll have no idea if they take him from here. If we stay, we cannot get help.

Silver will stay here and watch Doorie, Sunset replied calmly. *She will not leave her rider. She asks that we go back for Zornan's brother and then we can go get help.*

Sunset was right. They could go get the boy, nurse him back to health, and take him back to Bristrinia, probably via tunnel rather than giant flyer. The brother could recount what had happened up until that time. Silver could watch Doorie and track Zornan if he left. It would take weeks to return with a force sufficient to help (if that was what the Emperor wanted), but it was possible. He had failed, but there was still hope for his honor.

Tell Silver to keep watch. We will return as soon as we can.

Mizcarnon mounted Sunset, and they flew low, away from Doorie and back to where Zornan's brother lay.

37 | A TERRIBLE PURPOSE

C risdan finished packing his things, ready for tomorrow's return to Bristrinia. His work was done. Zornan had been cleared of the false accusations. Karzdiff had left in disappointment, deferring to Crisdan as if he knew the younger Investigator would soon be his superior.

Accolades came quickly. A letter of commendation arrived from the High Investigators, praising his delicate handling of a sensitive situation. What an unpredictable sea Crisdan navigated. Had he not found Stethdel's bag or been guided by Zornan's letter to Calla, he'd likely be returning in shame and facing reprimand at the hands of the High Investigators, maybe even expulsion. Now they covered him in praise like a rare jungle-river fish dipped in emperor berry sauce.

The whole affair played like a bard's tale. Zornan, the unwitting Peak Crosser, caught in the snare of a duplicitous High Magistrate. The hero of this tale? Crisdan Investigator.

A second letter arrived from his mentor Hykvan, Master of the Investigators of the High Trades and member of the High Investigators. The old man was effusive in his praise, hinting at Crisdan's eventual ascension to a High Investigator seat, exactly the sort of path Crisdan had tried to avoid. He had been too earnest, too honest, and too unconcerned by the political swirling of his High Trade to ever seriously consider rising to that level. But the moons favored Crisdan, delivering him an investigation that revealed treachery that only would have been more shocking if it had come from the Emperor's court.

First, he'd added Lascrill to his trophy wall and now Stethdel. Two of the highest-ranking men in the Empire proven to belong to the provocative Kuthraz. Hykvan wrote that Crisdan's next assignment would be to oversee a thorough investigation of the Kuthraz organization and to find more members and leaders. He was to return to Bristrinia at once.

However, he was no longer the man Hykvan knew, no longer honest and earnest. He was a puppet now, with strings reaching to an unknown enemy of the Empire, something worse than the Kuthraz. His ascension would mean incredible access for Trillia into the highest councils and activities of his High Trade. Crisdan would be a powerful tool, someone she could use to great effect. A deep, empty feeling wrapped darkly around him as he thought about just how effectively she could use him.

The only failure in Trillia's plan had been Calla, the one event he wished he could change. But it was good that he'd probably never see her again.

Where are the gods now! he screamed in his mind. *Have they forsaken me completely? I have been a valiant servant, but now I sit in a demon's hands doing a demon's work. Curse the gods, curse the moons, curse Trillia!*

Crisdan calmed himself. Fighting this would only lead to madness. Trillia reminded him of that often, and he believed her now. He had to learn to obey willingly, like an ox under a yoke, or he would go mad trying to fight against every action. Maybe madness was preferable to these bonds.

Blessedly, Trillia had been called to Bristrinia to testify in front of the High Magistrates, and during her travels, she had rarely intruded into his mind. Her previous commands still hung over him like the sun, casting their light into every corner of his soul. But at least he could think these thoughts without the foul woman chastising him for them. His thoughts were his for the moment, even if his actions weren't.

I need something to drink. Before Trillia, he'd almost entirely avoided spirited drinks, but the abstention seemed silly now. He finished packing the last of his papers and left the constable's office. It was time to drink himself into a stupor.

"Crisdan Investigator." He stopped short of the door of The Howling Dog, turning toward the man who called his name. He was shorter than Crisdan, though still tall and solidly built. His dusty blond hair was short, and he wore the light gray Peak Crosser uniform of an Imperial scout. He stood with a rigid posture and a sense of purpose, like Crisdan used to.

"Greeting, Peak Crosser," Crisdan said formally.

"Welcome greeting, Crisdan Investigator," the man returned, his accent betraying him as a native of Bristrinia. Not many High Tradesmen came from the capital. The man's feelings burned of urgency and pride. "My name is Mizcarnon. I am an Imperial Peak Crosser scout, and I need to speak with you urgently. I come with orders from the Greatest Emperor of the Peaks, Tothdarin, son of Gathrizdel." Crisdan's eyebrow rose at the Emperor's formal name. "We need to speak in private."

Crisdan nodded. "Follow me, Peak Crosser. We can speak in my office." Delightful drunkenness would have to wait.

Once inside Ninel's office, Crisdan took a seat behind the desk and asked Mizcarnon to sit as well, but the Peak Crosser refused. The man's rigid formality annoyed Crisdan, which birthed a slight, sardonic smile. The man was acting much like Crisdan would have. Why should that annoy him now? Had he been that pretentious just a week ago?

"What brings you to Fallindra, Mizcarnon Peak Crosser?"

"I bring a message from the Emperor himself, Investigator."

"I appreciate that. You can leave the letter of commendation with me. No need for you to stay longer than you need. Fallindra isn't exactly a place for vacation, unless you're a traitorous High Magistrate with a bastard daughter."

Mizcarnon's face wrinkled in confusion, though Crisdan could barely feel the man's emotions. The Peak Crosser had been taught well to control his emotions and reveal little to an Investigator or Counselor. Crisdan could feel some, but it was like comparing a small child's drawing to that of an experienced artist: the artist's lines and colors gave you a clear picture, one that imitated life, while a child's drawing was basic shapes and colors, a picture of a tree not differing much from a picture of a mrakaro. Mizcarnon's emotions were similarly blocky and obscure.

"I have not brought a letter of commendation, Investigator, though you certainly deserve one. I am an Imperial Peak Crosser scout; I only serve in military matters at the command of the generals and the Emperor himself. I do not carry letters."

Crisdan had offended the man with his assumption. *Foolish Peak Crossers and their sensitivities.*

"I apologize, Mizcarnon Peak Crosser. No offense was intended. I just couldn't imagine what military matters could possibly involve me."

"No apology necessary," Mizcarnon replied. "The matter I come for is extremely sensitive. The only letter I carry is a seal of the Emperor giving me the right to act in his name."

The Emperor's seal? Crisdan could think of no historic example where the seal was given to anyone outside of the Emperor's court—

certainly not to a Peak Crosser scout. Having the Emperor's seal in your possession made you his proxy—Mizcarnon's orders were to be obeyed as if they came from the Emperor himself. *Has the Fire Moon fallen from the sky and caused everyone, even the Emperor, to go mad?*

"First, I come with important news," the Peak Crosser continued. "Zornan Peak Crosser is alive, and we know where he is."

"Zornan is alive?" Crisdan blurted out. "That is good news, Peak Crosser." Despite his melancholy, he felt some joy at the news. At least Calla could be whole again. "But I don't understand why you had to come deliver that news to me, especially holding the Emperor's seal."

"Zornan is being held prisoner in a remote location. We believe he and Stethdel's daughter are held by the Dundraz. Are you familiar with that group?"

"Yes. A small rebel group, High Tradesmen who think our kind should be treated as gods and rule the Empire ourselves. Nothing much is known of their organization, if it truly exists at all."

"It exists," Mizcarnon stated emphatically. "And it's not a small, sleepy group anymore. They have a secret base of operations in the northern peaks, and Zornan and Stethdel's daughter are held there against their will. I believe Stethdel was assassinated by the Dundraz. And the Emperor believes that, like the Kuthraz, the Dundraz have buried themselves deep in the leadership of the High Trades."

"So you are going to raid the Dundraz base."

"Yes, that is our plan. We will attack in a few days' time and hopefully free Zornan and bring Stethdel's daughter into custody."

"Why is the military doing this? Shouldn't this be handled by the High Investigators and the Council of the Enforcers?"

Mizcarnon waved his hand dismissively. "All things related to the Dundraz have been declared a military matter and will be handled by the Emperor and his High Generals. The Emperor considered involving the High Investigators, but after the revelation that Stethdel was a traitor, he couldn't be sure a traitor did not sit in your High Trade's highest council as well."

Crisdan did not blame the Emperor for what would have seemed to him like paranoia just a few weeks ago. Unfortunately, this Peak Crosser and the Emperor had come to the most compromised Investigator in the Empire.

"I wish you luck in your raid, Peak Crosser, but I'm still not sure why you came to me with this information. Everything I know of Zornan is in the reports, and I know little of the Dundraz; less than you, it seems. I'm not sure how I can help."

"You are to come with us."

Crisdan coughed and shot forward in his chair. "Come with you? Why on earth would I come with you?"

"First and foremost, because the Emperor commands it. Also, this type of action requires an Investigator to witness that the military acted within the bounds of the law. Many of these Dundraz traitors could be High Tradesmen, either current or former. So we not only need an Investigator, we need an Investigator of the High Trades."

"But why me?"

"Because the Emperor trusts you." Though Mizcarnon's emotions were partially obscured, it was clear the Peak Crosser did not share the Emperor's assessment. "We discussed many options, and you were the only Investigator he was willing to extend this assignment to. His trust alone is a lifetime's worth of honor."

Bristrinians and their yearning for honor. Crisdan cared little for honor, even before Trillia had enslaved him. His desire had been justice. And freeing Zornan and capturing Stethdel's daughter was serving justice. Honor could be cast to the depths of the underworld; he wasn't likely to see any honor the rest of his days. But he might be able to ensure justice done in this case before Trillia buried him too deeply in her plots.

Mizcarnon looked at Crisdan, waiting for a response. How could the man not immediately respond? He'd delivered a command from the Emperor himself.

"You are right, Mizcarnon Peak Crosser," Crisdan finally replied. "I am greatly honored by the Emperor's trust. I will, of course, accept the command of my Emperor. What shall I tell my High Trade? They expect me back in Bristrinia the day after tomorrow."

"Tell them nothing." Mizcarnon cut off Crisdan's protest. "The Emperor will reach out to your council, if he hasn't already. He will tell them you have been borrowed for a military matter, and after the successful raid on Doorie, you may inform the High Investigators of what happened."

The Investigator fidgeted in his chair, clearly uncomfortable with the request for secrecy. Investigators lived their lives striving to bring secrets to the light; hiding something this important from his own High Trade must be unthinkable.

"Of course I will do it," Crisdan said after another moment of pondering. "It's an order from the Emperor, and it allows me to see justice to its end, which I don't always get to witness. Zornan deserves to have his life restored. When do we leave?"

"Tonight," Mizcarnon replied. "Meet me at the tunnel entrance at midnight. Bring only your weapon and a small travel bag. The rest of your things will meet you at your home."

"Very well." The Investigator stood. "I will meet you there tonight." The man finally had some energy after seeming so devoid of it since Mizcarnon met him on the steps of that tavern.

Mizcarnon nodded, left the office, and headed back toward The Howling Dog where he had rented a room. He'd only arrived a few hours ago, and he needed to get some rest before the journey.

Mizcarnon reviewed the plans in his mind. The assault on Doorie would be executed by a dozen Imperial Guards, the finest warriors in the Empire. They anticipated fighting the two Baldra and as many as a dozen Enforcers. Despite the lopsided numbers, the force should be sufficient. Imperial Guards were specifically trained to be able to handle the violent ferocity of Baldra. If they could attack under the cloak of secrecy, rescuing Zornan and capturing the Destroyer girl would be probable.

Crisdan had not been what Mizcarnon expected. He seemed nervous and unsure of himself, entirely different than the man the Emperor described. And his emotional state was perplexing. Mizcarnon did not have an Investigator's blessing, but the man seemed sad. Hadn't the Investigator just uncovered a great injustice and brought the villainous Stethdel to light? Shouldn't Crisdan be happy with his situation?

Mizcarnon chastised himself for not trusting the Emperor's choice of Investigator to accompany them; the Emperor was wise and knew what he was doing, much more so than Mizcarnon. Crisdan could be melancholy for a whole host of things. Maybe bringing down a High Magistrate, even in death, made the Investigator reticent. Stethdel's traitorous legacy tarnished not just his High Trade but all the High Trades and the Empire itself. And the Magistrates were like a brother High Trade to the Investigators.

When he reached his room, Mizcarnon slumped into the lumpy bed and reflected on the past three weeks since he and Sunset had left Doorie. Rescuing Zornan's younger brother Ballin had been the right thing to do.

They had flown the younger man to the small Fandrillan city of Dasnath where he'd recovered quickly, and they had made the journey by tunnel ferry across the Empire to Bristrinia. Once in the capital, Ballin had shared all the details of their journey with the Emperor and Lanthia. Mizcarnon would have dismissed the tale as fake if he hadn't known for himself that almost all the details rang true.

Ballin's story confirmed Crisdan's impressions and the Emperor's own suppositions. Zornan was not an agent of the Kuthraz or Dundraz, just a man who'd been caught up in their plots. Zornan could only escape by delivering Stethdel's daughter to her mother, an exchange Mizcarnon witnessed go horribly wrong. Mizcarnon shared what he'd seen after Ballin finished his story, and the young man fell into sobs, assuming his brother and the girl were lost.

Mizcarnon had been in Bristrinia less than a day when the Emperor and the High General of the Imperial Guard met with him in the Emperor's study and revealed their rescue plan. Mizcarnon would leave immediately for Fallindra and find and recruit Crisdan.

The next morning he'd met the man who would lead the Guards—Gahrshak. They met in the study, the younger man dressed in his full Imperial Guard armor. They'd talked a few moments about the assignment and Gahrshak even joked about how all the men were excited about facing off against Baldra and were taking bets on who would kill or subdue the two assassins.

With the pleasantries out of the way, Gahrshak became very somber and removed his helmet. Mizcarnon had closed his eyes; only the Emperor and the other Imperial Guards were to see their faces, and Mizcarnon was not worthy to be pulled into their trust. But Gahrshak was insistent, saying that if Mizcarnon was to lead them, he was now an adopted member of the Imperial Guard. After several minutes, Mizcarnon relented.

The guard looked very young, maybe younger than twenty. His brilliant blond hair had spilled from his helmet and past his shoulders. His eyes were a brilliant blue, like the ocean water Mizcarnon had seen while scouting in Croxshine. His features marked him as a man from one of the Kandrinian cities in the Empire's southwestern region.

"I needed you to see my face," he'd said. "You bring honor to the Emperor, the man we serve and protect. By showing you my face, I bring you into our brotherhood. You are one of us now, in spirit if not in name. By seeing my face, you are sworn to the Emperor. Your life is in his hands."

"I was already sworn to the Emperor," Mizcarnon replied, bowing his head deeply.

"We know."

His memory of his conversation with Gahrshak shook him from his half sleep. He was supposed to reach out to the man once he had successfully recruited Crisdan. He wasn't sure if the Imperial Guard would be close enough to mindspeak or not.

Gahrshak. He repeated the name a half dozen times in his mind.

Greeting, Mizcarnon Peak Crosser. Just like his real voice, Gahrshak's mind voice was vibrant, high, and formal.

Welcome greeting, Gahrshak. I have talked with Crisdan Investigator, and he has agreed to join our quest.

Did you order him to maintain secrecy?

Of course.

I don't think he is doing so.

What? How under the three moons would Gahrshak have any idea if Crisdan betrayed their trust?

He left the constable's office and headed straight for Zornan Peak Crosser's home. He is talking with the Lady Calla right now.

How do you know that?

I'm standing a hundred yards away, watching him. There's too much wind, so I can't hear their conversation. I would bet my armor he's telling the woman where we're headed and what we're doing.

Mizcarnon shook his head. How unlike an Investigator to break secrecy like that. Mizcarnon hoped Lady Calla could be trusted to keep whatever Crisdan revealed to herself.

He's leaving now, Garshak continued. *It was a short conversation. It appears he's headed back toward the constable's place.*

Are you going to keep tabs on him until we leave tonight?

Until about an hour before we leave. I have to slip back into the tunnel and retrieve my armor. I feel completely naked like this.

I thought no one could see your face but the Emperor and your own kind?

By law, yes. The Imperial Guard hesitated. *But that's a little impractical. The Emperor has changed the law somewhat, and we are allowed out of our armor occasionally. I left Bristrinia hours before you did. I've been here for a few days keeping tabs on both Crisdan and Lady Calla. I know the Emperor trusts Crisdan and believes Zornan innocent, but I trust no man or woman when it comes to the safety of the Emperor and my men. If he's not of the Imperial Guard, I assume him an enemy.*

I'm not of the Imperial Guard.

Not by law.

By appearance, Gahrshak was young, barely a man. But he spoke with the tone and perspective of a veteran soldier.

Very well, friend. I must get some rest. I will see you tonight.

Rest well, Peak Crosser.

Calla answered the door hesitantly. Through the window in the sitting room where she had been knitting, she saw Crisdan approach. She hoped against hope that he would walk past the house, but he veered toward their door.

She opened the door and looked up at him.

"Greeting, Lady Calla." His posture was rigid, and he made no movement to enter the house. Though she knew it was rude, she had no intention of letting him in.

"Welcome greeting, Crisdan Investigator." Her voice was strained, but she could fake nothing else. After their last meeting, any feelings she'd harbored had been dismissed. Whatever ill-conceived emotions she'd let grow were not for the viper she'd discovered but for a noble man who had never existed.

Crisdan's faced curved into regret. He probably sensed her strong feelings, but she couldn't actually believe he felt regret. He was an actor and a liar.

He looked down and then looked back into her eyes. "I have come with news of your husband. I am leaving very soon, but there's something you should know."

He did seem different this time. She didn't want to believe him, but she could feel her body relaxing at his remorse. *Stay strong, Calla! Do not believe him!*

"They have found your husband," Crisdan continued when Calla did not respond. "I cannot tell you where, but they are going to try and rescue him soon. If it works, Zornan will return. I can't say when for sure, but soon."

Calla's knees weakened, and she gripped the door. Crisdan did not move to steady her.

"He's alive?" The words escaped as a whisper.

"I don't know for sure, but we believe so. I've told you too much already. You must tell no one, including your parents. We're leaving tonight to find him, and we will to do everything in our power to deliver Zornan back to you."

Calla continued to hold the door for support. Could she really begin to hope beyond the dimming wishes she felt each day? Was this manipulative man stirring her feelings for some dark purpose?

She looked into his eyes and saw and felt the sincerity she'd seen when she first met him, not the cold man she'd encountered more recently. Despite her lingering fear, she believed he was telling the truth. She so wanted to believe.

"Thank you, Crisdan."

The Investigator blushed slightly, his gaze drifting to his feet.

"You owe me nothing, Lady Calla. There is so much I wish I could change."

Without another word, Crisdan spun and walked away.

Calla shut the door and slumped against it, sliding down to the floor. She cupped her hands over her face and sobbed. Was the old Crisdan back? Was he a man who could change personas like Calla might change a shawl?

She tossed thoughts of the Investigator aside. Her husband was coming back. Her girls would have a father again. Her fear of living a life alone, widowed and destitute, was replaced by blazing hope of a life restored.

Calla allowed herself a few more sobs, then stood and wiped her tear-traced cheeks with her hands. Zornan was coming back. She would hold to hope.

Get out of my head, cursed woman! Crisdan screamed in his mind as he stormed back toward the constable's office.

Calm down, Crisdan. Trillia's command immediately relaxed his muscles, and he slowed his pace. His anger was not gone, but it was diffused. *I ordered you to leave the woman before you revealed too much of your new self.*

At that moment standing at Calla's doorstep, he felt as if he could tell her everything, even things Trillia had ordered him to never repeat. He wasn't sure if he would have been able to or not, or if the empty, confusing feeling would overwhelm him, like it did whenever he tried to disobey the Magistrate's orders. But it didn't matter now; she'd reentered his mind before he could try defying her.

What is this about rescuing Zornan? she asked.

Crisdan related everything Mizcarnon had told him.

Interesting move by the Emperor. He is showing more initiative than I thought him capable of.

So am I going with them?

Of course. We want Zornan freed from the Dundraz. He should have never been involved in this. And a successful rescue will humble those idiots. This will work to our advantage. I already know how I can use this…

Trillia's thought trailed off, and Crisdan felt her withdraw from his mind. He sincerely hoped that none of this would be to that witch's advantage.

38 | TRANSFORMATION

Zornan sat in silence. He worked to suppress his ever-present frustration in what seemed like an eternal progression of sameness.

After being knocked unconscious by Maeltha, he had spent what he believed were twenty-nine days in a small, windowless, fifteen-by-fifteen-foot room. He'd measured it countless times, pacing back and forth. He believed he was still in Doorie, though they could have carried him anywhere in the Empire while he was unconscious.

He examined the room for the thousandth time. The floor, walls, and door were made of milky brown brastilia, the surfaces unnaturally smooth. The outline of the only door was barely visible against the wall, as was the outline of the slot where food was deposited and where he dumped his waste bucket. Besides the waste bucket, his only companion was the sickly light of an old and dying glow globe.

As he had each of the twenty-nine mornings he'd spent in this room (his body told him it was morning, though he couldn't be sure), he looked over himself. His wounds from the fight that day were mostly healed. He'd have a scar on the back of his head where Maeltha had struck him from behind, but it had been bandaged and well cared for; they obviously wanted him alive.

He ran his hands over his unshaven face. It was a scraggly, patchy beard, with more blank spots than grown-in ones. It must look terrible. He'd never worn a beard because his High Trade forbade it. If he ever regained his freedom, his first act would be to shave the cursed thing.

Zornan's body felt good, strong. Despite the terrible food and the isolation, he felt alert and ready for whatever his captors chose to do next.

The problem was that for fifteen days now, they had chosen to do nothing but feed him.

For the first two weeks, two or three men had come to visit him every few hours, usually when he was sleeping. He believed that at least one of the men was an Investigator. They asked him about Mairie. They asked about Stethdel. They were particularly interested in information about Loothdram. The questions always pointed back to the Kuthraz. Zornan answered everything honestly, except for questions about Loothdram's connection to the Kuthraz. He'd made a huge mistake in telling Maeltha about that, and he wasn't going to endanger his friend any more than he already had.

For days they had come, asking the same questions and hearing the same answers. The intense interrogation sessions left him exhausted. Without a bed or even a blanket, sleep eluded him for the first four or five days. He'd been tired all the time, and his body ached from what little sleep he had managed on the hard brastilia floor. His dreams were haunted as well, images of Baldra and demons and Maeltha. He would wake up screaming, always in the dimly lit room, always alone.

Thoughts of killing himself had come in his first hours of isolation, but he'd dismissed them almost immediately. Besides the impracticality of it (his only methods were starvation and drowning himself in his own filth), he held onto hope of returning to Calla and the girls. His hope seemed like a fantasy, but he used it to keep his darkest thoughts from overwhelming his soul.

When hope failed him, he dowsed his despair with rage, anger, and hatred. He would imagine Stethdel's face, and he'd be filled with sudden energy. He would remember Maeltha's betrayal and feel alive. He'd see his father standing above him, fists clenched and ready to strike, and he'd rise to his feet, his scream echoing in his small chamber. And finally he'd see all of his captors: the Baldra, the plump dark-haired woman, his questioners, and he'd imagine killing each of them, one by one. Despair sought to overcome him each day, rising anew with its dark corrosion. But he doused it with anger and hope. And that combination made him powerful.

The second week of questioning went differently. He had answered the questions the same way, but did so defiantly. He looked his questioners in the eye and even asked them about who they were and what right they had to question and imprison a High Tradesmen. They never did answer him, and their visits became less and less frequent, until one day they stopped. It had been fifteen days since someone had come to see him. His only interaction with the outside world came as two barely edible meals and a third visit when he dumped his waste bucket back through the same slot his food was delivered into.

He'd spent much of the first few days trying to reach out to Silver, but nothing had happened. At first he thought Silver was dead, as he felt nothing at all. Not a lack of response, but nothing. Then he'd tried, as he'd done hundreds of times before, to access the map of the Empire in his mind, to try and pinpoint his location. For the first time since he was blessed, he could not feel the map. Somehow, this room or this place blocked the magic that made mindspeak and the map work. He had only used mindspeak for a short while, but he desperately missed his mental connection with Silver.

The only sounds Zornan heard besides the footsteps of his guards delivering food and taking waste were Mairie's occasional screams. Usually once a day, she would scream loudly and painfully, begging her captors to stop. Zornan had not been tortured at all since he'd arrived. During one long and terrible torture session, her cries penetrating the walls, he'd tried desperately to escape his cell. Despite an hour of continued effort pushing and prying at the almost non-existent door seams, he could not escape. When her screams ceased, he collapsed, exhausted and crying. He wanted to help her, free her from whatever they were doing to her. That was five days ago.

Mairie no longer fueled his anger. It was more than just sympathy for what they were doing to her. She was not a monster any more than Silver was a monster for being a hawk transformed into a mrakaro. Maeltha had been right about one thing: the monsters were those who transformed humans into Baldra, Shantierd, and people like Mairie: the Empire, the Bendathdrans, even the Kuthraz. They were the monsters. Mairie was an unwilling participant, just as he was. She was a large rock picked up by a strong wind; she might crush the house, but the wind retained the blame.

He also felt anger when he thought of Lascrill, his old mentor, for not teaching him about his blessing and abilities, and Loothdram, his old friend, for not removing Zornan from this burden in Skathall. If Mairie was so important to his cause and to the Empire, Loothdram and his group should have stepped in when Zornan reached his old friend. Instead, the Kuthraz left Zornan and Mairie on their own, and Loothdram's negligence had resulted in their capture.

But his anger toward Lascrill and Loothdram was lighter when compared to the others who fed his hate. Lascrill's instruction had not been all bad. Zornan was leaning on the discipline the old man had taught. He meditated for hours each day, deep meditation bringing him his only real rest. He'd occasionally used that lesson in his Peak Crosser travels, but he'd abandoned it in favor of traditional sleep. But here he found that better rest could be gained in less time through meditation. He was also using Lascrill's strength exercises, pushing himself up and down with his arms, stretching in the different poses he'd been taught. He had worried that the exertion would drain him, especially with the two meager meals he received each day. But it was the opposite; the efforts created energy. He felt almost as if he hardly needed the food, that he was gaining energy and nourishment from the energy of the world around him this way. He couldn't explain it, but he was growing stronger.

As his strength grew, he'd started to practice fighting. He imagined himself with a hatari or a hatrindi, fighting an Enforcer or even a Baldra. Even without the weapon to practice, he was becoming fast. Not as fast as a Baldra or Mairie, but much faster than he'd ever been.

It was possible that the isolation made him delusional. He'd heard stories of men driven mad in prison, of delusions of greatness or paranoia. But he *felt* it was true. He could do things he'd never been able to do before, like leap into the air, flip, and brush the ceiling with his feet. Unless he was completely losing his grip on reality, he was getting stronger.

He would never be weak again. He would protect himself and his family from now on. He would not depend on the Empire or anyone else. He would use the Empire as it had used him, and he'd create a life insulated from their threats. He wasn't sure it was possible, but he'd try. The next time he faced off against Maeltha or an Enforcer or anyone, besides maybe a Baldra, he would win. Whatever magic blessed Mairie and the Baldra and the Enforcers coursed inside him now. He didn't know how it worked, but he could feel it growing in him, like a million tiny rivers flooding his skin, veins, and bones, creating something more than a common man, High Tradesman, or Peak Crosser.

Despite his rapid growth over the past several weeks, despair still tried to drown him each day. Now that his captors knew he was only a stooge of the Kuthraz and not their agent, he was expendable. They only had to stop feeding him to kill him. Even with his newfound strength, he'd found no way to escape. He was certain that his room was meant to contain Baldra and other powerful High Tradesmen. He may have become something greater but not great enough.

As if confirming his fears, it felt like a long time since the last meal, maybe as much as a day. It was almost impossible to know for sure—his only way of truly measuring time were the meals and waste pick-up. Everything about time, including the number of days, was a guess. Ever since he started meditating and exercising, hunger had transformed from insatiable to tolerable, so he could not judge the time based on his stomach's yearning.

So he slipped back into a deep meditation, focusing on the energy surrounding him. The room was filled with this energy, as if the brastilia was its conductor. He could feel it flowing through the chamber and into his body. He was becoming rested, stronger, borrowing sustenance from the world around him. The energy's flow was more intoxicating than Koofpashi vinewood liquor.

Zornan's meditation was interrupted by a distant sound. At first, he feared it was another torture session for Mairie. But the sound came from farther away than that. Even with his blessed hearing, he could only make out muffled shouts of nonsensical words, frantic and panicked. It was unlike anything he'd heard in the past twenty-nine days.

Next he heard footsteps in the hall outside, two sets, one growing fainter after a while, the other stopping outside his door. Zornan had imagined a hundred ways he would free himself the next time someone opened that door, unleashing the fury he'd built inside. Now was the time to put those thoughts into action.

Zornan opened his eyes, jumped to his feet, and hurried toward the door. He positioned himself flat against the wall next to the almost-hidden doorframe. The door opened inward, allowing for a good defensive position but blocking the view of the cell. Zornan stood by the door's hinge, where he could remain invisible to his visitor. The door opened slowly and noiselessly. The tip of a hatrindi slowly appeared, and then the whole weapon, followed by the maroon sleeves of an Enforcer uniform.

"Where are you, Peak Crosser?" the intruder said. "We need to move now."

As soon as the man's body came into view, Zornan grabbed the man's off hand and yanked, flinging the Enforcer into the center of the cell. The ease with which he moved the large man stunned Zornan, despite his mental preparation and underlying belief that his new skills were real. *I just tossed an Enforcer three feet into the air!*

Zornan's hesitation allowed the armed man to rise and charge the Peak Crosser, swinging his hatrindi at Zornan's chest. Zornan easily dodged the swipe, stepping and leaning back. It had been a slow weak blow, likely done to injure Zornan but not kill him. Zornan kicked the man's sword hand, knocking the hatrindi against the wall, the sickening crack of bone echoing in the small room. It was the Enforcer's turn to be stunned, staring down into Zornan's eyes. With the larger man's hesitation, Zornan struck him in the throat and then kicked him in the knee. The man collapsed suddenly, his eyes rolling back. Both attacks sent more echoes through the room, and Zornan bent down to examine his foe.

The Enforcer's neck was indented, and a slight gasping sound came from this throat, like a tea kettle about to boil. The Enforcer's knee bent in an unnatural position, and he slumped on the ground like a doll. The man was either dead or would be soon. Zornan had only intended to hurt and disable him, but his new strength was more than he'd been able to plan for.

Zornan scooped up the hatrindi and walked out of the room into the hallway beyond. Having never seen the rest of this mountain fortress, he took a few moments to gain his bearings. His room was at an intersection of two hallways, one to his left which then turned right, the other straight ahead and then bending right as well. He made out other doors to other windowless rooms, each with a strange recessed latch in place of a doorknob. The second hallway ended in a staircase, the passage lit by intermittent glow globes. The lack of proper light cast the intersection into dim light, similar to The Bowels. The greatest amount of light flooded down the stairs, where a much brighter glow globe or a window provided greater illumination.

From the hallway in front of him, a man came running into the intersection carrying a small figure over his shoulder. The man was another Enforcer, solidly built. He stopped suddenly upon seeing Zornan. The Peak Crosser recognized the man's cargo: it was Mairie, her curly blond hair dangling behind her. She was dressed in a rag, nothing more than an oversized pillow covering. The garment exposed her right side to Zornan from her bare feet to her waist; she wore no underclothing. Scars were visible on her exposed hip, calloused and infected. Her feet were bound together with brastilia cords.

"What are you doing out of your cell, Peak Crosser?" the Enforcer bellowed. "Where's Mookfra?"

"Put the girl down," Zornan responded, pointing the hatrindi at the man's chest.

"Demon's blood," the man mumbled, tossing Mairie off his shoulder. The girl landed with a thud, and the toss exposed her left side, butt, and lower back to Zornan. Her skin was dirty and bruised, covered in countless scars and scrapes. She did not move at all when she hit the ground, either dead or unconscious, her hands bound like her feet.

Zornan cried in rage and charged the Enforcer. The larger man extended his hatari, raising it to block Zornan's blow. The fury of Zornan's downward chop knocked the brastilia staff into the man's chest, and he fell backward onto the floor. Zornan swung the sword at his uprooted legs, but the Enforcer twisted away and rolled back onto his feet. Zornan's foe stood in a defensive posture, his eyes wide and disbelieving.

"But you're a Peak Crosser," the Enforcer mumbled. "You're not supposed to be able…"

Zornan cut off his words by advancing and striking. The Enforcer raised his hatari to block, but Zornan stopped mid-thrust, spun, and slashed the man's exposed chest. The sharp edge of the sword ripped the Enforcer's thick maroon tunic and his skin, the deep cut flooding with blood. The Enforcer dropped his hatari, and the staff shrunk to its smaller size. He fell to his knees and grabbed his bloody chest.

"Impossible," the man muttered. "Sweet demon blood."

Zornan stepped forward and stabbed him in the middle of the chest, taking off two of his fingers where his right hand rested on his body. The hatrindi went through the man and out his back, plunging all the way to the hilt. Zornan stepped back and withdrew the weapon. The Enforcer slumped onto his side, all life gone.

He'd done it. Unless this was the most real dream he'd ever had, he'd just easily killed two Enforcers, one of them without the aid of a weapon. He wasn't sure what he'd become, but he wasn't mad. Not yet.

Zornan set the hatrindi down and knelt next to Mairie. He leaned down close to her head and combed back her hair with his hand, revealing her face. She was barely recognizable. Her face was covered in a series of puffy purple bruises, and blood caked her swollen nose. One of her eyes was swollen shut. Zornan leaned closer and heard labored breathing. She was hurt beyond what any unblessed human could handle. But she was alive.

Free of his cell and the furor of battle, he could feel the world around him again. He closed his eyes and felt where he was. He was in Doorie, and near the entrance where they had been betrayed and captured.

Silver! he shouted with his mind.

Little rider! came Silver's instant and exuberant reply. *You live!*

Yes, friend, but I need your help. Mairie and I are in danger. We need to escape. I'm near the place where I last saw you. Can you meet us there?

Soon, little one. Sunset and I are dealing with two flying rodents and four accursed atacikics. I will be there soon.

Silver was here with the scout Peak Crosser's mrakaro? There was no time to query, so he pushed his questions aside.

Zornan tucked the hatrindi into his belt and scooped up the second Enforcer's discarded hatari. Despite his success with the hatrindi, he preferred the more familiar staff-like weapon. He would take both in case Mairie awoke. He sheathed the hatari in the holder on his lower back. His uniform was tattered, but the holster held. Next, he bent over and, as gently as he could, picked up Mairie and placed her on his left shoulder. She felt light, her weight reduced by weeks of deprivation.

He scaled one flight of stairs and then another until he reached the open doorway, leading to the plateau where they had landed weeks ago. The wind whipped ferociously, and he could feel Mairie's slight garment blow off her back and expose her wounds to the biting wind. When they got within a dozen feet of the plateau's edge, he laid Mairie down on her back on the smooth rock floor and pinned the garment under her legs and arms to keep the wind from exposing her further. He used the hatrindi to cut the cords which bound her feet and hands. He set the hatrindi aside and pulled out his newly acquired hatari. Still in its reduced size, he grew a sharp tip on one end and cut a series of aligning holes at the edges of Mairie's garment. Then he cut the brastilia cord into smaller segments and used the pieces to tie the garment together. It was a crude sewing job, which left too much of her skin still exposed, but it provided more protection and some dignity. She deserved both.

Zornan scanned the sky, but it was empty of any giant flyers, friend or foe. He'd forgotten about the archer posts, but when he glanced over, each one was empty. Whatever threat had entered Doorie, the archers had joined the fight below.

Silver, where are you?

We are engaged in battle, she replied. *I will come soon.*

Zornan cursed to himself. They needed to get out of here before anyone found them.

"Where were you planning to go, Peak Crosser?" came a brusque voice from behind him. "I hope you weren't contemplating jumping off the cliff. You can't fly without your stupid bird."

Zornan turned, extending his hatari to its full length and putting sharp pointed tips on each end. Standing ten feet in front of him was a Baldra, but not his sister. The creature was a little shorter than Zornan. His solid build was evident behind his dark, flowing robe, which danced in the heavy wind. His hatnuthri weren't visible yet, but Zornan knew they could be in an eye's blink.

"Leave us alone, demon. I just want to leave here."

"I cannot let you leave," the Baldra said, pulling back its hood to reveal its bald white head. Its face curved into a sickly smile, revealing jagged snow-white teeth. "My Shindar commands that I take the Destroyer girl to her. Two cosows are on their way to ferry us. Against my desires, I am also commanded to let you live. Nothing would bring me more pleasure than to deliver your severed head to your pathetic sister. She's weak, a disgrace to Baldra."

"Your cosows are not coming," Zornan shot back. "My mrakaro is killing them as we speak."

"Then your mrakaro will have to carry us," the Baldra replied, peering back at the door. "The Kuthraz and the Empire are both here, so I need to leave and take the girl. It's best for us all. If the Empire finds her, her fate will be no different than it will be with us."

"Whoever you people are, you will never touch this girl again."

Zornan struck quickly, swinging the staff toward the assassin's head. The Baldra's evasion was faster, as he ducked and rolled several feet away, bouncing to its feet.

"You cannot hope to defeat me," the Baldra snarled. "You are a Peak Crosser. Even if I cannot kill you, I will get you out of my way and take pleasure in each measure of your pain."

Zornan knew the Baldra was right. As fast and strong as he had become, he couldn't hope to defeat a Baldra who'd been training and fighting with these gifts for most of its existence. But he didn't have to beat it; he only had to buy time until the Kuthraz or the Empire or Silver arrived. Once he had help, defeating the Baldra might be possible. He had to distract it.

Zornan stepped forward with a jab, which the Baldra again easily dodged. The creature's movements were fast and fluid. It backed off and tossed its robe aside, two hatnuthri growing in its hands into their sharp, menacing form.

"So be it, Peak Crosser."

The Baldra became the aggressor, unleashing a flurry of strikes with both hands. The speed was faster than anything Zornan had ever faced, but he parried and blocked each blow, giving ground. The Baldra was pushing him back toward the cliff. After a block, Zornan swung his staff toward the Baldra's knees as fast as he could. The strike forced the assassin to step back, which gave Zornan space to spin and put his back to the north, the cliff more safely at his left. He could see Mairie, the cliff, and the door now. *Hold on,* he thought to himself. *Hold on.*

The Baldra struck again, even more aggressively. Again Zornan blocked each blow, but he was giving ground again, and he could feel fatigue grasping him. He tried twice to strike again, but each time almost led to disaster. The Baldra's left hatnuthri slashed Zornan's left hand. So he settled into a defensive posture. He blocked, parried, and maintained as much ground as he could. But he was now twenty yards from Mairie, and he would soon have another cliff to deal with. He was running out of space and time.

Suddenly, the Baldra stepped back and stopped attacking. Zornan kept his hatari up in a defensive posture, expecting another sudden series of attacks.

"What are you, Peak Crosser?" the assassin hissed. "I have never seen speed like yours, outside of my own kind and the Imperial Guard. What are you?"

"A man who is tired of being weak."

"Leave the girl to me," it said, pointing one of its hatnuthri back at Mairie. "She is not yours. The Kuthraz, my Dundraz, the Empire; they have conspired together to ruin your life. My will is the command of my Shindar. Yours is your own. Walk away. Take your mrakaro. Go back to your life. Do not bind yourself to this girl and her fate."

"I cannot do that."

"I'm sorry, then," the Baldra said, shaking its head.

The assassin leapt, flying through the air. Zornan raised his hatari and stepped back with one leg to brace for the powerful blow. The Baldra struck with only one hatnuthri, knocking Zornan's hatari from the grip of his left hand. It struck with the other hand as it landed, cutting Zornan's wrist and causing his weapon to spin out of his control. The Baldra stood between Zornan and his weapon now, which had rolled in its shorter form ten feet away.

As the Baldra smiled, Zornan reached up with his wounded hand, punching the creature in the face. The blow knocked the assassin back, blood erupting from its lip. It growled and brandished its sharp teeth. The hatnuthri disappeared into its sleeves, and it attacked with a renewed vigor.

Zornan blocked the onslaught of punches and kicks as best as he could, but after only a few blows, he realized just how much the creature had been holding back before in an effort to fulfill its command to not kill Zornan. As much as he had trained and focused, he would still fail. The Baldra was stronger, faster, better.

Fatigue overwhelmed Zornan, and he missed a block, the Baldra's fist colliding with the side of his head. He stumbled, stunned by the blow. He didn't see the next attack, but felt the creature's kick to his left shoulder, pain erupting as his left arm went limp. The Baldra's other foot landed in his stomach, and Zornan collapsed to his knees, gasping for air.

"You should have listened. What I wouldn't give for freedom. And you waste it—to protect a girl who's brought you nothing." The assassin struck him again, another punch to the side of his head. Zornan fell over, pain exploding anew in his left shoulder as he landed.

Zornan struggled to remain conscious, blue lights dancing in his blinking eyes. The pain nearly overwhelmed him, his shoulder, stomach, and head each clamoring for his attention. He could see Mairie and the Baldra. The creature was standing over the girl now, awaiting his ride. Zornan had failed.

Above the cliff rose a pair of wings, covering the sun and drenching the arriving creature in black shade. Was it a vision or his mind's frantic attempt to find help? No, it was Silver. She floated toward the Baldra, grabbing it by its shoulder and lifting it off the plateau, her talons sinking deep. The assassin screamed and flailed, but Silver was strong and held tight, lifting them higher into the air, away from the Baldra's domain and farther into hers.

Zornan wanted to call out to her, warn her just how dangerous this Baldra was, but he couldn't summon the energy to mindspeak. The Baldra suddenly grew a hatnuthri in its right hand, and plunged it into Silver's breast. She screeched, a piercing cry that echoed through the entire valley. As the Baldra withdrew its weapon and prepared to strike again, Silver twisted the assassin in her grip and ripped its left arm free from its body. She then tossed the arm and the rest of its body over the cliff face. The Baldra disappeared into the valley below.

Silver struggled to remain airborne, and finally landed awkwardly next to Mairie. She slumped to the ground, resting like a cosow, her wings spread out and her belly down.

We saved her, little rider, Silver spoke into his mind. *She is not a monster. She is our friend...I saved you both...*

Tears streamed down Zornan's cheeks. With all the energy he could muster, he thought to his friend, *You did well, old friend. You have always done well.* He tried to get up and go to her, but the pain froze his movement.

As do you, little one. Do not despair. We will be together again in the eternal flight...

39 | MASTERS

Sudden commotion broke Tha'Strukra from her meditation. She opened her eyes on the poorly lit barrack she shared with Dres'Dargpa. The barrack could house more than twenty soldiers, but Doorie was nearly empty save for the few Dundraz and their two prisoners. With many open barracks like this throughout the old military outpost, no one was going to share with the Baldra. They all knew the Baldra could only act under the direction of their Shindar, but fear overcame reason. All of the Dundraz here at Doorie avoided Tha'Strukra and Dres'Dargpa like they were diseased wretches. Maybe that was for the best.

The commotion came from a few stories below, near the tunnel entrance. It sounded like a struggle, not a brawl that might happen between Enforcers who've been cramped up in a military outpost for too long, but a mortal struggle.

Tha'Strukra sprang up, her two hatnuthri extending. She left the barrack and reached out in her mind to her Shindar, leaving her cloak behind—no need for discretion here.

Shindar, she projected. *What is going on?*

I'm not sure, pet, came the Shindar's reply. *I believe the Kuthraz or the Empire may have discovered us. Dres'Dargpa is headed to collect the prisoners and transport them to safety, you should join...*

Talalah Shindar's message was suddenly interrupted, and Tha'Strukra felt an intense stab of pain come through their bond. How could she be hurt? Talalah would have been far from the fighting and in little danger.

Sudden pain struck Tha'Strukra like a sword piercing her stomach, and her head erupted as if someone were ripping out her brain from the inside. She dropped her weapons and fell to her knees. She gripped her bald head and screamed, but nothing brought relief. Baldra were blessed to feel pain differently than humans. They knew they were hurt, and they understood a wound's severity, but "pain" was foreign, as it was an obstacle to their mission. That she felt this way meant only one thing: Talalah was dead.

She fell onto her side and screamed again. Baldra were driven mad by the constant pain that replaced the Shindar bond. Tha'Strukra had always thought these Baldra weak for letting pain drive them to madness, but now that she felt the intensity of the separation, she yearned for death or madness or a reconnection to her Shindar, anything to bring this to an end. She opened her clenched eyes and could see one of her hatnuthri within arm's length on the hallway floor. Talalah Shindar had commanded Tha'Strukra to kill herself if the bond was ever severed, and though Tha'Strukra remembered the command, she didn't feel the usual compulsion. She wanted to comply, to dig the pain out of her skull. But the pain was so debilitating she couldn't even do that.

"Look!" a voice above her said. "It's one of the Baldra. Is this what happens when its Shindar is killed? Where is the other one?" Tha'Strukra did not look up; it hurt too much.

"Get it to the blessing room," a second voice said. "Kisthana will meet us there."

She felt a hand turn her over and then someone lifted her off the ground. He was strong, probably an Enforcer. Despite the debilitating pain, she could still reason. She wasn't mad yet.

"Wait." It was the second voice. "Zandia? Cursed blood of the demons, Silver was right! Their sister *did* become a Baldra!"

"What?" said the first voice close to her ear. "I thought Baldra were chosen as infants."

"Apparently not, at least not all of them."

Tha'Strukra felt a hand brush her face. She wanted to slap it away, but she didn't, she couldn't.

"Oh, poor Zandia, may the three moons favor us today. Quickly, Mayfran, get her to the blessing room. Kisthana is her only hope."

Her pain intensified with each step as Mayfran sprinted down the hall. She felt them climb steps and run down another hallway. She kept her eyes shut and curled up like a young child in the man's arms. What would they do to her? Why didn't they just kill her? The Dundraz had tortured the Destroyer girl for weeks, subjecting her to every imaginable agony. Would these people do the same to her, testing the limits of the Baldra?

Mayfran came to a stop and set Tha'Strukra onto a hard surface. She turned over onto her side and constricted, cradling her piercing head as best she could in her body. It did little to ease the pain.

"What does he want me to do with *her*?" It was a woman's voice, calm and strong.

"I don't know. Help her. Cure her," Mayfran said.

"What? You don't cure a Baldra. If her Shindar is dead, she must be bonded to another High Tradesman, preferably a Shindar. Where is that foolish man?"

"Watch how you speak about him," Mayfran chided the woman.

"I am not a Kuthraz stooge, even if I've had to align myself with you idiots due to my own indiscretions." The woman paused. "Well, bind her up, and we'll carry her out of here with us."

"We cannot go back. The Imperial force has come in through the tunnel. Our only escape is by air. The Imperial Guards are coming."

"Juthrana," the woman cursed, in the ancient Bendathdran language. Tha'Strukra recognized the word but couldn't place its meaning, especially in her current state. "What have you fools gotten me into? And where is my daughter?"

"Loothdram is trying to find Mairie and Zornan."

"Do not waste time on the Peak Crosser! If he weren't an even bigger fool than all of you, Mairie would be safe."

Loothdram? Was Zornan's boyhood friend here? Maybe she *was* going mad. Little of what they said made sense.

"What do we do with the Baldra?"

"Kill her and be done with it."

If she hadn't been Baldra, Tha'Strukra might have been horrified by the priestess' suggestion. But it was what Tha'Strukra would have recommended herself.

"No, she is too valuable. We don't have any Baldra; she could help the cause."

"They have *you* Mayfran, and the others I've blessed beyond their blessings. And you don't come with the shackles a Baldra does."

"But Baldra are better than me, better than the others." Mayfran paused. "Bind her to me."

The woman went silent for several moments. "Fine. Lay down next to her on the table. How is your tolerance to pain, Mayfran?"

"I guess we'll see," he replied sardonically.

Through her pain-induced daze, Tha'Strukra heard the apparent priestess, Kisthana, chanting in Bendathdran. She imagined the woman twirling her hadbindhi in the air, performing a blessing of some sort. Was she to be bound to this Mayfran? To a Kuthraz? The irony was strong. Was he a good man? Would he treat her differently than Talalah had? No, she would be a tool, as she had been since her blessing day. The Kuthraz were the same as the Dundraz, the same as the Empire; only the names changed.

Like the sun breaking through on a cloudy day, the pressure in Tha'Strukra's head eased, and she straightened her body. She could feel a body next to hers, feel its muscles tense. Her head still ached, but the pain faded. She could think. She could move.

She sat up and opened her eyes. A man lay next to her, his eyes clenched in pain. Mayfran, her new Shindar. He was about her height, average for a man. His hair was dark brown, almost black, with flecks of gray on the temples. He was muscular like an Enforcer, though a little leaner. A hatrindi was sheathed at his side, and he wore a generic tan High Tradesman uniform.

"It worked," the woman said, her words almost a whisper.

Tha'Strukra looked over at the priestess. She looked nothing like her daughter, just as Zornan had said weeks before. She was average height, with long dark hair which hung to her waist. Despite her ageless air, the years heavily lined her face. She was also dressed in a nondescript tan High Tradesman uniform, pants instead of a dress or a Bendathdran robe. She still held her hadbindhi in her right hand.

"You should give her some basic commands. Establish that she must not kill herself, and for my sake, command her not to kill me. I don't like the way she's looking at me."

Mayfran sat up, shaking his head and blinking.

"Zandia," he said.

"Tha…" She stopped before finishing her name. Was she Tha'Strukra anymore? The name meant "wolf's tooth" in the ancient Bendathdran. All Baldra were given fierce names to reflect their purpose. What was her purpose now?

"No, Zandia, you are no longer Baldra, not in the traditional sense. I would like you not to kill Kisthana though, even if I've tired of her constant complaining."

"Now is not the time to discover a sense of humor, Mayfran."

"I wasn't joking, Priestess."

Mayfran stepped off the table, but began to collapse. Zandia slid off the table and supported him.

"Thank you," he said kindly. She started to smile, but thought better of it. She was still Baldra in appearance, if not in purpose. Her razor-like teeth would not convey the proper emotion.

"You are welcome, Shindar."

"You can call me Mayfran, Zandia."

"Can or must?"

"*Can*," he commanded weakly. "I only ask that you serve the Kuthraz and you only kill out of necessity. You will have your free will."

"You are all fools," Kisthana mumbled.

Mayfran stood tall. "We must go. Loothdram has found Mairie and Zornan. They are safe, but both are injured. We must meet the mrakaros above. The Imperial Guard are coming, and we don't have much time."

"What of the other Baldra?" Tha'Strukra asked, still unsure what name fit her now, or what title.

"I don't know. We haven't seen it."

Zandia hoped Dres'Dargpa was still alive, if only because she wanted to kill him herself. Mayfran's command not to kill unnecessarily certainly did not apply to Dres'Dargpa.

"We have to go," Mayfran insisted. "Guide us to the plateau, Zandia. I'm afraid we must go slowly; my legs are very weak." Mayfran took a step and almost collapsed again.

"I will carry you," she said. Her hatnuthri sat on the floor, so she scooped them up and sheathed them in her sleeves. Then she lifted Mayfran up and carried the man as he'd carried her. "Can you keep up?" she said, turning to the priestess.

"Probably not, Baldra. I do not have your blessing."

"Then you go first."

"I am watching you, Baldra," the priestess said, stepping close. "Mayfran is an idealist and may not realize how dangerous you still are, but I do."

"And I will be watching you," Zandia hissed back. "I am commanded to serve the Kuthraz now, and you don't seem to be completely with us. That could make you my enemy. Enemies of Baldra don't usually fare well." The command he'd given to Zandia not to kill Kisthana was weak and not binding. She could kill the woman now if she wanted, if she felt it served the purposes of the Kuthraz, a higher command. Commanding a Baldra was complicated, and Mayfran was new and untrained. In this, Kisthana had been correct.

"Easy, now, Zandia," Mayfran said. "Let's hurry."

They moved as quickly as Kisthana could through the halls toward the fortress's top floor. Zandia blinked away the bright light as they stepped onto the plateau. The scene was not what she expected. Zornan and Mairie were both lying near the plateau's edge, a man leaning over her brother and two others over the girl. All three were dressed in the same tan clothing. A gray mrakaro lay near Mairie. The creature's exposed torso was covered in blood, and its feet and claws looked like they had been dipped in it.

"You can set me down, Zandia," Mayfran said. "I have recovered enough to walk."

Zandia set him down doubtfully, assuming he was just ashamed to be carried. But he stood tall and walked ably, though slowly, toward where Zornan lay.

Upon seeing Zandia, the two men near Mairie pulled out their hatrindi and approached slowly.

"Easy now," Mayfran said. "She's with us."

The third man approached, his face a familiar shadow of a boy she'd known a long time ago.

"She's cured?" Loothdram asked.

"There's no cure," Kisthana said, looking anxiously toward Mairie. "May I see my daughter now?"

"Yes," Loothdram replied, his eyes soft. "But she is not doing well. I can't be sure she'll survive."

"She will," the priestess shot back defiantly. "She was born to survive." Kisthana turned and ran toward her daughter.

"What is going on?" Loothdram asked Mayfran, avoiding eye contact with Zandia. "You say Zandia's with us, but the priestess doesn't think so."

"Zandia is bound to me now, my lord. She serves the Kuthraz."

"By the Emperor's foolish bones, Mayfran! Bound to you? Are you an idiot?"

"People often ask me that."

"Well, it's appropriate. A Baldra?"

"I thought this was better than killing her."

Loothdram's eyes softened as he looked at Zandia. "Yes, I guess it is. Zandia, are you a threat to us?"

"I serve the Kuthraz."

Their conversation was interrupted by the cry of four mrakaros streaking toward them. Only one had a rider, the other three, riderless and saddled. Three had the white bellies so common among mrakaros, the fourth one with a mostly white belly and a black pattern of feathers that seemed to match the shape of its wings. After the four giant birds landed, they all looked at the dead mrakaro and bowed their heads.

"Can you guide a mrakaro?" Mayfran asked Zandia.

"Yes, Shindar." He had not commanded her not to call him that, so she used what felt most comfortable. Free will fit her like a garment that was several sizes too big. So she defaulted to what she knew.

"Help me mount that one," Mayfran said, pointing to the one with the unique belly pattern. The mrakaro was covered mostly in dark brown feathers, with black feathers covering most of its head.

Zandia helped Mayfran onto the giant flyer and turned to walk toward the edge of the cliff. As she helped Mayfran up, she saw Dres'Dargpa's cloak lying on the ground twenty feet away. She also saw one of his hatnuthri near the dead gray mrakaro. Few creatures could be considered predators to a Baldra, but an airborne mrakaro was one of them.

Zandia walked over to the edge and looked over. With her blessed eyes, she focused hundreds of feet below until she saw him. Dres'Dargpa lay at the bottom of the jagged valley floor, his lifeless body ripped in two. If the mrakaro separating his shoulder from his body had not killed him, the fall certainly had. Zandia wished she had been the one to kill him, but if it wasn't going to be her, then she was glad it was a mrakaro; Dres'Dargpa detested the creatures, despite the fact that his name in ancient Bendathdran was "hawk's talon."

"It is time to go, Zandia," Loothdram urged. She turned to see everyone on mrakaros now except for her and her brother, who still lay on the ground. Loothdram sat in the lead on one mrakaro with the priestess, Kisthana, sitting behind him, a nibrak in her mouth. The two men who'd been looking at Mairie were on another bird, and Mairie was propped up and tied to the Peak Crosser who'd guided the giant flyers to them.

"I am not leaving without my brother," Zandia replied defiantly, relishing her new-found free will.

"We have no room, Zandia," Loothdram said. "He will be safe with the Imperial Guard. They came to rescue him. Crisdan Investigator wrote a report declaring Zornan innocent. His life will be restored. He wants to get back to his wife and family. He won't want to come with us."

That was easy for Loothdram to say; he wasn't the wounded man lying on a cold plateau hundreds of miles from any civilization. But Loothdram had been Zornan's best friend. And her brother had a family? Children? She hadn't known. She had assumed he lived a celibate, or at least non-committed life, like most High Tradesmen. A family. Hopefully, Zornan had created the family they'd never had.

"As you say, Loothdram," Zandia said with a bow. Obedience felt so different given willingly. But despite Mayfran's weak orders, she felt bound to the Kuthraz (his only good order) and loyal to Mayfran for risking his life to spare hers. She sprinted toward the mrakaro and mounted it with a graceful leap.

The other three mrakaros launched into the air, cruising north away from Doorie. She looked at Zornan one more time. Her brother. The boy who'd been her protector during their long nights at the mercy of their father. He had been her hero before free will and human caring had been ripped from her soul.

But she was free to feel again, and it felt strange.

40 | JOYFUL NEWS

Eight days had passed since Crisdan had told Calla about the rescue attempt. The wicked anticipation hung over her, hope and fear mixing together to produce a bittersweet dread. Each time exuberance filled her, fear would crush it, fear that Crisdan had been wrong or that they would find Zornan dead.

The sun set over the high peaks, and Calla heard the girls squealing in the backyard, running around with their grandfather. The night before, Windsa had asked about her father, saying she missed him. Calla did not respond. She couldn't fill them with any more hope because she had so little to share. Calla's mother stepped into that role, assuring Windsa that her father would be home soon. The lies parents and grandparents told children weren't very much different than the lies they told themselves.

Calla skinned the last tuber and was about to start dicing them when she saw Trillia Magistrate standing in the kitchen doorway. Calla jumped; the woman's sudden appearance conjured Calla's dark dream of the Magistrate standing over Crisdan, chanting her dark magic.

It was only a dream, she reassured herself. But the feeling hung with her like dampness after a rain.

"Pardon me, Lady Calla." The older woman's face showed her age and wisdom, her power and grace. "I did not mean to startle you. I heard the children and came to the backyard. Your father said I could find you here."

Calla set down the tuber and the knife and wiped her hands on her apron. "Of course, Trillia Magistrate, please come in. You are always most welcome in our home."

Trillia followed Calla into the sitting room. Now that she had studied

High Trade law, Calla knew now that a lady like herself should wait for direction to be seated by a Magistrate.

So Calla watched Trillia sit in the chair next to the window and remained standing.

After a few moments, Trillia smiled, a deep smile, creasing her entire face. "You have studied well." The Magistrate waved her hand. "Please sit."

Calla quickly sat. "You know of my studies?"

"I do. Doothban came to me after your first day. He was nervous that it was unseemly for a woman to study the High Trade law, especially a woman who isn't High Trade herself."

Calla blushed. "I guess it was a little too bold."

Trillia shook her head. "Nonsense, child. Doothban is old, and he clings too tightly to convention. Besides, the law is free to be read. Your station or gender is not relevant." She frowned. "But I did not come to praise your scholarship. I have some news."

Calla's heart jumped. News of Zornan, for sure. She hoped Trillia's politeness did not portend evil news.

Trillia reached into a pocket in her skirt and pulled out a folded piece of paper, sealed with wax. "This is from your husband." Trillia extended the letter to Calla.

Calla took it, cradling it delicately like it might disappear if she gripped it too tightly. Her hands trembled.

"Open it," Trillia commanded. "The news is good, I promise."

Calla carefully lifted the seal, and Zornan's familiar scrawl opened before her. It read:

Dearest Calla,

I cannot share all my tale, not in a letter, but I will say the important things. I am alive, and by some miracle I can hardly fathom, I've escaped the dark cloud of Stethdel's false accusation. I am headed to the Imperial palace to meet with the Emperor himself, otherwise I would have come to you immediately.

Calla smiled through her tears. Shy Zornan standing in front of the Emperor. She could hardly picture it.

When I am done in Bristrinia, I will come to you. I may have to travel by tunnel, as this ordeal was not without loss. Silver died saving me, a heroic but terrible sacrifice.

Calla held back a sob. Her heart ached for her husband and the grief he surely felt.

I know you will have a thousand questions, but my time is short, and as you know, I'm not much for words, written or spoken. I will leave you with my undying love. I will be home soon. I cannot wait to hold you and to hug and kiss the girls. What I hardly dared to hope is now going to be real, the happiest reunion of my life.

Your dearest husband,

Zornan

Calla wiped away her tears, relief and joy exploding within her. He was coming home! She laughed a small laugh and clutched the letter to her chest.

"I am so glad for your fortune." Trillia's voice broke Calla from her happy trance; she'd nearly forgotten the Magistrate was in the room. "If I had not played a minor part in this story, I probably wouldn't believe it."

"Thank you, Trillia. Thank you for believing in Zornan. Crisdan said you were his only ally."

"The Empire is full of snakes," Trillia said, a sudden anger flashing across her face. "It's full of those who would take a good man like Zornan and use him, not worrying about the carnage left of his life. I cannot stand for that."

Trillia paused, her eyes distant. The letter had driven Calla's dark feelings toward the other woman from her mind, and now she banished them entirely. Trillia Magistrate was not the evil sorceress of Calla's dreams; she was a magnificent woman, a benevolent shepherd watching over Fallindra.

Trillia looked up and smiled. "You have changed, Lady Calla. I sense something different about you. Studying the law, using a deep hope to fuel you, I say you are not the woman you were even a month ago."

Calla shrugged. "I did what I believed I had to do."

Trillia nodded. "No, you went beyond what most would have done. And from what Crisdan and Doothban tell me, you could probably school both of them on the particulars of the law."

Calla blushed again. "They flatter me." The mention of Crisdan ignited feelings of shame, but she brushed them aside as quickly as they emerged. "I wish I had more schooling. It took me too long to figure out simple things."

"Then I have a proposal for you. After Zornan has returned, after your life has returned to normal, come see me. We should meet once a week to discuss the law. I can continue your education. There's no reason your intense study should flicker out and go to waste. And maybe someday, I could hire you as a clerk."

"Yes, I would enjoy that."

Trillia stood and walked toward the door, Calla following closely behind.

"Get some rest, Lady Calla." The Magistrate opened the door and then turned around. "Share the letter with your parents and your daughters. Celebrate Zornan's return. Welcome parting, Lady Calla."

"Welcome parting, Trillia Magistrate."

Calla closed the door behind Trillia and clutched the letter to her chest. The full emotion of Zornan's return overwhelmed her. The nightmare was over. She looked to the heavens and thanked the Moons for Zornan's safety and for delivering justice.

She wiped more tears of joy from her face and ran toward the backyard to share the news with her parents and her daughters.

41 | IMPERIAL AUDIENCE

The carriage bounced along the paved streets of Bristrinia, the city's brilliant buildings shining in the bright sunlight. Each bounce sent waves of pain through Zornan's various wounds. He was healing, but slowly. The healer had preached patience, and Zornan felt obliged to comply.

He looked out the carriage window and marveled, not at the beautiful buildings (which he'd seen many times on his visits to the capital) but at the animals pulling the carriage: horses. Skathall had no horses and neither did Fallindra. They were only common in the Plains of Bristrinia, the Jungles of Crazdar, and Kandrinal. The animals were said to be skittish in tunnels and were therefore extremely rare among the peak valleys. He marveled at their strength and their endurance. How much farming could be done with one of those animals? Maybe Zornan should save up his money and buy one for Calla's father.

He wished this ceremony surrounding his rescue could have waited until after he had seen his wife and daughters. But Mizcarnon Peak Crosser insisted that Zornan present himself to the Emperor and speak with the Investigators about his experience.

It had been two weeks since he had fought the Baldra at the top of Doorie. He'd awoken in a room to Mizcarnon Peak Crosser and a group of Imperial Guards hovering over him. Zornan repressed tears as he thought of Silver, lying there dead, a noble sacrifice. According to Mizcarnon, the Kuthraz had entered Doorie less than an hour before the Imperial Guard arrived. All the Dundraz had been captured or killed, but the Kuthraz and Mairie had escaped before the Imperials reached the plateau. Zornan had never been asked to explain about the two men he had killed, and he kept many details to himself.

In those first few minutes of consciousness, Mizcarnon explained that Zornan was free, proclaimed innocent by Crisdan Investigator. The tall, dark man who had interrogated him those months before in Fallindra appeared at that moment over Mizcarnon's shoulder, smiling.

"You can return to your home now, Zornan," the Investigator had said. "You are free. Cherish that freedom."

He'd written a letter to Calla, and a Peak Crosser had taken it to her. Their tunnel ferry had even passed right by Fallindra, but they did not stop. As his mind became aware of their proximity to his home, his heart ached to be with Calla again.

Ballin would be in Fallindra as well. His younger brother left a letter in Bristrinia, explaining that the capital city was suffocating him. The letter had been written with the hope that Zornan would be alive to read it. He smiled at the faith of his little brother, a trait that had allowed him to see past Mairie's blessing and fall for the young woman underneath. Ballin was a better man than he.

Zornan awoke from his daydreaming and turned to Mizcarnon. "What is the Emperor like?"

"He's an incredible man," Mizcarnon replied reverently. "He is wise and kind. He is young, though I think his wisdom stretches well beyond that of almost all men."

Mizcarnon was an oddity. Zornan had encountered other scouts, and while Mizcarnon shared their serious nature, the other Peak Crosser also exuded kindness and justice. He had risked his life to help rescue Zornan, and he'd been kind and supportive during Zornan's recovery in Dasnath and throughout the tunnel journey across the Empire to the capital. Like Crisdan, Mizcarnon did not seem to fit the mold of his class.

They arrived at the Emperor's palace and were escorted through its grand entrance and into its ornate hallways. Zornan had been past the palace but never inside. A lowly Peak Crosser wasn't likely to ever have reason to enter its ancient halls. Yet here he was, a visit with the Emperor moments away. The quiet boy from Skathall had indeed come a long way.

Lost in thought, Zornan hardly noticed anything until their Imperial Guard escort stopped in front of two large brastilia doors. The doors opened, and Zornan stepped forward to enter, but Mizcarnon held him back.

"This is where we part, Peak Crosser," the scout said.

"Thank you for everything, Mizcarnon. I owe you a great debt."

"You owe me nothing, Zornan," Mizcarnon said with a wave of his hand. "Crisdan freed you from the accusations. The Emperor decided you were worth fighting for. And the Imperial Guard fought valiantly for your freedom. My part was insignificant."

"Regardless, Peak Crosser, I owe you. Fly free, Mizcarnon."

"Fly free, Zornan Peak Crosser." The man bowed his head slightly, and walked back the way they'd come, escorted by one of the Imperial Guards. Zornan breathed in deeply and stepped inside the throne room.

He gasped once he was inside, the majesty and size weakening his composure. It wasn't much of an exaggeration to say that most of Fallindra would have fit in this room. Large pillars supported the ceiling which hung in the air above them, more like the sky than a ceiling. Brastilia accents were everywhere, and the massive throne was made from the magical element. The Emperor sat still on the throne. He looked exactly as Mizcarnon had described him: dark curly hair, a hawk-like nose, and a young face, almost like a young actor playing the part of a great king. He was dressed in a dark blue flowing robe with a black cape attached at the shoulders. His ankles were bare, and his feet were adorned with golden sandals.

Zornan heard the doors close behind him, leaving him alone with the Emperor, or so he would have thought if Mizcarnon had not warned him about the Emperor's High Counselor. He glanced to his left at Lanthia. She had long dark hair, two brilliant gold bands pulling it back into tails behind her head. Her face was thin, and her cheekbones looked as if they'd been carved into her face. Her tight black dress shimmered in the sunlight. Zornan nodded to the woman, as he'd been told to do; she did nothing in response. Mizcarnon had been wrong: her beauty did indeed match her reputation

"Welcome, Zornan Peak Crosser." The Emperor's deep voice snatched Zornan's attention. "We look forward to your report of your unfortunate interaction with the Kuthraz and the Dundraz."

"Welcome greeting, Greatest Emperor of the Peaks, Tothdarin, son of Gathrizdel." Zornan bowed deeply after finishing the formal greeting.

"Please tell us, Zornan Peak Crosser, how all this happened. Give as much detail as you can remember. And please relax. This is not an interrogation." The Emperor smiled warmly, but Zornan couldn't help feeling that this was indeed an interrogation.

Zornan started at the beginning and told most of what he remembered. The first part was easy to tell: Stethdel had arrived in Fallindra and forced Zornan into his scheme. He told of his escape with Mairie and reluctantly told of the abilities she demonstrated in Skathall. Like he had with Crisdan in their interview in Dasnath, he left out Loothdram and the Kuthraz he'd met in Skathall. He then told them of their escape through the tunnels, the visit to The Bowels, and their flight with the deceitful Maeltha. It took most of two hours for Zornan to tell the Emperor and his Counselor the tale, ending with him waking up in Doorie with Mizcarnon, Crisdan, and the Imperial Guards. He also left out his newfound abilities he'd discovered (or developed) during his isolation.

"What an amazing tale," Lanthia said as he finished, her voice dipped in incredulity. "You just so happened to get involved with the Kuthraz by accident, even though your mentor Lascrill is the leader of the group?"

"If I was a member of the Kuthraz," Zornan snapped, "I would not have needed to be manipulated by Stethdel to assist him. And I would not have fallen into Maeltha's trap, as I would have known she was not Kuthraz. If I am Kuthraz, as you seem to suggest, then I'm the most incompetent rebel in the Empire's history. I should be set free to do more damage to their movement." Part of Zornan regretted his sharp tone, but it was a small part. He would not be bullied by anyone ever again.

Lanthia's face lit up in anger, her eyes narrowing dangerously. "How dare you, Peak Crosser. I am Lanthia, High Counselor to the Emperor himself, and I will…"

"Enough." The Emperor's voice cut Lanthia off, and she stopped immediately, though her seething eyes never left Zornan. He locked eyes with her. "Zornan is my guest, Lanthia," the Emperor continued, "and this is not an interrogation."

Zornan turned back to the Emperor, keeping the scornful Counselor at the corner of his vision.

"Thank you for your tale, Peak Crosser," the Emperor continued. "While this is not an interrogation, you must understand that these rebels represent a serious threat to the Empire, and we must guard against the possibility that you are an agent of either organization, cleverly disguised as an innocent man."

"My apologies, Greatest Emperor." Zornan turned toward Lanthia. "My apologies, Lanthia Counselor." The woman again gave no response, which suited Zornan; he felt no remorse.

"What are you plans now?" the Emperor asked.

"I will return to my family in Fallindra," Zornan said, stunned that the most powerful person in the Empire seemed sincerely interested in Zornan's personal life. "Then I will try to secure a mrakaro and a new Peak Crosser assignment. I can only assume that my previous assignment with the Priests of Cazdanth has been given to another."

"Indeed it has," the Emperor replied, his voice echoing down from his elevated throne. "But I reached out to the Council of Peak Crossers and to the Priests of Cazdanth; your former commission will be restored. It should not be taken from you when your failure to execute it was due to the manipulation of rebels. It would set a bad precedent if you lost what was yours."

Zornan fought to keep his jaw from dropping. He had assumed he would have to find another commission, a very poor one, ferrying communications across the Empire. A low commission would likely mean more time away from his family and less coin in his pocket. He had only hoped he would one day regain a commission that was a fraction of the one he'd had.

"Thank you, Emperor. I don't know what to say. I am not deserving of your grace."

"That is not all, Zornan Peak Crosser. Mizcarnon Peak Crosser told me of the death of your mrakaro, Silver. I am sorry that she, too, was caught in this nefarious plot. As soon as you are able, you are to travel by carriage out to the Cliffs of the Peaks to the Peak Crosser Aviary and select any bird you would like of those currently not assigned."

He would get to choose his mrakaro? He'd never heard of such a thing. Mrakaros were assigned by the Aviary Priestess, a Bendathdran who oversaw the raising and assignment of the giant flyers. Zornan wasn't even sure that members of the Council of Peak Crossers were able to select their own flyers.

"I am honored by your offer," Zornan uttered. "Again, your grace is too much." Zornan agreed with Mizcarnon's assessment of the Emperor as a singularly great man.

"Nonsense," the Emperor replied. "You have endured much, mostly because we, as the Empire's stewards, ignored the threat of these rebels for too long, assuming they were nothing more than querulous High Tradesmen whispering dissatisfactions in distant corners. But the willingness of the Kuthraz to ruin the lives of the Empire's citizenry is appalling. And the lesser-known Dundraz maintained a secret military base, building strength for some unknown strike against us. No, Zornan Peak Crosser, it is the Empire that owes you. We failed to deal with this threat before it began overturning lives."

The smile was gone from the Emperor's face, replaced by a firm determination, his eyes afire with righteous anger. When the Emperor was raised four years before, his reputation had been that of a spoiled, weak boy. Most felt that Lanthia was the force behind the Emperor. If that had been true then, it was not now. The Emperor seemed to wield every fraction of his power. The stern look made Zornan worry for Loothdram. If his role in the Kuthraz was discovered, the Emperor would hunt him mercilessly.

"Thank you, Emperor."

"Return to your family, Zornan Peak Crosser, and rest. When your health returns, send a letter to the Priests of Cazdanth, and they will welcome you back. And if you ever return to Bristrinia, you are free to seek my audience. Consider yourself a friend of the court."

"Though I would not want to relive my ordeal, it is almost worth it to be placed in the light of Your Honor's grace and wisdom."

The Emperor nodded.

"Graceful parting, Zornan Peak Crosser."

"Graceful parting, Greatest Emperor of the Peaks, Tothdarin, son of Gathrizdel." Zornan bowed as deeply as his wounded body allowed, smiling up at the Emperor. The Emperor returned his smile tenfold. Zornan turned toward Lanthia before leaving and bowed respectfully. The anger was gone from her face, replaced with a blank expression, her eyes focused away from Zornan.

As he turned to walk away, joy overwhelmed him. Like a hero's tale, his return would be glorious. His commission restored, a new mrakaro of his choice, and he'd be with Calla, Windsa, and Caldry within days. As deep as his despair had been, his happiness eclipsed it. Everything would be as it should be.

And he had changed, become something that apparently no one suspected. If someone like Stethdel ever tried to disturb his life in the future, he would be ready. Enforcers, Magistrates, Baldra, not even the High Counselor of the moon-blessed Emperor, would control his fate.

. . . .

Sign up for Adam's mailing list to get news about his stories right to your mailbox. http://www.adamjmangum.com/mailing-list

www.ingramcontent.com/pod-product-compliance
Lightning Source LLC
Chambersburg PA
CBHW070847260626

47170CB00007B/2534